PENGUIN BOOKS

BED & BREAKFAST

Lois Battle is the author of seven novels, including *Storyville*. She lives in Beaufort, South Carolina.

Praise for *Bed & Breakfast*

"[Lois Battle] manifests throughout a sort of fundamental decency—a compassion for human frailty—that makes her book especially appealing." —*The Washington Post*

"The Tatternall family will seduce you from page one of *Bed & Breakfast*. . . . It's a tender sigh, glad-I-read-it, perfect-for-Christmas kind of book." —*San Antonio Express News*

"Like a cup of high voltage coffee, *Bed & Breakfast* will jolt you awake."

—Rita Mae Brown, author of *Hounded to Death* and *Rubyfruit Jungle*

"Lois Battle's *Bed & Breakfast* is pure delight: touching and witty, sympathetic and shrewd. It's the kind of book I'll rush to tell all my friends about; it's the book I can't wait to give my mother!" —Nancy Thayer, author of *The Hot Flash Club*

"I loved it—it's truthful and benevolent and entirely recognizable. It's also a wonderful portrait of the fractured nature of the modern family, and proof that however much we wish we could get along without one, we simply can't."

—Joanna Trollope, author of *Friday Nights*

"An engrossing [and] emotion-filled story."

—*Newport News Press*

"A heart-tugging drama." —*The Beaufort Gazette*

"A literate, witty, and affectionate tale." —*Kirkus Reviews*

"There are no heroes in this family drama, no villains either—just regular folks, drawn with sympathy and keen-eyed humor." —*Booklist*

Lois Battle

Bed & BREAKFAST

Penguin Books

PENGUIN BOOKS
Published by the Penguin Group
Penguin Books USA Inc., 375 Hudson Street, New York, New York 10014, U.S.A.
Penguin Group (Canada), 90 Eglinton Avenue East, Suite 700, Toronto, Ontario, Canada M4P 2Y3 (a division of Pearson Penguin Canada Inc.) • Penguin Books Ltd, 80 Strand, London WC2R 0RL, England • Penguin Ireland, 25 St Stephen's Green, Dublin 2, Ireland (a division of Penguin Books Ltd) • Penguin Group (Australia), 250 Camberwell Road, Camberwell, Victoria 3124, Australia (a division of Pearson Australia Group Pty Ltd) • Penguin Books India Pvt Ltd, 11 Community Centre, Panchsheel Park, New Delhi – 110 017, India • Penguin Group (NZ), 67 Apollo Drive, Rosedale, North Shore 0632, New Zealand (a division of Pearson New Zealand Ltd) • Penguin Books (South Africa) (Pty) Ltd, 24 Sturdee Avenue, Rosebank, Johannesburg 2196, South Africa

Penguin Books Ltd, Registered Offices: 80 Strand, London WC2R 0RL, England

First published in the United States of America by Viking Penguin,
a division of Penguin Books USA Inc. 1996
Published in Penguin Books 1997
This edition published in Penguin Books 2009

1 3 5 7 9 10 8 6 4 2

Grateful acknowledgment is made for permission to reprint
excerpts from the following copyrighted works:
"Stardust" by Mitchell Parish and Hoagy Carmichael. © 1928 (renewed) EMI Mills Music, Inc. and Hoagy Publishing Co. in the USA/EMI Mills Music, Inc. for the rest of the world. All rights reserved. Used by permission of Warner Bros. Publications U.S. Inc., Miami, FL 33014.
"The Biggest Difference" from *Alchemy* by Dana Wildsmith.
By permission of The Sow's Ear Press.

PUBLISHER'S NOTE
This is a work of fiction. Names, characters, places, and incidents either are the product of the author's imagination or are used fictitiously, and any resemblance to actual persons, living or dead, business establishments, events, or locales is entirely coincidental.

THE LIBRARY OF CONGRESS HAS CATALOGED THE HARDCOVER EDITION AS FOLLOWS:
Battle, Lois,
Bed and breakfast/Lois Battle.
p. cm.
ISBN 0-670-86074-3 (hc.)
ISBN 978-0-14-311643-1 (pbk.)
I. Title.
PS3552.A8325B4 1996
813'.54—dc20 96 17258

Printed in the United States of America
Set in Bembo Designed by Junie Lee

To Colleen Battle, my sister and beloved friend

Acknowledgments

THANKS TO MY editor, Pamela Dorman, for her Penelope-like patience and continued guidance; to my dear friends Will Balk, Christine Stanley, Dana Wildsmith, Brewster Robertson, Shirley Carson, Meg Ruley, Gene Jones, and Pat Thelma Latimer, for their unflagging loyalty, humor, and affection. And to John W. Patterson, "Rat-Boy," jokester, Guardian, Master of the Revels . . . and of my heart.

Bed & Breakfast

Prologue

IT WASN'T AS though Josie'd had a premonition. Nothing as strong as that. Just a sense that *something* was going to happen that would be more than she could cope with. She'd had it from the moment she'd opened her eyes and realized that the girls were coming to her house for their weekly bridge game. She'd tried to shrug it off but the feeling had persisted, undeniable as the sneezes and aches that signaled the flu, right up until the moment it had happened. Then she'd been totally involved but totally surprised, as though she were watching an old movie she'd seen many times.

The four of them—she, her sister Edna, Peatsy Gibbs, and Mary Gebhardt—had been playing bridge on her sun porch. The grandfather clock in the dining room, which she'd had repaired just last week but which was still running about seven minutes fast, had struck three. Peatsy had just trumped Mary's ace and said she was feeling dizzy. " 'Course you feel dizzy," Edna had said, "you're a dizzy broad." But instead of the tight little smile Peatsy usually showed when Edna talked slangy, Peatsy'd closed her eyes and got a strange look on her face, as though someone had just come up behind her and whispered, "Guess who?" Her hand had wandered up to her pearls, forgot where it was going, and pawed the air. Then she'd plunged forward, her head hitting the table with an awful thud, one arm flung out scattering cards and Mary's glutted ashtray. "Mother of God," Mary cried, and ran to her, hauling her back by her shoulders so that her arms flopped to her sides and her head snapped back, mouth open, showing her bridgework. "Mother of God!" Mary cried again. Edna got up as though someone had lifted her by the hair, stared at Peatsy, doused iced tea on the smoldering cigarette that had rolled out of the ashtray, then sat down hard. But she, Josie, had known just what to do.

She'd walked straight to the kitchen telephone and dialed 911, and when she'd said, "This is Mrs. Josephine Tatternall, over at The Point. We need some help here," she'd sounded so calm as to be sociable.

She'd answered all the questions, speaking slowly and enunciating carefully because the girl sounded young and not too bright, and when the girl told her that the ambulance was on its way, she'd even remembered to say, "Thank you. And Merry Christmas."

PART *One*

One

SHE'D WOKEN AROUND seven, shut off the alarm she always set as a precaution, and turned to look past the bedpost to the windows. They were undraped because her bedroom was on the second floor where no one could see in and she liked to be woken by natural light. The sun was already making a shy appearance, and it looked like a seasonable day for mid-December. She would like to have lingered in bed, but that was out of the question. When you ran a bed-and-breakfast, you had to get up. Hooking her arms behind her head, she ran her mind over the day's tasks: she would fix breakfast for last night's guests, see them on their way, do the dishes, garden while Cuba did the laundry, then make a quick trip to the Azalea-land Nursing Home to see Mawmaw. Her sister Edna said there wasn't any point in visiting because Mawmaw wouldn't even know she was there, but just last week as she'd been about to leave, Mawmaw had said, "So glad you dropped by. You know, I've always thought of you as one of the family." So even if Mawmaw no longer recognized her as her daughter, she at least seemed to appreciate her presence.

When she got home from Azalealand she'd toss some leftovers together for lunch, then she'd decorate the tree. She'd carried boxes of ornaments down from the attic over a week ago when Edna's husband, Dozier, had set up the tree in her living room, but she just hadn't been able to face the prospect of decorating it alone. If Cuba helped her . . . that is, if Cuba came in. When it came to Christmas, or "the birth of our Baby Jesus" as Cuba called it, Cuba went hog-wild. She strung every bush and tree around her own house with colored lights, put little statues of the Three Wise Men on her scrubby lawn, and fixed a black-faced Santa, ready to crawl down the chimney, on her roof. She plaited wreaths, baked mounds of cookies and coconut cakes, drove her dinged-up '83 Olds on a daily round of Wal-Mart, Kmart, and the Bay Street stores, and went into hock for every toy and gewgaw her grandchildren saw on TV. And this year Cuba was making new robes (actually dashikis) and headgear for her choir at First African Baptist, so she'd told Josie straight out that she wouldn't be putting in her regular hours until after the New Year. So . . . if Cuba didn't come in, she'd do the laundry, then she'd fix lunch, then . . . then she remembered that the girls were coming to her house for their weekly bridge game, and she allowed herself a single but heartfelt "Damn!"

They usually met out at Mary Gebhardt's place on Dataw Island on the third Wednesday of each month, but last Wednesday Mary had asked if someone would switch with her because her children and grandchildren were coming "from all over the country" for the holidays. Peatsy had said she couldn't possibly switch because she was supervising the wrapping of Toys for Tots and singing the *Messiah* at St. Helena's Episcopal before she took off to visit her son, Waring, in Washington, D.C. Edna, predictably, had begged off, too, saying she was keeping her gift shop open extra hours to catch the Christmas trade, then she and Dozier were driving up to their son's place in Columbia. So the lot had fallen to Josie. How could she possibly refuse when they all knew she had no special plans? None of her three daughters was coming home for the holidays. On Christmas Day her daughter, Lila, would just drive over from

Hilton Head to pick her up. They'd go back to Lila and her husband Orrie's place, open a mountain of presents, then Orrie would take her, Lila, and the kids out to some expensive restaurant. So Josie'd said, "Why, sure, you girls can come back here again."

Edna, who'd gotten religion about the women's movement since she'd gone into business, had said, "We're not *girls,* Josie, we're *women.*" She could have pointed out that Edna, who was two years her senior, still lied about her age, whereas she always told the truth (partly because in a town the size of Beaufort most everyone knew your real age anyway, partly because when she confessed to seventy-three, most people said she didn't look it), but she'd just said, "Well, y'all are more than welcome to come here again."

At the time she'd meant it, but now she could hear the conversation in advance, the gush about holiday plans, the updates on children and grandchildren that were really just an accepted form of bragging (less happy topics—bankruptcies, unwanted pregnancies, and divorces—being reserved for one-on-one conversation). With a bright smile that only served to point up her underlying pity, Mary would ask if Josie had heard from her eldest daughter, Camilla, now known as Cam. Mary had never even met Cam but she knew (though Josie had never personally told her) Cam had sworn, some ten years ago at her father's funeral, that she would never come back to Beaufort or speak to Josie again. She also knew that though Cam had relented to the point of making obligatory monthly phone calls, she had held to her promise never to come back home. Since Cam was unmarried, lived in New York, and worked for a publishing company, Mary thought of her as some sort of soap-opera siren—glamorous but hard as nails. Josie sometimes thought of her that way herself.

Then, Mary would ask about her youngest daughter, Evie, a onetime runner-up in the Miss South Carolina contest. Evie wrote a column in the Savannah paper in which she shared the most intimate details of her private life, including her "dysfunctional" childhood. She wrote under the byline "A Good Ol' Girl" but that, as Cuba had pointed out, provided about as much concealment as Saran Wrap.

Josie focused on the bedroom windows, comforting herself with the thought that she could talk about her daughter, Lila. Lila had achieved the old-fashioned Southern ideal of being the well-cared-for wife of a successful man. Her husband, Orrie Gadsden, was a real-estate developer who'd been elected to the state legislature just months before. Lila had money, social position, a beautiful home, and two lovely teenage children. She called Josie daily; they saw one another at least once a week. They shopped and occasionally even traveled together. Lila was everything a mother could want. Or so everyone believed. And Josie wasn't about to disabuse them of that notion. Still . . .

Thank goodness she had only that nice Canadian couple to cope with this morning, and they'd been so grateful that she'd bent the rules to let them keep their little dog in their room that they'd said they'd only want tea and toast before they got back on the road to Florida. But since most of her guests came through word of mouth, she'd make the effort and fix the homemade sausage, pan-fried gravy, biscuits, and peach preserves for which she was rightly famous. Maybe she'd even sell them a copy of the Lowcountry cookbook she'd published years before and kept on the kitchen counter. She was too polite to push the book, but guests often wanted to buy it after they'd tasted some of the recipes, and the extra cash was always welcome.

Hearing her dead husband, Bear, command, "Reveille! Up and at 'em," she flung back the quilt, grasped the bedpost, and stood up. The floorboard's creak seemed to be a cry of protest coming from her feet but she straightened, pulled her jade satin robe over her flannel nightdress, tucked her hands into her armpits to warm them, and moved to the window to look down on her garden. In the early morning light it was like an Impressionist painting—a misty blur of greens, blues, grays, and white limned with pale gold. The paperwhites she'd planted for the Garden Club's Christmas tour of historic homes—"Snow in the South"—were so thick that they really did look like snow and her mind drifted to the first time she'd seen snow—when she'd gone to visit Bear at that base in New Jersey right after they were married. When he'd said "up and at 'em" in those days, he'd meant something entirely different. He'd made love to her first thing every morning, and again when they'd come back to the inn after the walks he'd said were bracing but she'd sworn would give her frostbite. He'd undress her, pulling off her hat, gloves, galoshes, and socks, teasing her for being a hothouse flower, chafing her hands and feet, then massaging them, telling her in a husky voice, "I'm a gentleman. I always start with the extremities." It had been a wonderfully arousing form of foreplay, though at the time she'd been such an innocent she hadn't even known the word, let alone realized that he must've perfected his technique on other women.

Thinking about those long-ago mornings put her into a sort of daze. Her fingers moved, gently kneading her breast, until the memory of the lumpectomy she'd had three years ago came across her like a shadow. The cyst had been benign and, perversely, she'd stopped all self-examination after she'd had the operation. She refused to think of her breasts only as a danger zone. If something went wrong, then it was up to that boy doctor to find it when she went for her semiannual checkup. True, she hadn't kept her last appointment, and she'd ignored the nurse's phone call and follow-up postcard, but she wasn't going to think about that either. At least not until after the holidays.

As she reached into the chest of drawers for fresh underwear, her eyes caught the two silver-framed photos on the dresser top. She found her glasses next to the bowl of potpourri, put them on, and studied the pictures.

She had never, not even in the early years, been able to look at her wedding portrait without regret. There was Bear in his dress whites, wholesome yet somehow dangerous, already the embodiment of the World War II hero he was to become. His eyes under his brimmed hat had that "I can take on the world" look that had magnetized her when she'd first seen him, while ladling out nonalcoholic punch at a local "Support Our Troops" social. Only his nose—broken in a fight when he was ten and one of the boys at the Baton Rouge orphanage had called him a bastard and told him what it meant—stopped him from being movie-star handsome. And there she was, always notoriously unphotogenic, but just this once looking truly beautiful, her light brown hair flowing around her shoulders, her eyes shining, her smile bright, with just a whisper of sensuality.

The photo was in black and white but she always saw Bear's chocolate eyes and hair, the gold buttons on his uniform, her suit—"dusty rose" the saleswoman had called it and she'd loved the name. It had been an expensive, well-tailored suit and the cream hat and gloves and her purple-throated corsage had complemented it nicely. But it wasn't a wedding gown. It would have taken only another few weeks of preparation to have a real wedding. Why had she crumbled under Bear's insistence and forgone all the pomp and celebration she'd dreamt about? Because, at the time, as Mawmaw had said, she would have walked off a cliff if Bear had told her to. Her fault, not his. "We create our own reality," her daughter, Evie, was always saying. "We always get what we secretly want." But that couldn't possibly be true. She had never gotten anything she'd wanted except this house, and she'd had to drive the final wedge between her and Bear and threaten divorce to get it.

The other photo, taken some ten years later, was a typical studio portrait of a typical (though certainly better looking than average) well-bred, well-fed, well-groomed American family, circa 1950s, when being typical was a badge of honor. At one time the photo had filled her with pride, but over the years she'd come to see it differently. In it, she and Bear, his uniform now decorated with medals, were seated with Cam and Lila between them. Evie, who was only a few weeks old, was held in her lap. Bear was, if possible, even more handsome than he'd been in their wedding photo, but he looked a bit too rigid. Playing Daddy had never been an easy role for him and he'd had a terrible hangover the morning the photo had been taken. When she looked closely she could see the nick on his left cheek and remembered rushing around the house to find his styptic pencil. But that had been back in the days when two-fisted men had been expected to tie one on at weekend parties, when booze had increased rather than diminished his sexual prowess, when she'd denied that he had a problem.

She was still in maternity clothes (that teal suit with the bow at the neck, which she'd come to hate). Her face was fuller and her hair was gathered into a chignon, because in those days there were definite styles that corresponded to each phase of a woman's life and a young matron didn't go around looking like a teenager. Her smile had lost the hint of seductiveness it had shown in her wedding portrait but was still trusting and open. You didn't see such innocent expressions anymore, not even in very young girls, but back then she'd still believed everything her husband, her government, and the newspapers had told her. And if she'd had any doubts, she'd hidden them, because that was her duty as a military wife.

She hadn't planned on being a military wife. When they'd married during the war it had been impossible to plan anything. She'd just prayed that he would come back alive and whole, and when he did, he'd probably go to college on the G.I. Bill. But by the time the war had ended he wasn't Ted Tatternall anymore, he was what his admiring buddies had christened him: he was "Bear," a fearsome career warrior. And she'd known, with a jealousy she hadn't been able to admit, that the military had become not just his profession, but wife and mistress to him as well. Asking him to take an office job or sit in a classroom would have been like asking Tarzan to put on a three-piece suit. So she'd accepted his decision, as a loving wife was supposed to do. Bear was climbing the promotional ladder and writing a book about his experiences in the Pacific. When the book was published (and she'd never doubted that it would be), she would get the home she'd always wanted. In the meantime she'd be stoic about her homesickness and overcome her panic at being constantly uprooted and having to make a nest in strange towns, even in foreign countries.

During the long periods when Bear was away she was expected to, as he put it, "hold the fort." Her appearance and behavior, and even that of her children, would be written up in Bear's periodic fitness reports. Any misstep could damage his chances of promotion (because, the reasoning went, if a man couldn't keep his family in line, how could he be fit to command men?). She'd studied the wives' reference manual. The rigid and detailed instructions made her want to laugh ("answer the phone in a low, well-modulated voice. . . . Place an ashtray at the top of each plate to the left of the water glass, and in it put two or three cigarettes and a book of matches. . . . When making a social call at a commanding officer's house *never* stay more than twenty minutes. . . ."), but she kept the joke to herself. Any hint that she didn't take all the conventions seriously might put Bear at risk. So she joined the appropriate organizations, spearheaded fund-raisers and welcoming committees, kept herself, her children, and her home ever-ready for white-glove inspection. When Bear returned, they'd joke about his giving her an A on her periodic evaluation. He rewarded her with gifts from wherever he'd been deployed, but her real reward came after the girls had shown him their report cards, new teeth, drawings, and merit badges, when he'd give her his thousand-watt smile and say, "Dammit, call that babysitter. I want to paint the town with my best girl."

And he could paint the town as no one else could. From the best hotels and nightclubs to roadside juke joints, if there was a place to laugh and cut loose, drink and dance, Bear Tatternall could find it. He could coax the best table out of a snooty maître d', get a bartender in a country tavern to reach under the counter for the white lightnin' on a Sunday, set an entire table laughing at the officers' club. And dance! In the slow numbers he led with a light but masterful touch, and when he jitterbugged he had such swivel-hipped, athletic vitality that couples would stop and applaud. He was, quite literally, the life of every party. But when he gave her the look they called "the eye-melt" and touched her leg under the table, she couldn't reach for her coat fast enough.

Their lovemaking had all the thrill and excitement of the first times, without her initial shyness and fumbling. What joy it was to have him back! To have what she'd remembered, thought about, longed for. In the mornings, she'd wake to the sound of the kids stirring, say "Rest," pull on her robe and go into the kitchen. She'd be turning the bacon or brewing coffee and he'd saunter out, showered and shaved, looking none the worse for wear, to tell the girls that he expected them to be especially dutiful while he was away because she was both Mama and Daddy, to which Cam had once giggled, "No, she's not the daddy, she just pretends to be tough." In a way this was true. Josie coaxed obedience, but Bear's word was law.

In the photograph, Camilla, then almost six, stood next to Bear, one of her arms around his shoulder, her face close to his, pointing up their remarkable resemblance. Lila was at Josie's side, trying-to-be-a-big-girl at four, with her hands laced obediently at her waist. Both girls were wearing identical white eyelet, puff-sleeved dresses she'd made them for Easter, with white gloves and tiny gold crosses she'd bought at the PX. Lila had a bow in her hair, but Camilla had taken off her bow, saying it was babyish. Josie had reasoned and cajoled, then Bear had brought Cam into line with an order to "shape up," and the photographer had arranged them.

In the picture there was no hint of disagreement. All—even milky-eyed Evie—seemed to be smiling and focusing in the same direction, as though they all saw the same bright and limitless future. Actually, they'd been focusing on a toy bird the photographer was holding up next to his right ear. A yellow plastic bird with a single, bent feather in its tail. And to keep the children's attention, Josie'd quoted the Emily Dickinson poem she loved: " 'Hope' is the thing with feathers—That perches in the soul—And sings the tune without the words—And never stops—at all—." But how long could one hope?

"I'm a mother," Peatsy had once said to her, "because I was born with female equipment in the days before the Pill. But you're a different kind of mother. No matter how old your children get, you're still watching them for signs of improvement." Josie knew this was true. Despite all sense and reason she couldn't give up worrying about her children, couldn't give up wondering where she'd failed. Hadn't she birthed, nursed, and cuddled them? Hadn't she tucked them in, read to them, kissed their hurts, taught them manners, disciplined them even when it had hurt her to do so? Hadn't she watched, hawk-eyed, for their individual tastes and talents, and fostered those talents as best she knew how? Even after they'd left home, hadn't she called and written, fiddled with the bank account to send them money, taken them back in whenever they'd wanted? Hadn't she scaled down all her great expectations to a tepid "Whatever makes you happy" that secretly stuck in her craw? But none of her understanding, compromises, or maneuvering had helped. All of her children (even, if she looked beneath the surface, Lila) were lost to her. It was one thing that her marriage had started on a tidal wave of love, then shipwrecked, and bleached and dried to bitterness. That happened to so many women. But her failure with her children—that was the ache for which there was no painkiller, the foghorn she heard on the sunniest days.

"Stop this," she said out loud. She tightened the sash on her satin dressing gown and turned to make the bed. She maintained her weight at a respectable 135, so it must be the dressing gown, a slinky Jean Harlow affair with swirling skirt and wide sleeves, that made her feel fat and foolish. Lila said, rightly, that it was old and tatty and her inability to throw it out was a sign of her "Depression mentality." Lila gave her a robe almost every Christmas, expensive but practical, grandmotherly robes in pastel colors, with ruffles, pockets, and zippers. But she couldn't bear to throw out this old jade satin one. It was the last gift Cam had given to her out of love and it had come with a note saying, "For the secret you." None of the others would have guessed that she'd want something so glamorous and impractical.

Even as a child, Cam'd had that uncanny ability to sniff out what was really going on. When she was no more than four, Cam could sense Josie's upset and unhappiness. She would comfort her, touching her hand or her cheek, giving her a "make-it-better kiss." But all that had changed when Cam was about twelve. Then she'd turned with a fury, seeming to blame Josie for everything. There'd been that awful Christmas when Bear had called from Okinawa at the last minute and said that his commanding officer had canceled his leave, so he wouldn't be coming home as planned. That was the first time she hadn't been able to deny her suspicions that he really *didn't want* to come home, when she'd known undeniably that he was lying.

She'd struggled to make the holiday special—the tree, the presents, the twelve-pound turkey. But on Christmas morning Cam had refused to get out of bed, and when Josie had ordered her to get up, she'd yelled, "Oh, tell us about the old days when you were grateful to get an orange in your Christmas stocking," and Josie had slapped her—not a don't-run-out-in-the-street wallop on the butt or a swift stop-being-sassy flick on the arm—but a real across-the-face slap, as though they were mortal enemies. Child abuse, they'd call it nowadays, though at the time she'd been so desperate, so beside herself with worry that she was lucky she hadn't picked up a knife and killed them all. "Childrens," Cuba had said last week when her youngest daughter (who'd run off to Philadelphia and left a child in her care) had called to say she couldn't make it home for Christmas, "might as well raise a flock of blackbirds to peck out y' eyes."

She finished making the bed, deciding that she would have the jade satin robe cleaned one last time. Then she'd wrap it in tissue paper and mothballs and put it in the storage room, along with Mawmaw and Grand's useless furniture, the christening gowns, the prom dresses, the butter churn, the windup gramophone, the boxes of papers dating back to great-grandfather Marion's enlistment papers for the Civil War, the diplomas, the photographs, Bear's unfinished memoirs, and his gun collection. Sometimes she wished she could be more like her sister Edna, who lived next door with her husband, Dozier. Nothing was sacred to Edna. She made a clean sweep every two or three years, throwing out clothes, appliances, furniture. She'd even changed the lovely veranda that wrapped around the side of her house into a "Florida room," replacing screens with louvered windows, painting the ceiling (which, in keeping with the tradition of most of the historic homes, had been a pale aqua) a midnight blue and pasting it with luminescent stars. But she could never be like Edna. Decades of moving from one base to another had changed Josie's natural desire to nest into a compulsion to hoard and preserve. Part of the reason she'd wanted this five-bedroom antebellum house was so she could save it all. And if she ever had to give it up (a recent *60 Minutes* segment about an old woman who'd been stripped of her belongings and shunted off to a nursing home came to mind), she'd just set a match to it.

Alarmed at such incendiary thoughts, she stripped off her nightdress and went into the shower. She gave herself a shampoo, singing "I'm Gonna Wash That Man Right Outta My Hair," toweled and powdered herself, put on her underwear and pantyhose. Twisting her long salt-and-pepper hair into a topknot, she pulled out a few strands and curled them with mousse, the way Lila had taught her to do. Moving so close to the mirror that her nose was almost touching it, she examined her face. She didn't really think of it as her face anymore—her real face was left behind in that family portrait—this face was just something she had to deal with, like the weeds in her garden. She plucked a wiry white hair from one of her eyebrows, stroked a tad of blusher high on her checks, touched her mouth with rose-colored lipstick, and muttered, "That'll do."

She put on her gray, pleated skirt, buttoned up her paisley blouse, threw a cardigan over her shoulders, and slipped her feet into her sneakers. Her mouth was watering for some of her homemade sausage and it was good to think that she'd be sharing it, even with paying guests. Most of her friends were financially better off than she and felt sorry that she had to run a bed-and-breakfast, but she didn't mind. At least she wasn't an old woman rattling around her house like a marble in a coffee can. She'd gotten used to sleeping alone, doing most everything alone, way before Bear had died, but eating alone was downright uncivilized.

* * *

After the Canadian couple had breakfasted and gone, as she was carrying dishes to the sink, Josie looked out the window and saw her brother-in-law cutting across her backyard. Though Dozier had retired years ago, it still surprised her to see him in work clothes instead of his three-piece suit. She watched as he stopped, stuffed his hands into the back pockets of his jeans, looked up at the largest live oak, and sighed so deeply she could see his shoulders heave. When the last hurricane had snapped off some of the tree's outer branches, Dozier had wanted to cut it back. But Edna'd said that an old man up a ladder with a chainsaw was just asking to be made an amputee and, "If you think I'm gonna spend the rest of my life playing nursie, you've got another think comin'." Josie knew Edna was right. From this distance, despite near baldness and a slight paunch, Dozier looked rangy and fit, but his grip was not as strong as it had once been, and his new glasses couldn't restore his vision to its former sharpness. But she sympathized with Dozier. Like her, he wanted to keep on keepin' on, even if it involved a certain amount of risk.

She knew he'd never liked the lumber business he'd inherited but he'd taken his role as provider so seriously that he'd worked for decades to turn the company into a lucrative tri-state firm. All those years he'd been in harness, he'd fantasized about retirement. But retirement had proved to be a disappointment, like some beautiful girl he'd longed for from afar but found he didn't much like once he got to know her. Always handy around the house, he channeled his restlessness into carpentry and repair. He hammered creaky stairs, built bookcases and windowboxes, carved wooden toys for kids who preferred Nintendo. He haunted secondhand stores, scrounging for broken lamps, busted ceiling fans, old radios, which he fixed and donated to church bazaars where, Edna pointed out, they were sold (if at all) for the same price he'd paid for them.

But his handiness was a blessing for Josie. Bear had mastered aerodynamics, radar, and complex weaponry but he'd hated household maintenance so much that he'd griped if she'd asked him to change a light bulb. But Dozier anticipated repairs and fixed things without being asked.

In return for all the work he did around her house, she'd taught him about gardening and, on the q.t., slipped him the spicy, cholesterol-heavy delights Edna had banned from her table. "You two belong together," Edna would say. "You're both as housebound as neutered cats." But Dozier was far from neutered. Sometimes when their eyes met, Josie felt a current between them. Not the blood rush of youth, but a deep fondness, all the more tender because they both knew that it would never be spoken of, let alone acted upon. She didn't think she knew Dozier better than Edna did, but she knew him differently. Sometimes a wife didn't see the forest for the trees. Sometimes a wife didn't appreciate.

She busied herself with the dishes as he came through the back door. He said, "Morning, sister," and she smiled at the country greeting and told him to help himself to the last of the sausage and biscuits. He picked up a knife, reached for the butter, decided against that indulgence but couldn't resist the peach preserves. "Waited till I saw your last night's guests leave 'bout ten minutes ago," he said. "Saw they had Canadian plates."

"All the way from Toronto," she told him, taking off her rings and putting them on the shelf above the sink. He offered to load the dishwasher, but she said, "I don't mind doin' them by hand if there's just a few." She actually enjoyed the feel of the warm suds, the squeak when she rinsed the plates, the sense that she could make something visibly better in the space of fifteen minutes. "They were a real nice couple," she told him. "He's an engineer and she's an art teacher, or at least she was. They've been trying to get pregnant for about five years, and now she's expecting, so she's taking a leave of absence to . . ." He nodded. It always amazed him how women managed to find out intimate details of strangers' lives.

"I wonder," he said, "why so many young people have trouble conceiving these days. Do you s'pose it's because they put it off for too long, or do you think it has something to do with pollution?"

"Can't blame the women for putting it off. You know how hard it is for young couples to make it financially these days and—"

The bleat of the telephone cut her off and Dozier watched as she dried her hands on her apron and went to pick it up. She was the only women he knew who still wore an apron and seeing her in it gave him the nostalgic, relaxed glow he got from listening to Golden Oldies.

Josie said, "Hello," and, not even waiting for a response, "Cuba, is this you?" She knew it would be Cuba, saying she wouldn't be in on time, possibly saying she wouldn't be in at all, so she just went, "Uh-huh, uh-huh," while Cuba told her that her youngest grandchild, Antoinne, had a fever so she wouldn't be coming in till late afternoon when the other childrens would come home to watch over him. In all the years they'd known one another, Josie had never been able to coax Cuba away from misplaced plurals (childrens instead of children, mens instead of men) any more than she'd been able to get her to say "asked" instead of "axed." "I axed the gentlemens," Cuba would say, and Josie would picture a crashing guillotine with aristocratic heads tumbling into baskets.

She told Cuba to come in when she could, hung up, and reached into the closet for the cleaning caddy. "I've got to go make up the room," she told Dozier.

"Can't you leave it?"

She shook her head. "Didn't I tell you that Mrs. Beasley's coming in this afternoon? She'll want the lavender room because it's got its own bathroom and TV, and Mrs. B.'s got to have a TV, and I put the Canadians in the lavender room last night."

"Didn't know we were getting Mrs. Beasley. That's like getting a lump of coal in your Christmas stocking."

"It surely is, but you know things are always slow this time of year, so I couldn't tell her no. I'll be back down soon's I can."

The lavender room had the usual detritus—shells and pinecones from the beach at Hunting Island, real-estate brochures the tourists always picked up and left behind—but was otherwise neat. She wiped down the bureau and dressing table with lemon oil and looked at the carpet. Since she didn't want to bother Dozier to lug the vacuum cleaner upstairs, she decided to give it a miss. She was getting that tense, queasy feeling she'd known since childhood: too much to do and not enough time to do it in.

As she scoured the toilet, basin, and tub and collected the towels, she thought about Mrs. Beasley and began to feel more queasy. Mrs. Beasley had a condo in Boca Raton but her only relative, a niece, lived out on Fripp Island. Mrs. B. visited several times a year and always stayed at Josie's, saying she didn't want to stay with her niece because she valued her privacy. It hadn't taken Josie long to figure out that Mrs. B.'s niece, who had her eye on a sizable inheritance, couldn't afford to reject Mrs. B. entirely but simply couldn't stand to have the woman in her house. Josie understood why. Mrs. B. watched Oprah and Montel and Sally so much that she'd adopted their style, asking the most intimate questions as though she were merely asking the time of day. She was also a terrible snoop. The last time she'd stayed, Josie had caught her lurking in the hallway, eavesdropping on Josie's phone conversation. It was a rudeness she would not have tolerated in a friend but she'd pretended not to notice. Mrs. B. was a regular guest and she couldn't afford to alienate a regular guest.

As she stripped the bed, she realized that she would have to decorate the tree before Mrs. B. arrived, otherwise Mrs. B. would notice it and, hoping for a refill on the complimentary glass of sherry Josie offered guests upon arrival (no one, she'd noticed, scrounged freebies more avidly than the wealthy), Mrs. B. would ask why none of Josie's children were coming home for the holidays, mutter some cliché about "we poor lonely widows," and offer to help her decorate it. She couldn't bear the thought of Mrs. B. touching ornaments that had been in the family for generations. Couldn't bear the thought of Mrs. B. herself.

Feeling winded, she sat down on the bed, the soiled sheets in her lap. She could hear, almost verbatim, the terrible fight she and Bear had had when he was getting ready to retire and she'd said she wanted to buy the house. What, he'd wanted to know, did she want with "a goddamn plantation"? They couldn't afford it. He wanted to travel. *Travel?* she'd said in a whisper; then her voice had gone into a yowl of protest. Travel? When she'd spent her whole adult life being shunted from base to base, when he'd destroyed her life, their childrens' lives by constantly uprooting them? And it wasn't as though they had the money to travel in style, sit in front of some whitewashed hotel in Portugal, and watch the fishermen. If they traveled, it would be in a camper where she couldn't even fix a decent meal! She didn't have to remind him how he'd squandered their savings and thrown away their security because she knew, after a lifetime of arguments, that if she made him feel too guilty he'd just walk out and she might not see him for days. She did remind him of his promise, the promise that had kept her at his side, the only promise he hadn't broken: when he retired she would get a real home, a fine home. Or was that another sop he'd thrown her? A lie, as she'd said then, "like all the other lies in this rotten marriage?" (Why was it that ugly words, words that could never be taken back, stuck in the mind so clearly?) She wanted *this* house, next door to the house her brother-in-law had bought for her sister, in this town where she'd been born, wanted it so much that if he didn't let her have it, she'd leave him and get every damned penny she could get out of him.

She'd softened that threat with a practical plan: she knew the house was too big for the two of them, understood that they couldn't really afford it (though it was going for a ridiculous price and a blind man could see that the town was expanding), *but* she'd be willing to work to make it possible. She'd turn it into a B & B, not with a vulgar sign out front (neighbors on The Point wouldn't have stood for that anyway), but a graceful, comfortable place that would provide them with a cash flow. Despite her reasoning, he'd walked out anyway. It was the first time in years that he'd stayed out overnight, and the last time he would ever do so.

When he'd come back the next morning, he'd just said, "Do what you want. It doesn't matter anymore," and she'd known that she'd won the final battle but had lost him for good.

Remembering that awful morning, she put her hands to her mouth, lowered her head, took a deep breath. Since the thought of preparing food usually calmed her, she turned her mind to lunch. "I'll fix spinach salad for lunch," she thought. "Peatsy likes spinach salad." But she still felt a hum of fear, not a memory of past troubles but a sense that something terrible was going to happen that day. "You're crazier than a bedbug" she said out loud, and, picking up the cleaning caddy, she left the room.

Two

Dozier had finished putting the dishes away and was sitting at the kitchen table reading the classifieds in the *Gazette* when she came back downstairs. "You okay?" he asked as she tossed the dirty sheets and towels into the laundry room.

She retrieved her rings from the windowsill, studying her hands as she put them on. "I'm all behind like the cow's tail. The girls are coming here for bridge so I've got to run over to the Winn Dixie and pick up something for lunch." When he rolled his eyes to the ceiling she added, "I know you think I'm a sucker."

"No, you're just a tad too accommodating. Always have been. Can't help it. It's your sweet nature."

Being told that she was sweet when she felt she couldn't do anything right made her eyes moist. "Do you ever have one of those days," she began. "From the moment I opened my eyes this morning, I knew . . ."

He folded the paper and stood up. "Steady as she goes, sister. You'll get through it." The most natural thing would have been to bring her head to his chest, put his arms around her, and give her a comforting hug, but he pushed his glasses higher onto the bridge of his nose and said, "Saw an advertisement for a moving sale over in Port Royal. 'Divorce sale' they call 'em now. Print it right in the paper. Anyhow, I think I'll drive over. Might could find a bargain. 'Member when I found that Art Deco wall sconce you liked so much?"

"Uh-huh. And I remember you near electrocuted yourself installing it."

"I guess there'd be worse ways to go. By the by, I noticed that one of your porch lights is burned out."

"You know . . ." She tilted her head and smiled up at him. "When I was young I always thought that those songs about a woman needing a handyman were dirty, but since I've had this house I've come to realize that when a gal's crooning about needing to have her furnace fixed maybe she really *does* need to have her furnace fixed."

Dozier patted her shoulder. "I'll check out that porch light soon's I get back. If you win at bridge you can tip me."

At 11:45, as she was tossing the spinach salad, the doorbell rang. She knew it would be Mary Gebhardt. Mary had been a high-school principal in Cleveland before she and her husband, Mort, had retired and come South and Mary still conducted her life as though bells rang every hour. "I came a little early," Mary explained, raking her hand through her close-cropped white hair, "because I want to copy your recipe for cornbread stuffing. Now that Mort and I take most of our meals at the clubhouse, I can barely remember how to fry an egg." Mary had lived out on Dataw Island for years but she still wore outfits that made her look like a tourist. This morning she was in Reeboks, an aqua velour running suit and, in lieu of a purse, had a fanny pack strapped around her waist. Why was it, Josie wondered as she ushered Mary into the kitchen, that people nowadays, even people with money, wore what amounted to an exercise uniform but usually looked out of shape? And in Mary's case it really made no sense, since her leathery complexion came not from outdoor exercise but from lying next to the pool, cigarettes close at hand.

She had no more than settled Mary at the kitchen table, given her pen and paper and a copy of her *Lowcountry Cooking* (which Mary was always saying she was going to buy but never did), when the bell rang again. "That," Josie predicted, "will be Peatsy." On her way to the front door she paused as she passed the hall mirror, smoothing both her hair and her skirt. Unnecessary gestures, since she knew that Peatsy had an aristocratic disregard of convention and wouldn't have cared if she'd come to the door buck naked. When Mary had first met Peatsy she'd pulled Josie aside and said, "I heard this joke, that there are only two kinds of South Carolinians: those who have never worn shoes, and those who make you feel that *you* have never worn shoes. I mean, I've got a master's degree and Peatsy Gibbs never went further than high school, but she makes me feel like I've never worn shoes. Is that because she was married to a general?" To which Josie had replied, "That's part of it, but Peatsy . . . well, Peatsy's from Charleston." Mary didn't get it, so Josie'd tried to explain that to Charlestonians like Peatsy, who could trace their lineage back to buddies of King Charles II, the question "Who are your people?" was more important than how much education, talent, or even money you might have.

Peatsy, in a velveteen blazer and violent silk dress, tottering on heels no sane woman in her seventies had any business wearing, came in on a mist of Youth Dew. Josie could tell she'd just come from the beauty parlor because her hair, which had the weight and color of chicken feathers, had been puffed into flossy fullness, and her face beneath her makeup was as flushed as if she were still sitting under the dryer. "Are you feeling all right?" Josie asked.

"Fine, fine," Peatsy assured her, "just the usual Christmas rush." One of her hands, now so bony that her diamond rings were loose, fished her pearls from the neck of her dress. The other was outstretched, her purse and a battered Harrod's shopping bag dangling from her wrist. "Be a sweetheart and stash this somewhere till we've finished the game, will you?" Josie took the shopping bag and saw that it contained three small boxes wrapped in gold paper. She didn't have to be clairvoyant to know they contained Estée Lauder perfume. She could even guess that it would be Cinnabar for Mary, White Linen for Edna, and Beautiful for her. Only Mary would have taken their agreement not to exchange gifts seriously. Josie had bought each of them a book on South Carolina history, which Mary claimed to be interested in and Peatsy could have written if only she'd had the discipline.

Since the weather was so balmy they decided to play on the sun porch. They'd already settled themselves at the table when Edna came though the back door, letting it slam behind her. Peatsy jumped and Mary said, "What the hell!" but Josie was used to Edna's entrances. Ever since she'd been a child she'd felt as though she melted into the wallpaper when her sister Edna entered a room. "Sorry I'm late," Edna said, dropping her shoulder bag next to her chair and stripping off the jacket of her cerise pantsuit. "That new girl I hired to work in the shop is about as reliable as a politician's promises." Peatsy smiled but cut her eyes over to Josie, giving her an "Edna's late again" look, then she reached for the cards and began to shuffle. Josie set a glass of iced tea next to Edna's place and went into the kitchen. "I'll never know how you can drink iced tea year-round," Mary said with a mock shiver.

"Do you think we could start?" Peatsy asked. "I haven't near finished packing and you know I'm flying up to D.C. tomorrow. And I've still got to do some shopping."

"Shopping," Mary groaned as Edna shucked off her gold bracelets and called for Josie to bring her some Sweet'n Low. As Josie set the salad plates before them, Mary said, "I read Evie's column in the paper today. She's so right about these godawful Christmas holidays." Josie braced herself, hoping Evie hadn't written about some miserable family scene from their past. "And all the psychologists agree with her," Mary went on. "They say more people go into depressions around the holidays than at any other time of the year. The holidays induce trauma. I'm glad I married a Jew. At least we never had to go overboard celebrating Christmas, though when the kids were little . . ."

"Trauma?" Peatsy interrupted. "Why should a holiday celebration induce trauma?"

"Well, you know," Mary insisted, "everyone has such unrealistic expectations of love and togetherness, and then there's the pressure to buy gifts—"

"We're not drafted into celebrating," Peatsy reminded her. "If people don't want to do it, then they just shouldn't bother."

"But the social pressure," Mary insisted.

"Oh, social pressure!" Peatsy scoffed. "I simply don't understand all this fiddle-faddle about social pressure." For Peatsy, conformity was not a straightjacket but a shield, and she'd understood since girlhood that you could do anything you damned pleased if that shield was in place. "Are we playing cards, or what?"

After the fourth rubber they'd finished their salads and settled down, playing with killer concentration. The conversation had meandered down the usual back roads—the weather, diets, the commercialization of Christmas—and hit the highway of serious gossip. "I dropped by Beaufort Memorial yesterday to see Grace," Peatsy said. She lowered the cards, which she always held stiff and close to her mouth like a geisha's fan. "George told me they're going to have to take her up to Charleston for the next operation, but they haven't told her yet."

Mary rearranged her hand with her usual swift precision. "I think it's downright criminal to hold out on people when they're that sick. On some level people always guess when they're going to die and when those around them won't admit it, it just isolates them."

"You sound like Shirley MacLaine," Edna said. "How the hell does anyone know when they're going to die?"

"I just think they do," Mary insisted. "After Grace had that first operation and went through chemo, they said they'd got it all, but now, just six months later, she's back in the hospital. She's got to know. If people'd just have the guts to tell her the truth she'd at least be able to prepare for it."

"How could she prepare for it?" Josie asked.

"Well, she could get that lousy son of hers to come visit. He's so neglectful. He hasn't been to see her in years." Realizing that she'd touched a sore spot, Mary quickly looked away from Josie. "She could arrange her will," she stumbled on. "She could say goodbye. She could . . . well, not that I'm a believer, but she could prepare herself spiritually."

"I can tell you," Peatsy said, "you won't catch me going through chemotherapy."

Edna laughed. "Oh, Peatsy, you're so vain you'd rather die than have your hair fall out."

"Maybe so," Peatsy agreed, "'cause I feel that the *quality* of life is important. If you're just holding on by your fingernails, being snatched bald by chemo, so sick you can't eat or drink . . . I just don't see the point of it."

Josie said, "I guess none of us can know what she'd do unless she was confronted with the real situation." She hated it when the conversation turned, as it invariably did, to sick friends, doctors, and medical bills, but she supposed that at their time of life this was as natural as teenage girls talking about dates. "I'll swing by and visit Grace this afternoon," she said. Then, standing up, "Everyone ready for dessert?"

"What are you offering?" Edna wanted to know.

"Just some thawed-out coconut cake and strawberries."

"I'll pass," Peatsy said. "I've been chasing around since early morning and I'm feeling a little woozy."

"And you're the only one who doesn't have to watch her weight," Mary complained. "I guess I'll just have the strawberries. Remember when we were kids and only rich people ate fruit out of season? We were lucky we didn't get scurvy during those winters in Cleveland back then. And speaking of winters, I was watching the Weather Channel last night and I saw where New York's supposed to get a big storm. I hope Cam's prepared."

"Oh, Cam's still too young to worry about the weather," Josie said as she gathered up the salad plates. As was usual when someone mentioned Cam she stiffened and looked away, like a kid getting ready for a shot. "You want both cake and strawberries, Edna?"

"Mary," Edna said, "if you knew Cam you'd know she wouldn't give a damn about the weather. I remember back when she was no more'n ten or eleven and we had that hurricane and Cam ran out in the yard. No one could stop her. She just broke away and ran into the yard and stood there, laughing like crazy, waving her arms."

"Is she staying in New York for the holidays?" Mary persisted.

"I think she's going up to Connecticut to be with some friends," Josie lied. The truth was that during their last phone conversation, Cam hadn't said anything about Christmas. Or her boyfriend. Or her job at Athena Press. Josie knew better than to ask, but because she hadn't wanted the conversation to end, she'd fallen into her usual trap of yammering about guests and recipes and Lila's kids, knowing she sounded as small-minded as Cam thought her to be. "Edna, I've asked you twice. Do you want cake and strawberries?"

Edna said, "Oh, all right. You've twisted my arm."

As she carried the salad plates into the kitchen, Josie heard the other women's voices drop into what she thought were sympathetic whispers. *I'm just being paranoid,* she told herself as she set the plates on the sink and took the dessert from the refrigerator. Their voices suddenly rose enough for her to hear them: Mary said that her granddaughter's SAT score was so high that Wellesley had offered her early admission; Edna bragged that her son, Skip, had just closed a big lumber deal with a Japanese company; Peatsy said she couldn't wait to get up to D.C. because her son, Waring, who owned an art gallery, had just bought several paintings of backwoods baptismal ceremonies from a Georgia primitive who promised to be as hot as Grandma Moses. Josie wondered how far you'd have to go into the Georgia woods to still find preachers dunking folks into water holes. Probably a lot farther than most Northerners thought. To drown out the conversation, she turned on the faucet and began to rinse the plates, wondering what Cam *was* doing for Christmas.

The last time she'd seen Cam, over a year ago, when Lila had taken her along on a trip to New York, Cam hadn't even invited them to her apartment. They'd met for brunch at the Waldorf, where, thanks to Orrie's generosity, she and Lila were staying. When Lila excused herself to go to the ladies', Cam had ordered another Bloody Mary (her third) and lit another cigarette (Josie had lost count of those). She'd thought she'd made her face blank, but Cam had said, "I don't see why you're worrying about me, Mama. You don't seem to worry about Lila and she's like a glazed doughnut—all puffed up and shiny, but with a big hole in the middle. Do you think she's on tranks or antidepressants?" And all that afternoon, while she and Lila were at the matinee of *Phantom of the Opera*, Josie had watched Lila and thought about Cam.

"Forget the dessert for now, will you, Josie?" Peatsy called. "You girls can have it after I leave. I'm fifty cents down and I want to play this last rubber before I dash." Josie had refilled the coffee cups and Edna's iced tea and taken her place at the table. Then Peatsy had trumped Mary's ace and said she was feeling dizzy, then . . .

The speed with which the ambulance arrived had amazed her. They'd barely concluded their argument about whether or not to move Peatsy to the couch—Edna repeating the "never touch an injured person" theory, Mary yelling, "Bullshit! I can't keep propping her up like a sack of potatoes," then ordering Josie to take Peatsy's shoulders while she took her legs. The three of them had lifted Peatsy and moved to the living room slow and crab-style because she was so light it seemed she might shatter if they dropped her. Josie tried to find Peatsy's pulse while Mary and Edna traded guesses—had she just fainted? Was it a heart attack? A stroke? Mary said she felt *she* might faint and rushed back to the sun porch for a cigarette. Through clenched teeth Edna said, "You'll be next if you don't give up those damn cigarettes." And then they heard the wail of the siren.

A husky black man in his thirties and a young white woman, both in uniform, were at the front door. Josie stepped back, answering questions, admiring the efficiency with which they pulled out instruments, checked Peatsy's vital signs, and strapped her onto a stretcher.

Neighbors had gathered at the front of the house. Josie looked for Dozier but didn't see him and watched as the attendants lifted the stretcher into the back of the ambulance. She started to climb in with them but they told her she should follow in her car. Mary left off giving the neighbors the lowdown, said she was going out to the country club to find her husband, Morty, and would then be over to the hospital. Edna, who had apparently gone over to her own house, returned, cursing that Dozier was never there when she needed him, and said she was going back to her shop, so would Josie please call her there.

Josie walked back into the house, got her car keys from the hook near the back door, started out, then turned back to get Peatsy's purse. She was halfway to the hospital before she realized that she'd left her own purse behind.

She told the volunteer behind the admissions desk, a woman of her own age who looked vaguely familiar, who she was and why she was there. The woman told her to sit down and wait. Josie asked where the telephones were located, took a seat, and opened Peatsy's purse. Its contents were a jumble—balled-up, lipstick-kissed tissues, an address book, a parking ticket torn in two, upholstery samples on a metal loop, a battered eelskin wallet, a roll of breath mints, a folding brush, a bottle of blood-pressure pills, a Waterman pen, discount coupons for Broad River Seafood, a cosmetics bag—and, as she dug to the bottom, a bunch of keys on a ring with a gold Palmetto charm, quarters, dimes, pennies, a single garnet earring, and a couple of safety pins. She took out several quarters and the address book. The book was butter-soft, navy leather with the initials PWG, for Peatsy Waring Gibbs, pressed into it in gold. Quintessential Peatsy, Josie thought, then she remembered that she herself had given it to Peatsy for Christmas year before last. She also remembered that she'd spent more money than she'd wanted to but, Peatsy being Peatsy, she wouldn't have felt right giving her anything but the best. From the first time she'd met Peatsy, when she was just sixteen visiting a cousin in Charleston and the cousin had let her tag along to a moon-dance coming-out party given in Peatsy's honor, she'd been in awe of Peatsy.

Even then, Peatsy had seemed to come from another era. She was an F. Scott Fitzgerald golden girl (though her cornsilk hair came out of a bottle), she was a Gershwin tune (though actually it was her mama who was rich and her daddy who was good-looking), she was filmy dresses and slim hips and the keys to a convertible. She was smart and, perhaps what Josie envied most of all, confident.

A lifetime's friendship, or more accurately, association, had taught her that Peatsy was stylish rather than beautiful, more wily than intelligent, and probably incapable of real friendship with another woman, but against her better judgment, she still held Peatsy in awe. Perhaps, perversely, she did so because Peatsy had hurt her so many times. There had been that awful time at Josie's engagement party when she'd gone upstairs to go to the bathroom, had passed the bedroom she shared with Edna, and had seen, through the partially open door, Edna sitting at the vanity while Peatsy sprawled on the bed, and heard Peatsy say, "Of course he's a knockout, but I'll bet he didn't have a suit of clothes before Uncle Sam issued him that uniform. I mean he could put his boots under my bed anytime, but *marry* him? Josie's got to be crazy."

And all those years during the war, when she was using leg paint and Peatsy, miraculously, had nylons. And even after the war. Bear had finally become an officer, she an officer's wife, but by that time Peatsy had become "the general's lady." And that time—Lord, she hadn't let herself think about it for years—when they were all in their late thirties and she'd known that Peatsy finally *had* let Bear put his boots under her bed, and General Gibbs's finding out about it had blocked Bear's promotion and put him on a downward spiral from which he'd never recovered. And yet, if anyone had asked her she would have said, unequivocally, that Peatsy was her friend. Why was she thinking about all this now, when Peatsy might be dying? Her stomach flip-flopped. She turned her attention back to Peatsy's address book.

She couldn't find Waring's number under either "Gibbs" or "Waring." On the first page of the book, under "In Case of Emergency," she was surprised to see her own name and number printed in a spidery hand. Finally, at the top of the S's, she saw "Son:

Waring Gibbs, III," the number of the Green Carnation Gallery, a home number, then "Waring's companion," a name and number crossed out, and "Alonzo?" and another number.

She went to the desk and asked a second time where the phones were located. She sat on the plastic stool near the phone, wishing they still had actual booths where you could close the door and have some privacy. Deciding against using the quarters, she found a telephone calling card and punched in the torturously long series of numbers, incorrectly. She tried again, finally reached the Green Carnation Gallery, started to talk as soon as she heard a voice, then realized it was an answering machine and hung up in panic.

She tried, in vain, to remember if she'd given the emergency people Waring's name and number. Then she tried again, punching in the numbers as slowly as a preschooler playing with a new educational toy, and after the beep, she said, "I don't know if you remember me, Waring. I'm Josie Tatternall. Your mother's been taken ill. Please call me at—" For a split-second she couldn't remember her own phone number. What if her brain were short-circuiting? What if she were having one of those—what did they call them—pinpoint strokes? *Well, I guess I'm in the right place for it,* she thought, and when she laughed, her phone number rolled off her tongue.

When she dialed Alonzo's number she got another machine, with grinding rock music in the background and a message in a heavily accented voice: "You're there. I'm not here. You know what to do, *amigo.*" The machine started to repeat the message in Spanish, so she gave up. She sat very still, then dialed Lila, reaching Lila's answering machine at the same time she remembered that, since it was Wednesday, Lila would be at the Volunteers for Literacy. Her heart was thrumping as though she'd run up a flight of stairs. She hated answering machines as much as she hated computers. For one wild moment she thought of calling Cam, then she went back to the seating area, and lowered herself into a chair, smiling reflexively at the little boy who was wiggling around on the lap of his dozing father.

She didn't expect Edna to turn up—Edna was bad as a man when it came to illness. Maybe Dozier would come by. But why was she thinking that Edna was "just like a man" if she expected Dozier, who *was* a man, to come? Lord, her mind was turning to pluff mud—that soft squishy ooze she'd stepped into as a child when they'd gone harvesting oysters. She could see that her smile had made the wiggling child think that she might play with him, so she closed her eyes. Pluff mud, she thought, imagining its fecund, clean smell, feeling its cool mush sucking at the soles of her feet.

"What . . . ?" She jerked up, recoiling as she looked into Mort Gebhardt's face, not ten inches from hers.

"It's us," Mary said, patting her arm.

"I was just resting my eyes," she said defensively, realizing that she must've fallen asleep.

Mary nodded. "Some people have that reaction to shock. I was in Los Angeles once when they had an earthquake, and right afterwards I just crawled into bed and slept for hours. We're here now, so you ought to go on home. Peatsy's stabilized, whatever that means."

"She—?"

"Uh-uh. It *was* a heart attack. That's what I said, wasn't it? The doctor came out and told us when we came in just a little bit ago. They reached Waring and he's coming down soon's he can get a flight. You're done in, Josie. You ought to go on home. They won't let you see her anyway. Mort'll drive you."

Mort smiled and offered his hand. He had, Josie noted, not for the first time, a gentle gallantry you wouldn't have expected from a man who smoked cigars, weighed two hundred pounds, and had made big money in the meat-packing business. "C'mon, Miss Josie," he kidded her in a drawl, "let me carry you on home."

"No, no. I'll go on," she said. She noticed that the light had been turned on and, looking at the wall clock, saw that it was almost six. She must've been dozing for over an hour. "So Peatsy's all right?"

"Stabilized, that's what they said," Mary answered dubiously. "I'm gonna put in a call to our son, David. You know he's an internist. He'll give me more information than I'll get out of them here. Let Mort take you home, Josie."

Driving after dark made her nervous, but she said, "No, no. I'd really rather go in my own car. I'm fine. You know my house isn't but ten minutes away. Believe me, I'm fine. I'll go on home. But promise to let me know how she's doing."

Mort started to insist that he drive her, but Mary, in a tone that suggested she was working out some ongoing personal dispute, said, "Mort, you don't listen! The woman said she wanted to go alone. Why can't you respect what she says and let her go alone?"

"I respect it. I respect it," Mort insisted, throwing his beefy arm around Mary's shoulder. "How come I married a *shiksa* and she still ends up sounding like my mother?"

Josie smiled as she got up. "You'll call me?" She handed over Peatsy's purse, which she'd been holding tight to her chest. Mary took it and promised she'd call.

As she passed the reception desk Josie looked back. Mort's arm was around Mary's waist, her head was on his shoulder, she was talking a mile a minute and Mort was nodding with a "yeah, yeah, I hear you" acceptance. Then he pulled her close and she stopped talking and nestled into him. Josie felt so lonesome she thought she might cry. "Oh, miss," she said to the receptionist, wondering how she'd been so addle-brained that she hadn't asked before, "I believe

I have another friend here. A Mrs. Grace Koch." The woman, who'd been fixing the curling M from the "MERRY CHRISTMAS" tacked to the wall behind the desk, turned to her. "A Mrs. Grace Koch," Josie repeated. "Oh," the woman said, glancing around. She checked a roster, smiled as she punched a number into the phone, then turned away. Her brief conversation concluded, she turned back and said, "I'm sorry to tell you, ma'am, but Mrs. Koch died yesterday morning. Her family has been notified, so I guess you might get in touch with them."

Pulling into her driveway, Josie saw that lights were on in the kitchen, the living room, and the lavender room upstairs. She let herself in through the back door, moving as quietly as a burglar, inhaling the pine scent of the Christmas tree. The sun porch and the kitchen had been restored to order. There was a note from Cuba in the middle of the kitchen table. She'd gotten no further than reading "Dear Miz Tatternall . . ." when she heard movement on the stairs and Mrs. Beasley's whining voice. "Is that you, Mrs. Tatternall?"

Oh, dear, not now. "Yes, Mrs. Beasley," she called out, trying to keep the annoyance out of her voice. "No need to be alarmed. It's just me. No need to come down."

"I've just been frantic, Mrs. Tatternall. Your housekeeper said you'd had an emergency and you'd be right back but . . ."

"Everything's all right, Mrs. Beasley. I'll be with you shortly."

"I was just frantic. Whatever happened? Your housekeeper said—"

"Mrs. Beasley," she called again, not bothering to hide her irritation, "you'll have to excuse me for a few minutes. I have to make some phone calls, and then I'll knock on your door and we'll have our sherry, all right?"

Mrs. Beasley responded with a miffed, "Then I'll just go take my shower. I suppose we can talk afterward." Josie listened to Mrs. B.

make a grudging retreat to her room, then read the note: "Dear Miz Tatternall, Mr. Dozier tolt me what happen. I clent up and got Miz Beastly in her room." Josie smiled. Despite Cuba's chronic misspelling, she suspected that "Beastly" instead of "Beasley" was deliberate. "I strung the lites on the Xmas tree," the note continued. "I pray Miz Peatsy will be O.K. I pray for her and for you. See you in the morning, Cuba."

Still holding the note, she walked through the semidark dining room into the bright living room, flicking off the wall switch, then the lamps, so that only the twinkling lights on the tree remained. Sinking onto the couch, she stared at the boxes of ornaments she'd left at the base of the tree. Grace Koch dead. She had never been close to Grace Koch, but she'd known her for, oh goodness, perhaps fifty years. That a life could be snuffed out, gone from the world so suddenly. . . . And perhaps Peatsy, who'd sat in this very house a few short hours ago, getting peevish because she'd lost fifty cents at bridge, Peatsy might be dying at this very moment. And Peatsy was only a few years older than Josie.

She smoothed the note on her lap. Cuba was going to pray for her. How comforting it must be to believe in an all-powerful and protective God who was always on call. She'd been raised Methodist and, at Bear's request, had taken religious instruction and "converted" when they'd married. She still went to Mass because she liked Father Lazeret, but when she got right down to it, she had to admit that she'd stopped believing in a Daddy god who took a personal interest in your life even before she'd met Bear—when she'd been a high-school senior and stopped praying for victory in basketball games. Probably there was a God—or at least an intelligent force in the universe—but such a force was beyond her understanding, and she couldn't expect that He, She, or It cared about whether your team won, or if you paid your bills on time, or even if you had cancer. You had to rely on family and friends for that sort of concern. Nevertheless, she felt a powerful urge to pray. "Please," she began. But then she just stared up at the tree, thinking of Christmases past.

There'd been that Christmas right after they'd been transferred when she'd been six weeks pregnant with Evie and having the worst morning sickness she'd ever experienced. The base housing was cramped and shoddy; she hadn't known a soul. It had been the first time they hadn't had a real pine tree, and when they'd bought the boxed plastic tree at the PX, she'd almost started to cry. She now knew enough to understand that she'd been going through hormonal changes and suffering depression, though at the time she'd just said she was homesick and had the blues. Oh, she had been miserable. Yet it had turned out to be one of the happiest Christmases she'd ever had.

That Christmas Eve, after she'd put Cam and Lila to bed, she and Bear had put out the presents, danced to Armed Forces Radio in their pajamas, and made love on the fold-out sofa that served as their bed. Afterward, as they'd whispered and laughed, she drinking the milk and eating the cookies the girls had put out for Santa, Bear having another toddy, she'd looked up to see Lila, standing in the doorway, her face puffy from sleep, staring wide-eyed at the presents. She'd got up to put her back to bed, but Bear had opened his arms wide and said, "Yep, Lila baby, Santa's already come." And when Lila asked, "When? When did he come?" Bear had dropped his voice to a suggestive whisper, kissed Josie's hand, and said, "About fifteen minutes ago. So"—he'd pulled on his pajama bottoms and gotten out of the bed— "wake up your sister and let's have Christmas right now." And despite Josie's protestations, Lila had run to get Cam.

Then it had been happy confusion—shrieks of delight, ribbons and boxes and—she would never forget this—when all the presents had been opened and Bear had gone in to take a shower and

Lila had been squatting on the floor changing the diaper on her new Betsy Wetsy doll, Cam, who couldn't have been more than five, had sidled up to her and whispered, "I know it's not Santa. I know it's just you and Daddy." She'd started to remonstrate, but Cam had given her that precociously grave look and said, "It's okay, Mama. I won't tell Lila. She's only a child and I don't want to spoil her fun," and Josie had pulled Cam to her and laughed so hard she'd started to wet her pants.

She got up from the couch, walked through the dining room and kitchen and opened the back door. The hair on her arms stood up as the chilly air and the earthy smell of the garden hit her. Her girls had never lived in this house, yet she opened her mouth as though to call them, as she'd called them from countless back doors, on countless evenings when the light had faded and the weather had turned cold, "Camilla! Lila! Evie! Stop playing and come on in. Come home. Now!" She stood for another full minute, blank and dazed. Then she shuddered, turned, closed the door, and walked to the kitchen telephone. She would call her girls, call them now, tell them that life was short, that time was running out. No, she couldn't say that. She would just tell hem that they must come home for Christmas dinner. And they couldn't refuse her. Not this time. This time she wouldn't take "no" for an answer.

Three

Cam never cried. Absolutely. Never. Did not cry, she told herself as she ripped the plastic cover from a roll of paper towels, wiped her eyes, and blew her nose.

She hadn't cried on Sunday when Sam, her lover of three years, had told her that he was moving back to Atlanta, and she hadn't cried on Tuesday when her boss, Elaine, had told her that the grant money hadn't come through, so there would be cutbacks, maybe even layoffs, at Athena Press. But she was crying now. Not just crying but blubbering, howling, moaning. And why? Because she'd dropped a bag of groceries.

It was already dark and beginning to sleet as she'd come out of the office. Standing in the building's lobby, peering through the glass doors at the crowd swollen with Christmas shoppers, she'd wondered why she'd been dumb enough to believe the weather report ("cold but sunny, with temperatures in the mid-twenties") and to wear her best hat and coat and her red suede boots. But she knew the answer to that: if you were on the wrong side of forty, worked in an all-female office, and had just lost your lover, you knew that if you didn't make a conscious effort to groom yourself you could turn into a bag lady faster than Cinderella's coach had turned into a pumpkin.

She took a small mirror from her makeup bag and moved it from side to side, looking at her face. "Faded" was the word that came to mind. Her cheeks were pale, her eyes dull, her mouth seemed to lack definition, except for those tiny lines of disappointment that pulled it down on either side. She had never thought of herself as pretty (only her mother, and men who were on the make, had described her as pretty) but "interesting" and "sexy" (especially sexy) had been used to describe her, even in the recent past. But it was winter, she reminded herself as she put on lipstick, and everyone looked pasty in winter, and the lobby had fluorescent lights and everyone looked sick in fluorescent lights, and she hadn't been sleeping well, and—she rolled down the lipstick and clicked the mirror shut—and sooner or later, you faded like an old Polaroid. And you never realized how vain you were until it started to happen.

"You know, Cam, you really don't need makeup." Her assistant, Maria Giacomini, came up next to her, dropping her backpack to the floor so she could button up her overcoat. "Makeup is so retro, and you look great without it. If you don't mind my saying." Cam did mind, but smiled and said, "That's one girl's opinion." Maria rolled her eyes at being called a girl and stared out the glass doors. "Oh, shit," she said, "will you look at that sleet! The sky god is pissing on us again." Cam nodded. Maria, or Young Maria, as she thought of her (because lately anyone under thirty-five seemed young), had the apple cheeks, liquid eyes, and finely etched brows of a Renaissance madonna, a natural beauty she seemed determined to obscure by wearing a spiky crew cut and baggy clothes. When answering the office phones, Maria was as polite as her grandmother would have been when serving biscotti and espresso to the priest, but as soon as she dropped her office persona, she sounded like a sergeant in a Marine barracks. "And will you look at the fuckin' traffic," Maria went on. "It's those goddamn suburban consumers. Why don't they stay home and shop in their malls? Screw Christmas anyway."

Though Cam wouldn't have put it that way (constant profanity, like a fondness for computers or the ability to program a VCR, seemed to be a generational difference), she was inclined to agree. What did Christmas mean except clogged traffic, short tempers, Muzak carols in elevators, tacky decorations, and office parties where people got drunk and tried to lay their co-workers? At least she'd be spared the office party, since four of the ten women on staff at Athena Press were Jewish, one was a converted Buddhist, and the other two, "women of color," as her boss, Elaine, would say (the term always made Cam uncomfortable because it sounded dangerously close to her grandmother, Mawmaw, talking about "coloreds"), had shucked their Baptist heritage and were planning instead to celebrate the newly created African-American feast Kwanzaa.

"And I have to go shopping," Maria groaned, " 'cause if I turn up at my brother's house without presents for his brats, my mother will fry my ass. You finished shopping yet?"

"I generally just order from catalogues," Cam told her. She was past the rebellion of ignoring Christmas altogether, so she thumbed through museum catalogues, then ordered over the phone. This year she'd sent her family books: *Victorian Gardens* to her mother, *Mary Cassatt* to Lila, *Fashion Through the Ages* to Evie. She'd only ventured into the stores to buy a fancy frying pan for her best friend, Reba, and cashmere sweater for her lover, Sam. She still hadn't decided if she'd send Sam's sweater on to Atlanta or return it to Brooks Brothers after the holidays.

"Wish I'd had the sense to order from catalogues," Maria said. "Now I'll be stuck in the kids' department at Macy's, spending money I don't have. Shit! I just hope I don't see a bunch of kids lined up for some wino playing Santa Claus. Ever considered the significance of little girls sitting on the lap of an old guy in red underwear and begging him for presents?" Cam laughed, but a quick look confirmed that Maria was deadly serious, twenty-two-year-old graduates of Rutgers's Department of Women's Studies not being known for their frivolity. "Well, here goes Dick Tracy," Maria said, raking her hand through her crew cut, pulling her thirties-style man's hat low over her ears, and shoving open the door.

Cam braced herself against the freezing blast, watched Maria shoulder her way into the crowd, then headed in the direction of the bus stop, her head turned to the side to avoid the needles of sleet and one shoulder pulled down by a bookbag heavy with manuscripts. *Lordy,* she thought, *I must look like Quasimodo. And why am I lugging these manuscripts home when there isn't a snowball's chance in hell that Athena Press can publish them?* She wished she could write a letter telling the truth: "Dear Author, Word may not yet have reached Lincoln, Nebraska, but small presses are in a bad way. By the time you receive this, I may be out of a job." But she would read the manuscripts, write a critique, and, if either of them was any good, add some words of encouragement. She knew how much it took to write a book, even a mediocre book. Especially a mediocre book. And as her father, Bear, had always said, you didn't desert the field because the battle wasn't going your way.

When the bus finally arrived, the crowd squeezed onto it like meat forced into a sausage casing, and she was pushed to the back, poked by elbows, crushed by shopping bags, boxes, and umbrellas. Some fifty blocks later, sweating and dizzy from the diaper smell of wet wool, she pulled the cord for her stop. The bus rolled on. In a throwback to an earlier self she called, "Oh, sir? Sir?" in a sweet Southern voice, but when she was ignored she switched to a louder, "Hey, mister, I want out!" The teenager in the Malcolm X cap who exited in front of her let the door slam in her face. She shoved it open and stepped into a bank of slush. Now her red suede boots were really gone.

The sleet had been replaced by an icy, cutting wind. Shifting her bookbag to her other shoulder, she turned the corner of Broadway and moved toward Amsterdam, past the Japanese take-out, the Korean grocery, the newsstand, the baby furniture store she knew must be a numbers front (why else would so many men hang out in a baby furniture store?), and Blockbuster Video. She slowed down as she passed "Discount Air Fares," wondering when she'd joined the ranks of people who complained about winter and gawked at sunny travel posters. Walking by Ray's Pizza, she caught a whiff of hot pepperoni and her mouth watered, even though she'd met her friend, Reba, for lunch at a Cajun restaurant where they'd eaten large bowls of gumbo and a disgusting amount of cornbread.

She and Reba had been buddies since they'd met at a temp agency when they were college students. In the intervening decades they'd been roommates (briefly), loaned one another money, supported one another through changes in hair color and careers, nursed one another through viruses, hangovers, minor surgery, broken hearts, and family deaths.

There had been a line of customers waiting to be seated but Reba had already found a table, unbundled herself, and put the menus aside. "It gripes me to pay twelve dollars for okra gumbo and cornbread when I know the ingredients only cost a dollar ninety-five," she said by way of greeting.

"But the value of the chef's expertise is incalculable. Isn't that what you always tell the customers of your catering business?" Cam teased.

"Yeah, that's what I tell them. Because I'm afraid they'll realize the ingredients only cost a dollar ninety-five. Sit. Sit. I took the liberty of ordering because I know what you like and I know you have to get back to the office." Leaning across the table, she took one of Cam's hands. "You don't look too good," she said with an honesty so concerned and open-faced it was impossible to take offense. "So. Tell me again about Sam."

Cam said, "There's nothing to tell," and when Reba rolled her eyes in an aw-come-on expression, amended it to, "I've already told you everything."

"But, Cam, it's not like he's leaving you. I mean, he's been offered this big promotion back in Atlanta. What's he gonna do? Turn it down?"

"Of course not. I wouldn't expect him to do that. After all, his kids live there."

"Exactly. And he didn't say he wanted to break it off with you, did he?"

"Of course not. Men never have the guts to tell you when they want to break it off. They just start playing around with other women, or turning up late, or going into a noncommunicative funk that forces *you* to break up with *them*. That way they don't have to accept any emotional responsibility."

"But Sam didn't do any of those things, did he? We're not talking about the generic male here. We're talking about Sam. Sam's not like that."

"You know him better than I do?" Cam challenged, lining up the utensils.

"Yeah. Maybe I see him better than you do. Love being blind and all."

"Do I seem visually impaired?" Cam asked, shaking out her napkin as though it had bugs on it.

"Oh, no. You're a regular Cassandra. You always see the worst first." Reba shook her head. "I just can't believe you and Sam are breaking up. You're in love with one another. It's as plain as the nose on your face. As plain as the nose on *my* face," she added with characteristic self-deprecation.

"Reba, you've seen too many of those old Disney movies where cute little animals mate for life."

"But you and Sam . . ." Reba almost squawked in frustration, digging in her hand into her Brillo-thick hair, then lowering her voice and staring at Cam as though she were a defense attorney making her final summation. "Let me put it this way: one Sunday morning last year when Cheryl and I were on the outs, I came over to your apartment. I was in a bad state and I had your keys so I just let myself in the front door of the building and came up the stairs, and I was standing at your door getting ready to ring when I heard the two of you. I couldn't exactly hear the words, but I could pick up the tone of it, you know. You were both talking and laughing and I remember just standing there, eavesdropping, feeling a little jealous, thinking 'This is it. They've really got it.' I mean, Sam's a mensch. He looks straight-arrow, but he's got this private, quirky side. Plus, he's got great legs."

"You mean, if you weren't gay, you'd be in love with him?"

Reba shrugged. "Of all the guys you've been with, Sam's the best. I just don't believe Sam would bullshit you." She interrupted herself long enough to say thanks as the waitress set down the bowls, then charged on. "How many guys have I seen you break up with?"

"Well, let's see." Cam shook some hot sauce into her gumbo and said, with sarcastic wistfulness, "There was Fred."

"Ah, Frederick the Weasel—a classic youthful misjudgment."

"Agreed. And Richard."

"The Prince of Darkness. What a phony. I'll never forget what a creep he was."

"And Jeffrey."

"I saw through him from the beginning."

"And—"

"I remember! I remember them all." Reba shook her head, tasted, considered, and swallowed the gumbo, "A little heavy on the bay leaf, otherwise fine," she pronounced, then said, "Cam, I know you. Whenever things get shaky—or sometimes if they just seem too calm—you always want to get your licks in. You always want to be the one who says good-bye first, because you have this deep, unresolved fear of being abandoned."

"You're right," Cam agreed, wiping the corner of her mouth with her napkin. "There is a tad too much bay leaf."

"You're giving me indigestion," Reba accused, throwing up her hands, then, after a few moments of silently tucking into the gumbo, "Tell me again what happened."

Cam put down her spoon and stared out the restaurant window to a street crammed with Christmas shoppers. "I knew the promotion was a possibility. Sam told me about that when it first came up, maybe two months ago."

"So. He wasn't hiding anything. He wasn't looking for an excuse to break it off. He said he wanted to stay together, right?"

"Sure. Sure. He said we could keep it going. I could fly down, he could fly up." She hadn't bothered to ask how often, hadn't bothered to point out that long-distance love affairs usually collapsed under the weight of massive phone bills, delayed flights, hasty sex, and the constant rip and tear of separation. Hadn't bothered to say that she couldn't bear the loneliness and the suspicions that would inevitably, if unjustifiably, creep in when she called and he wasn't there.

"But after all this time! I mean, you could at least have tried to work something out."

"Reba, believe me, the notion that separation increases love is a myth." And the pain of a clean break was preferable to the agony of watching something vital wither and die.

"But he loves you. Didn't he tell you that?"

"Sure. Oh, sure. He loves me the way . . ."

"He once told me he could never have survived being here without you."

". . . the way any long-married man loves the woman who sleeps with him while he's going through a divorce. But now the divorce is final and he has his freedom . . ."

"He was getting the divorce even before he met you!"

"Sure. But I think, and I think *he* thinks, that it's time for him to move on, to another place and to another, probably younger, woman."

"So you just said 'Curtain' and took a bow, and that was that?" Reba demanded.

Cam shrugged and took up her spoon. She couldn't bear to admit—even to Reba—that when Sam had told her he was leaving she'd made that shamefully bitchy, self-pitying remark: "I guess I'm just like my mama. I run a bed-and-breakfast too. Only difference is I provide sex, and I don't get paid for it." That had made him so angry, she'd thought he might hit her. After she'd regained control and apologized, she'd said she'd wanted to make a clean break and she'd walked him to the door and said good-bye as though he were going around the corner for a carton of milk. Then she'd collapsed on the couch, feeling as though a hole had been punched in her heart. "Trust me, Reba. He sounded relieved when I asked him not to call me."

"Well, what else could he do? Beg? He'd never do that. He's got as much pride as you have."

"Now you're giving me indigestion. Do you mind if we talk about something else?"

"Like what? The weather?" Reba scraped the bottom of her bowl and offered the last square of cornbread to Cam. "Remember that first New Year's Day party you and Sam gave? Cornbread makes me think about Sam."

Cam accepted the cornbread and took a bite, feeling stuffed but somehow unsatisfied. "Reba, when you've lived with someone for three years . . ." Not that she and Sam had actually lived together. Because of his long hours at the pharmaceutical research lab, he'd kept his own apartment in New Jersey, but their relationship had an undeniable, and for her, surprisingly pleasant domestic streak from the very beginning. Except for those weekends when he flew back to Atlanta to see his children and talk with lawyers about his divorce, it was his habit to drive into the city on Friday evenings and stay for the weekend. They'd make love, then go out to dinner, or go out to dinner, then make love, depending on which appetite was stronger. On Saturday mornings they'd drop off the laundry, go for long walks, and shop, usually for food. In the evenings they'd see a movie, meet friends, or go to a concert. But Sundays they'd spend alone, sleeping late, eating the goodies they'd bought from Zabar's or Citarella's the previous day, reading the paper, lolling in their robes, chatting and making love until it was time for Sam to go. "When you've lived with someone for three years," she repeated, "*everything* makes you think about them."

If she and Sam were still together, she thought as she passed the bodega with *"Feliz Navidad"* spangles over the door and a crêche nestled in the window amid boxes of green bananas, Pampers, and Tide, she'd have a refrigerator full of gourmet leftovers. As it was, she'd have to stop by Food City, where she'd been a customer for eight years but had never once heard "You're welcome" in response to her "Thank you," or she'd go into a salad bar where lonely-looking people shuffled around the layout of rabbit food as though they were filing past a coffin. If Sam hadn't left her she wouldn't be looking and feeling like Quasimodo. At least she wouldn't have to face the holidays alone. Reba was going to be in town too because Cheryl, Reba's partner in their catering business, and "significant other," was going home to visit her family in Raleigh. "I wonder how I can continue to love someone who's so gutless she can't bear to crawl out of the closet at age forty-five," Reba had lamented at lunch. "But since you and I are both gonna be grass widows, we can spend some time together. We'll go watch the skaters at Rockefeller Center, or listen to the choir at Riverside Church, or maybe just rent *It's a Wonderful Life* and get drunk." *I'll get through it,* Cam thought, trying to believe it.

A warm soapy smell belched from the open door of the Mekong Delta Laundry and she stepped inside to ask Mai if they'd found the sheet they'd lost last week. Mai shook her head and said, "Sorry. Never find. Never lose before." This was true. Though the place was tiny, crowded, and seemingly chaotic—laundry dumped in great mounds, churning in machines, tumbling in dryers, sitting wet in plastic baskets, lying in heaps on the Formica table where Mai's sister and cousin shook and smoothed and folded it—they'd never lost so much as a sock of hers. "Sorry," Mai apologized again. "I keep looking. You go way for Chissmas? Go see folks?" Cam shook her head, wondering if the sheet had gotten mixed up with Sam's things, in which case she'd never see it again. And it wasn't just any old sheet. It was part of a set. The most expensive sheets she'd ever owned: pale blue, 100 percent Egyptian cotton, purchased at Bloomingdale's White Sale two years ago when she and Sam were celebrating their first anniversary as lovers. That sheet was special. That sheet had seen some action.

She told Mai she'd check back later in the week and walked out, almost colliding with a couple carrying a Christmas tree as she turned toward Central Park. Suddenly she knew she didn't have the energy to face the lines at Food City. She'd just have to duck into the deli on the corner, then she'd go home, lock the door, take a long bath in that herbal oil Reba had given her, put on her flannel nightgown, button it to the neck, make cocoa or a toddy. If she was lucky, there'd be a nature show on TV, and she'd turn down the sound and sit on the couch with her feet, in Sam's socks, tucked under her, and read manuscripts, glancing up occasionally to be comforted by the sight of a polar bear training her cubs or a middle-aged anthropologist, who still looked good in shorts, talking to a gorilla. "When there's no one to baby you, you have to baby yourself, otherwise you'll go under," Reba had lectured today at lunch. "And ain't that the truth," Cam muttered, as she slogged toward the red neon deli sign.

When she came out, the homeless woman she'd nicknamed Maria Callas was standing next to the entrance, jiggling a Styrofoam cup and singing "Joy to the World" in a cracked soprano. The woman's eyes seemed sightless as marbles and the light from the neon sign made her face and hands the color of veal. "You need gloves," Cam told her as she fished in her purse for change. "Gloves," she repeated, dropping fifty cents into the cup and waving her gloves in front of the woman's face. The woman stopped singing and nodded in passionate agreement, then her eyes changed back into marbles and she started to sing the carol from the beginning, in frantic double-time, trying to find her way back to the place where she'd left off. "What the hell," Cam said impatiently. She looked at her gloves—one of many pairs of eight-dollar Weber's discount specials she bought in multiple sets because she was always losing them—and tucked them into the pockets of the woman's army coat. As she walked off the woman began to sing, again from the beginning, "Joy to the world, the Lord is come, Let earth receive her king, Let every heart . . ."

"Prepare Him room . . ." Cam joined in, then stopped and muttered, "Get a grip!," not sure if she was talking to the woman or to herself.

God, how she hated the sweetness and light, the false promise of Christmas carols! And hated this one in particular because it reminded her of when her father, Bear, was dying, and she'd left her mother, Evie, Lila, and Lila's husband, Orrie, slumped in orange plastic bucket chairs outside the intensive care ward, saying she was going out for coffee when she was really going out for a cigarette and a drink. A group of carolers had been standing in front of the Christmas tree in the hospital lobby warbling about joy and redemption and she'd hated their inexhaustible cheerfulness and their blind faith because she'd known that she was going to have to make the decision and tell the doctors to pull the plug and she didn't think she was up to it. But neither of her sisters, nor her brother-in-law, who usually claimed the male prerogative, would be capable of that decision. And certainly Josie couldn't: the guilt would be too great for her. She, Cam, would have to talk them around. They'd waffle and be tearful but in their heart of hearts they'd all be relieved.

After nervously driving Orrie's new BMW around a small town she no longer knew, she'd finally found a hole-in-the-wall bar and taken a stool next to an old black guy, so ramrod straight and enormously polite that she'd known he must've been in the military. With Elvis and Aretha blaring in the background, they'd made small talk about what he called "The Big W," and she'd thought about something Bear had told her when she'd been old enough to imagine what he'd had to do to become a hero: it was all right to be scared. Only stupid people weren't scared. Courage meant facing down the fear, and if you couldn't do that—she could see his face breaking into that wide, challenging grin—you just went ahead and acted brave. It amounted to the same thing. Bear had never said what she'd known—that he'd wanted a son—but from the time she'd been about six or seven, whenever he'd left home, he'd always told her that she was second in command. She wished she'd been able to do something to make him proud of her, but at least she wouldn't fail him in this. She was the only one who really loved him, so there seemed to be a tragic rightness that she would be the one to decide to end his life.

Dodging a taxi and crossing the street, she remembered her first winter in the city, when she'd seen whirling snowflakes from the window of a Fifth Avenue bus and become so excited that she'd gotten off and walked all the way to the ratty apartment she'd shared with two other girls in the Village. She'd sung as she walked, nodding at strangers, getting smiles in return, and a good-looking young man, coming out of a florist's shop, had pulled a yellow rose from his bouquet and presented it to her, saying, "Merry Christmas, beautiful." Well, she thought, as she trudged the last block to her apartment, both she and New York had changed. If a man approached her on the street these days he'd probably be asking for a handout.

"Damn your lazy ass, Rodriguez," she muttered as she got close to her apartment building and saw that the super hadn't put salt on the pavement. "No Christmas tip for you." Approaching the entrance, juggling bookbag, purse, and groceries, digging into her coat pocket for her keys, her feet went out from under her as though she were on roller skates, and the bag of groceries went flying. She was down on all fours. Tampax, Woolite, a roll of paper towels, a pack of Marlboros, a carton of cranberry juice, and the roast beef on rye that was to have been her supper scattered in the slush. Letting out a jet of curses that would have done Maria proud, she wiped off each item and dropped it back into the grocery bag, readjusted her bookbag, reached for her purse, and started to get up. Then the bottom fell out of the grocery bag. Suddenly, it was too much and she crumpled to her knees. Her head sank until it almost touched the pavement, and she heard herself cry, "Help me. Somebody please help me." She tried to get up but couldn't seem to move. There was nobody to help her and she knew it. She sobbed like some refugee who'd been left by the side of the road. Twisting her head to the side, she saw the man who lived upstairs rounding the corner. Frantic, she stuffed the scattered items into her bookbag, shoved the roll of paper towels under her arm, staggered to her feet, and thrust the key into the lock, praying it wouldn't stick. Letting the front door slam behind her, she ran up the stairs.

Her apartment was dark except for the glow of the street lamp shining through the windows. The only sounds she could hear were the hiss of the radiator and her own sobs. Moving to the counter that separated the kitchenette from the living room, she tore at the roll of paper towels, wiped her face, and blew her nose. She took a deep breath, dug in the bookbag for the Marlboros, felt for the box of wooden matches above the stove, lit one, inhaled, coughed, and took another drag. She had just cracked up. Cracked up on the street. Because she'd dropped a bag of groceries. Sweet Jesus! She was in worse shape than she'd thought. It was one thing when you felt it coming—that Edvard Munch *The Scream* panic—quite another when it mugged you from behind. When that happened they came and shot you full of tranquilizers and carted you off to the loony bin.

She yanked open the refrigerator door and reached into the freezer for the bottle of wine, splashed some into a cup that was sitting on the counter, took a slug. Mixed with what must've been the dregs of that morning's coffee, it tasted so foul that she swung toward the sink and spat it out. The sobs bubbled up again. She was hopeless. Lost. She didn't even know how to wash out a cup! But she knew she wasn't crying because she'd dropped a bag of groceries or neglected to wash out a coffee cup. She was crying because she, who'd believed she was going to have it all, had ended up with nothing.

She'd come to New York at eighteen, giddy with the triumph of having escaped her crazy family and the life of a small Southern town. She'd won a scholarship to Columbia and she'd already published a short story. All she had to do was experience life and write The Great American Novel. When she did that she'd fulfill not only her own dream but her father's, because she knew that's what Bear would have done if he hadn't been boxed in by her mother's stifling domesticity.

She'd understood that writing would be something of a challenge—no doubt she'd have to suffer some and she'd probably be pretty jaded by the time she was famous, but that was a price she was willing to pay because it was her Destiny, capital D, to write. In her imagination she was already Carson McCullers (but with a lot of male lovers), Eudora Welty (only prettier), Flannery O'Connor with good health, Truman Capote without the lisp. Mostly she was like Truman Capote because the story she'd been lucky enough to publish was closest to his early work—a childhood reminiscence, dripping eccentric Southern charm, about an aged relative. Her grandmother, Mawmaw, had been the model for the central character but she'd taken pains to disguise her (making her a hardscrabble-poor, snuff-dipping, maiden aunt, whereas in real life, Mawmaw was unrelentingly middle class, had borne five children, and would have put her head in an oven before she'd taken snuff). But in those days, tell-all exposés and "sharing" confessions on talk shows had still been considered to be in bad taste. She'd believed (really, still believed) that if you criticized, let alone trashed, your relatives in public, no amount of fame or money could ever make up for your shame. "I just invent these stories," she'd told the reporter who wrote the Local-Girl-Goes-to-the-

Big-City piece for the paper the week before she left for New York. At the time she'd envisioned triumphal, though rare, visits back home. She'd drive into town in a convertible, wearing some wild expensive outfit the locals had seen only in *Vogue*, and all the girls who'd said she was loose and the boys who'd said she was crazy would look at her in cow-eyed admiration. Even her mother would be proud. Not that she'd really cared about that.

Almost as soon as she'd arrived in the city she'd known it was all too much for her. Her fellow students were generally better educated and much more polished. Her professors managed to convince her that trying to write without syntax, style, and being able to define intent was as hopeless as trying to breathe without lungs. (She would never forget that awful moment in her Freshman Comp class when Dr. Ehrlich—who'd later put the make on her—had asked her to describe stream of consciousness and she thought he was talking about an actual stream.) She'd felt like an explorer who'd stumbled upon a dangerous tribe whose language and customs she couldn't understand. They'd all read Faulkner as well as Camus, but in their minds Southern still equaled dumb. The Vietnam War was raging and everyone she met believed that men in uniform were at best a joke, at worst an abomination. She'd engaged, to the point of tears, in arguments, but when facts had brought her around to thinking that the war was wrong she'd felt as bereft as a devout Christian who could no longer believe in God. The only things she'd written that year were love poems to a handicapped, narcissistic, anti-war veteran with whom she was having an affair.

By the middle of her junior year she'd let her grades slide and had lost her scholarship. Not that she'd cared. Being a college student didn't seem to have much to do with the real life of teach-ins and demonstrations. She hadn't had the courage to tell her parents, so she'd gotten a part-time job to pay for tuition and had found herself in a making-ends-meet scramble of work and school. Writing had fallen by the wayside. What stories did she have to tell? What could she possibly understand, let alone express? When she'd look at the drift of papers on her desk, all she could hear was her mother's voice saying, "Camilla, clean up your room." She couldn't clean up her room, let alone her life.

Of course, she wasn't unique in thinking, at eighteen, that she had a clear path to the top of the mountain and, at thirty, finding herself in the flatlands without a map. Betsy, who'd thought she'd be a filmmaker, had ended up in advertising; Shelley, who'd come to New York to be an opera singer, had returned to Santa Fe, where she'd become a fund-raiser for the local symphony; and Reba, who wanted to be a sculptor, found her way into the catering business where the only thing she sculpted was the frosting on expensive cakes.

But, Cam reminded herself, no matter how tough things had gotten, no matter how close to the brink she had come, she'd never given in entirely because she could always hear those voices in her head: Mawmaw telling her, "Don't let anyone but the Lord catch you crying," or Bear commanding her to hold the line, never to give in no matter how the fight was going; or even Josie saying, "Now, Camilla, is this any way for a lady to act?" She could hear those voices even now, as she gave her watery nose a final swipe, took another deep breath, and went back to the front door to turn the locks and flip on the lights.

Pouring wine into a clean glass, she noticed that her knuckles were grazed, and heard Reba's voice saying, "You've got to baby yourself," but she didn't have to look in the bathroom cabinet to know that she'd find a twenty-five-dollar bottle of Rejuve face cream, but no Band-Aids or peroxide. Still, she was safe in her burrow now, and if she ignored the clutter of last Sunday's *Times*, books that overflowed shelves, discarded clothes, trash waiting to be taken out, flowers that had wilted because Rodriguez insisted on keeping the temperature close to that of his native San Juan, it didn't look half bad.

The living room cum kitchenette had twelve-foot-high ceilings with good original molding which gave an illusion of space. One wall was exposed brick, with a beautiful (though nonfunctioning) turn-of-the-century fireplace with a large antique mirror (a flea-market find) over it. The walls were painted in a dove-gray semi-gloss (it had taken two coats to cover the cracks just as Sam, who'd helped paint it on that miserably hot day last summer had predicted). And if you focused on the large abstract painting (a gift from an old artist boyfriend who'd hit the big time), the antique map of the South Carolina barrier islands she'd bought with her first raise at Athena Press, the framed covers of books she'd edited and was proud of, the Kiva-Bhokara carpet in deep reds and blues (inherited from her friend, Wally, who'd died of AIDS two years ago), or the sleek chrome-and-glass coffee table Betsy and Josh had left behind when they'd moved to Connecticut and gone country, it looked like the dwelling of someone who had good taste if limited means. At least that was the way it would look to her New York friends, some of whom lived in conditions that were only slightly better than those in Eastern Europe.

Of course she knew that neither her mother, who thought "a lovely home" was life's crowning achievement, or her sister, Lila, whose Hilton Head home had been featured in *Southern Living*, would see it that way. To their eyes it would look cramped and grimy, "bohemian." She could imagine Josie, smiling while she tried to find something complimentary to say about New York brownstones, or Lila, looking around and trying to locate the nonexistent dishwasher, or ducking her head into the tiny bedroom, seeing the Japanese erotic print over the bed, then pronouncing it "really cute and artsy." Which was why she hadn't invited them here during their last visit. Better to let them think she was rude than to have them condescend or feel sorry for her.

She moved to the couch, pulling off her hat, shrugging out of her coat, and sitting down to unzip her ruined boots. The answering machine's light blinked twice. Maybe Sam had called, even though she'd told him not to. She punched PLAY and stood, chanting, "Sam, let it be Sam" like a mantra, until she heard Reba's voice: "Cam? Cam, you there? Pick up. Come on. I can see you there sulking and lurking. Pick up . . . Okay. I guess you're not there. Listen, when I came back to the store after we'd had lunch, Cheryl was in a guilty snit-fit about not taking me along when she goes to see her family in Raleigh. We had this awful fight. I won't use up the tape giving the gory details, but the upshot is that she's decided to screw her courage to the sticking place and asked me to go with her. So I'm going to go. I know I told you I'd be in town, and I know you're going through a bad patch, so if you want me to I'll stay. Fact is, now it looks as though I'm going to get what I want I'm getting cold feet. I wouldn't mind using you as an excuse to stay in town. So . . . give me a call as soon as you get in, will you?"

Cam punched the STOP button and stood perfectly still, biting her lower lip. So. Wimpy Cheryl, whom she'd never thought was deserving of Reba's affection, had actually come through. Reba's offer to stay in town sounded klutzy, but she knew it was sincere: if she asked Reba to stay, Reba would stay, and there'd never be any reminders about the sacrifice. Still. It wasn't as though she didn't have other friends. She'd had lots of invitations. But she knew she was too emotionally rocky to be with anyone but Reba. Surely by the time you were approaching menopause you could act like a big girl and get through the holidays alone.

Besides, she hadn't played the other message. The other message might be . . . She punched the PLAY button and heard: "Hi, Cam, it's Betsy. Gee, I miss you. Seems like ages since you've been up to visit." Cam shook her head, steeling herself against more tears, and moved to the kitchenette to look for the roast-beef sandwich as Betsy continued: "The only friends I have in East Haddam are women from the environmental action committee and the other mothers in the play group, and it's just not the same. I was just saying to Josh the other . . ."—a yowl and a crash were heard in the background—"Oh, Cam, hold on a minute, will you? I'm cooking supper and Terrence . . . Terrence!" Betsy's voice rose in motherly command, "Terrence, I thought we'd agreed—Josh, will you—Oh, hold on, will you, Cam?" Imagining Betsy rushing to stop two-and-a-half-year-old Terrence (whom she and Reba had christened Little Napoleon) from strangling the cat or yanking down the draperies, Cam picked up the sandwich, saw that it was crushed and soggy from having been dropped in the snow, and realized she'd have to settle for a working girl's supper of scrambled eggs, toast, and glass of wine.

"Cam?" Betsy resumed her message with a sigh, "Cam, it's me again. Terrence knocked over the fire screen. Since we told him that Santa is going to come down the chimney, he tries to crawl into the fireplace every time our backs are turned. Anyhow, so, what was I saying? Oh, yes. Josh and I were talking the other night and saying how it's been months since we've heard from either you or Sam. So, how are you two getting along? Still a hot item?" Betsy's voice dropped to the sly tones of a matchmaker, natural enough, since Cam had met Sam at Josh and Betsy's apartment.

Betsy and Josh had thrown a big party to officially announce the success of their $10,000 high-tech conception of embryo Terrence. It had been a uniquely contemporary and strange celebration, reminding her of nontraditional weddings in the early seventies, when hippie couples with flowers in their hair had gotten married in public parks, sounding like actors improvising lines instead of a man and woman exchanging vows. Much as she'd disliked the all-female, hush-and-giggle cookies-and-punch showers of her mother's generation, where pregnancy was coyly referred to as "having a cake in the oven" or "swallowing a pumpkin seed," she'd felt even more ill at ease munching macrobiotic hors d'oeuvres and listening to men discuss episiotomies and postpartum depression. When Josh had toasted "our gestating son" and downed a glass of champagne (which, naturally, Betsy couldn't drink), then added, "I feel just great about being pregnant," she'd turned her head and suppressed a smile.

Her eyes had met and held those of a tall stranger standing in the corner, and their "I know what you're thinking" amusement had been so undeniable that she'd smiled as though she'd seen an old friend. For a half second, she'd thought perhaps she actually *did* know him, from way back, because Southern, basketball, and military flashed through her mind.

As the guests had broken into applause and shouts of congratulations, she'd looked away, wondering why he'd prompted such a host of associations, and as she'd moved to the buffet table she'd unraveled it. The basketball part was easy enough to understand: he had a basketball player's body, six-two or -three, with lanky arms and legs, still slim, though thickening around the middle. The military hint had probably come from the erect posture and the "barber shop" haircut. The Southern part? Maybe the intimate look instantly softened by the deferential smile. And what a look, what a smile. Brownish green eyes that could make a girl's socks roll up and down, and, if she wasn't mistaken, his smile said his socks were rolling up and down too.

She didn't see him again until everyone had settled themselves informally to eat the buffet supper, and she'd found herself sitting two people away from him. The conversation had, thankfully, shifted from sperm samples and Lamaze classes to food, particularly holiday food. She'd heard him say to a woman with red hair who was sitting at his feet, "We always serve Hoppin' John for good luck on New Year's."

"Are you Southern?" the redhead wanted to know.

"I'm so Southern I've got a cousin I call Aunt Sister," he'd joked, but no one except Cam laughed, so he'd gone on to say, "To make Hoppin' John you take about a pint of cowpeas . . ."

"What kind of peas?" the redhead asked.

He made eye contact with Cam again, and said, "Dried local field peas, black-eyes would be okay," and she'd nodded.

The next thing she could remember was standing next to him outside the apartment while guests took their coats from the rack Betsy had put in the hall. He'd reached to help her but, out of habit, she was already putting on her own coat. Then, with a gesture so intimate that it had made her feel as though he was undressing her, he'd reached over and done up the top button of her coat. They'd been crammed into the elevator with other guests and when they'd reached the lobby, the redhead, who clearly had her eye on him, grabbed his arm and pulled him aside. "You don't even know this guy's name," Cam reminded herself, feeling an absurd twinge of possessiveness, but she'd stalled, moving to the doorman to ask him to get her a cab, even though she was perfectly capable of getting her own cab and generally did so. On the street there was the usual milling about and leave-taking, people deciding if they'd share cabs and who should be dropped off first, and just as she was about to climb in with a crowd who were going to the West Side, he'd come up behind her and said that he had a car and would be happy to take her home.

"You have a car?" she'd asked, incredulously. "Either you're rich or you haven't been in town too long."

"Sorry, it's the latter," he said, looking around. "Now can you tell me which way to Lexington Avenue? That's where I parked."

As they walked toward the garage, he taking her elbow because he was afraid she might slip in the snow, he told her he'd recently been transferred from Atlanta to head up a medical research lab in New Jersey. He'd met Josh, who was making an industrial film about the company, and Josh had been kind enough to invite him to the party. "I accepted," he told her, "because I've been here for two months and still don't know a soul I didn't meet through work. When I got the invitation I thought, 'What the hell is an amniocentesis party?' "

"It was a first for me, too."

"I didn't quite get Josh's speech about *people* getting pregnant. Even in New York, it's still only women who get pregnant, isn't it, Miss—?"

"Tatternall. Cam, short for Camilla, Tatternall. And I prefer Ms."

"Why?"

"Because when men use Mr. it doesn't tell you whether or not they're married, and Ms. gives women the same *advantage*." As soon as the words left her mouth she realized that she sounded as though she was pumping him to find out if he was married. Which of course she was.

"As you please."

"And what shall I call you?"

"Dr. Samuel Magruder. Not a real doctor, as my mother would say. A Ph.D. in chemistry. Sam will do." They had stopped under a streetlight. The snow was coming down powdery soft as confectioners' sugar. "Cam and Sam," he said. "It rhymes, but can we dance to it? And when did you come to the Big Bad City, Miz Cam?"

"Ah, back when I thought Utopia was a place on the map."

"Where from originally?"

"Hard to say, really. I was born in Quantico, Virginia, while my daddy was stationed there. He was from Lou'siana. My mother's family is from Beaufort, South Carolina. That's where they met while he was in training on Parris Island. We always went back there when we weren't traveling with him, so I guess that's as close to home as I get. My mama's the earthbound type. She's got tap roots deeper than a live oak's, but me . . . I've lived on bases all over the world. I'm just a military brat."

"I knew there was something about you. I'm a military brat, too." Oh, that smile had wattage. "My mother was from Brunswick, Georgia—that's where I was born—and my daddy was from Waxahachie, Texas. But by the time I entered college I'd gone to twelve different schools and lived in about eighteen different places."

"I know what you mean. You'd just get used to one place and—whoops—there you'd go again—being transferred. You got pretty good at psyching out new places. But you always knew that even when you made friends, it wasn't going to last."

"But it was exciting to travel," he said. "Especially when you were a kid and didn't have to do the packing. My grandaddy never got more'n thirty miles from the farm where he was born and he always told us only rich people got to travel around the world like we did. So what's wrong with being like a turtle and carrying your home on your back? Home is where the heart is. Home is where you *make* it. All this stuff about the trauma of rootlessness sounds like a Woody Allen movie. Then again, I'm not the introspective type."

"We weren't trained to be introspective. We were trained to follow orders."

"Nothing wrong with discipline. Lots of military brats were top of the class."

"Or complete screw-ups."

"I'll bet you were top of the class."

"Actually, I was both. Sometimes I think I still am. Okay, Sam," she went on, trying to make her point, "tell me the first thing that comes to your mind when I say the word 'secure.' "

" 'Secure' is a verb, as in 'secure' meaning to batten down the hatches."

She laughed. "See what I mean?"

He laughed too. "Sure, I know what you mean. If my mama's to be believed, the first words I ever said were 'hup-hup' 'cause we lived near the parade ground. I didn't mind getting a transfer up here, but my wife just couldn't bear the thought of leaving our place in Atlanta. I thought, 'It's a house, it's just a house.' 'Course I'd known for a long time that property was about all we had in common. That and the kids. But the kids are almost grown. And, truth to tell, I've never cared much about property, or things, or money."

"Nor have I," she said archly. "Which may explain why I work for a nonprofit organization and hence don't have much of it."

"I'm making more money than I ever thought I would. Money's not my problem." He stopped abruptly as they reached the corner and the light changed, then he looked up at the street signs, muttering, "So, this is Lexington and Eighty-third, only another block to go to the garage," as though the need to secure his geographic position was foremost in his mind.

She wanted to ask more about his marriage but she knew better. She didn't think he was a man who talked about his relationships or his feelings. In fact, she was surprised that he'd said as much as he had. With a man like this—"a man like Bear" flitted across her mind—you never got anywhere by pushing. That was something her mother had never understood. Her mother simply didn't understand men, whereas she. . . . Yet did having countless affairs but never finding a real mate qualify as understanding? She'd have to think about that tomorrow. She looked both ways, then stepped off the curb and started to cross the street against the light, saying, "Come on. This is New York. Pedestrians still have some rights here." But he waited for the light to change before catching up with her.

"Yeah, this is New York," he said. "That's why it's gonna cost me fifteen dollars to park for a couple of hours."

He took the FDR uptown, turning the Volvo's heater on high, but leaving the windows open a crack, so that her feet were warm but her face tingled with cold. She said how much fun it was to be in a car instead of a cab and as they approached the Triborough Bridge, he suggested that they keep driving north. He asked if he could turn on the CD player. She said, "Sure," and hoped to God he wouldn't play country-western. He surprised her with a pumping, erotic Argentinian tango, and they fell silent, acutely aware of each other's presence.

They found a dilapidated roadside diner with Edward Hopper *Nighthawks* lighting and a hatchet-faced waitress from central casting. She ordered coffee, but he said the macrobiotic food at Betsy and Josh's hadn't really done it for him and ordered hash browns, eggs over easy, sausage, and white toast. They went through the "Where were you when Kennedy was shot?" and "What did you do during Vietnam?" questions that still seemed so important to their generation. "You know, if we'd met when we were in our twenties we'd never have been able to talk like this," he said. "You'd have thought I was a baby killer and I'd have thought you were a nutcase who was undermining the country."

"But I was right. About Vietnam, I mean," she said.

"I know that. I knew that before I went."

"Then why . . ." But she already knew the answer. Southern boys whose fathers were in the military did not say no to duty.

Thinking that she looked washed-out, she excused herself and went to the ladies', relieved her bladder of the cider she'd had at the party and the two cups of coffee she'd drunk while they'd been talking, brushed on blusher, touched her mouth with Vaseline and thought she didn't look half bad. The smile he gave her when she rejoined him at the table reaffirmed her confidence. Since she'd mentioned that she missed driving, he asked if she'd like to take the wheel. She said yes and he handed her the keys, moved the passenger seat back to accommodate his legs, and stretched out with his eyes half shut. "I figure you for a fast woman, Miz Camilla. Don't be gettin' us a ticket."

"You guessed right," she told him. "I'm the original lead-foot. I love to drive fast." And cruising along a nearly deserted highway at two in the morning made her feel excited and peaceful and very young.

"Going home for Christmas?" he asked.

"No. I haven't been home since my daddy died."

He waited for her to elaborate but when she didn't, he confessed, "This Christmas is going to be strange for me. I'm flying down to see my kids, but since my wife and I are legally separated now, I guess I'll be staying in a hotel, so I won't want to stay for long. And then there's New Year's Eve. No matter how old you get, you still feel queer as a red-headed stepchild when you don't have plans for New Year's Eve."

"I figured out years ago that no one has plans for New Year's Eve," she told him nonchalantly, "but they think everyone else has so they feel too embarrassed to mention it. Then, around December twenty-ninth, people start making phone calls. At first the conversation is casual, then one of them breaks down and confesses that they don't have any plans. People always find something to do, but it's usually at the last minute."

He shifted his weight and turned to look at her. "I suppose you already have plans. If you don't," he added quickly, "then what say we get together and make some Hoppin' John?"

"That'd be fine. I was planning to ask some friends over," she said, though that had been no more than a vague possibility, a last resort if she didn't have a better offer. "You could invite anyone you wanted, come early, and help me cook."

"Can't think of anyone I'd invite, and I can't cook, but I'd be happy to provide the liquor, come early, and stir the pot at your direction."

"Then it's settled."

"Right. It's settled." He stretched his legs and touched her hand lightly. "Well, life is full of surprises and this has been a helluva day. Mind if I turn on that tango again?"

Listening to the music, they slid into conversation that slowed, then trailed off into silence, like pillow talk. She didn't feel ignored or rejected when she realized that he'd fallen asleep. She eased up on the accelerator and rolled down the window to help her stay awake, amazed at how comfortable she felt with him snoozing beside her. When they got to her neighborhood, she circled her block looking for a parking place. Just as well there aren't any, she told herself as she double-parked in front of her apartment—because he looked so damned wonderful stretched out next to her, the line of his neck and jaw strong and sinuous in the moonlight, his big hands curled on his thighs—that, against her better judgment, she wanted to invite him up.

She shook him gently. He insisted on walking her to her door, but they were spared the decision of handshake versus kiss because a van came up behind his car and revved its motor. "The city never sleeps," she said, turning her key in the lock.

"And when I get home I'll bet I won't either. I'll call you in the morning."

"But you don't know my number."

"Sure I do. Got it from Betsy when I first saw you back at the party." He pulled to attention and gave her a wink before turning away. "No flies on this country boy."

They talked several times during the next ten days, ostensibly to arrange details for the party, but staying on the phone, chatting and making jokes long after the arrangements had been made.

On New Year's Eve, yo-yoing between sexual anticipation and denial of same, she bathed, shaved her legs, shampooed and dried her hair, spraying it with lots of Volumize. She slipped into her winter-white slacks and satin blouse, turned and looked at herself in the full-length mirror, saw the expanse of her backside in white and decided it was enough to make anyone snow-blind, so tore through her closet looking for something that was festive but loose enough to camouflage her love handles. In dark green slacks and matching sweater—after all, she was going to cook, not do a nightclub act—she returned to the bathroom.

Putting on her makeup, she wondered if she was demonstrating a sexist inability to accept herself as she really was. But F. Scott Fitzgerald had said that the test of a first-rate intelligence was the ability to hold two opposing ideas at the same time. "Damned straight," she told the mirror. "I accept myself as I am; but I also accept the fact that Estée Lauder can give me a little help."

Returning to the kitchenette, she saw a confusion of groceries, pots, pans, silver polish, flowers still in their wrapper. Why did she always leave everything until the last minute? She washed and picked the greens, scrounged in the back of the refrigerator to find the ham hocks, put them in the pot to boil, found the napkins in the back of the linen closet—cloth napkins because she agreed with her mother that a lady always had cloth napkins—and the silverware, lit the candles, arranged the flowers, and whipped up the cornbread. When things seemed under control, she went back to the bathroom.

She'd licked off her lipstick and spilled oil on her sweater. Steam from the cooking had made her hair mangy as the MGM lion's. Why had she been so dumb as to dress before she'd finished cooking? No doubt about it, this party was going to be a disaster. It would be like her sixth birthday party, right after they'd moved to Okinawa. She hadn't been there long enough to have any real friends, so Josie had invited the entire first-grade class and Josie had made a carousel birthday cake with tiny plastic horses around the edge, their ribbons twirling into a central flagpole that had a little banner saying, CAMILLA. Oh, the work her mother must've put into that stupid cake! And only half the invited guests had come. It would probably be like that tonight. Maybe even Sam wouldn't turn up.

By the time the intercom rang at ten o'clock she'd had two drinks, her hair was pinned up with plastic barrettes, she was wearing fur-lined slippers and a T-shirt saying, in Russian, VODKA IS THE ENEMY OF PRODUCTION, which Reba had given her, along with a bottle of Stoli, for her last birthday. After she'd buzzed Sam in, she opened the door and stood there, watching him come up the stairs. He was hatless, wearing a winter suit with a sweater, but no overcoat. She didn't say "Welcome" or "Happy New Year" or anything she'd expected to say. She said, "Hey, you need a coat."

"Yeah, well," he said as he reached the landing, "I don't normally need winter clothes and I gotta tell you, I hate to shop. I never learned how to shop. Didn't I tell you my mama died when I was ten and my daddy ordered everything out of catalogues? So don't expect me to make the centerfold of GQ."

He was carrying shopping bags and an oversized book was tucked under his arm. "Seeing as you're an editor, I guess a book is the last thing you need," he said as he followed her into the apartment, "but I thought you might like this one." It was *Jericho: The South Beheld*, painted by Hubert Shuptrine and text by James Dickey, a hard-to-find book, published in the seventies, that she'd seen once and coveted.

She couldn't remember the last time she'd been so delighted by a gift. "Oh, you have ESP," she said, embarrassed that she hadn't thought to buy him a little something. "I've always wanted this book. You must've gone to a lot of trouble to find this."

"I hunted for it at the Strand. I've found two things I like in New York: the Strand and . . ." He smiled at her and took a deep breath. "Sure smells good in here. Cornbread already done?"

"Uh-huh. I think this oven predates Boss Tweed, so I don't bake often, but I don't think you can ruin cornbread. Drink?"

He lifted the lid on the greens, sniffed, and gestured for a spoon. "Pot liquor before real liquor, if you don't mind." She handed him a spoon and watched as he ladled some out, blew on it, sipped, and pronounced it "Perfect!" She was tempted to say, "So's the shape of your mouth," but she said, "My mother taught me and my sisters to cook, sew, crochet—all that suffocating domestic crap. I used to avoid it like the plague."

"But you still cook?"

"Not often, God forbid. And only because a couple of years ago I discovered that I actually enjoy it."

"Maybe we have to wait until we're a certain age before we have the wit to know what we really like, instead of either conforming, which has been my problem, or rebelling, which was more likely the case with you."

"Uh-huh. Finding out what you're *really* like. I think that's called a midlife crisis. Would you like that drink now?"

"Sure. Bourbon and water, please. Can I help you do anything here?"

"The kitchen, so to speak, is too small for two people. Just make yourself comfortable," she said, pouring his drink and nodding toward the living room. "Go through my music and see what you'd like to hear."

He moved to the other room and looked at her bookcases, nodding his approval, taking off his jacket and squatting with the grace of a peasant to examine her records and tapes. He selected an early recording of the Preservation Hall Jazz Band, and stretched out on the couch. She stirred the pots, put out the butter and hot sauce, and arranged the napkins.

When it was close to eleven he turned on the TV to the yahoo mayhem of Times Square. "Sure glad we're not there," he said, patting the space next to him. She sat down. He smiled, said, "Thank you for inviting me," and brushed her hair back from her forehead. Her voice came out husky. "Most of my friends said they'd be dropping by on their way home from other parties, but I wonder what we'll do with all this food if nobody comes."

"Oh, they'll come. They'll all come. And when they do, I'll bet we'll wish they hadn't." And then he kissed her. And she agreed with him.

"So, Cam"—Betsy's voice jolted her back to the present—"the real reason I called—well, I hardly know how to put it, so I guess I'll just come out with it: Josh and I were wondering why we hadn't been invited to the annual Cam and Sam Hoppin' John party. Anything wrong? Or are you just too busy to throw a party this year? We thought . . . Terrence! Oh, shit, he's into the fireplace again. Give me a call when you can, okay? And Merry Christmas." The machine beeped and rewound.

Cam leaned back on the sofa. She wasn't making a sound but tears were running down her cheeks. Nothing like recalling a happy time in the midst of present misery. What was she going to do? When the phone rang she didn't move until the answering machine clicked on and she heard, "Cam? It's your mother. If you're there, please pick up."

Four

Lila started up, ears pricked, sure she'd heard the sound she'd been waiting for. But no. It wasn't a car pulling into the drive. Just a strong wind tossing the trees so their branches moved against the house.

She sank back onto the king-sized bed, feet together, hands crossed over her breast. Orrie, who always slept as though he'd been poleaxed, lay beside her in much the same position, close enough to touch if she extended her arm to its full length. "Here we lie, still as stone," she thought, and the thought brought a vision, ghostly as the shadows playing on the ceiling, of two prone, life-size statues, a knight and his lady, lying side by side. Where had she seen them? What country? Which trip? New York. That was it. That medieval museum Cam had recommended, the Cloisters. She and Orrie had gone there soon after they'd been married, Orrie under protest, making jokes about rusty armor and chastity belts. The statues, adorning the tops of matching stone coffins, had been the only objects in a small, dark room with parallel stained-glass windows. Orrie had said they must've been the hotshot couple of their time, and after he'd walked away she'd lingered, touching the stone lady's cheek, wondering if she and the knight had loved one another, how many children they'd had, who'd died first, and if their bones were there inside the coffins. She could see them quite clearly, lying straight, feet together, hands crossed over their chests, in much the same posture she and Orrie were in now. The image frightened her so much that her breath stopped and she felt paralyzed.

She wanted to wake Orrie and tell him how scared she was. She'd say she'd had a nightmare she couldn't remember, otherwise he'd think she was crazy. But it wouldn't be fair to wake him. He'd been so tired when they'd gone to bed. Besides, she was all right now. She rolled toward the night table and looked at the luminous dial on the digital clock. 11:10. No use listening for their son Ricky's car this early. Ricky, who was home from Clemson for the holidays, was supposed to be grounded because he'd gone over the limit on his credit card, but Orrie had relented (as usual), saying it would be mean to keep him from seeing his friends. She'd set Ricky's curfew at eleven; Orrie had stretched it to midnight, so that meant Ricky would drag in around . . . well, there was no telling. It was stupid to wait up. You didn't wait up for an eighteen-year-old male, even if he had wrecked two cars in the last two years. On the other hand, if you were his mother, you didn't go to sleep.

She could hear Josie saying, "When you're a mother you'll understand." Josie had said that about a lot of things, but Lila had known all about waiting up long before she'd become a mother. When she'd had breasts no bigger than chestnuts and pimples that burned like pepper, she'd wake up in the night and even before she'd open her eyes to see that the twin bed next to hers was empty, she'd know that Josie was waiting up for Cam to come home from one of her dates. When Bear was home, Cam respected her curfew, but when he was gone . . . She could sense Josie in the kitchen, sitting at the table in her blue candlewick robe, leafing through magazines and cookbooks because she didn't have the concentration to read a real book. Sometimes Josie would play the radio while she kept vigil, or sometimes she'd try out a new recipe and it would be the sweet smells of cakes or cookies that would bring Lila downstairs. She'd sneak past Evie's room (nothing but a fire alarm could wake Evie) and go to the kitchen. Mostly Josie would tell her to go back to bed, but on rare occasions she'd let her stay up. She'd fix cocoa or tea for both of them, and the warmth and light of the kitchen and, Lila liked to believe, her company, would almost overcome her mother's anxiety.

When Josie finally heard a car she'd turn off the light and station herself behind the front door. Sometimes she had to wait a long time between the motor being turned off and the little click of the front-door lock. By that time, Lila was usually back in bed, but she could see and hear what was happening as though she were standing right there at the door: Josie clutching the front of her robe, demanding in a furious whisper if Cam knew what time it was, Cam offering wild excuses or sometimes just being sassy, sailing past, saying if it was so late then why didn't Josie go to sleep? Some nights there were real brouhahas—Josie's voice rising, Cam screaming, lights going on, pots crashing—but more often it was a ritual confrontation of whispered accusations and hissed denials, followed by silence, a soft padding up the stairs, a doused hall light, and then Cam would come into their bedroom and close the door.

It almost seemed as though Cam glowed in the dark. Sometimes she'd undress quickly and slip into her bed without a word, but sometimes she'd say, "You awake?" and get into Lila's bed, her face and body hot, but smelling like she'd just come out of the ocean. She'd hug Lila and whisper to her about the dance, the party, the boy she'd been with. Lila would feel excited by the attention but confused. It hurt her when girls at school said Cam had "a reputation." Maybe Cam was boy-crazy, but the boys were crazy about

Cam, too. She'd wonder how long it would be (if they ever did) before boys looked at her like *that,* and how she'd be when she grew up. But even then she'd known she'd never do the things Cam did, because she couldn't bear to see her mother's face contorted with such anger and grief. It wasn't fair to make your mother suffer like that, not when she had to go through so much with your father. Even then, Lila'd known she would always be a good girl.

She glanced over at Orrie, then sat up. Maybe a cup of chamomile tea would help. Especially if she used it to wash down a Halcion. Swinging her legs to the floor, she moved her feet through the thick carpet, feeling for her slippers. The house was kept at a uniform 72 degrees the year round, but her feet and hands felt unaccountably cold. Her toes came up against the front of the silk slippers Orrie had brought back from his last trip to Japan. They were a tad too small and her big toe had already pierced the embroidered dragon on the left one. Maybe this was the largest size they made in Japan. Maybe he hadn't remembered her size. Did he even know her size? To turn her mind away from visions of shattered windshields and emergency road crews milling around in the glare of Ricky's overturned headlights, she mentally recited Orrie's, then Ricky's, then Susan's, clothes and shoe sizes.

She closed the bedroom door behind her and stood a moment. The length of the hallway and the recessed lights made her feel as though she were in a hotel, a sensation that remained when she finally reached the living room. It was a huge open area designed for entertaining, with a free-standing fireplace, a wet bar, and couches ranged around low marble tables. She didn't need to turn on any lights because glass panes, tall enough to have trees planted next to them on the inside of the room, rose, in lieu of walls, on either side. The lights nestled in the shrubbery at the front of the house, and the glow from the pool at the rear gave a silvery illumination to everything. Even the artificial snow on the twelve-foot Christmas tree looked real.

Moving into the north wing of the house, she saw the yellowed NO TRESPASSING. THIS MEANS YOU! sign on Ricky's door. Years ago, when he'd first put it up, she'd thought it was cute. Now it struck her as another reminder of how alarmingly immature he was. She knew he wasn't in his room but she opened the door just the same, wandering into his bathroom and flicking on the light. After the pristine order of the living room it was a shock: the countertop of the sink was choked with shampoo, hair gel, a dryer, aftershave, cologne, a tube oozing toothpaste, a pile of loose change, some crumpled bills, CDs. Toilet paper trailed to a carpet littered with cast-off clothes, wet towels, barbells, a tennis racket that looked as though it had been purposely smashed, magazines. It was worse than the mess he'd left in his nursery when he was two years old. *Dear God,* she thought, *if Mama saw this.* How was it that she, who'd tried to bring up her children with the same standards of neatness that Josie had taught her, had failed so miserably? She knew there was no point in trying to discuss it with Ricky. When she'd mentioned it to him the other day, he'd said, with that aggressively bored expression that his friends of both sexes affected, "If I cleaned up after myself, the maid wouldn't have a job, would she?" What bothered her more than either his sloppiness or his rudeness was that he'd referred to Sarah, who'd been their housekeeper for six years, as "the maid."

Turning, she stepped on a magazine, looked down, and saw a nude model in a pose she could only associate with the gynecologist's office. She'd *told* Ricky, or rather, she'd asked Orrie to tell Ricky, that she didn't want *Hustler* magazine in the house, but if she brought that up again, she'd have to admit that she'd been snooping in his room. She turned out the light and went back into the hallway.

The door to her daughter Susan's room was open a crack, and she pushed it ever so gently. Susan, in boxer shorts and T-shirt, was curled up, knees close to her chest, arms around a pillow, her hair pulled tight in a ponytail. She wanted to sit on the bed and loosen that lovely hair—no longer the cornsilk color of childhood, but, owing to sun and chlorine, still blond—but she was afraid she'd wake her. *Susan's all right,* she told herself. *Susan's a good kid. I don't have to worry about her.* At fifteen Susan was still more interested in books than in boys, but mostly she was interested in sports. She'd inherited Orrie's looks as well as his coordination and had gone from being a tomboy to being a fiercely competitive teenage athlete. Though Susan's disposition was more purposeful than sunny (ever since she'd been a child she'd thrown temper tantrums when she didn't win), she didn't have any *real* problems. Of course she was too thin, obsessed with her diet, and she groused about the groceries Lila or Sarah bought, weighed herself every morning, even weighed her portions of food, but that wasn't so unusual. All the mothers said their daughters were obsessed with diets, but then, so were the mothers. She herself ordered salads when she wanted potatoes, played golf though she didn't really enjoy it, went to aerobics classes when she'd rather be reading.

She pulled the door to and continued down the hallway. Passing the smaller guest room where she'd wrapped and stored the Christmas gifts, she went in, lifted wrapping paper, scissors, and tape from the wing chair and sat down. Light from the hallway shone on the mounds of presents, a virtual cornucopia of gifts wrapped in gold foil tied with white and gold ribbons, small vellum cards attached that she'd personally inscribed with gold ink calligraphy, "Warmest wishes from Orrie and Lila Gadsden." The sight of them made her feel warmly secure. She didn't care if people thought she was a softie; she loved Christmas, loved being generous and hopeful. There were presents for everyone—first and foremost for the family, but also for friends, for Sarah, for Orrie's business associates and campaign staff, for the women on the Arts and Culture Council, for the gardener, the pool man, Susan's tennis and swimming coaches. She even had a stack of personality neutral gifts—boxes of stationery, little pots of jam, sets of imported teas and soaps—in case she needed extras, but most of the gifts had been chosen with care and, she liked to believe, sensitivity for each person on her list. She'd searched for months to find just the right robe for Josie, something that would make her give up that old green satin thing that looked like a costume for a Tennessee Williams play, and she'd finally found a tailored, cashmere, Stewart tartan, made in Scotland, though there was nothing Scotch about the price.

The only person for whom she hadn't been able to come up with a gift was Cam, and that, she knew, was because she didn't really want to give Cam a gift. Josie always said, "Cam is difficult to buy for," but Lila thought that should be amended to "Cam is just plain difficult." She could hear Cam's voice—that low, sexy (actually cigarette-damaged), subtly derisive Southern drawl now spiced with a Yankee twang—saying Christmas didn't mean a damned thing to her. Why should she buy for someone who wasn't grateful, who didn't care? After their last meeting, that disastrous brunch, Lila'd decided, not for the first time, that she didn't care either, didn't care if she ever saw her sister again.

She could still remember sitting in the Waldorf's Peacock Alley, waiting for Cam, who was late as usual. She'd watched Josie unfolding and folding her napkin, trying to smooth over her hurt because Cam hadn't asked them to her apartment, saying that since they had matinee tickets and Cam had to go back to work, it was "so much more convenient to meet at the hotel." She could still see Cam striding across the lobby, eyeing the tourists and the foreign businessmen and the swans carved out of ice on the buffet table as though they offended her, wearing an all-black outfit with black high-heeled boots, a large, peasantlike paisley scarf draped around her shoulders, and a Russian Cossack hat.

She'd kissed Lila on the cheek, hugged Josie, then settled into the booth, making a slight gesture that instantly brought the waiter, who'd been doing a good job of ignoring Lila, to their table. Cam had gone through another of her transformations and it had taken Lila a moment to absorb the changes: the last time she and Cam had met, perhaps three years earlier, Cam's hair had been short and showing the first traces of gray, her face had been bare of makeup and she'd talked about the virtues of "the naked face" and declared that she would never dye her hair. Lila had come away from that meeting feeling that her own face was clogged with paint and that the streak and highlight job on her hair, which had cost $150, looked obvious. Now Cam's hair was shoulder length and just a tad more auburn than her natural brown, her eyes were accented with kohl, and her complexion was so even that Lila knew it had the benefit of a good base. Lila had felt somehow betrayed because Cam's changed appearance reminded her of all the times while they were growing up when Cam had adopted a style or a belief, insisted on its importance, talked, actually badgered, Lila into adopting or believing in it, then changed her mind. When Cam was twelve she'd told Lila that God ("not God like they tell us in church, but a real presence, close as I am to you") was the center of existence, but as soon as Lila'd started to really pray, Cam had reversed herself and said there wasn't a God after all. Cam had said eating meat was wrong, but when Lila had sworn off hamburgers, Cam had told her that vegetarians were wimps. The list was endless: integration was the only possible future for the country/integration was a shuck; women and men should be friends/women were crazy to think that they could ever have friendships with men. If Lila had pointed out any of these turnarounds, Cam would just say something about foolish consistency being the hobgoblin of little minds. Of course, Lila's sense of confusion and hopelessness was nothing new. She'd felt it from the time she'd been no more than four, and six-year-old Cam had clicked off the Daisy Duck night-light Lila had wanted kept on and told her, "Just remember, I'll *always* be the big sister."

"So you've got tickets for *Phantom of the Opera,*" Cam had said that day at the Waldorf, and Lila had instantly felt that the show wasn't "in." Later Cam'd said, "Well, I'm not exactly Leona Helmsley, but at least I earn a living," and Lila had felt diminished, as she always did when she put wrote down "homemaker" as her occupation. The worst of it was that she couldn't trust herself to know if she'd actually heard a mocking tone in Cam's voice or simply imagined it, but by the time Cam had her second Bloody Mary, she'd sounded so much like Bear, so simultaneously full of charm but overbearing, that Lila had excused herself and gone to the ladies'. When she'd gotten back to the table, Cam had already picked up the check.

Josie hadn't talked much while she and Lila were on their way to the theater, but afterward, in the taxi, she'd said in a plaintive voice, "I just wish I knew more about what's going on with Cam." "Mama," Lila had told her, not bothering to hide her impatience, "we've never known that and we never will." Josie had stared out the window, her face as confused as Mawmaw's, and said that blood was thicker than water. It sure is, Lila had thought: blood is sticky, it stains you, and it frightens you. Which is what Cam had always done and always would do. "If only Cam'd come home. Just for a visit," Josie had said as the cab had pulled up to the curb. *You still care about Cam the most,* Lila'd thought as they'd crossed the lobby, *you still hope she'll be there for you, but let me tell you, she won't be there, any more than Daddy ever was, any more than Evie ever will be. I'm it. In every family there's one who's "it," just as surely as there's an "it" in a game of tag. I'm the one you'll rely on when the time comes.*

The bitterness of her thoughts had amazed her, because she loved her mama, sometimes loved her more than she loved her husband or her own kids, but how, she'd wondered, could Josie think of Cam coming home, even for a visit? Hadn't Cam caused trouble every time she'd come home? When Lila and Orrie had gotten married, Josie had insisted that Cam be a bridesmaid and Cam—she'd never forgive her for this—had missed her flight, turned up at the last minute looking like the cat's breakfast, refused to wear bows in her hair as the other girls were doing, and refused to wear a girdle, so that even as Lila had walked down the aisle she'd known that people weren't watching her, they were watching Cam's sassy ass wobbling behind her. And at the reception she'd found Cam in a clinch with Orrie's father! And that speech at Bear's funeral. Cam had been like some crazed actress going for an award. Afterward, at home, after the humiliating public display, the things she'd said, the accusations she'd made . . . as though Josie, and everyone in the family—Cam being, as always, the significant exception . . . had blighted Bear's life and shoveled him into an early grave. Lila felt sick just thinking about it, and not even the sight of all those lovely Christmas presents helped. She stood up, letting the wrapping paper, tape, and scissors fall to the floor, and left the room without picking them up.

In the kitchen, she put on the kettle, then reached into the spice rack for the earthenware jar labeled SANTA FE SPECIAL CHILIES and tipped the contents into her hand. The Halcions were small and smooth, the gray-white of an early morning sky; the Valiums were smaller yet, with that tiny heart shape in the middle; and the Percodans were the palest yellow, the color of her first prom dress. One or two? And which one, or two? Everything was basically under control, she told herself. The wall clock said 11:50. No need to panic. A single Halcion would be enough. She'd have her tea and wander back to bed. She swallowed without water, feeling somehow proud, as though she'd done her homework on time. She stared across the sink at the delicately painted ceramic fruits and vegetables she'd special-ordered from Provence when she'd decided that the copper molds were out. Waiting for the kettle to boil, she picked up the remote control, punched it, hit the MUTE button, and started to click through the channels. News, news, and more news. A talk show with some transvestites. A rerun of *The Lucy Show*. The Weather Channel. The stock-market crawl. An infomercial about exercise machines. A World War II movie that, naturally, reminded her of Bear. Though not exactly an up-to-date, concerned parent, he'd limited their TV time, but they'd always watched *Victory at Sea* and she hummed its theme song as she flipped to the buyer's channel offering tacky gold-plated bracelets. *Click*. There was Madonna, feeling herself up again. Hadn't they seen everything except her dental X-rays? A woman lawyer in a designer suit facing down a judge. A couple, buck naked, in bed, sharing a tortured open-mouthed kiss. Another woman hiding in a closet while a man wielding a knife crashed through the wall. Some black rappers in baggy pants and skewed baseball caps, leaping around a garbage dump, shaking their fists at the camera. Fifty channels and nothing but . . . what was that Yiddish word Cam always used? Dreck. America was drowning in dreck.

She reached for the kettle just as its whimper went into a squeal. Putting her tea bag in the trash can, she saw an ice-cream carton of double fudge with a smear of chocolate inside. Susan, who always refused dessert, must've eaten it after they'd all gone to bed. And she hadn't bothered to hide the evidence because she'd expected Sarah to empty the trash first thing in the morning.

Was Susan sneaking food all the time? How could Lila possibly ask her about it? She knew Susan would look her right in the eye, say she was crazy and point to the fact that she had organized her fellow students to petition the school to have healthier lunches, that she weighed her food, that she was on a training diet. But who could have left the ice-cream carton if not Susan? She would have to ask Sarah about it. It was humiliating to ask your housekeeper about your daughter's secrets.

She sat down heavily and stared into her teacup. When the phone rang she jumped and lunged, picking it up on the second ring. "Hello." She hoped it might be Ricky but she heard her mother's voice.

"Lila, it's me. I hope I didn't . . ."

"No, you didn't wake me. I was just sitting in the kitchen having some tea."

"I wouldn't have called so late, but I left a message on the machine late this afternoon and again this evening, and when I didn't hear back . . ."

"I think we have to blame Ricky for that. After he's listened to his own messages, he erases everything. I was going to call you when we got in from—" She stopped in midsentence. "Is anything the matter? You sound funny."

"Peatsy Gibbs had a heart attack while we were playing bridge today."

"Oh, no!"

"They took her to Emergency. Last time I checked they said she was stable, but you know what they say about women surviving heart attacks."

"Oh, no!" Lila said again, wondering why she sounded so insincere. She didn't particularly like Peatsy—Peatsy was such a snob, a living example of the adage that South Carolinians were like the Chinese because they ate rice and worshiped their ancestors. Peatsy was always saying how developers had ruined the coastline, even though she knew that Orrie's family had made their money as developers—but she didn't wish the woman any harm. "Tell me what happened," she said, taking a sip of tea. She expected Josie, who could turn a trip to the Piggly Wiggly into a saga, to give her a long-winded story, but all she heard was Josie's breathing. "Mama, are you all right?"

"I guess so."

"You don't sound all right."

"It's just . . ." A pause "It's just that it set me to thinking, Lila. Really thinking, you know?" A longer pause. "About death and dying."

"Oh, Mama, please," Lila said with cheery admonishment, "don't be so morbid."

Another pause, so drawn out that she asked, with real concern, "Mama, *are* you all right? Because I can throw on some clothes and drive over."

"At this time of night! Don't be silly. I'm fine. It's just . . . I know I should have spoken to you first, Lila, because I know you've made all sorts of plans, but I decided I want to fix an old-fashioned Christmas dinner, here in my own home, and I think we should all be together, so I called Evie—"

"I already told Evie we'd be happy to have her join us." That was an invitation it'd been hard to make since she was still annoyed with the let-me-spill-my-guts-about-my-family columns Evie had written while Orrie was running for office.

"Evie said," Josie went on, "that she'd made tentative plans, but she could probably change them." That means, Lila thought, that she'll come if her married boyfriend isn't in town, which he's not likely to be during the holidays.

"And," she went on in a rush, "I called Cam."

"You what?"

"I called Cam."

After an intake of breath, Lila said, "I heard you the first time. I just couldn't believe my ears. Why would you call Cam?"

"I told you. I've been thinking about things and—"

"Mama, Cam won't come."

"She said she would."

"She also said she'd never come back and she's held to it for ten years."

"She said she'd come."

"Mama, what in the world's the matter with you?" Her voice was more incredulous than angry. "Mama, don't you remember all the times before? You know what it'll be like. She'll stir everyone up. Especially you." She waited, hoping Josie would see the truth of what she was saying. "Mama," she went on, softly, reasoning, "I know you want to do the right thing. I understand that but, remember, last year when I had to give up tutoring that black boy in the literacy program? Remember that? I told you how upset that made me. I told you how I hated to give up on him, because I really loved that boy, but after a while Mama, unless you're blind in one eye and can't see out of the other, you have to admit defeat." And now her voice came out loud. "*Don't buy heartache!* You're in good shape but you're not as young as you used to be. You . . ."

"Do you know what it's like when you're older, Lila? You don't sleep the same. Sometimes, when you only sleep for a couple of hours at a time, the night seems so long, you tell the whole story of your life, tell it ten times over, waiting for the dawn to come, but other times, when you think about your life, it just spins out so fast it's like a spool of thread you've dropped and you're watching it roll across a polished floor."

Lila put her head in her hand. "Mama . . ."

"I've already asked her and she's coming."

"She won't be able to get a flight this close to the holiday.

She . . ." The choking sound she made sounded close to a laugh. "I guess I'll just have to think about that tomorrow. I'll just wait to think about it when we get Cam's flight number, because, frankly, Mama, it wouldn't surprise me if she doesn't come, no matter what she's said. And just tell me the truth, when you spoke to her, had she been drinking?" This was the thing she wasn't supposed to say and, as she'd expected, the response was a long time coming.

"I don't know. She sounded a little . . . I think she just has a cold."

"Well, dollars to doughnuts, Mama, she's not gonna come." And now she wanted to finish up the conversation so she could call Cam and *tell* her not to come. "Listen, Mama, I'm kinda tired. I'll call you first thing in the morning, okay? And we'll arrange a time to go see Peatsy. Now, get some rest."

She found her phone book and checked Cam's number. Didn't matter if it was after midnight. She wasn't going to let her mealy-mouthed manners stand in the way now. She was just going to put it to Cam. Stand up to her for once. Tell her not to come. She punched in the numbers hard. She was geared up, she was ready. But on the first ring, she hung up.

Five

At 5:30 the next morning Cam jerked out of a fitful sleep, fumbled for the OFF switch on the clock radio, and started to slide back into a dream in which she was wandering through underground tunnels of a Bram Stoker–type castle trying to find someone she was supposed to rescue. Some little girl . . . or maybe it was her mother . . . or . . . She opened her eyes, struggling to untangle herself, and reality hit her like a wave she couldn't surf. Her mother had called the night before because Peatsy Gibbs had had a heart attack. Her mother had asked her to come home for Christmas. And she had said she would. Which was worse? The nightmare or waking reality? She turned the clock radio back on and the vibrant trilling of a flute seemed like needles drilling into her brain. *I can't face it,* she thought. *I can't face anything.*

Then she could hear Bear's voice bellowing, "Up and at 'em," and as she shivered, pulled on her robe, and straggled out to the kitchen to grind coffee, she remembered all those mornings when Bear had roused the family before dawn to go on camping trips. He'd stride through the halls, flicking on lights, pounding on doors, commanding them to come front and center, and she, usually a slugabed, was always first to answer his call, sometimes she even slept in her clothes so she could get the jump on the others. "You're the only volunteer in this operation," Bear would tell her as she helped him load the car with camping gear, "the others are just draftees." And she'd glow with pride, knowing it was true. Lila would obey orders as she always did, her general willingness to conform slowed by resentment that made her complain about a sore throat or a tummy ache. Evie would whimper that it was still dark and sit helpless on the edge of her bed waiting for someone to help her dress. And Josie would be in the kitchen, simultaneously fixing breakfast and packing groceries, pots and pans, a first-aid kit, and other necessities, her face resigned, even though she couldn't understand why Bear wanted to sleep in a tent, cook over a wood fire, and eat out of tin plates when he could enjoy the comforts of clean sheets, flush toilets, and good china. But, even as a kid, Cam had understood that the seeming hardships of camping out were better than staying at home. When Bear stayed at home too long he got antsy, then downright morose. He'd settle into his big chair, reading, then staring into space. It was better to escape, to sweep all problems and miseries aside by making decisions about where to go, what route to take, what to pack. "Just as I'm doing now" she thought as the whir of the coffee grinder zapped her into full consciousness.

She wasn't so much going toward something as running away, she thought as she stood under the shower, but leaving was better than sitting by the phone waiting for Sam to call, or sinking into a full-blown holiday depression. Stepping out of the shower, she caught her reflection in the full-length mirror. What had possessed her to buy a full-length mirror for the bathroom? Toweling herself, she examined her throat, arms, and breasts. Her breasts were still beautiful. "All the women in our family have pretty chests," Mawmaw had told her when she was just sprouting. The birthright of a pretty chest had eluded Lila, but Lila had inherited—presumably from Bear's side of the family, about which nothing was known—a pair of remarkable legs, whereas Cam's legs had never been more than average. Only Evie, first runner-up in a Miss South Carolina contest, had both legs and chest, but that, Mawmaw said, believing that the Good Lord distributed assets with an eye toward equality, was only fair because Evie had "been born dumb and had a relapse."

She did a half-turn, looking over her shoulder and examining her legs and buttocks. Why did she still have these wild fluctuations of feeling about her body? Just a few weeks ago, after she and Sam had made love, she'd looked at herself in this same mirror and thought, "You're holding up just fine, girl," but now she noted the dimples in her thighs, the little pouches and sags, the tiny starburst of broken veins, the general softening. "Women are supposed to be soft," Sam had said, but now soft disgusted her. Soft meant vulnerable. Soft equaled weak. And—she stepped closer to the mirror and examined her face—there was gray showing around her hairline. She'd have to do something about that. Patrick, her hairdresser, would probably squeeze her in for an appointment. She'd be damned if she'd not go home looking her best. Pulling on her underpants, hooking up her bra, she reminded herself to call Sabra, the car service, because in this weather she might not be able to get a taxi.

Crawling up onto a chair to retrieve her suitcase from the top of the closet, she wondered if she shouldn't call and tell Josie that she'd changed her mind. But she couldn't do that. She remembered calling a friend of hers in the travel business, last night, who'd juggled a computer for over an hour to find her a flight. She was committed. "You ought to be committed," she muttered to herself, "to an institution."

By 7:30, after stopping for more coffee and an Egg McMuffin, she hailed a gypsy cab and arrived at her office, where she talked her way past the new security guard. By 9:45, as the other women started to arrive, she'd cleared her desk of the most pressing work and was waiting for her boss, Elaine, so that she could ask her—or rather, tell her—that she'd be taking the week off.

Elaine came in late, as usual, rushing through the outer office, tearing off her scarf and coat as though she were a beekeeper running from a swarm. "No calls, no interruptions," she snapped, waving away a handful of messages Maria held out to her, "Just make a pot of coffee when you get the chance, please." As soon as Elaine's office door closed, Maria, whose talent for mimicry had helped Cam through many otherwise unfunny days, snapped her arm into a *"Sieg Heil!"* salute, then, imitating Elaine's Bronx accent, "No interruptions. Unless it's Gloria, Betty, or Hillary." Cam couldn't help but laugh. Elaine lectured about equality and sisterhood and the importance of destroying hierarchical structures, but she could name-drop with the best of them. "And make a pot of coffee," Maria sputtered. "It's just like working for a man. I mean, I'm on the team but I'm not going to be her PMS chew toy."

"I'll make the coffee, Maria. Making coffee is a spiritual exercise for me. Besides, I want to talk to her." Cam knew Elaine was fighting not only hot flashes but a terrible sense of failure. Elaine had founded Athena Press twenty-five years ago. She'd devoted her considerable intelligence and all her energies to it and it wasn't going well. So if Elaine had to shore up her ego by mentioning her association with Gloria, or Betty, or other women who'd become more famous, not to mention more wealthy, while she was barely holding on to her business with the help of ever-smaller grants, then Cam felt, at least in her more generous moments, that she should cut her some slack.

Fresh coffee in hand, Cam knocked on Elaine's door, entered when she heard an impatient "Come," took the chair in front of the desk, and studied a dying philodendron while Elaine, ear glued to the phone, grunted, "Uh-huh . . . uh-huh . . . okay, see you

Friday," then, with dripping sarcasm, "Well happy holidays to you, too." She hung up and rolled her eyes to the ceiling. "That was my daughter, Sheila, calling from Brown. She's bringing her boyfriend—the one I told you is remarkably *un*remarkable—home for the holidays, and now she wants to bring her roommate, who is too depressed to go home to *her* parents, too. Sheila and the jerk will stay at my ex-husband's apartment, but I get to babysit her depressed roommate. Oh, and I'm also supposed to pay the roommate's bus fare down. I swear, it's gimme a nickel, gimme a dime, write me a check, it's Christmas time! Oh, thanks for the coffee." She took a sip. "Hey, why don't you come over on Christmas Eve? Have some mulled wine and help me entertain a suicidal sophomore?"

"Oh, that sounds festive, but I can't. Because I'll be out of town. My mother called last night. A dear friend of hers has had a heart attack and she's pretty wobbly, so I'm going home for Christmas."

"Who's wobbly? Your mother or her friend?"

"Both, I expect. I'd like to leave at lunchtime."

"But there's—"

"I know, but you don't need me here for the staff meeting. You've already read my memo, and you know how I'd vote." How she despised those interminable staff meetings, staged to create an illusion of democracy when all decisions were preordained. "I'm caught up on most of my work."

"You'll never get a ticket at this late date."

"I have a friend who's a travel agent. Called her last night, and she managed to get me something."

Elaine looked dubious. "I just wonder why you're bothering. In all the years I've known you, you've never . . ."

"I just feel I have to."

"Anything else the matter?" Cam shook her head. "But Cam, you're the one who always said you can't go home again."

"Actually, that was Thomas Wolfe."

"Yeah, and Garrison Keillor said the wonderful thing about Christmas is it's compulsory. We all have to go through it—like a thunderstorm. Really, Cam, you know what it'll be like," Elaine persisted. "The first day you'll feel all warm and runny, the second day you'll resent having to be on your good behavior, and the third day, all the reasons you left in the first place will come crashing down and you'll be climbing the walls to get out, but you'll be stuck. Believe me, I know. That's why I don't go home to my mother's."

"You're probably right, but I'm going anyway. Hey, just stuff the turkey with Prozac and everything'll be fine."

By two she came out of Patrick's salon, her hair bright and smooth, the balance of her checkbook reduced by a whopping $150 ($105 for the foil and blow-dry, $20 for the tip because he'd squeezed her in at the last minute, and $25 because he'd hit her up for another AIDS benefit). By four she'd eaten two hot dogs, gone to the bank, had a manicure and pedicure at a walk-in nail salon, her pleasure at being pampered over-shadowed by her concern for the Korean girls who worked there for a pittance and a green card, ruining their health by breathing noxious fumes all day.

She battled rush-hour crowds to get to Lord & Taylor to buy a gift for Josie. On the first floor she was jostled from counter to counter as she considered, then rejected, perfume, a leather handbag, a silver brooch in the shape of a frog. Feeling sweaty, encumbered with hat, coat, and purse, helpless as a piece of flotsam on a raging stream, she bounced along with the tide of shoppers surging toward the elevators and got off at the second floor, not with purpose but because the elevator made her feel claustrophobic. She looked at a gray wool sweater, was nudged aside while pricing a silk blouse, then drifted toward the escalator, bumped into someone, muttered a polite "excuse me" that was instantly rejected with a gelid stare. Had it been *The Pumpkin Eater* where Anne Bancroft had cracked up in a department store? In the lingerie department she watched an affluent, worried-looking man study a black-lace teddy, turned quickly when he caught her eye because she felt like a voyeur, and saw a mannequin dressed in a clingy rose-colored dressing gown with pleats running from embroidered shoulder pads to a cinched waist and a cut-on-the-bias full skirt. She remembered how pleased Josie had been when, years ago, she'd given her that jade satin dressing gown.

Even as a child she'd had a precocious awareness of sexy women. She'd always wished that Josie, who she knew was pretty but who always dressed like, well, like a mother, would be more like the women she saw in movies and magazines and occasionally in real life. Like Peatsy Gibbs. She didn't know if Peatsy had actually been sexy, but Peatsy had always been vain and in her child's mind that had amounted to the same thing. Peatsy, in her heyday, had been the sort of woman men watched. She remembered watching Bear watching Peatsy, or Mrs. Gibbs, as she'd then called her, at some family function at the officers' club and seeing an expression on his face that she'd never seen before.

The slithery rose fabric invited touch and she ran her hand down the sleeve, surreptitiously feeling for the price tag, remembering how, when she was only twelve or thirteen, she'd saved babysitting money and bought Josie a black lace slip for Christmas. It had been that awful Christmas when Bear was supposed to come home but hadn't, and when Josie had opened the package she'd said how much she loved the slip but she'd looked as though she would burst into tears. And the next morning, when Cam had refused to get up to go to church, Josie had slapped her, right across the face, with a stunning blow that had marked the beginning of hostilities that had raged, with occasional but ineffectual truces, ever since. And ever since, except for those times when she was so broke or so estranged as to ignore Christmas gifts, she'd bought Josie practical gifts. The exception being the jade green gown . . . and that had been a fluke. She and Reba, reasonably flush at the time, were coming from an office party and slightly tipsy, and had ended up at Bergdorf's. She'd wanted to get Josie something but couldn't think what, and Reba had said that if you couldn't come up with a gift that reflected the recipient's tastes, then the next best thing was to give something that you wanted to own yourself. She'd loved the green gown and, much to Cam's surprise, Josie had been delighted with it.

"Would you like to try it on?" a salesgirl who looked as angular and glassy-eyed as the mannequin asked.

"No. It's a gift. For my mother." The girl's eyebrows, already plucked and shaped to resemble half-moons, rose even higher. "If you have it in a, oh, I guess a size twelve, I'll take it," she said with a touch of defiance, because she understood that the girl thought the gown too seductive for an older, or, in her eyes, just "old" woman.

"I'll check," the girl told her and sauntered off while Cam pulled out her wallet and realized that she hadn't bothered to check the price because she was thinking not just about her mother's age, but her own. In the last few years she'd found herself looking at older women with intense curiosity, mentally congratulating the few who could bring off a stylish look without making fools of themselves. Even Sam, notoriously indifferent to fashion, had noticed—but what man wouldn't—that miniskirts were in again and had suggested she buy one. She'd said, "If you're old enough to remember the first time, you're too old to wear one now."

At what age did you give it up entirely, throw in the towel, so to speak? When did the desire for love, and sex, the need to be attractive, pride and vanity, begin to fade? Just asking the question meant that she was on the cusp, but aging was an intensely individual experience. She'd once asked Josie if she missed sex and Josie, her face on fire, had said only, "I miss dancing. I did love to dance." Did her mother really miss dancing more than making love? She wondered what it would be like to have known only one man, and never to have experienced sex outside of marriage. Not an uncommon situation for women of her mother's generation, though Aunt Edna, who'd joined the WACs during World War II, had hinted that she'd had a few flings before she'd settled down with Uncle Dozier. But Edna had always been the more adventurous sister; Josie, the house mouse. Maybe the older sister was automatically the dominant one. She remembered all those childhood years when she'd lorded it over Lila because Lila couldn't tie her shoes, or read, or fix her own hair. Little Lila, who'd always begged to come into bed with her. Suddenly she wanted to see Lila so much that tears came to her eyes. She wanted to see Evie, and Uncle Dozier, Aunt Edna, and Mawmaw . . . she wanted, needed, to see them all. But mostly she wanted to see her mother.

She could remember coming home as a child. Some places she could remember with great clarity—that awful base housing in Camp Lejeune when she'd been in the second (or was it the third?) grade—the place that had always smelled of mold and the pine-scented cleaner Josie had used to try to get rid of the mold. It had patchy linoleum, rickety front stairs, an oven that had to be lit with a match, and a yard with dirt so poor and hard-packed that Josie hadn't been able to get it to yield a single carrot or geranium.

But they'd been transferred so often. Trying to remember all the places they'd lived was like trying to remember local subway stations when you were on the express train. Coming home had never meant any particular place. Coming home had always been

Mama, fresh from the afternoon bath she took even when Daddy wasn't around because she liked to look pretty for her children, Mama in a cotton housedress, smelling of the White Shoulders dusting powder she had Mawmaw send her, Mama with her hair pinned up and her lipstick on, working in the yard or, more likely, peeling vegetables for supper—Mama wiping her hands on her apron, taking Cam's face in her hands and asking, "How's my angel today? Were you a good girl at school?"

"We do have that in a size twelve, miss," the salesgirl told her. "Do you want it?"

"How much . . . ?" she began, then shook her head and blotted a tear that was running down the side of her nose. "I mean yes. Yes, I'll take it."

The buzzer sounded and she hurried to the intercom. An accented voice said, "Sabra Car Service." She swallowed the last of her coffee, felt as though she might heave it up, and put the mug in the sink. She went into the bathroom, checked her face in the mirror, started to zip up her cosmetics bag, then reached for the box of tampons on the toilet top. Mustn't forget those. She was bound to start in mid-flight. She was already several days late. She stopped dead. How many? Four? Okay. She hadn't been regular for months. Stress. Or maybe she was starting to go through the change. Reba had started over a year ago and she'd told her all the symptoms. But . . . she'd been eating like a hog. And what about this crying jag? Well, who wouldn't cry? Christmas. Her job. Sam.

The buzzer sounded again.

"All right! I'm the one who has to catch the damn plane. *Just wait,*" she bellowed before she punched the SPEAK button, then, barely audible, "Please, wait. I'll be right down."

She shoved the box of Tampax into her cosmetics bag, went to the couch to pick up the carry-on she'd decided to take instead of a suitcase, and stood perfectly still. If she held herself very still and remained quiet—the way she had years ago after that accident, when she'd been thrown from the car and had lain on the icy road, dazed but knowing that if she had a concussion, it would be better not to move—if she remained very still she'd be all right.

She couldn't be pregnant. All those years, all those affairs—sure, she'd been vigilant about birth control—but she'd had friends who'd been careful and not one of them had escaped without being caught. She'd even thought she might be sterile.

A bleating horn startled her and caused her to look out the window. A truck was backed up behind her hired car, its driver leaning out the window, middle finger raised. Her driver, a Sikh wearing a turban and a red windbreaker, shrugged and gestured toward her window with his cigarette. She slung her travel bag over her shoulder, sagged with its weight, picked up her purse and keys, went to the front door, saying, "Checked the gas, checked the lights . . . It's not true. It can't be."

Six

"Well, Merry Christmas, sugar!" For a split-second Cam didn't recognize the woman in the bright green pantsuit who pushed through the crowd at the Savannah airport and headed toward her, arms outstretched. "Aunt Edna," she said as she was pulled into an embrace, felt a cool cheek, a well-trussed bosom, and hair stiff with spray. Edna, so sharp-eyed she could spot a designer knockoff at fifty paces, said, "You didn't recognize me, did you? Not that I'd expect you to. It's been what? Ten years? And I guess the old gray mare ain't what she used to be."

Cam laughed. Part of the reason she hadn't recognized her was because Edna's hair, now multitoned blond, *had* been gray the last time she'd seen her.

"You remember how riled your aunt gets when she fishes for a compliment and doesn't get a bite," Uncle Dozier said, putting his arm around Cam and giving her a squeeze, "so you'd better tell her she's looking good."

Cam said, "She's looking great. And so are you, Uncle Dozier," though it was hard to reconcile this near-bald man wearing glasses, consciously resisting the sag of age by throwing back his shoulders, with the younger Uncle Dozier she'd kept in her mind's eye.

"Well, you surely haven't changed," Edna gushed. "You're as snappy-looking as ever."

"And so are you," Cam repeated, remembering that Southern women of her aunt's generation complimented one another's appearance with a compulsion usually reserved for people in show business. "It's just that . . ." She realized they were blocking traffic and stepped out of the flow of emerging passengers, "just that I wasn't expecting you. I thought Mama was going to pick me up."

"Your mama's memory isn't what it used to be," Edna told her.

"None of our memories are what they used to be. What was your name again, girl?" Dozier joked.

"Josie clean forgot that Lila and Orrie are giving a party tonight, so she's over to Lila's place, giving Lila a hand. Not that Lila needs the help, but you know Lila and your mother. So we volunteered to pick you up."

"Truth to tell," Dozier gave Cam a wink, "we volunteered to pick you up 'cause it was the only way Edna could get herself invited to the party."

"Dozier, you know that's not true," Edna snapped, making Cam wonder how it was possible to be married to a man for fifty years and not understand his sense of humor. "So," Edna went on, "we're going to drive over to Hilton Head to the party before we go home. That way you'll get to see Lila and Orrie, and Evie, too."

"You all right?" Dozier asked.

"I'm fine. Just that I was expecting . . ."

The fear that she might be pregnant was like a constant hum, audible only to her, which kept her from concentrating on what was going on. She knew she'd crack if she had to get through the next few days without knowing for sure, but how would she get a doctor's appointment at Christmastime, and on such short notice? She could hardly picture herself sitting in the waiting room of Planned Parenthood with a slew of hapless teenagers. Of course there were those home pregnancy tests, but how reliable were they?

During the flight she'd remembered Josie's obligatory "facts of life" conversation when she'd started her period. She'd felt smugly superior at the time, convinced that between slumber-party secrets and library research (she'd read *The Kinsey Report*, biology texts, and every other book about sex she could get her hands on), she knew as much, probably more, than her mother did. But Josie had finished her little lecture by saying, "If you're ever in trouble"—pathetic euphemism!—"come to me," and as the plane had touched down and Cam's stomach had flip-flopped, she'd decided if Josie asked what was going on in her life, that she, who prided herself on honesty but rarely told Josie the truth, would make a new start, finally come clean and tell her everything. It was too tiring and confusing not to.

". . . expecting Mama to pick me up," she concluded, unable to keep the disappointment out of her voice.

"Well, if all this traveling has made you tired," Dozier continued.

"She's all right," Edna answered for her. "She was born traveling. She'd been halfway around the world when she was knee-high to a duck." Seeing the perspiration on Cam's forehead, she added, "Cam, sugar, shuck off that heavy coat. You don't need that here." And, with a deadly sideways glance at a man who'd bumped into her without excusing himself, "We're having glorious weather."

" 'Cause if you're tired," Dozier kept on, "we could go right on home to Beaufort."

"No, we could not," Edna insisted. "I swear he's like a hibernating bear since he's retired. Can't budge him to go anywhere but to the blessed hardware store. And this isn't going to be a fancy party. Just cocktails and hors d'oeuvres from six to eight. Lila's trying out this new catering service that I've heard is real good. A little overpriced, but that wouldn't matter to Lila. I guess you know they're in high cotton now. Who would've thought that Orrie would make something of himself? I don't mean to be hateful, but he didn't look like much of a catch when Lila married him."

Dozier said, "Still doesn't look like much of a catch to some."

"Well, I'm sure I don't know what it takes to impress you, Dozier," Edna said. "After all, Orrie's going to be in the state legislature."

"Representing every developer who wants to turn a marsh into a golf course or a jetty into a marina," Dozier croaked.

"Oh, Dozier, hush up. Take Cam's coat and bag and let's get this show on the road." Edna eyed Cam's black turtleneck sweater and slacks. "Don't worry about how you're dressed. People don't dress up the way they used to, not even for the holidays. Why, I remember when Mawmaw wouldn't let us go shopping without we put on white gloves. You look just fine. Doesn't she look just fine, Dozier?"

"Pretty as a picture, but a little tired. Like I said, we could go on home, put our feet up, talk some."

"Personally, I don't care what we do," Edna said with martyred patience, "but I know Cam would like to see Lila and Orrie's place and Lila and Josie are expecting us, and I just think it would be selfish to mess up their plans." This, Cam remembered, was quintessential Aunt Edna. Edna never said, "I want"; she always got what she wanted by seeming not to defer to the wishes of others. "We'll only stay for an hour or so, then we'll carry you and your mama back home. Now let's go get your luggage."

"I was afraid it might get lost, so I just brought this carry-on and this shopping bag." She handed her carry-on to Dozier, folded her coat over her arm and followed her aunt into the crowd. Edna pointed out the features of the new terminal and commented on the crush of people as though it were an accomplishment. "You won't believe all the changes, Cam. We're getting bigger and bigger. We're on the map now."

"Guess that explains why all these fool Yankees want to come down here," Dozier grumbled. "Did your mama tell you that they've got tours goin' around our neighborhood now? Can't step out your own front door without a carriage full of tourists gawking at you. One of them was so bold she came right up into our garden with a camera."

"Those fool Yankees, as you so ungraciously call them, are what's keeping me in business, Dozier. Wait'll you see my gift shop, Cam. You'll be so proud of me."

"They'll buy anything. Shells they could've picked up on the beaches, bags full of moss they could've snatched from the trees."

"And speaking of buying foolishness, who bought a paddle fan with one of the blades missing last week?"

"I've got a blade sitting in the attic will fit right into that."

"Sitting next to the windup gramophone and the ice chest you retrieved from Mawmaw's? I swear, Dozier . . ."

The terminal doors opened and Cam caught the pervasive smell from the paper factory. People always said it smelled like rotten eggs, and though the odor was undeniably foul, it hit her like the olfactory equivalent of an old song—so full of associations that it almost seemed pleasant. She and Edna stood on the curb while Dozier went off to get the car. "Oh, how's Peatsy?" she asked.

"I've been too busy to get to the hospital, but your mother and Lila went this morning and they say she's hanging on. Doctors are still trying to decide if she should have a bypass, but women do much worse than men when they have a heart attack. Did you know that?"

"I guess I did."

"Did your Mama tell you that Grace Koch died?"

"I don't think so." Cam scoured her memory. Who the hell was Grace Koch?

"I tell you, Cam"—Edna shielded her eyes, looking past the parking lot to where the sun was setting beyond the rim of trees, and dropped her voice as though she were talking to herself—"when you're over seventy it's like you're in a war zone. All of your friends are going or gone. It may sound cold but I'm not in any hurry to be visiting hospitals. I mean, what good can you do there? You've just got to ignore them—ignore *it*—otherwise you can't keep on."

Cam did think it sounded a little cold. And she had never heard Aunt Edna say anything that smacked of this sort of introspection. She reached out to take her hand, but Dozier drove up in his late-model black Lincoln, Glenn Miller's "String of Pearls" blasting from the radio. "For mercy's sake, turn that down, Dozier," Edna said, getting into the front seat and gesturing for Cam to get into the back. "His hearing's going," she informed Cam loudly, as though Dozier weren't there.

"It's okay," Cam said, "I like the big bands." It had been years since she had ridden in such a gas-guzzling boat of a car and she relaxed into the soft upholstery as they pulled in behind a van with a bumper sticker showing a Confederate flag and warning I DON'T CARE HOW YOU DID IT UP NORTH. At the tollbooth Dozier paid his ticket and talked about the weather with the black attendant in the purple nail polish, then they drove though straggly pines that only partially masked an industrial park, across the railroad tracks, past the Dixie Crystals sugar factory, through the sleepy collection of houses, gas stations, churches, and schools that made up Port Wentworth. Accustomed to Manhattan's glitzy advertisements for fur coats, Broadway shows, museum exhibits, concerts, men's designer briefs showing bulging crotches, Cam smiled at a billboard asking REMEMBER WHEN WE SAID "GOD BLESS AMERICA!" AND MEANT IT? and another advertising a turkey shoot at a Baptist Church.

In the gold and crimson sunset the river shone like a mirror and as they crossed a little bridge, Edna pointed to the Savannah skyline downriver. "You haven't seen that new big bridge, have you?" she asked. "It's really something. 'Course your mama and Dozier are tree-huggers. Hate to see any progress. They'd like us all to be laying in hammocks and driving buggies." They passed the WELCOME TO SOUTH CAROLINA sign, driving through what had once been the richest rice paddies in the British colonies and was now a wildlife preserve, then crossed a new freeway and took old Highway 17.

She could remember driving this road right after she'd got her license, barefoot and racing hell for leather across the state line to the bright lights of Savannah in a car full of friends so dumb and hungry for excitement that they'd thought "Live fast, die young, and have a good-looking corpse" was a funny line. On summer nights that big fat moon would shine like a spoon, the air would be heavy with honeysuckle and desire, the ferns and vines so fast-growing they'd threatened to snake right over you if you stood still. That verdant lushness was dormant now, but to Cam's eyes the muted greens, browns, and grays still looked summery. The crude roadside stands and lean-tos promising "Fresh Peaches," "Home-Grown Tomatoes," and "Vidalia Onions" on signs that looked as though they'd been painted by a child had always been there, but now there were full-size billboards advertising time-shares, retirement "plantations," discount stores, and malls. She took it all in, paying just enough attention to keep the conversation going with an occasional question—not a difficult task since Aunt Edna was of the generation that confused tireless vivacity with charm. The wooded road was slashed by a superhighway and in the waning light she saw the turnoff sign to Hilton Head.

"They're gonna push this highway all the way west to join up with I-95," Edna told her, "so we'll be able to get here even quicker."

"So we'll be able to hurry up and wait," Dozier mumbled. " 'Fore I die they'll probably have Japanese trains crisscrossing the islands."

"In addition to the golf classics, they have these Renaissance retreats here now," Edna said. "Even the president comes down. Not that we particularly want to see *him*." The median was well planted and tended, the signs, pointing to the markets, the library, the post office, hotels, and restaurants, were partially concealed by palmettos and tastefully discreet shrubbery.

After a few miles they turned off a traffic circle and stopped at a kiosk. Dozier told the guard that they were going to a party at Orrie Gadsden's, the guard checked a list and waved them on. They cruised by stables, a golf course, man-made ponds silvery in the moonlight. The lights of sprawling houses twinkled through banks of trees. This was her sister Lila's life—a timeless round of sunshine, shopping, cocktail parties, volunteer meetings, golf, and boating. Of course it wasn't "the real world," but so what? Where had adventurousness landed her?

"So you must be, mustn't you?" Edna said.

"Must be what?" Had she been talking out loud?

"Hungry. I said you must be hungry."

"A little." If anything more than a saltine cracker passed her lips she'd upchuck. Late-model cars, mostly of U.S. manufacture, were parked on either side of the road and a young man in black pants, white shirt, and a black bow tie waved them down. "Guests for the Gadsdens' Christmas party?" When Dozier nodded, the young man said, "I'll park the car for you, sir. The house is right there. The one with all the lights."

"We know," Edna said with sweet condescension, "we're relatives."

Dozier held his arms akimbo, waited for each of the women to take one, and they started walking toward the house. A middle-aged couple, the woman's gold sweater set and the man's plaid sports coat bright in the decorative lights of house and shrubbery, walked ahead of them up the circular drive.

"Edna, honey," Dozier said, steering her toward a flagstone path at the side of the house, "don't you remember Lila asked us to come through the back door?"

"Why should we go in through the back door? We're not the help."

"Lila said she wanted us to come to the kitchen first, that way the family can all say hello without disrupting the party."

But the front door had already opened, emitting a bray of laughter, and Orrie, glad-handing the man in the plaid sports coat but looking past him, called out, "Well, if it isn't Cam."

As Lila looked in the kitchen door, her smile, wide and bright as her lipstick, froze. Josie was fiddling with the garnish on a platter of shrimp while the caterer, tense with impatience, hovered behind her. "Mama," Lila said, "you really aren't needed in here. Come out and circulate."

Cuba, wiping down an already spotless countertop, said, "Sure. Go on out, Miz Tatternall. Nothin' for you to do in here."

Nothing for you to do either, Lila thought, angry with herself because she'd given in to Josie's entreaties to hire Cuba for the evening because Cuba needed the extra cash for Christmas. There were several leaders from the black community, mostly educators or ministers, on her guest list and, being sensitive to what they might feel if the only other blacks were those serving food, she'd specifically hired this caterer because she knew her helpers were young white men and women. Cuba had showed up looking like the maid in some colorized forties comedy, wearing an aqua rayon uniform tight as sausage casing, with a starched white apron bigger than a salad plate that pouched out over her belly. She said she'd bought the outfit specially for the party and had looked hurt when Lila had told her to just help out in the kitchen.

"I was wondering if there's trouble with Cam's flight," Josie said. "It's already six-thirty, so they should be here by now. Maybe I got the time of the flight wrong. I guess I should've written it down."

"Short-term memory loss, Miz Tatternall. Saw a program 'bout it just the other day. At our age it best to write everything down."

"But I'm sure it was supposed to arrive at five," Josie repeated. "So they should have been here by now, shouldn't they?"

Lila said, "I don't know. And I don't care. I've got over a hundred guests to see to." She knew she sounded snappish but she didn't care about that either. Even with the responsibility of the party, she'd devoted most of the day to her mother. She'd taken her to the hospital to visit Peatsy and sat for what seemed like hours with Peatsy's son, Waring, and his "companion," a darkly silent Santo Domingan who could barely speak English. Peatsy, drugged out in a bower of tubes and machines, hadn't even known they were there. Then her mother's bridge partner, Mary Gebhardt, had turned up and she'd been roped into going to lunch at Plum's. That had taken another hour and a half because people kept stopping by their table to ask after Peatsy. Lila'd been so impatient her throat had constricted and she'd barely been able to swallow her she-crab soup. Sometimes when she was with her mother and her mother's friends, listening to their "who's married, who's dead, what's the price of detergent" conversations, she felt as though she were being buried alive.

Years ago, when Mawmaw had first started to lose it and Aunt Edna had distanced herself and let Josie shoulder most of the responsibility, she'd thought Edna terribly selfish. Middle-aged people weren't that far away from being old themselves, she reasoned then, so why couldn't they show compassion? But now that she was over forty herself she understood the awful sense of time running out that made you want to distance yourself from the older generation. She'd wanted to yell, "Y'all are *retired,* but I have things to do!" Her impatience had made her feel so guilty that she'd suggested that she take Josie back to her place, let her pick up her things, then carry her on back to Hilton Head so she wouldn't have to drive over by herself.

While Josie had been collecting her party clothes, Lila'd been cornered by that disgusting Mrs. Beasley. Then, on the way back to Hilton Head she'd gotten behind some octogenarian who crawled along at thirty miles an hour, apparently unaware that he was causing traffic to back up for miles, and when she'd said, "People that age should be kept off the road," Josie had given her that "if you can't say something nice, don't say anything at all" look that made her feel about eight years old.

They'd stalled again as they'd driven by the new retirement community under construction and when they'd finally arrived at her house she'd found her son Ricky and one of his college buddies wallowing in the debris of his room like pigs in a trough. She'd given Ricky a piece of her mind, slamming the door on his room as she'd heard his friend say, "Hey, your mom's really wrapped tight." She'd rounded up her daughter Susan and driven her over to a friend's for an overnight, then returned to the house just as the caterer was arriving to set up and found the refrigerator's ice maker was on the fritz. She'd gone to a local liquor store and bought extra bags of ice. As she was getting out of the shower, Evie had shown up, plunked herself down on the toilet seat as though they were still kids sharing the same bathroom, quizzed her about why Josie had called Cam to come home, then talked about her hair, her dress, her life. Then Orrie had come in, not alone as she'd expected, but with his father, Jasper, in tow. She'd decided she didn't have time to paint her toenails and, still in her terry-cloth robe, she'd settled Jasper into the living room and poured him a weak bourbon. (She knew by the way he'd slammed his glass down on the smoke-mirrored table that he'd already had a few before he'd arrived.) As she was struggling with the zipper on her champagne-colored hostess dress, Josie had come in and asked her to fix the back of her hair, and fussed about Cam's flight. In desperation, she'd suggested that Josie go to the kitchen and see how the preparations were coming.

Alone at her dressing table, she'd eyed her reflection sternly, alarmed at the lines that dragged down the edges of her mouth. She'd had a chemical peel only eight months ago, but its smoothing affects were already diminishing. *You're somebody's daughter, and somebody's mother, and somebody's wife, and somebody's sister—there's no you here at all,* she thought. And then she'd heard the doorbell and got up, shaking herself like a dog coming out of water, and gone to meet her guests.

"Mama," she said again now, eyeing the canister of Santa Fe chilies that contained her stash of pills and wondering how she could divert attention long enough to get herself a Valium. "Come on out and circulate. Mrs. Bethune from the Garden Club has been asking where you are. And you've hardly even talked to Evie."

"Tell Evie to come out here. You know I'd rather keep my hands busy when I'm nervous."

"Mama. Please." Lila inclined her head to the caterer, who was spooning caviar and sour cream into pastry shells she'd just taken out of the oven. "Too many cooks . . ."

"Oh, I am sorry," Josie apologized, realizing that she was in the way. "Where did I put my sherry?"

"Right here." Cuba, who usually disapproved of liquor, handed the glass to her with a smile. Josie tucked her blouse into the waistband of her velveteen skirt, pulled in her stomach, followed Lila through the dining room where the servers were setting up the buffet, but stalled in the doorway to the living room. "It seems to be going well," she assured Lila.

People were laughing, chatting, generally refusing the hors d'oeuvres but lapping up the drinks, moving from the living room to the patio, which was warmed by torches set around the lighted pool. The majority (most of whom Josie knew more by reputation than real acquaintance) were high rollers who'd contributed to Orrie's campaign, but, as a goodwill gesture, representatives of opposing groups—a couple of embattled Democrats, some women who worked with Planned Parenthood, and a few environmental activists (or "shit-disturbing tree-huggers" as Orrie called them in private) had also been invited. One of the latter stood out: he was the only man wearing jeans (albeit with a Brooks Brothers sports coat), and he lolled against the patio door, talking to no one and viewing the proceedings with lynx-eyed calm. "There's Bedford Bethune," Lila said. "Do you remember him, Mama?"

"I surely do," Josie answered lightly. How could she forget? He'd been one of Cam's high-school boyfriends and he'd caused a lot of arguments in her home. Bear hadn't trusted him because of his politics. She hadn't trusted him either. She'd thought him too cool, too self-interested. And she'd suspected that he'd been the one who'd claimed Cam's virginity.

As though he'd heard them talking about him, Bedford Bethune looked in their direction. Lila said, "He looks lonely. I'd better go over and say hello to him."

Josie said, "Yes, do," but as Lila walked away she thought, "He isn't lonely. He's just chosen to isolate himself so he can be the center of attention." Bedford had been one of the first boys in the county to wear his hair long. (It was hard to believe the furor young men's hairstyles had caused back then.) He still wore it long, though now it was salt-and-pepper and pulled back into a ponytail. Bear had called him "a little hippie prick" and refused to let him come to the house, and when Bedford had gone off to Yale or Harvard or one of those Eastern schools the local gentry sent their sons to before the Southern colleges had started to gain prestige, Cam had moped for weeks. Word had it that Bedford had moved to Canada to avoid the draft, lived there for some fifteen years, returned to the States, and made a killing on Wall Street, then had given up the fast track to return home.

He'd reappeared on the local scene just a few years ago, writing and editing a newsletter called *The Swamp Fox*, championing the rights of migrant farm workers, trying to get the bomb plant on the Savannah River cleaned up, and generally making himself troublesome to the powers that be. He'd even turned up at onc of his mother's garden club meetings to enlist the members' support. Fundamentally, Josie agreed with his politics (as she had, secretly, way back when), but there was something about him. . . . She watched his expression as Lila talked to him. He was a shade too seductive, a tad too condescending, and certainly self-satisfied enough to be called, well, what Bear had called him.

Josie turned her eyes to the bar, where Orrie, his father, Jasper, and Evie were standing. Except for some thinning of his hair, Orrie's appearance had barely changed since Lila had brought him home in her junior year of high school, when he'd been all Adam's apple and hangdog lust. Bear had always said Orrie lacked the manly virtues. Orrie had professed to be patriotic but he'd avoided (Bear'd said dodged) military service—though Josie could hardly blame him for that. She knew Orrie's idea of courage went no further than a fullback going through the line at a football game and that if it hadn't been for Jasper's money and influence, Orrie might have been a gas-station attendant, but the qualities a woman looked for in a son-in-law weren't necessarily the qualities she respected in men generally. She'd known from the beginning that Lila would be safe with Orrie, and Orrie hadn't disappointed her. He was patient, indulgent, and affectionate toward Lila, and though Lila rarely showed outright meanness or bad temper, she was not—no one knew better than Josie—the easiest person to get along with.

Orrie had gone from college jock to businessman to politician. As far as Josie knew he'd never played around. Jasper had set him up in business, he'd always been a good provider, and now he was something of a celebrity. He was no leader of men and wasn't particularly ambitious, but Jasper was. He, many of Orrie's backers, and even Lila seemed to think that Orrie'd just put his foot on the lower rung of the political ladder and had a high climb ahead. He was a good ol' boy like his father, but with all the edges knocked off.

Jasper, in contrast, was the genuine article. He had a broad back and a big, hard belly. His head was the shape of a root vegetable and his cheeks were a patchwork of bourbon blossoms. He laughed too loud, whacked men's backs too vigorously, still genuinely grieved for his sweet, dead wife but never greeted any woman under seventy without commenting on her sex appeal. He had a reputation for ruthlessness in business deals—as Cuba had once said, "He'd take a worm off a sick hen"—but, Josie had to admit, he had a certain rough vitality that Orrie lacked. His personality, like his red sports blazer, was in primary colors. Just now he was slipping his arm around Evie's waist and Evie was bobbing her head and laughing in a way that made Josie's heart sink.

At a distance Evie looked at least ten years younger. She still wore her hair long and fluffy, and tonight she had little red satin bows that matched her dress tying it back. Her mouth was a glossy pout and her false eyelashes were so artfully applied that if Josie hadn't watched her making little shushing sounds punctuated by curses as she'd glued them on in one of Lila's guest bathrooms, she wouldn't have known she was wearing them. In a photograph Evie would have been, hands down, the most beautiful woman in the room, but there was something about her actual physical presence—the slightly pigeon-toed stance and strained cheeriness of her laugh—that condemned her to being "First Runner-Up, and Winner of Miss Congeniality" just as she'd been in the Miss South Carolina contest over twenty years ago.

Bear had always been against Evie showing herself off in beauty contests—anything that called undue attention was a mistake in a military family, and beauty contests, Bear insisted, were something only "chippies" did. Josie hadn't much liked the idea herself, but she'd argued that Evie had a right to shine in any way she could, because she'd known from the time Evie'd been a little girl that looks were the only thing about her that ever would shine. She'd never believed that Evie was actually unintelligent, but somehow Evie'd made a habit of seeming so and didn't know how to break it.

By the time Evie had been conceived—an accident after the annual Marine Corps Birthday Ball when Josie'd neglected to put in her diaphragm—Josie had been less into "the miracle of birth" than a hardheaded calculation of what it would be like to raise another child virtually on her own. It had been a difficult pregnancy and Bear had even tried to get his orders changed so that he could be with her, but—not for the first or last time—he'd had a poor relationship with his commanding officer and he'd been overseas for most of her pregnancy.

After the birth, when he'd finally come home, he'd joked that she must've found Evie under a rosebush. If Evie had been the son he'd wanted, both she and Evie might have redeemed themselves, but though Bear had never shown any outright disappointment, she'd known that he held a deep superstition that there was something wrong with a couple that couldn't produce a son on the third try. She didn't like to reduce things to the pop psychology that had made Evie's columns popular, but Evie had always suffered from Bear's—and perhaps even her own—neglect. Evie was the "accident" child who didn't get the attention given to the firstborn, or the discipline imposed on the second.

But there was something beyond that, some flaw Josie had noticed from the very beginning. Evie was—what better words could she find, even though she'd never say them aloud?—a born sucker. At two she'd handed over her toys and backed off at the first sign of bullying. At four, when most children insisted on the fairness of taking turns, she'd step aside and let the kid behind her go on the slide. By first grade she'd give up her cookies for tuna sandwiches and, even though Josie'd explained the difference in the value of coins, she'd still trade a quarter for a nickel because, "Kids like me better when I trade the way they want."

In high school Cam had blazed a trail of flash and sass and Lila's light had shone, less brightly but more consistently, in honor societies and student government, but Evie couldn't compete as either star or solid citizen. She'd become cheerleader, "Sweetheart" of boys' clubs, homecoming queen, but surprisingly, perhaps because boys assumed she already had lots of suitors, she'd had fewer dates than either Cam or Lila. Her best friend, and sometime escort, was Lance, the team mascot, a frail, bright boy-man cursed with a terrible case of acne and a mordant wit. Josie hadn't given much conscious thought to Lance's sexual proclivities. She'd only known that she had no objection to Lance and Evie being alone in Evie's room.

In her first year of college Evie had been pursued by a couple of overly confident "big man on campus" types, but they hadn't stayed around for long. And who could blame them? Despite Josie's warnings that she should go slow and use her head instead of her heart, Evie would start planning the color of her bridesmaids' dresses after the second date.

In her sophomore year, after being dumped by a boy to whom she'd been unofficially engaged, Evie'd run off to the West Coast with Lance. By then, Bear had lost interest in everything but his memories and his bottle, and hadn't seemed particularly concerned when Evie'd written to say that she and Lance had been married in Las Vegas. They'd gone on to live in San Francisco where Lance found work in a florist shop and Evie went back to school, their meager income supplemented by whatever Josie could scrounge out of her housekeeping money. After a couple of years, Evie'd announced that she was coming back home. She wouldn't discuss either her marriage or her divorce with Josie, but her relationship with Lance remained surprisingly amicable. So much so that when, to everyone's surprise, Lance went into the mail-order business selling artificial centerpieces and made a small fortune, he'd continued to support her, both financially and emotionally, through her two subsequent marriages and divorces.

During the last few years Evie had seemed to develop a hard shell. The popularity of her newspaper column was due, at least in part, to her complaints about male behavior, but when, as now, she was in the company of the opposite sex, she reverted to cute mannerisms and showed such naked vulnerability that Josie sometimes wanted to rush over and throw a blanket over her. And though Josie had no evidence to support it, she suspected that Evie was involved in another hopeless affair.

Feeling hopeless herself, she stepped back into the dining room and went to the table, moving a fork into alignment so that it formed a semicircle with the other forks. Was it her fault that Evie was unhappy? It seemed unfair that you were expected to assume responsibility for everything you'd done—or hadn't done—as a parent. Sometimes when she woke up in the middle of the night she thought about the inscription on a gravestone she'd seen on St. Simons Island. The marker said, "She did the best she could." At first she'd laughed at it because it seemed such an acknowledgment of defeat, but when she'd mentioned it to Dozier, he'd had a different take. He said it was a sign of wisdom to accept that you'd done the best you could. "We've only got so many years left ourselves, Josie. If we've really done the best we could, we'd better just give it a cosmic shrug." She'd loved the cosmic shrug part. Went to show that Dozier was still reading philosophy, or at least sci-fi. She wished Dozier was here with her. Not *with* her—clearly he couldn't be *with* her—but just in the same room, standing across from her and giving her that special look of understanding. And who was she to chastise Evie for weaknesses about men when she, at her age, was longing for the presence of her own brother-in-law?

"Look at these benne straws," Cuba, who had come up beside her, whispered. "Caterer says they homemade but I know they store-bought. And see that?" Cuba inclined her head to a large platter of rare roast beef. "That's just for show, 'cause how peoples gonna eat it without cuttin' it and how's they gonna cut it when there's no sharp knives an' no bread or biscuits to stick it in?"

Josie agreed, "You have a point, but the table does look beautiful."

"Know anybody who eats with their eyes?"

"Why, yes, people do eat with their eyes."

Cuba shut hers. "Wonder what's the bill, that's what I wonder."

"Well, we can always eat up the leftovers."

"Miz Tatternall, what we want with leftovers *before* Christmas?" Cuba sighed. "Seem like these days you can't teach young people the value of money. Like my grandchildrens carrying on 'bout a special brand of sneakershoes . . ."

"Yes. Well." Josie glanced into the living room. Lila, still talking to Bedford, slid her eyes over to them with a look that made Josie feel uncomfortable. When she and Cuba were alone in her home, they had the ease of old friends, but she didn't know how to balance their relationship when they were on Lila's turf. "Maybe we ought to go back into the kitchen and see what we can do to help."

"Oh, it's all ready to go. Caterer 'bout to tell Miz Lila to call everyone in to supper. Soon's she do, I'll go to the living room and start picking up glasses."

The caterer, edging her way through the crowd, reached Lila, who nodded, signaled Orrie, disengaged herself from Bedford with a smile, announced that the buffet was being served, and started toward the dining room. As guests began to follow her, the sound of chimes was heard over the din of voices and Orrie made his way to the front door, admitting some latecomers. As though the crowd had been restlessly waiting for a parade and someone had spotted the first float, the collective attention shifted to the front door. "I guess it's them," Josie said, craning her neck, her heart thrumping.

"I specifically asked Aunt Edna to bring her in the back way, but she would make her entrance just I'm getting ready to serve," Lila muttered as she swept past Josie into the kitchen and reached to take a jar of chilies from the spice rack.

Seven

"Hey, sis, long time no see!" Orrie gave Cam what she called an A-frame embrace; his lips touching her cheek but his body held away stiffly at an angle. Evie came toward her, arms outstretched, looking like an advertisement for a collector's doll in a regional Sunday supplement. "Oh, sis. My oldest sister, Camilla!" she said in a little-girl voice, kissing Cam on both cheeks, stepping back to shake her head and catch a tear on the tip of a fuchsia fingernail. The toss of her head looked studied and the touch of finger to eye seemed more like checking mascara than controlling emotion, but there was an echo in the childish pronunciation of "Oh, sis" that reminded Cam of the times Evie had begged her to come into her bed or play with her, and she found herself smiling. "Oh, Cam, it's been too long! How long has it been?" Cam started to speak but was tackled from the side. This was no A-frame embrace. The man was pressing her to him from neck to knee, asking, "Don't you remember me? I'm Orrie's daddy, Jasper."

"Of course I remember you." The old goat had chased her into a corner at Lila's wedding and Lila had blamed her for it.

"And this"—Jasper gestured to a couple in the semicircle that had already formed around them—"is Jerry and Ruth Cremoni, remember them? They've been neighbors of mine for years. You and Jerry did a tarantella at Lila and Orrie's wedding." Cam nodded uncertainly, wishing they'd come in the back door as Dozier'd suggested. "And this here is Orrie's special assistant, Jennifer." Cam extended her hand to the woman with the oversized glasses and protruding teeth, who said, "I've heard so much about you, Miss Tatternall," before Jasper interrupted with, "So whatta you think of your brother-in-law becoming a politician, huh?"

"Congratulations, Orrie."

"Could be governor someday," Jasper persisted.

"Today Beaufort County, tomorrow the world." Cam smiled and scanned the crowd. "Where's Mama?"

"I'm right here."

For a moment she saw her mother as though she were a stranger. Few women over seventy could honestly be described as pretty, but there was a softness about Josie that made her so. The tension and disappointment that had spoiled her features when she'd been middle-aged had relaxed, so that, Cam thought, she actually looked better than she had ten years ago. But all objectivity vanished as Josie took her in her arms. Cam clung to her, thinking, "This is my mother. This is the body I came out of," feeling slightly dizzy. Josie released her and took her chin in her hand, asking, "Are you all right?" It was both a question and a reminder to behave, like the soft pinch Josie would give her arm when she was a child and they were at a public ceremony and she wasn't standing up straight.

"I'm fine." She caught a glimpse of Lila over Josie's shoulder. Lila was hurrying toward them, one hand raised, looking slightly miffed, as though she'd been hailing a taxi that had just whizzed past.

"So you're finally here," Lila said. "We'd almost given up on you." She kissed the air next to Cam's cheek, smiled all around, then, as though realizing that her embrace had been too swift and perfunctory, added, "It's good to see you. Merry Christmas. I'm in a bit of a dither because we were just about to go in to the buffet."

"Bet you didn't eat on the plane," Ruth Cremoni said. "Knowing you'd have all this fine Southern food waiting for you. I just don't know how you stand to live in New York."

"Sometimes I wonder myself." *Oh, no, please don't start in with the clichés about the big, bad city.*

" 'Course we go up there a couple of times a year for the culture. To see the shows and exhibits, you know."

"They don't feed you on planes anymore," Jasper informed them. "Cutbacks. Throw a bitsy bag of peanuts at you like you're a monkey."

"The last time I was on a plane . . ." someone else put in, retelling a story Cam had heard on some late-night comedy show. Everyone laughed dutifully. Orrie took her by the arm and started to steer her through the room. "Cam, I'd like you to meet . . ." She was moving in slow motion through a gauntlet of people dressed in bright, paint-box colors. Their faces were mostly middle-aged, uniformly well cared for (though some hadn't gotten the message about sun damage in time), their smiles made her think about advances in cosmetic dentistry. Here was eternal summer—or at least eternal autumn. But really there were no seasons here, she thought as she looked over people's heads to the swimming pool and the lighted patio. "I-know-we've-never-met . . ." and "We've-heard-so-much-about-you," and "You probably don't remember but . . ." She thought she remembered, or said she did, Mrs. So-and-so from her mother's garden club. And there was a fit-looking man with snowy hair and a needle nose who looked familiar, but he was such a Captain of Industry type that she wasn't sure if she'd actually met him or just seen him, or someone who looked like him, on the cover of *Forbes* or *Business Week*. Josie was next to her, a hum of concern underneath her social voice. "So glad you're here, darlin'," Josie whispered. "We'll be able to talk soon." Then, glancing around, Josie saw Lila trying to shepherd guests to the buffet. Knowing how much it bothered Lila when things weren't going according to plan, Josie said, "I think I'll set a good example and fill my plate. See you in a bit," squeezed Cam's hand, and left her side.

". . . and I hope you brought some lighter clothes," a woman in a dress vivid as a Gucci scarf was saying.

"Well, it's pretty cold in New York," Cam replied, pulling at the neck of her sweater. A little later, after Orrie had been buttonholed by a short and insistent black man who wanted to talk about funding for a Gullah Arts Festival, someone else commented on her dark clothes and said they made her look like Anne Rice. A few steps further on, in response to still another comment about her outfit, she said, in a throaty, accented voice, " 'I wear black because I'm in mourning for my life,' " and seeing the look of bewilderment that produced, added, "That's a quote from Chekhov." *Oh, get a grip,* she told herself. She lowered her head to compose her face, put a smile on it, raised it, and found herself looking at a man with a ponytail.

Bedford Bethune. She'd been on the debating team with him. She'd gone skinny-dipping with him. She'd smoked dope and talked politics with him. She'd even made love with him at the beach on Hunting Island. And she'd let him think he was the first when the fact was that she'd lost it to Chet Sumter in a tussle in the backseat of his daddy's Olds. And she'd never even liked Chet Sumter. Chet was a beefcake, dumb as a post. She'd known that at the time. What had she been thinking? Well, she hadn't been thinking at all. After her fine officer's daughter upbringing, all the rules and injunctions and warnings—the things she'd done! At the time she'd thought promiscuous meant "wild," but now she knew the real definition, and it was even more shameful: indiscriminate;

casual; lacking in standards. She, who'd wanted to define her own standards for everything, had been totally lacking in standards when it had come to boys. And poor Josie must've known and it must've made her frantic. Why had she put her mother in the miserable position of constantly lying and covering up for her? Why had she risked Bear's anger? Because if Bear had found out it wouldn't have just been anger, it would have been wrath, rage, The Death of a Thousand Cuts. But oh, those big ol' daddy cars with their roomy backseats, the smell of gasoline and leather, the steamed-up windows . . .

Bedford cut through the crowd. "Remember me?"

"I do indeed. You've hardly changed at all."

"Nor have you. But then, I have a theory that strong personalities don't change all that much."

Was he putting her on or had he morphed into some New Age guru? "I knew you were back in the States but I certainly didn't expect to see you here."

"Didn't you know this is the place to be? Yankees retire down here, even blacks who went north are coming back."

"And you got homesick?"

"Not so much for the people, I know 'em too damn well, but for the Lowcountry itself. Want to see the sun go down over those marshes while we've still got 'em."

"But what do you do with yourself down here?"

"I'm a country gentleman, or maybe rabble-rouser would be a better description. I run a little newsletter on environmental issues. Try to convince the local politicos to do the right thing, and in some cases," he said, sotto voce, nodding in Orrie's direction, "that's no small job. Yes, ma'am, things have changed. Land grab is called development and management, fanny-patting has given way to family values, hunting has been replaced by golf, the preachers' wives wear false eyelashes, and we're growin' our own lawyers. So . . ." He paused. "How long are you going to be in town?"

"I'm going back to New York right after Christmas."

The man standing next to them said, "I just don't understand how anyone can live in New York."

"It's a dirty job, but somebody's got to do it," Cam answered.

The man laughed. "You're in publishing, right? So I guess you've got to live there. I do a little writing myself. I wonder if you could . . ."

Lordy, Cam thought, *if you met a dentist at a party could you open your mouth and show him your molars?* "I'm afraid I can't help you much. I work for a feminist press."

"You only publish women?"

"Not exclusively, but mostly so. We publish books dealing with—"

"You're not a femi-Nazi, are you?"

"A what?"

"Femi-Nazi," a woman with her arm looped through the man's arm explained. "That's what Rush Limbaugh calls them."

"Calls who?" Cam asked.

"Hey, we'd better join that chow line or we won't get anything to eat," Bedford said, though there was enough food to supply a small army. "Saved you," he said, moving close behind her after she'd excused herself and they'd headed for the dining room. "How long is it since you've been back?"

"Since my father died. About this time of year, over ten years ago."

"Lotsa changes, Camilla. Lotsa changes." As he guided her through the crowd she heard snatches of conversation.

"If they close the bases the economy of the whole state . . ."

"They close Parris Island, we ought to secede again."

"Too damned cold to play golf, so . . ."

"Of course you know Peatsy Gibbs! I heard she's not expected to pull through."

"I already opened it. The most darling little solid gold teddy bear with ruby eyes and . . ."

Bedford said, "Well, this is no place to have a civilized conversation. I think I'll skip the food, pay my respects to your sister, and hit the road. You'll be staying at your mother's?"

"Yes."

"Okay if I drop by?"

"Please do."

"Maybe we could take a drive out to Hunting Island. I've got a place out there."

"That would be nice. I like the beach best in winter."

"You would." Praise or criticism? She couldn't tell. "So I'll call you," he promised, starting to leave. "Give you the real skinny on everything that's happened since you left. Great to see you."

"Oh, Cam . . ." Evie, at the head of the candlelight buffet table, waved a napkin. "Come on over here. You don't mind if my big sister cuts in, do you?" she asked the bald man next to her with coy charm. " 'Course not," he said, stepping aside. Cam thanked him, picked up a plate, and felt her mouth water at the barbecued shrimp, roast beef, smoked turkey, vegetables, crudités, and assortment of breads and cheeses. "You're not going to stay at Mama's the whole time, are you?" Evie asked.

"I'm not going to be here that long, so I guess I'll just try to fit in with whatever holiday plans are going."

"Why don't you come on in to Savannah? You could see my apartment, we could do some last-minute shopping, or just have lunch—we've got some really first-class restaurants now—and play catch-up. It's just sinful to think we've gone so long without quality time together." Evie's voice was just a tad louder than was necessary, like an educated supermom talking to her child in public and showing the bystanders what a fine job of parenting she was doing. The buzz and chirp of conversation kept up all around them, but Cam was aware that she and Evie were the focus of attention.

Don't be paranoid, Cam told herself. *People aren't just looking at you. They're looking at her. Little Evie's a local celebrity.* Her eyes swept the table and met those of a tall black man about her age who was standing across from her. He was possibly the most conservatively dressed man in the room, in a dark suit, pale blue button-down shirt, and striped tie. Though she couldn't imagine where or how they might have met his eyes were warm with recognition.

"I love your columns," a woman with a helmet of gold hair who was helping herself to the asparagus said to Evie. "They're just so *honest.*"

"I try," Evie said with an appropriate mix of pride and humility. "I guess writing's in the genes. My great-grandaddy on Mama's side wrote these wonderful Civil War letters, and my daddy tried to write a book about his experiences in World War II, and Cam published a short story just before she went off to New York."

"I remember that," the black man said, giving Cam another don't-you-remember glance.

The woman with the gold hair turned to him. "Oh, H.A., where's Constance tonight?"

"She wanted to come but . . ." He made a palms-up, apologetic gesture. His hands were large but had an almost feminine grace. ". . . our daughter's flying home from Howard for the holidays, so Constance and I flipped a coin and Constance lost, so she's gone to pick her up." His head, like his hands, was beautifully shaped. "Positively Rodin," as Reba would have said. But she was still trying to place him. Had she ever known anyone called H.A.?

"And," Evie went on, recapturing the floor, "after they fired that political consultant, Lila wrote some of the copy for Orrie's campaign literature. Whoops," she covered her mouth with mock horror, "I don't think I was supposed to tell that. And of course Mama published a book. Just a cookbook, but they sell it at local bookstores as well as the Chamber of Commerce and she gets some little royalty checks."

"That's nice," the woman agreed, giving Cam a sidelong glance as she reached for the hollandaise sauce.

"Cam, you aren't putting anything on your plate," Evie noted.

"I'm slow tonight. Jet lag, I guess."

"Jet lag from New York?" the woman asked. "We're in the same time zone."

"I didn't sleep much last night." And the pressure of making small talk with so many strangers was making her feel positively catatonic.

"Would you like a drink?" one of the servers who was replenishing a bread basket asked her.

She laughed. "How about a double scotch with a hemlock chaser?" But if she were pregnant, she shouldn't drink.

"Say again?"

If she were pregnant. The bottom dropped out of her stomach again. "Just some seltzer, please."

" 'Scuse mc, ma'am?"

"Uh—club soda."

"Club soda," the server repeated, and turned away.

"Oh Cam," Evie said, "I'm so glad you've given it up. What with the history of alcoholism in our family . . ."

Cam moved her head, part question, part protest. What the hell did Evie think she was doing?

"I know they've yet to prove a direct genetic link, at least with daughters, but what with Daddy's drinking problem . . ."

Cam's mouth opened. When the words finally came out she sounded as censorious as a toffee-nosed matron in a British comedy. "Evie, I don't think . . ."

Evie was as wide-eyed as a four-year-old who didn't understand why it was wrong to point out the hump on a stranger's back. "But it's the truth, Cam. There's no point in staying in a state of denial."

Cam's look of disbelief hardened into one of recognition. Here was Evie the Innocent, the "I don't know why you're mad 'cause I told" tattletale, the kid who'd started acting dense at such an early age it was impossible to tell if she were really stupid or deeply conniving—or if she knew the difference. "Our father . . ." Cam began, aware that the chatter around them had all but stopped. Her throat closed and she felt a prickly flush come over her neck. "A lot of military men are hard-drinking," she said offhandedly. "It goes with the territory."

"Not anymore," a barrel-chested man standing next to her said with a chuckle. "At least not in public. Not after the Tailhook mess. The brass frowns on it now. Hurts their image. You can go to the officers' club on a Friday night and it'll be all but empty."

Evie nodded. "You can call it hard-drinking if you like, but that's just a euphemism. Daddy might have made it to general if it hadn't been for the drinking and"—she gazed at the ceiling—"other things."

"Evie!" Cam shot her a look that would have frozen a rabbit in its tracks. Evie looked surprised and hurt. The gold-headed woman started talking about cut-rate flights to Cancun, but no one was listening. Cam felt as though she couldn't breathe. Evie said, "Well, Cam, if you're not drinking, you should have something to eat. You must be starved. Here, take mine," and offered her plate, piled with food, with a conciliatory gesture. The barrel-chested man, seemingly unaware of the tension, persisted with, "Fellow at my local liquor store tells me his sales are up because servicemen would rather pay full price than be seen loading up at the PX."

"Don't know why I piled all this on my plate," Evie chatted on with forced gaiety, " 'cause I'm watching my waist."

There was an instant of silence, then the black man across the table said, "A waist is a terrible thing to mind." Apparently Cam was the only one who got it, because she was the only one who laughed, but others joined in just to be polite, and conversations resumed. When she made eye contact, the man gave her a complicitous smile. It was that shy but sly expression that jolted her memory: Hannibal Attucks Staples. To say they'd been good friends would be an exaggeration. More properly, because they'd recognized the similarity of their experience and circumstances, they'd been unspoken allies.

They'd met on the first day of high school. The school had just been integrated and though everyone was exceedingly polite, the tension was palpable. A tall, scrawny kid with big ears, he'd been standing behind her in the line waiting for locker assignments. At first they'd only shared looks of impatience at the long wait, then he'd asked, "Your father in service?" When she'd said yes and how did he know, he'd pointed to the scars on her bare arm and said, "All your vaccinations. I've got 'em, too. I bet we've got shots for diseases most of these kids don't know exist." She'd said, with a world-weary shrug she'd been perfecting in her bathroom mirror, that they'd probably been to *countries* most of the locals didn't know existed. As far as she could recall, they had never even eaten lunch together, but across Formica tables in a cafeteria that reeked of rendered lard, or at school assemblies, they'd cut their eyes to one another and share knowing looks when foolish things had been said.

She gave him such a look now, across her sister's candlelight buffet, and mouthed his name, "Hannibal." He nodded and started around the table. She met him halfway, already saying, "The minute I saw you I knew that I knew you, but I just couldn't place you. And when that woman called you H.A. . . . I just didn't put it together."

"If your folks had christened you Hannibal Attucks," he said softly, the sly smile cracking, "wouldn't you be looking to change it to initials that made you sound like some guy on *Dynasty*?"

"But you've changed so much."

"Am I supposed to say you haven't?"

"Hardly. But you were so skinny in high school."

"Yeah. I was a long drink of water back then."

It was hard to untangle what she'd actually thought of Hannibal at that age. She realized that it must have been some unrecognized taboo that had prevented her from realizing that even as a painfully thin, shy adolescent, he'd been potentially very handsome; but the notion of dating him had never even occurred to her.

She hadn't been brought up with redneck racial prejudice. Bear had always been a firm believer in meritocracy: a man was judged by his character and his performance on the job, not by the color of his skin, and Josie had shared his sentiments. Even Mawmaw, who, despite Cam's arguments, had voted for George Wallace, had said she didn't so much object to integration as she objected to "fools in Washington telling me what to do, when I never let my own flesh and blood dictate to me." Cam no longer believed that this had been Mawmaw's only objection. Mawmaw had wanted to perpetuate the Southern "way of life." Hearing the word "nigger" hadn't raised Mawmaw's moral hackles, but she had given her children and grandchildren to understand that such terms were definitely déclassé.

"So, Hannibal . . . I mean, H.A.," she teased. "Lord, this is like being in a time warp. I saw Bedford Bethune about fifteen minutes ago."

"Yeah. Bedford just said good-bye to me. I wouldn't exactly say we're buddies, but we're on each other's lists—you know, he calls me to sign a petition or make a charitable contribution, six months later I call him. Bedford's still living in the seventies—but who can blame him?"

"And you? Can you catch me up on the last thirty years in ten minutes?"

"I'd sure like to try. But you go first. Don't see a wedding ring. You divorced?"

"Never been married."

He chuckled. "No surprise. I always thought, 'Cam Tatternall—either she'll have no husband or she'll be tying Liz Taylor's record.' "

"I'm flattered that you thought about me at all." She hadn't thought about him in decades.

"Oh, sure. I always wondered how you'd end up. It was a big deal when you went up to New York after graduation. You got out. You made something of yourself." Cam grunted, stepping aside for a woman who was going for the pastries. "Well, you did," H.A. persisted. "You're a New York editor, right? It's no small thing to be an editor."

"Smaller than you think—at least in terms of money—at least if you work for a nonprofit organization."

"Ah, money. That's the thing that makes me feel old. Worrying about money all the time."

She arched an eyebrow. "You don't look poverty-stricken."

"Like ol' LBJ, I keep looking for the light at the end of the tunnel. My daughter's only got another year to go in college and she's a real hotshot. But my son—we're talking about a black boy with SATs in the upper fifteenth percentile, could've chosen any college he wanted—and what does he do? He drops out and goes to Africa. Africa! The most pitiful damned continent on the globe. I went there in the Peace Corps 'bout twenty-five years ago, so I should know."

"And what are you doing now?"

"Oh, I'm an administrator in highah education," he said with an Amos 'n Andy drawl. "That be why I'm playin' the political circuit at parties like this. You can't imagine how prickly it is—Brer Rabbit in de briar patch."

"I'm feeling a little prickly myself. Want to go out on the patio?"

"Actually, I was about to leave. Why don't you walk me to my car?"

"You've got a deal." She looked around. "I already made more of an entrance than I wanted to. Maybe it'd be less obtrusive if we went out through the kitchen."

"I cain't be leaving by the back door, missy. I'll do my round of good-byes and meet you in front of the house."

She started toward the kitchen but saw her mother at the sink, hands plunged in suds, chatting to Cuba, who stood next to her, slowly wiping plates while servers who looked like they'd just climbed off surfboards sailed around them. She decided against leaving through the kitchen, turned and made her way through the crowd to the patio. Even the torches hadn't succeeded in taking the evening chill from the air and it was virtually deserted. She looked around, saw a break in the hedges, and after a backward glance, slipped through and came out near a man-made stream with a small waterfall and, beyond it, what appeared to be a golf course. She stood for a moment, taking in deep breaths of the sweet-smelling night air and staring up at the stars. She didn't see the stars all that often in Manhattan and looking at them now made her feel not so much insignificant as wondering about her place in the larger scheme of things, and wishing Sam was here with her, his arm around her.

After her eyes had adjusted to the darkness, she figured out that she was next to a triple garage. She circled it, surprised to find her boots sinking in some muddy places, and came out on the side of the house, near a giant Christmas tree.

H.A. stood, smoking a cigarette, farther down the drive near the street. "You made it," he said, waved away the parking attendant who'd rushed up to aid them, and looped her arm through his. "It's that old Honda just up the road under the big live oak." They walked in silence. He opened the door on the passenger side, moved some books from the seat, helped her in, then walked to the other side, got in, closed the door, snuffed out his cigarette in the ashtray, and started to laugh. "Makes you feel like a kid again, sneaking out of someplace and getting away with it. Remember when you talked me into cutting class?"

"I have no recollection of that. Where did we go?"

"*We* didn't go anywhere. I think you were going off with friends. It was a beautiful day and you said you didn't want to waste it in class. I must've looked shocked because you dared me to do the same. I thought maybe I'd go fishing but I was so afraid the truant officer would catch me that I just sat in the woods for a while, then went and hid out in my room and when my mother came home from work I told her I had a stomachache. Not exactly *Ferris Bueller's Day Off*. But you, hey, nothing stopped you. You were already taking off for another planet. You were a real inspiration. 'Provincial' you used to say when anything displeased you. 'Provincial,' in this sophisticated drawl."

"I spent a lot of time in front of the mirror working on it."

"You said it once when some guys had made some smart-ass racist remark and I was getting ready to bop them. Growing up on bases—well, you know what it was like—there was discrimination but it was more subtle. Everyone followed the same rules. Rank was more important than race. And when these guys at school called me 'jungle bunny' or whatever it was, it really knocked me back. And you overheard them, and just as I was getting ready to jump on them, you said, 'Oh, Hannibal, don't pay any attention to those yahoos. They're so *provincial.*' "

"Not exactly Joan of Arc."

"Yeah, but it did the trick. That's why I remember it."

"I always figured you'd go into the military."

"My dad wanted me to. He used to say, 'your grandparents were shrimpers who lived in a two-room shack. The military's the only institution that's given us a fair shake. Why you want to turn your back on it?' Even now he'll say, 'General Colin L. Powell is the only black man who could make a real run for the presidency'—as though I could've been Colin Powell if only I hadn't wanted to spite him. Hell, he only made sergeant but he had it in his mind from the time I was a little kid that I'd be an officer. But I went to college and had my consciousness raised. I was reading Franz Fanon and wearing a Huey P. Newton T-shirt and letting my hair go natural. You ever had your consciousness raised, Camilla?" he asked with a grin.

She smiled back. "Oh, sure. It was my principal occupation for about ten years."

"So," he knocked another cigarette out of the pack and gestured to ask if it was all right to smoke. She nodded, he rolled down his window and continued, "So, there was no way I was goin' in that man's army." He draped his arms over the steering wheel, shaking his head and looking straight ahead. "And I was so proud of Daddy when I was growing up, even though he used to whup me if I stepped an inch over the line. He always looked so neat. Creases in his trousers, pomade on his hair, shoes shined, tie straight. Spit and polish all the way. 'Yes, ma'am. No, sir. If you make a mess, clean it up. If you borrow it, return it.' "

" 'If you value it, take care of it. If it's none of your business, don't ask questions. If it will tarnish someone's reputation, keep it to yourself.' " Cam laughed. "There were about fifty of those rules, weren't there? What're your folks doing now?"

"My mother died just as Daddy was getting ready to retire. It was hard for him at first—the retirement, even more than her death, I think. But I think he's happy now, or would be if he could still order his kids around. He's got himself a little farm down near Waycross, where his sister lives. Raises his own chickens and hogs, plants vegetables, even puts up pickles and relish and gives 'em to people for Christmas."

"I don't think my father would ever have been happy as a civilian. At least not the sort of domesticity my mother wanted. Since he'd been brought up in an orphanage, I guess the idea of home and family always appealed to him—but the reality?"

"I remember your daddy," he said. "He looked like he belonged on a recruiting poster. I always figured he'd come from a long line of distinguished warriors."

"If he did, he never knew them. Funny, but I never even thought it was strange that I only had one set of grandparents until one morning at breakfast there was a particularly bad argument . . ."

"My parents always argued over breakfast too. I still can't get more'n a cup of coffee down at breakfast."

"My mother called him a 'bastard.' I'd never heard her use that word before. I guess I was about ten. I knew what the word meant because I liked to read histories of royal families, but I'd never related it to anyone I knew. When she called him that I thought he was going to kill her—and that made me put it all together." She stopped, thinking perhaps she'd revealed too much. "Nothing that is said in this house goes further than the door" had been the rule, and she still respected it, which is why she was so appalled at Evie's conduct. But this was different.

Perhaps it was sitting in the darkness of the parked car under the big live oak, the cool breeze coming in the window and moving the Spanish moss so that it made shadows on the windshield that made her want to talk. Or maybe it was because she and Hannibal sensed a mutual trust, and knew they were unlikely to see one another again.

"Yeah, Daddy loved the idea of home and family," she repeated, "but, oh, how he hated the reality! The military wasn't just an adventure or an obligation to him, it wasn't even a way of life—it was his natural element. He suffered when he was away from it the way a dolphin would suffer if you took it out of the ocean. When he'd first come home, he'd seem real happy to be there, but it never lasted for very long."

She could remember the excitement, the holiday feeling of his homecomings, how Josie would do everything to make the occasion special, but after a few days she'd start with little "please don'ts"—please don't smoke cigars in the house 'cause they smell up the draperies, please don't put your feet on the furniture, watch out you don't get hair oil on the back of the couch. He'd go along at first, but pretty soon he'd be looking at doilies as though they were insects he wanted to slap away. And he'd sit there in that ratty leather recliner, staring at the TV without seeing it, trying to read and not being able to concentrate. And the level of the bourbon bottle kept going down, but no one talked about that. Sometimes he'd get so restless he'd start doing push-ups in the living room. Josie would want him to prune hedges or mow the lawn, but he'd just sort of pace in the yard, like it was a preserve in a zoo. Sometimes he'd say he was just going to the store and be gone for hours. Sometimes he drove to the beach or a movie and took Cam with him. And she was more than happy for the opportunity to be alone with him, to try to entertain him, to get out of the stifling atmosphere of the house.

"I wasn't much for the home fires either. I always wanted"—she said the words as though they were enclosed in quotes—"a 'life of adventure.' I asked him once why he'd gotten married and he said—I'll never forget this—'Oh, a man isn't complete until he's married; and then he's finished.' "

"Did you ever think of going in the service?"

"Never. Not once. Guess my consciousness wasn't raised that much."

"My younger sister went in as a nurse, but that didn't quite make it for my daddy. She can bust her hump till the day she dies and it still won't quite make it for him. But she still lines up with him against me every time. Go figure."

"Sometimes," Cam went on, because there was no sense of his having interrupted her, it was more like they were singing a duet, "we'd go camping, and when they were really on the outs, he'd just pull a frying pan and a sleeping bag out of the cupboards and go camp out by himself, and that'd really hurt her feelings. At the time I never saw it from her point of view." She sighed. "When he came home, it was a sort of invasion. There was that anxiety—wondering what he'd look like and how he'd be—and that bit of resentment, knowing I'd have to take orders from him too. But when he left again—oh, sometimes I'd cry for days. I'd be afraid he'd never come back."

"Yeah, that coming and going was some kind of rip and tear. Even now, I hate good-byes. I always have to cut 'em sharp and cold. Like a salute."

"I'm the same way." She thought about that last meeting with Sam. "Mama always talked about how wonderful things would be once he retired, but I don't think I ever bought that. 'Course I was long gone by that time. But I came back to visit just as he was getting out and she was pressuring him to buy the house on The Point. He really didn't want it, and they really couldn't afford it."

Strange, she thought, perhaps for the first time, that her parents should have been so strapped for money when Josie had always been so careful about not spending it. "That's when she came up with the bed-and-breakfast idea. And that was the thing that broke him. That was what killed him. The notion of spending his last years as a goddamn innkeeper. I don't think I'll ever be able to forgive her, forgive any of them, for that. 'Cause Lila was there with her 'anything you say, Mama,' and Evie was there with her golly-gee-I-can't-figure-it-out. And when he had the stroke I just said, 'Pull the plug,' because I knew he'd be better off dead than living like that."

She wasn't aware that her body had gone rigid and her hands had balled into fists until he put his arm around her. "I know what family quarrels are like," he said in a low voice, drawing her to him. "Bitter. Oh, so bitter. Not so much a wound as a split in the skin that can't heal. I didn't talk to my daddy for eight, maybe ten years after we had the big blowup about my not going into service. And it was Constance, my wife, who finally bridged the gap. Started sending him pictures of our kids. Even he couldn't hold out against grandchildren. Is there anyone in your life now? Any man, I mean?"

"No. Yes." She shook her head. "If I sound confused, it's because I am. There's my boyfriend, Sam." She gave a little laugh. "Boyfriend! Now that sounds dumb at our age. On the other hand 'friend' doesn't quite make it, 'lover' sounds like you're crooning a torch song, and 'significant other' sounds like a joke."

"Are you in love?"

"Sometimes I think I just miss him like a habit; other times I have this . . . now this sounds like a torch song, too, but this . . . yearning. So, I guess the answer is yes."

"I wish I felt that way about Constance."

"Well, after twenty-some years you can't expect it to be heavy breathing and pounding hearts."

"It never really was with us. Constance was cute and smart and ambitious. Still is. We had the same goals, personally and socially, and figured it would be easier to attain them if we were together. But pounding hearts? No, it was never like that. If I had to pick a business partner I'd still pick her. Trouble is, the mortgage is almost paid off and I don't care anymore—I don't care about the house or the pool or the cars, and I've had it up to here with all the racial jockeying in highah education. Constance is still out there fighting the good fight. She's so involved in this committee and that organization I don't think she notices whether I'm home or not. But me . . . It's not like I'm interested in other women, but I sit in my office and have these bizarre fantasies—I'm a beachcomber or a bartender in a little place in Tierra del Fuego. Nobody knows me, I just pour rum and watch the surf roll in and the bougainvillea climb up the whitewashed wall."

"Midlife crisis," she offered, with no sarcasm.

"Can a black man afford to have one of those?" He answered his own question. "I don't think so. At least not if he's turned himself into a role model—ideal family man, pillar of the community, educator. I may not be Colin Powell, but I know what it means to be 'a credit to my race.' I'd disappoint a whole lot of people, myself included, if I ducked out on my responsibilities."

She nodded, her head moving on his shoulder. At one time she might have said more, but she was now at an age when she knew that a willing ear was often the best a friend could provide.

First one, then another set of headlights flashed in the rear window and they could hear voices. "I guess"—he quickly moved his arm from her shoulder—"the party's breaking up."

She straightened, suddenly conscious that they'd slumped into what might be mistaken for an embrace. "I hope so. I'm so tired, I'm punchy. Hannibal . . ."

"Hannibal," he said in a sing-song schoolboy's recitation, "crossed the Alps with forty thousand men and a pack of elephants. He defeated the Romans in one of the most famous battles in history, but when he couldn't defend Carthage, he took poison and died, rather than be taken prisoner."

"You're not thinking of taking poison are you?"

He laughed. "I think I'll try Tierra del Fuego first. But it's a helluva namesake to live up to." He turned to her. "Cam. Talking to you like this . . ."

"You don't talk to anyone?"

"You know men only talk about stuff like this with women. And talking to someone I know from way back . . ."

"Someone who doesn't live here anymore."

"Sure. That, too. Makes me feel safe. This is probably the best Christmas present I'll get."

She opened her door. "Not counting the subscription to *Sports Illustrated*."

"Yeah. Not counting that. I might be in Beaufort before Christmas. Would it be all right if I dropped by your mother's?"

"I'd like that." She started to get out, turned back, and pecked him on the cheek. "It was so good to talk with you. I hope I do see you again. At least call so we can exchange addresses."

"Yes, ma'am." He gave her a swift salute.

"Good night, Hannibal."

She shivered and wrapped her arms around her chest as she made her way back to the house. Cars were starting up and a gaggle of guests loitered at the front door, prolonging their good-byes. One of the men, much the worse for drink, was weaving around the Christmas tree on the front lawn asking, "Isn't this the prettiest tree you've ever seen, Eleanor? Why can't we have a Christmas tree like this, Eleanor?" while the woman Cam supposed was Eleanor tried to steady him, reassuring him, "Our Christmas tree is pretty too, Fred. Come on home and I'll show it to you." Cam decided to go around the back way.

Lila stood, arms at her sides, staring into the pantry. Behind her, the catering crew was packing up and Josie was helping Cuba into her coat. "Hey, moron," she heard one server whisper to another, "don't pack that. It belongs to the client." She knew she should be overseeing the operation or settling up with Cuba, better yet, she should be at the front door with Orrie, saying her so-glad-you-could-comes to departing guests, but she moved through the kitchen, paused at the door, then turned and walked quickly down the long hallway to her bedroom.

She hadn't meant to slam the door but it shut with a wallop. She walked around the bed, retraced her steps, then lay down, pressing her hands to the middle of her chest. Why hadn't she put her foot down? Why hadn't she said she wasn't going to change any of her holiday plans, that she didn't even want Cam coming to her party? A bitter phlegm came into her mouth, as though a pill had dissolved in her throat and she couldn't swallow it. Well, she'd expected trouble and she'd been right. She literally wanted to gag.

There was a tap on the door and Josie's voice, "Lila, may I come in?" She didn't bother to answer. When your mother asked if she could come in to your bedroom, could it be anything but rhetorical?

Josie left the door open so that a wedge of light shone in from the hallway, and came to sit at the foot of the bed, putting her hand on Lila's instep, resisting the impulse to tell her that her shoes might soil the cream sateen comforter. "Lila? Is anything the matter?"

Lila shook her head.

"There are a few stragglers in the living room. I think maybe they're waiting to tell you good night." Lila said nothing. "I thought the party went well. People seemed to have had a good time," Josie went on in a quiet voice. "And," she added, though she secretly agreed with Cuba that the spread wasn't worth the price, "the caterer did an excellent job, but there're lots of leftovers. This time of year everyone's already had too much of everything."

"She did it again," Lila said in a strangulated voice, "I knew she would and she did."

"What . . . ?"

"Don't pretend you don't know, Mama. Don't make me draw you a picture. She always disrupts everything. Always."

"Lila, she couldn't help it if the flight was late."

"She makes her grand entrance just as I'm getting ready to serve. She's barely civil to the other guests. She goes into her whisper-and-flirt act with Bedford Bethune, then she has a fight with Evie at the buffet table. Evie told me about it. Cam jumped down her throat just because she mentioned booze."

"I know for a fact," Josie said quietly, ashamed to admit that she'd been watching, "that Cam wasn't drinking."

"And then . . . and then"—Lila raised herself on her elbows—"she leaves the party and goes out and necks with H.A. Staples!"

"Lila! I don't believe—"

"When it comes to Cam, Mama, you can see it with your own eyes and not believe it."

"I know she left the party but—"

"Mama! Liz Heffernan told me. Liz and Sid went out to their car and they saw them. Liz left her shawl in the house and when she came back in to get it, she told me. They saw Cam and H.A. Staples making out in his car. Liz just made a joke of it—said, 'I know they walk faster and talk faster in New York, but I didn't know they moved quite that fast.' Cam would choose him, wouldn't she? First night back and she just had to shock everyone, just had to rub our noses in it." She sat up, pulling her foot away from Josie's hand, crossing her arms over her chest. "Everyone knows that H.A. and his wife are on the rocks. Cam doesn't look so great to me, but then, I'm not a man. Men are purblind when it comes to some woman who's putting it out there."

"Lila! How can you talk that way about your sister?" A shadow fell across her, causing Josie to turn.

Orrie called from the doorway, "Hey, sweetheart, you in there?"

Josie said, "She just has a little headache and we were talking about the party."

"Great party, honey. Sorry you don't feel well. Can you come out long enough to say good-bye to the Pearsons?"

"Of course." Lila got up, flicked on the light on her dressing table, took a Q-Tip and wiped away a smudge beneath her eye, ran a brush through her hair, and left the room.

Josie continued to sit on the bed. She could hardly believe what Lila had told her, but there must be some kernel of truth to it. A great sense of weariness came over her—the same bone-weariness she'd felt as a young mother living in the confines of a Quonset hut, all the kids down with colds at the same time, fetching and carrying and trying to referee the constant rivalry and bickering—"Mama, it's not fair," "*She* started it," "It's all her fault"—until she thought she'd lose her mind. Now they were middle-aged women, and they were still at it. And she had neither inclination nor energy to referee. She'd left that Quonset hut once, just taken off her apron, locked the front door, and left them to it. She'd walked down to the water. She'd wanted to keep on walking until the waves swallowed her up, but she'd sat on the pier instead, gazing out at the ocean until she'd noticed some men looking at her. A madwoman in house slippers, with her arms wrapped around her chest. And then she'd got up and walked back to the Quonset hut.

She got up now, straightened the comforter, turned off the light in Lila's dressing table without looking at herself, and started to walk back to the kitchen, hoping against hope that Cam could be found and Dozier would be ready to take them home.

"Dozier, you're too old to be driving this fast," Edna said for the second time.

"Want to know my definition of old, sweetheart?" Dozier asked. "Old is fifteen years past whatever age I am." But he eased up on the accelerator anyway.

Cam cracked the window and looked over at Josie. It was going to be a long drive home, and not just because Dozier was now limping along at forty miles an hour. She sensed something was amiss but didn't know what. Josie's explanation that Lila had a migraine couldn't quite account for the chilliness of Lila's good-bye, both to Cam and to Josie. Edna had noticed it too, and ever since they'd been in the car, she'd been trying to ferret out the reason. When Josie ignored her questions, Edna started talking about various guests as though they were produce on display at a roadside stand: Orrie's assistant was well preserved, Marge Larson looked overripe, and Evie was positively blooming. "Didn't you think Evie looked marvelous?" she asked no one in particular. "Well, I thought she looked marvelous," she answered herself, then, "I thought she was going to come back to your place tonight so she could visit with Cam, Josie."

"She was going to," Josie said, "but those friends of Jasper's, the Cremoris, were going on to another party and they invited her to come along."

"I see," Edna said.

"Actually, Jasper convinced her to go along with them."

"Yes, I see," Edna repeated slowly, implying that she saw a great deal more than anyone else did.

Dozier turned on the radio. The oldies station was wailing with "Take the A Train." Edna switched it off, saying, "I think we're all too tired to be listening to that." Dozier nodded and began humming softly to himself. Edna turned toward the backseat to ask, "Where were Lila's kids, Josie? I would've thought Susan and Ricky would be there."

"I don't think either of them are at an age where they want to be at their parents' parties," Josie said.

"Mmmm. Having their daddy in the spotlight is going to be hard on them. People are always looking for some dirt on a politician's family. Did you see the family portrait in Orrie's campaign literature, Cam?"

"No, I didn't," Cam mumbled, sounding as though she were half-asleep, and wishing she were.

Edna clucked sympathetically. "You could tell Ricky wasn't too happy in that picture. I guess it's hard on kids that age."

Cam gave Josie a sidelong glance and patted her hand. They both knew that Edna's expressions of concern about problems in their family would be followed by a comparison to the happy normalcy of her own, and she didn't disappoint them. "Now my grandson, Chip," Edna went on. "He's Ricky's age but he still likes to be in on the family doings. He told me that the big family reunion we had last summer was the most fun he'd had all year."

"I wouldn't doubt it," Cam whispered in Josie's ear and even in the darkness she could see her mother's face, which was looking extremely tired, crinkle into a smile.

"How's Chip doing?" Cam raised her voice to ask, knowing that topic would be good for at least five minutes of bragging. Similar questions about her other cousins kept Edna going all the way to the Broad River. As they crossed it, Cam looked out on the expanse of moonlit water and rolled down the window to smell the salty-sweet clean air. Maybe Bedford Bethune was right: maybe the best thing about this visit would be the country itself.

"And that," Edna told her when they'd gone another few miles, "is the new Cross Creek shopping center. That must've just been virgin land last time you were here." Cam noted the huge, sterile parking lot where pines had once grown, the strip-mall stores with the Wal-Mart anchor illuminated by ghostly lights, the security guard napping in his Chevy, lone protector of the stand of "Last Minute Sale" Christmas trees. "Maybe I can take your car and drive over here tomorrow, Mama," she said, feigning interest. "I need to pick up a few things." Like a pregnancy test kit.

"Almost home now," Dozier assured them, softly humming "String of Pearls" as Edna pointed out the sprawl of characterless government buildings on what had been another wooded site. They caught a glimpse of water as they rounded onto Cartaret Street, passed the college and the new library, then turned into the almost deserted streets of The Point, an enclave of dignified and beautifully eccentric houses shadowed with live oaks. "Just pull into your drive, we'll walk across to my place," Josie told him.

"No nightcap?"

"Not tonight." Josie noticed that her house was ablaze with lights. Her heart sank when she remembered that Mrs. Beasley was there. "I have a guest at the house, Cam's been traveling all day, I want to get up early to go visit Peatsy, and I know y'all have lots of things to do tomorrow, so I think we should all just call it a night."

"What *was* the matter with Lila?" Edna almost exploded as Josie reached for the door handle. "She sure seemed to have her nose out of joint when we left."

"I told you," Josie said calmly, "she had a migraine. This time of year everyone tries to do too much. Everyone's stressed out."

"Maybe she was annoyed because Cam left the party." Like the indominable huntress she was, she'd been stalking her prey for over an hour and had to get in her last shot. "Where *did* you go, Cam?"

"Oh, a fellow I went to high school with was there. H.A. Staples. I don't think any of you knew him. He never came to the house."

"That black man who looks like Harry Belafonte?" Edna asked.

"Uh-huh," Cam said, though Hannibal didn't look anything like Harry Belafonte. "We were talking about old times. It was good talking to him." She pushed open the door, then turned back in, "Uncle Dozier, would you please unlock the trunk? My bag and that sack of presents is in there."

Dozier helped Edna, then Josie, out of the car. The sisters wandered down the driveway, having a desultory discussion about the next day's plans, then walked through the gardens of their respective houses to their back doors. Cam stood as Dozier hefted her bag out of the trunk, looking from house to house. "I'm sure I don't know what was the matter with Lila," Cam said, stifling a yawn.

"Wouldn't have to be anything special," he said as they moved down the drive. "Relatives rile one another. You know what Linus said—'Big sisters are the *crabgrass* in the lawn of life' and . . ." He looked from one house to the other, "I know that to be true. Sure you don't want me to help you in with these bags?"

She shook her head, then kissed him on the cheek. "See you tomorrow, Uncle Dozier. I am sure glad to see you." He said, "Likewise, I'm sure, Miss Camilla," then shambled away. She turned and walked into her mother's garden. The banks of paperwhites looked phosphorescent in the moonlight and gave a sweet smell to the chilly air. Josie had left the back door open and as she mounted the stairs and stepped into the enclosed veranda she heard a woman's voice, high-pitched and anxious, as though she were telling about an accident: ". . . and I thought it might be a prowler, so—"

"No, Mrs. Beasley," Josie soothed. "You've met that neighbor cat before. She belongs to Mrs. Smiley, two doors down, remember?" Hearing the door close, Josie broke off and turned to Cam. "Cam, this is my guest, Mrs. Beasley." She nodded toward the woman sitting at the kitchen table. "Mrs. Beasley, this is my eldest daughter, Camilla. She's home from New York for the holidays."

Mrs. Beasley stared at Cam as though she might have been given false information.

"Pleased to meet you," Cam said, though she wasn't. Mrs. Beasley had the squashed face, protruding eyes, and hostile look of a spoilt Pekinese. Her hair was set in tiny sponge rollers covered with a net cap that matched her baby blue dressing gown and fluffy slippers.

"Oh, there was a telephone call for you," Mrs. Beasley told her.

"For me?" Cam was surprised. "I don't know who . . ."

Josie sighed. "Mrs. Beasley, I told you I have an answering machine so you don't need to bother yourself with the phone."

"I thought it might be something important. It was—" She got up from the kitchen table, waddled over to the telephone, and checked the notepad on the wall. "A woman by the name of Reba. The number's here. It's in North Carolina."

"You remember my talking about Reba, don't you, Mama?" Cam reminded Josie. "She's a good friend. Down visiting her partner's folks in Durham."

"She sounded upset," Mrs. Beasley warned, handing her the slip of paper before turning back to Josie. "I 'bout jumped out of my skin when I heard that scratching at the back door. I've never been left alone in this house before."

"Well, Mrs. Beasley, you know the neighborhood is safe. Would you like a cup of herb tea to take up to bed with you?"

"No. No. I'll be all right now that I know there's someone else in the house."

"Good. Well, then," Josie began, taking off her jacket and moving into the dining room to turn off the lights. Cam covered a yawn, waited for Mrs. Beasley to say her good nights, and checked her watch to see if it was too late to return Reba's phone call.

"Lord and Taylor!" Mrs. Beasley exclaimed, pointing to the shopping bag Cam had put on the table. "That's one of my favorite stores. Christmas gifts?" Cam said "Yes," and picked up the bag, afraid that Mrs. Beasley might actually reach in and start shaking the boxes.

"I'm up here visiting my niece," Mrs. Beasley went on as though she were imparting delicate information. "I don't like to stay at her house because she has small children and I don't like to interfere. Still, they always want me to come for the holidays so I always stay here with your mother."

Cam nodded, said, "That's nice," paused, then moved to the phone, muttering, "I think I'll return that call." She had no sooner punched in the number than she heard Josie return and Mrs. Beasley say, "Maybe I *should* have a cup of herb tea to help me sleep. Maybe we should all have a cup of tea," and, lest her suggestion be ignored, Mrs. Beasley picked up the kettle and began to fill it with water. "As I was saying, I always stay here with your mother," she rattled on. "This place has such a homey atmosphere."

"Apparently," Cam said, allowing herself a heavy dose of sarcasm because she knew it would be lost on Mrs. Beasley. It was not lost on Josie, who shot her a warning look. "Chamomile or raspberry?" Mrs. Beasley asked brightly. Now that she was riffling through Josie's kitchen cabinets her mood seemed almost festive. Cam cupped her hand over her ear as the phone was picked up on the other end of the line and a man's voice, gruff and sleepy, barked "Hello" as though it were a curse.

"I hope I haven't disturbed you," Cam began, checking her watch to reaffirm that it was only 10:20. "I'm trying to reach Ms. Reba Golden." She was about to offer her apologies for having dialed the wrong number when the man said, "They're not here right now," and hung up. "And happy holidays to you too, jerk," she muttered, replacing the receiver.

"Anything wrong?" Mrs. Beasley asked hopefully.

"I didn't reach my friend," she said, stifling another yawn.

Josie was setting out the cups and saucers, an expression of resignation on her face. Good manners, Josie always said, were made of petty sacrifices, but just now Cam didn't feel like making even the most trivial sacrifice. She said, "I'm real tired, Mama. I think I'll go on up to bed."

"But I wanted to talk with you, dear." Josie looked at Mrs. Beasley, foolishly entertaining the hope that she might get the message and leave them alone.

Cam said, "I guess we can talk in the morning. Which room do I sleep in?"

"First right at the top of the stairs. Here, let me help you up with your things."

"Don't bother. I'll find it." Cam picked up her case and shopping bag.

"There's a bottle of lavender bath salts on the sink," Josie informed her. "Maybe after you've had a bath . . . "

Cam said, "Thanks," gave Josie a kiss on the cheek, and headed toward the stairs. Mounting them, she felt a disappointment close to resentment. Josie was so damned unselfish that she made herself available to everyone. Just as Bear had operated within a chain of command, Josie operated in the military wife's "chain of concern." Her door had always been open and her ear always available to those in need. Flowers or cards were sent at deaths and illnesses, births or promotions, she arranged kaffeeklatsches, helped women find secondhand baby carriages or raise money for the school board. And she expected the same code of conduct from her children. To be ill-mannered was as bad as wearing soiled underwear. "It's more comfortable for me to be polite," Josie would say, *but,* Cam thought, *the opposite is true for me: I'd rather be rude than polite, at least to the likes of Mrs. Beasley.* "Dear Daddy, thank God you didn't live to be an innkeeper," Cam muttered, dropping her bags and shutting the door.

She didn't have the energy to take a bath in lavender salts, didn't even bother to turn on the lights, just sat on the four-poster bed in the moonlight, scrunching off her boots, stripping off her slacks and sweater, pulling back the coverlet, and climbing in between sweet-smelling, smooth sheets.

Some twenty minutes later, after watching Mrs. Beasley drain a pot of chamomile tea and wishing she'd dosed it with arsenic, Josie watched her toddle off, then rinsed the cups. She allowed Mrs. B. time to settle, then climbed the stairs, knocked softly on Cam's door, and waited.

"She's probably asleep already," Mrs. Beasley said, poking her netted head out of her room up the passageway.

"I suppose we should all be asleep now."

"Sweet dreams," Mrs. Beasley said, shutting her door.

Damn, the woman was everywhere, like ugly on an ape!

Josie sighed, checked the thermostat, washed her face and hands, cleaned her teeth, hung up her clothes, and pulled on her nightdress, all the while thinking about Cam. Something was wrong with the girl. Those circles under her eyes weren't just from flying down from New York. And there was something strange about the way she held her body, contained and concentrated, the way she used to look just before she'd go off the high dive in a swimming contest. Something was definitely wrong. Not that she had a hope of finding out what it was.

She was so bone-tired that just lying down seemed like a wonderful gift, but she'd barely settled herself when the phone rang. She lunged for it on the first ring, afraid it would wake Cam or Mrs. Beasley, and almost tipped herself out of bed.

"Mama, it's Lila."

"Yes, dear," she whispered, thinking perhaps Lila had called to apologize. "How's your migraine?"

Lila ignored the question and went on in a businesslike voice. "I've called to firm up plans. I won't be coming over tomorrow, but the day after—Christmas Eve day—we'll all come over in the afternoon. Evie's coming too. And Jasper. I'll help you cook, we'll decorate the tree, and go to Cuba's church service like you want us to, and we'll stay all night. That way we'll already be there Christmas day."

Josie said, "Fine," despite her exhaustion, already juggling the sleeping arrangements in her mind. She would give Susan and Ricky separate rooms, Evie could go in with Cam, and since Mrs. Beasley had the lavender room, she'd put Lila and Orrie in the yellow room. She didn't relish the idea of Jasper sleeping over—she made a mental note to get another bottle of bourbon—and since Lila really didn't enjoy cooking, she would have preferred to fix

Christmas dinner alone, but she was willing to do anything to make things go smoothly. "Fine," she said again. "Everything else all right?"

"It's almost midnight and Ricky's not home yet."

"Well, at that age . . ."

"And Evie called. She's still out with Jasper and the Cremoris, and she wants to come back here to sleep."

She knew she daren't give any advice about ignoring both Ricky and Evie. "I do think the party went well, Lila. Everyone seemed—"

"Please, Mama. No post mortem. I need to get some rest." And with that, Lila hung up.

Josie pulled the comforter up to her chin. Lila was never going to forgive her for changing the Christmas plans. Lila was never going to forgive her, period.

She heard Mrs. Beasley's toilet flush. As a younger woman, waiting for Bear or Cam to come home, Josie'd walk the floor, bake cookies, read recipe books, or listen to the radio when she couldn't sleep, but by the time Evie had entered high school she'd weaned herself away from anxious vigils. Problems, like dirty dishes, would still be there in the morning. She turned onto her side and willed herself to go to sleep. But tonight, willing herself didn't work.

The wind blew the branches of the chinaberry tree against the window. She couldn't stop thinking about Cam. A pipe in her bathroom made a burping sound. She remembered Dozier'd said that the hot-water heater would make it through the winter, but the air-conditioning system would definitely have to be overhauled before next summer.

She heard the grandfather clock downstairs strike one.

A car cruised past, its stereo turned up so loud that she could hear the thrump. Certainly none of her neighbors were driving around The Point at this hour playing rap music. This was some in-your-face intrusion, a none-too-subtle expression of hostility, like the MALCOLM X RULES graffiti Edna had found on the side of her shop a few months ago. Edna had wanted to report it to the police but Dozier had said no. He'd mentioned the incident to a black man he was friendly with who owned a little market on Green Street where teenage boys hung out, hoping elders in the community would deal with it. Then he'd gotten up at dawn, painted it over, and said that was the end of that.

She moved her feet to warm them, curled up, and pulled her nightdress over them, wondering if it would be too tacky to put space heaters in the rooms.

She'd prefer to fix a fresh-killed turkey, but it was probably too late to get one. If Cuba could give her a couple of hours tomorrow, she'd be able to do last-minute grocery shopping. Creamed turnips. Cam had always loved them and they went so well with turkey. She mustn't forget to buy turnips. Of course, she had to visit both Mawmaw and Peatsy . . .

She hoped to heaven Ricky had come home. She'd seen trouble coming with Ricky from the time he'd been in diapers. Like so many parents of their generation, Lila and Orrie had been child-centered. They'd always indulged both Ricky and Susan, pretending to give them free choice when they'd needed firm guidance, if not outright orders. How could you raise a child properly if you weren't prepared to be hated once in a while? They'd never reined Ricky in, and here he was at eighteen, without a hint of manhood, going through money as though they minted it in the garage. "Correct thy son and he shall give thee rest; yea, he shall give delight unto thy soul." She remembered the quote, but for the life of her, she couldn't remember its chapter and verse. No doubt about it, she was losing her mind.

After five minutes of acute frustration (her Bible was downstairs and she was sure to wake Mrs. Beasley if she went in search of it) a voice that seemed to come from nowhere said "Proverbs 29:17" out loud. She sighed with relief and rearranged the pillows.

Hearing Mrs. Beasley's toilet flush again, she wondered why she'd been stupid enough to let the woman drink an entire pot of tea. She knew Cam was angry with her because she'd humored Mrs. Beasley. What Cam didn't understand was that Mrs. B. was a paying guest. But even more than that, Mrs. B. was a lonely woman. And loneliness wasn't just a word, it was a naked terror. No human being could really feel it without going mad.

Wondering if she had enough pecans to make three pies. . . .

Eight

CAM WOKE THE next morning churning through the covers, knocking aside pillows as though she were being suffocated. Coming up for air, she blinked at the canopy, then turned on her side and looked at the room. It was like waking up in a dell—all greens, roses, and browns kissed with sunlight. Against a background of William Morris wallpaper in a lovely vine and pomegranate design there was a walnut wardrobe and matching chest of drawers, a marble-topped dressing table and oval mirror, standing towel rack, nineteenth-century drawings of local flora, a crystal bowl of potpourri—a place for everything and everything in its place—save the pile of clothes she'd dropped on the floor. No doubt about it, her mother had exquisite taste, but such carefully planned Victorian domesticity made her feel queasy. The possibility of her pregnancy crashed over her. Yes, she definitely felt queasy. But also ravenously hungry. She opened the door to the hallway and got a more powerful whiff of the coffee and cinnamon she had only been vaguely conscious of smelling. Closing the door and going into the adjoining bathroom, she checked her underpants, felt her heart sink when she saw nothing, slapped water on her face, and put on the white terry-cloth robe hanging on the back of the door. She opened the hall door again and looked from left to right.

Relieved to see that Mrs. Beasley wasn't lurking, ready to pounce, she went downstairs.

The brightness and warmth of the sun coming through the kitchen window was both shocking and delightful. She shielded her eyes as though she had a hangover and picked up the note on the kitchen table.

Dear Cam—

You seemed so tired I didn't want to wake you. I've gone over to the hospital to visit Peatsy. Be back by eleven, then maybe we can go visit Mawmaw—

Love, Mama.

She poured herself a cup of coffee, picked up a cinnamon bun from the tray on top of the stove, and moved slowly into the next room. Since she had never lived here, she had the almost disembodied sensation one feels when walking alone through a stranger's deserted house. The walls of the dining room were a rich ivory, the woodwork Charleston green. A Queen Anne table that could seat a dozen people shone in the light from the tall windows, which were draped in heavy fabric with a palmetto-and-pineapple motif. Like the rest of the house, the room had both understated beauty and a sense of comfort. Josie finally had the dining room she'd always wanted, and it seemed sad to Cam that paying guests rather than family sat at her table.

She paused next to the sideboard, licked the cinnamon frosting from her fingers and touched a bowl of holly and berries. Something familiar struck her and she realized that the sideboard had been one of Mawmaw's prized possessions—a massive piece of furniture that came from a time when people didn't jump on planes and fly halfway round the world in a single day, when living in one house for a lifetime was not unusual. On the wall was a framed letter from Mawmaw's great-grandfather, written during the Civil War, that began: "My dearest and most cherished wife . . ." Cam thought, *Sam would appreciate this.* If he were there she would tell him about the first time it had been shown to her, when she'd been about six years old. Mawmaw had told her that it was one of the most valuable things she owned and when she'd asked how much was it worth, Mawmaw had told her, with a sternness that still stuck in her mind, that truly valuable things had no price.

Wandering into the living room, she saw the green, cream, and red antique carpet Josie had bought, over Bear's objections, while they were traveling through Turkey. Carpets, Josie'd insisted, were a good investment. They could be moved anywhere, shipped, and stored. Since they'd never had a house big enough for this one, it had been stored until they'd retired. Cam sat cross-legged, next to the Christmas tree, running her hand back and forth over the nap of the carpet, staring at the boxes labeled ORNAMENTS. The first one she opened had the usual tinsel and brightly colored balls. The next one was marked SPECIAL—HANDLE WITH CARE. All its contents were protected with Styrofoam peanuts. There was a little silver plane (a gift from Josie to Bear), a lacquered butterfly from Kyoto, a hand-carved rocking horse, no doubt a legacy of some distant relative who had whittled, and, at the bottom, wrapped in pink tissue paper, an angel doll Mawmaw had made, with cloth body, bisque face and hands, and human hair. Touching it gave her a shiver. The baby-gold hair had belonged to one of Mawmaw's children, Christina, who'd died of some old-fashioned disease—scarlatina? whooping cough?—when she was just four years old. Mawmaw had always put Christina on top of her Christmas trees, saying that she had her own private angel.

She had always thought that her mother's obsession with houses and decorating was small-minded, "feminine" in the most narrow sense. She had even suspected that Josie'd wanted this place, next to her sister's, because she was envious of Edna's home and possessions. But now it struck her that Josie's desire for a home wasn't just acquisitive, and her need to save things wasn't just hoarding. It was Josie's way of creating a center, trying to hold things together. A beautiful home was permanence in an impermanent world, a little utopia where she tried to give herself and those nearest to her a sense of comfort, beauty, security. The nesting instinct was not just "feminine" but deeply female.

She rewrapped the angel, put it back into the box, went back into the kitchen, checked the notepad, and dialed. The line was answered by a man who said "Merry Christmas" in the same cheery tone one might hear when listening to "This is a test of the emergency broadcast system. This is only a test."

"Sorry, if I've disturbed you," she began. "May I please speak to Reba Golden?"

"She's not here." The same response she'd gotten the last night, but this time, there was a weight to it, not just "She's out," but "She's gone."

"Ah . . . when do you expect her back?"

A pause. Then a terse, "I don't."

"Then could I please talk to Cheryl?" she asked quickly. But the man had already hung up.

She was sitting by the kitchen window, sipping a third cup of coffee and staring out the window, when the phone rang. As she picked it up she thought, stupidly, that Sam might have tracked her down. Instead she heard a familiar throaty voice laced with a Bronx accent. "Good morning. This is Reba Golden. May I please speak to Cam Tatternall?"

"Reba, it's me. I just tried to call you."

"Then I needn't have said good morning. I could've told the truth and said shitty morning."

"Where are you?"

"I'm in a Motel 6 in someplace called Spartanburg, and believe me it is."

"What are you doing there?"

"Eating Doritos for breakfast and watching infomercials on TV."

"No, I mean—"

"They kicked me out."

"Who?"

"Cheryl's family. Okay, that's an exaggeration. They didn't kick me out. They just made me feel like something the cat had dragged in, then Cheryl and I had a fight, so I left."

"Oh, Reba. I'm sorry."

"Yeah, well. I knew it wasn't going to be a cakewalk, but we'd talked on the drive down about how we were gonna handle things. I mean, we weren't gonna do a mad tango and turn it into their first gay Christmas. I promised not to discuss politics, sex, or religion—which, as you know, are the only subjects that really interest me. And Cheryl agreed that she'd at least admit that we're roommates, so I wouldn't have to watch everything I said. But when we get there, Cheryl goes all soft and runny, doesn't mention a thing—even about us living together—just says we're business partners. I'm bent out of shape, but I figure I can deal with it."

Cam heard the crackle of cellophane, and a quick intake of breath. "Reba, you're not smoking again, are you?"

"So what if I am?"

"But you haven't smoked for a year and a half."

"I'm in the South. The health Nazis haven't got control here yet. It's like France. Well, not a lot like France, except that the natives treat you like shit. Anyway, are you listening?" Without waiting for an affirmation, Reba plunged on. "So, soon as we arrive we sit down to dinner with all these cousins and aunts. It was like a cross between a funeral and a church social. We say grace. As you know, I don't have any problem giving thanks for food, but this food! Lime Jell-O with Miracle Whip—that's supposed to be the salad—white bread the consistency of angel food cake slathered with margarine, lima beans mushed up like pond scum, chicken that's been deep-fat fried then smothered in beige gravy. I mean! 'You are what you eat' is probably one of the smartest things anyone has ever said."

"That's not real Southern food," Cam said defensively, but since Reba was one of the most accomplished chefs in Manhattan, she added, "but I know it must've been difficult for you."

"Difficult? Difficult? Have you ever tried to smile, chew, and stop yourself from upchucking simultaneously? Then one of the cousins with two first names turns to me, oozing pity, and says, 'You're Jewish, aren't you? You've never had Christmas.' And I say something like, 'We don't have Christmas, but we have Hanukkah,' and she says, 'Besides bagels, what are your traditional foods?' I tell her that foods associated with Jews are just Eastern European, that we only eat traditional foods for Passover. All eyes drop to the table and the cousin says, like it's the tag line on an *X-Files* episode, 'What kind of ritual foods?' I was tempted to say roasted Christian babies with Béarnaise sauce garnished with parsley. I mean, Cam! I had no idea such ignorance existed. You'd think they'd have watched *Seinfeld*, or seen a Woody Allen movie."

"This is redneck stuff, Reba. It's not representative. One of the oldest synagogues in America is in Charleston. I can show you—"

"Then, then," Reba plowed on, "after the banana pudding and the peach cobbler—which, by the by, wouldn't have been half bad if we hadn't had to wash it down with Gatorade and iced tea—they turn on the TV. Actually, they don't turn it on, 'cause it's never been turned off. It's on twenty-four hours a day as a safeguard against conversation—but Cheryl's daddy turns it up—way up. Cheryl and her mother and the two female cousins with two first names clear the dishes. I offer to help but Cheryl's mother says, 'Oh, no. You just sit in the La-Z-Boy.' Like I'm too lazy to help."

"No. She wouldn't let you help because you were company."

"The La-Z-Boy is mustard-colored velveteen with the plastic cover. Must be Daddy's throne 'cause he looks some kinda pissed when I sit in it. So the TV is turned way up to a preacher show, with this guy yelling, 'Je-sus,' as though it was a curse. Then Cheryl's sister and her husband come in with this endomorph infant dressed in green and red rompers with 'Happy Birthday Jesus' on the bib, and snot hanging from his nose like candles. The kid starts beating on my chest with a plastic M-16 gun and the whole family's giving me the fish-eye, especially when the TV preacher yells, 'Do you want to be born again?' I say, by way of a joke, 'cause believe me, this assemblage is in sore need of a joke, 'I don't think my mother would let me be born again. From what she tells me she didn't enjoy it the first time.' Nobody laughs. Anything make you feel more lonely than saying something funny and nobody laughs? I tell you, Cam, I started doing some serious thinking about Passover. The escape from Eygpt never meant more to me than it did then. I needed a scotch and a cigarette and a guzzle of Pepto-Bismol real bad. So I go out to the kitchen, where I catch Cheryl with tears in her eyes, scarfing down a second helping of the barfy banana pudding. I suggest that we go to a store and get some cigs. Why don't I go alone, she asks? Because I don't know where the hell I am, I tell her. So we leave. I can feel all of them peeking at us through the ruffled curtains, as though we're gonna duck into the bushes and start necking. As if anyone could feel anything vaguely affectionate, let alone sexual, in that atmosphere! Then, the minute we start to drive away Cheryl goes ballistic and turns on me."

"Did you say anything to make her mad?"

"Of course not. Well, I did say I could see where she'd had to run away from home to get a decent meal."

"Reba, you've got to understand—"

"But I meant it as a compliment. I really did. Never in my wildest dreams had I imagined what she'd come from."

"People get very defensive about their families. They may put them down, but when anyone else, even a lover, does—"

"But when I took Cheryl to visit my grandmother and she almost gagged on gefilte fish, we laughed about it. And at least I had the guts to admit our relationship. I'll never forget that one: Grandma looked at Cheryl, then looked at me, then shrugged, and said, 'Homosexual, heterosexual—I hear about it on the TV but they never had those things when I was a girl,' then she put our hands together, told us to live and be happy, and got up to fix coffee. I mean, acceptance I don't expect, but tolerance is the foundation of civilization."

"You're sounding like a letter to the editor. And of course you wanted acceptance. Who wouldn't? How did Cheryl take it when you decided to leave?"

"She said maybe it was for the best. Whenever someone says maybe it's for the best, you can be damned sure it's not going to be. So I grab my bag and get back on the road to New York, then I ask myself, what am I going back to? We've closed the business down for two weeks . . ." Reba made a hissing sound. "When I think of all the parties we missed doing! We could've made an extra payment on the condo. Besides, you're out of town, everyone else I know has already made plans. So, I said to myself, you're in the South for the first time, why not see it all? Why not check into the slave quarters in a Confederate theme park or something? So here I am in Spartanburg."

"Why don't you come on down here?"

"I wouldn't want to butt in. You're involved in a family thing."

"Am I ever. Lila's already so pissed off at me that she's spitting nails, though I'm sure I don't know why. Please come on down. My mother has all kinds of room and I could use an ally."

"I don't know, Cam. It doesn't seem like such a hot idea."

"Reba." Cam used her pay-attention voice. "My period's five days late."

"Five days," Reba scoffed. "At our time of life . . ."

"Reba, do I have to remind you that I'm not a lesbian?"

"Oh, you mean . . ." There was a pause. Cam could feel rather than hear Reba taking a deep drag on her cigarette. "So have you seen a doctor?"

"How the hell can I see a doctor? I flew down from New York. It's Christmas. My mother's gone to visit a friend in the hospital and when she gets back we're supposed to go see my grandmother in the rest home, then I'm going to try to sneak out and get one of those pregnancy tests they sell in the drugstores. Do you have any idea how accurate they are?"

"Have you heard anything from Sam?"

"Why should I hear from Sam?" Cam snapped. "Especially since I told him not to call me? Reba, please come down. You know Mama runs this bed-and-breakfast—there's plenty of room."

"I'd be glad to pay her."

"Don't be ridiculous. Please come. I miss you. I think I-26 goes from Spartanburg to Charleston, and crosses I-95. You'll see signs to Beaufort. You'll have to check a map but you can't be more'n four hours away. Please come. I need you."

"Well, if you put it that way I guess I'll just have to shove aside all the others who're clamoring for my attention. Four hours?"

"Something like that. Just call when you get close and I'll give you the address. 'Bye. And thanks."

As she hung up the phone, Cam had a prickly sensation around her shoulders that made her feel she was being watched. Mrs. Beasley was standing in the door to the hall, still swaddled in pale blue fleece. Her nylon sleep cap and sponge rollers had been removed to show a topknot of orange curls that made you want to call Clairol's hot line for emergency advice. "Are we going to be having another guest?" she asked, eyes bulging.

"That's—" Cam stopped herself from saying, "none of your business." This was her mother's house. "Coffee?"

"I already had a cup with your mother. But I wouldn't mind another." She settled her bottom into one of the kitchen chairs and helped herself to a cinnamon roll. "Your mother usually fixes a complete breakfast. That's one of the reasons I always recommend this place to friends. But this morning . . . I suppose, what with the holidays and all . . ." As Cam set a cup of coffee before her and turned to leave, she whined, "I was cold last night. Weren't you cold? I don't think the thermostat was set high enough. And the hair dryer in my bathroom isn't working, so I went into your mother's bathroom. I don't suppose she'll mind."

I'd certainly mind, Cam thought, but said, "I don't suppose she will."

"A close friend of yours?"

"Excuse me?"

"The guest who's coming—is he a close friend of yours?"

"Mrs. Beasley . . ." It was hopeless. Some people were dense because they chose to be dense, apparent stupidity being the only weapon in their arsenal. "If you'll excuse me."

But the back door was opened after a *dum-de-dum* knock and Dozicr, cheery and red-cheeked, wafting a hint of Old Spice and carrying a large box, came through the door. "Mornin', sweetheart," he said to Cam. "And to you too, Miz Beasley."

Mrs. Beasley clutched the front of her robe and pressed her lips together as though she were controlling an attack of gas. "Oh, Mr. Robido, I am ashamed to have you find me in *en déshabillé.*" Dozier and Cam exchanged a quick glance.

"Please forgive me," Dozier said, gallantly diverting his eyes. "I didn't mean to intrude. Cam, is your mama gone?"

"She's at the hospital visiting Peatsy."

"But she's coming back to collect you before she goes to see Mawmaw?"

"I guess so."

"Edna and I were supposed to go along with you, but Edna's running around like a headless chicken. Says she's got too much to do to visit Mawmaw. She's down at her store already. Wants you to drop by later so she can show it off to you. I don't have much to do, so I figured I'd go along with you and Josie." He placed the package, wrapped in white wedding paper with a silver-bell-and-heart motif, on the table. "Guess Edna ran out of Christmas paper. Don't suppose Mawmaw will notice. I think it's a nightdress or a bed jacket. I wasn't with Edna when she bought it. I said we might as well donate the money to Alzheimer's research, but Edna said that would be cold."

Sure, Cam thought, *Edna's so warmhearted she doesn't have time to visit Mawmaw, so she eases her conscience with a $100 gift.* But who was she to criticize? She hadn't bothered about Mawmaw in years, though she still had the postcard Mawmaw had sent when she'd gone to the rest home. "Dear Camilla, They're putting me in the other place. I hope you'll come visit. I remember you as a girl. So much like me." Cam couldn't imagine what similarity Mawmaw had been referring to. Mawmaw had always been hard on her, but then Mawmaw had been hard on everybody, including herself. "Oh, Mawmaw," Cam said, shaking her head. Mawmaw had gone no further than the fifth grade, but Cam had always believed she had what philosophers would call "a world view." She'd witnessed births and deaths and she knew how to kill and pluck a chicken, but was a stickler for the finer points of etiquette. She liked starched petticoats, white gloves, ironed handkerchiefs, and a recognizable part in the hair. When she got what she called "gussied up," she could talk the county council into voting the way she thought they should vote. She could get the best price on everything from antique silver to roadside watermelons, could diagnose most childhood illnesses faster than a pediatrician, follow stock-market reports, and dance the Charleston. She could quote the Bible but preferred to read John Steinbeck or Pearl Buck. She held office in the Daughters of the Confederacy but gave her money to the League of Women Voters. She said she knew everything there was to know about men and children because, basically, they were the same. "I'm looking forward to seeing her."

"You know she probably won't recognize you. Your mama thinks she sees a glimmer now and then, but I reckon that's just wishful thinking," Dozier told her.

She nodded. "I guess I'll go upstairs and shower."

"Not going to fix any real breakfast?" Mrs. Beasley asked.

"No. The cinnamon bun was enough." More than enough. It was rising in her gullet and making her feel swoony. She could see that Dozier was torn between wanting to sit and enjoy coffee and cinnamon buns and an equally strong desire to escape Mrs. Beasley. "Think I'll go check out the garden," he decided. "Once the holidays are over, your mother and I both have got some serious work to do in our yards."

"Oh, Dozier, I do appreciate your coming along," Josie said as she and Cam got into his Lincoln. "I just don't think I'm fit to drive any more today. You know the last time Mary Gebhardt and I were out together she was fussing, 'I didn't move to a small Southern town to sit at stoplights.' I told her to calm down, but you know she's right. I've never seen traffic like this." Josie didn't want to tell them that she'd hit the brake instead of the accelerator when coming out of the hospital parking lot, but she did confess, "You know I haven't honked my horn but a couple of times in my entire life but today, coming along Bay Street, I got behind these tourists with New Jersey plates who were rubbernecking, going about ten miles an hour, and I just leaned on the horn."

"Good for you, sister. Got to assert yourself. You buckled up, Cam?" Dozier asked, turning to the backseat. Cam nodded and he pulled out of the drive. "So, sister, how's Peatsy comin' along?"

"They say she's stabilized."

Dozier grunted. "Peatsy Gibbs stabilized? If she is, it'll be the first time since I've known her."

"She seemed much more like her old self." Very much like her old self. Even before Josie had reached Peatsy's room she'd heard Peatsy's sweetly demanding voice telling her son, Waring, to "Take some of these flowers home, I feel as though I'm already at a funeral. There's some thank-you notes in my desk in the library—not the heavy parchment ones, the regular ones with the blue monogram will do—write something simple like 'Mother thanks you. She's recuperating and wishes you a happy New Year.' "

The room looked like a florist shop. Waring, his face as rumpled as his suit, was slumped in a chair. Peatsy, in an écru satin bed jacket, was propped up on a bank of pillows, holding a hand mirror and applying bright pink lipstick while Waring's companion, Alonzo, brushed her hair. "It still looks flat," Peatsy complained.

"Chure, because you need a champoo," Alonzo assured her, giving another flick of the brush. "But you're lookin' charp, lady. Lookin' charper every day." Alonzo's long sooty lashes, sweetly cheeky face, and the way he worked his mouth around the words reminded Josie of Lamb Chop.

"Why, Josie," Peatsy exclaimed, noticing her, "aren't you a darlin' to come by again! Waring, where're your manners? Give Josie that chair."

Josie told him not to bother, but Waring got up, saying that he and Alonzo were on their way out for brunch. Was there anything else Peatsy needed? Strange, Josie thought, as Peatsy went through her list—baby powder, emery boards, a bologna sandwich with pepper relish and mustard that she wasn't supposed to have, so they'd have to sneak it in—that Waring seemed so adoring. The kindest thing Peatsy had ever said about him was that he'd inherited her brains if not her looks, and, even in Waring's presence, Josie had heard Peatsy go into shocking detail about the agonies she'd suffered giving him birth ("Your head was the size of a football"). When he'd been no more than an infant, Peatsy had taken trips for months at a time, blithely leaving him in the care of others, and she'd sent him to boarding school as soon as they'd take him. Yet Waring was more devoted and less critical of Peatsy than any of Josie's own children would be of her.

"Just leave those long-stem yellow roses. Take all the rest. Especially the poinsettias. Never could stand poinsettias." When Waring said he wasn't fond of them himself, Peatsy said, "Then leave them on the steps of some church or other. Only get them out of here. And while you're at it, throw that dime store Santa in the trash."

When a nurse came in to give her a shot, Waring and Alonzo made their getaway, toting pots of flowers in both hands. Josie pulled the chair up to the bed and listened while Peatsy, her voice still vivacious but her face chalky, gossiped about the staff, and asked about Cam, and Lila's party. As the drug started to work, her eyes closed to half-mast and her speech slowed and slurred, so that by the time she was telling Josie what arrangements Waring was making for her recuperation, she sounded more than a little tipsy. "Go on home, dear heart. I'm still getting my strength back and this medication makes me dopey, so I nap most of the time." Her hand flopped onto Josie's and gave it a half-hearted pat. "It really is good of you to come." She yawned. "I know what it must do to you to be in a hospital this time of year. Memories of Bear and all." Her expression turned dreamy. "Bear. Now that was a man. I still have a photo of him somewhere, standing in front of his Grumman Wildcat. The wind is lifting his hair and he's wearing one of those long aviator scarfs, like the Red Baron." She shut her eyes, rolled her top lip over her bottom lip and squeezed them together. Josie couldn't tell if she was reliving an unpleasant memory or was in physical pain. "He was twice the man Gibbs was, and Gibbs knew it. Bear was a real hero, and no matter how long they actually live, heroes always die young."

Peatsy's touch suddenly felt abhorrent. Josie slid her hand out from under Peatsy's and stared out the window to keep herself from saying, "How dare you speak so knowingly about my husband." But she knew how Peatsy dared.

She had known almost from the beginning—at least a decade before she been willing to admit it consciously—that there were other women. One night, soon after they were married, they'd been at a big going-away party. A buddy of Bear's, in his cups as Bear had been, had been swearing eternal devotion to his girlfriend, and Bear had said—she'd never forget it—"Don't listen to him, girlie. Just ask yourself: if you knew you might die tomorrow, what would you want to be doing tonight?" The crowd had roared with laughter, and Josie'd laughed too, but she'd thought, "I'd want to be with you. And if I couldn't be with you, I'd want to be alone to think about you and pray about you." And she'd actually believed, or had kidded herself into believing, that he felt the same way.

Over the years she'd shrugged off excuses she didn't quite believe, and refused to challenge him on explanations that didn't quite ring true. She'd usually been able to talk herself out of her fits of doubt and jealousy, reasoning that if you were married to a charismatic, highly sexed flying ace who was gone for months on end, a certain amount of insecurity went with the territory. She'd forgiven the flirtations she'd witnessed—easy enough since they were usually initiated by women—and struggled to build her own self-confidence. But sometimes, alone after she'd put the girls to bed, she'd be powerless to put the awful "What if . . . ?" out of her mind. "What if Bear is having . . . a dalliance?" She always used that word because it made the threat seem trivial. A dalliance couldn't really hurt anything but her ego; besides, she probably wouldn't know about it. She was sure that she was first in his heart, that he'd never do anything that would directly threaten their marriage. Hadn't he told her that she was the great love of his life? And didn't we all survive by putting the dreadful "what if's?" out of our minds?

But there was no denying the reality that Christmas he'd called from Okinawa to say that his commanding officer, who happened to be General Gibbs, had canceled his leave. She still didn't understand how she'd known—had it been his tone of voice, the unnatural pauses in the conversation, the static crackle that made her feel as though he were on another planet?—but she had known, undeniably, that he was lying. Why, she'd sputtered, would Lamar Gibbs (who was, after all, a friend of sorts) cancel his Christmas leave unless there were a military emergency? When would she learn, he'd answered, that a CO was a CO, not a friend? She hadn't said any more, hadn't even been able to feel anything. But after she'd hung up. . . .

That awful fight with Cam! Cam seemed to feel it was Josie's fault that Bear wasn't coming home, and her you-can't-control-me attitude and look of defiance were so much like Bear's that Josie'd lost all control and slapped her face. But it was she, not Cam, who'd burst into tears. Shaking and ashamed, she'd ordered Cam to her room, then bundled up Lila and Evie and sent them to play at a neighbor's. She'd gone into the living room, shut the door and drawn the shades, sat on the secondhand chair she'd reupholstered, and put in a call to Bear, dialing the long-distance operator, as one had to in those days. Even though she said it was an emergency, it had taken such a long time for the operator to make the connection that she'd almost calmed down. He was probably just as disappointed as she was, and how could she burden him with the problems of raising kids when he was thousands of miles away? She was ready to say, "Darling, I was so upset I just had to hear your voice again. . . ." But the voice at the other end of the line, Bear's master sergeant, told her that Captain Tatternall had left base without giving a destination.

Then she'd done something she knew Bear would never forgive her for: she'd put in a call to his commanding officer. This time, to her surprise, the operator made a direct connection. Josie gave her name to Lamar Gibbs's secretary and scrambled to think what she would say, but General Gibbs picked up immediately, shocking her even more by saying, "Mrs. Tatternall—Josie, my dear—I've been meaning to get in touch with you." In that high-pitched voice the men all made fun of, he'd asked how she was doing, how the girls were doing, his unprecedented warmth making her feel she was sinking into quicksand. "Now, Josie," he'd said, after the miserable preliminaries, "you know and I know that men like Captain Tatternall—Bear—are only in their element during a war. Peacetime training bores them. But they have to understand that despite the great service they've performed for their country, despite their popularity with the men, they are not exempt from getting with the program." She murmured assent. "I don't suppose it will surprise you," he went on, "to hear that your husband has had a lot of UAs." (She went blank, then translated UAs as unauthorized absences.) "Apparently Bear has an off-base"—she heard him search for the euphemism—"*interest* that is consuming a good deal of his time. . ."—an interest? Lightning translation: another woman—"and possibly a good deal of his money. Let me ask you, ma'am . . ."—she was no longer Josie, or even Mrs. Tatternall, she was *ma'am* as he cut to the chase—"about your recent allotment checks. How much have you been receiving?" There was no point in withholding information; if he didn't already know, he could find out. "Ah-huh, ah-huh," he'd said, when she told him, "well . . . I thought so. I'm going to check that out as soon as Captain Tatternall returns to base." He'd inquired about the girls again, told her she was a fine example of a devoted military wife, said he'd convey her best wishes to Peatsy (though she hadn't mentioned Peatsy), wished her a merry Christmas—then hung up.

She'd written to tell Bear that she knew about the other woman. By the time she'd finished writing it, the letter was tear-stained, making it look trashy and melodramatic, but she put it in the mail before she could change her mind.

A week or so later she'd received a belated Christmas card from Peatsy and Lamar Gibbs, Peatsy's scrawl telling her that Okinawa was so boring she'd spent the holidays in Tokyo on a shopping spree ("Wait'll you see the kimonos I bought!"), and a terse P.S., printed in block letters, from Lamar, saying, "Situation under control. Best wishes for the New Year." She knew neither Bear nor General Gibbs would tell her what had transpired in their confrontation, but she assumed Gibbs had given Bear a proper dressing down and told him to increase her allotment, because a few days afterward she'd gotten her monthly check, with a fifty-dollar increase, from the paymaster's office.

She'd written to Bear again, a businesslike letter informing him that she'd received the increase and asking what, if anything, he had in his savings account.

Bear had called about a week after that, dodging her questions about money and saying that he'd be coming home by the end of the month. And what about "her," she'd asked? He'd paused, then said in a flat, dismissive voice, "You know that didn't mean anything. It's over. There's nothing to discuss." And when she'd howled, "Don't tell me there's nothing to discuss," he'd said, "Nobody talks to me like that, girl. Not even you," and hung up, leaving her screaming, "Who the hell are you! God?" at the living room wall.

She'd imagined the woman as everything from a young but unexceptional camp follower to a sophisticated beauty, but strangely, the fact that Bear been squandering money pained her even more. She'd believed that she and Bear were partners, making mutual sacrifices to save for the future. When she thought about the times she'd struggled onto buses instead of taking cabs, used Mawmaw's birthday checks for household necessities, done her own hair instead of going to the beauty parlor, bought beans instead of steak . . . then pictured him paying the rent on a shack-up, or buying a round of drinks for a roomful of strangers . . . her sense of injustice bubbled like lava.

She'd thought about divorce, but she'd never mentioned it. She had three children to raise. She'd never worked. Where would she go? What would she do? The military would guarantee her some money, but not enough. She would have to go home and live with Mawmaw, and be reminded, every day of her life, that she'd made a tragic mistake.

There had been times when she'd wanted to scream his guilt from the rooftops. He hadn't just betrayed her. He'd willfully, irretrievably tarnished his own reputation. But no matter how she cursed him in her heart, she couldn't bring herself to belittle him in front of his daughters. The girls thought he'd hung the moon, and she couldn't bear to rob them of that illusion.

When he'd finally come home, it had been the worst period of her life. She'd hoped, against all prior experience and knowledge, that he'd talk to her about what had happened. But of course he hadn't. (It was only after his death that she'd understood not that he wouldn't, but that, because of his nature, he simply *couldn't* talk to her.) But her trust had been violated in the deepest way. She would never recover. She would never be able to take him back into her bed, let alone her heart. And yet . . .

The wound had started to heal. The scar remained, but she would never let anyone, even Bear, see it. If she was going to live with him she wasn't going to reheat his sins for breakfast.

Habit, necessity, and a mutual concern for their girls, fueled by some still-burning coal of love she'd thought must be dead, had brought them to an unspoken acceptance. After a year, they were almost back on track. She had almost gotten to the point where she could acknowledge her physical desire for him without feeling like a masochist. All marriages suffered storms, she'd told herself. Theirs had been more destructive than most, but there was a certain pride in knowing that they'd weathered it. After such havoc, what could hurt them?

It had been a New Year's bash at the Parris Island Officer's Club. They were sitting at the head table with three other couples, including Peatsy and General Lamar Gibbs. Bear had given her an orchid corsage and, while they were dancing, he'd come as close to an apology as he would ever get, smiling down at her, his eyes moist, saying, "It doesn't matter if you crash; what matters is getting up and walking away from it." They'd gone through the worst; their love was strong as steel. That night, she thought, when they got home, she wouldn't put in her diaphragm. She'd take this one last chance and gamble with fate, and maybe give him the boy-child he'd always wanted.

When Peatsy, wearing a silver dress that fit her like fish scales, had asked Bear to dance, Josie fiddled with her swizzle stick and smiled at General Gibbs. She tried to talk to Gibbs, but he was so galvanized by the sight of Bear and Peatsy gyrating and bouncing that he barely acknowledged her. When the fast number had finished in a blare of trumpets, the dancers applauded, broke, drifted back to their tables. But Bear and Peatsy stood, inches apart, not talking but waiting, then rolling like quicksilver into one another's arms as "Mood Indigo" started up. Josie virtually pulled General Gibbs to the dance floor, pressing her breasts (in a strapless outfit she was afraid might fall down) against his medalled chest. Gibbs dipped and twirled her, his mouth creasing at her little jokes, but his eyes continually strayed to Peatsy and Bear, who danced in wordless, unsmiling bliss.

Dear God, Josie'd thought in panic, what are Bear and Peatsy doing? Peatsy clearly was settling some of her own scores by humiliating Gibbs, but Bear? Didn't he realize that he was gambling with his career as much as if he and Peatsy had actually stripped and had carnal knowledge on the dance floor? But then she'd understood, as through a glass darkly, that Bear, the foundling boy who hated all authority, was deliberately saying "screw you," daring General Gibbs to punish him. And she'd known at that very moment that Gibbs was past forgiveness and would oblige. He would block any promotions and make sure that Bear finished his days as a flight instructor, waiting for retirement. Which is what had happened.

Josie'd accepted more than her usual glass and a half of champagne, and when the New Year was toasted, raised her glass with the rest of them, but she'd been deep in desperate and befuddled thought. Some things, broken, could not be mended. No matter how she loved the man, she must never trust him again. If she stayed with him—and even then she'd known that she would—her wifely duties would only be a pose. She'd have to make her own plans. She'd been silent all the way home. Bear, expansively singing along with Guy Lombardo's broadcast from Times Square, seemed oblivious. The TV was still on, showing the test pattern, and the coffee table was littered with Coke bottles and a bowl of popcorn, but the girls were all asleep in their beds. She went into the bathroom, took off her makeup, and put in her diaphragm. Bear made love to her passionately, but she felt an emotional distance that was entirely alien to her nature. She knew that she would never be able to abandon herself to him again. Afterward, when he'd fallen asleep, she got up to check on the girls, then went into the bathroom, washed herself carefully, and sank to the little bath mat. And wept.

She watched Peatsy's chest rise and fall but she was certain Peatsy wasn't asleep. *I could ask her now,* she thought. *I could say, "Did you have an affair with my husband, Peatsy? It doesn't matter anymore. You can tell me now."* But even at this late date she couldn't rely on Peatsy to tell the truth. And of course she, too, would be lying, because it *did* really matter. Strange, she'd thought as she stared at the tubes and bottles, the vase of yellow roses, the trees outside the window, all of which looked flat and two-dimensional, that what two people, one of them now dead, might have done alone in a bed forty years ago could still pain her so savagely.

"But she still seems very tired," she told Dozier, pulling herself back into the present. "She was sleeping when I left. They're going to delay surgery until after the holidays. Then they're going to do that procedure where they put balloons into your veins and blow them up."

"Angioplasty," Cam said.

"Yes, I think that's it. And it turns out that Alonzo, that good-looking young foreign man who lives with Peatsy's son, is a registered nurse, so he's going to come down here and help while she recuperates."

"He's a *nurse*," Dozier asked, his squint into the rearview mirror showing that he thought nursing a gender-specific occupation.

Cam said, "Walt Whitman was a nurse during the Civil War."

Dozier snorted. "I don't doubt it."

"Does it ruffle your feathers because he was gay, a nurse, a Yankee, or a poet?" Cam asked.

"None of the above. I didn't even know he was a queer."

Cam sighed dramatically. Josie realized that Cam and Dozier were going to have one of the teasing-verging-on-argument discussions that they so enjoyed. "Can't you say 'gay' or 'homosexual'?" Cam asked.

"I can't say 'gay,' because gay means something else to me. It means happy or full of delight. I don't take it kindly when people change words on me. It's like the Negroes. First they want to be called blacks, then when we get used to that, they tell us they're African Americans. Soon's we start callin' 'em that, they'll want to change it to something else. It's like you when you were a little kid"—he raised his eyebrows and smiled over at her—"you wanted to pick your own name. Remember that, Josie? When Cam was 'bout six years old she insisted that kids ought to be able to pick their own names? For a while there you wanted to be Rosa, then you had us all callin' you Esmeralda. Lord only knows where you came up with that one."

"Actually, I think Esmeralda suits me fine. Language is constantly changing," Cam said, "you say 'Negro,' but your folks would've said 'colored' without blinking an eye."

Dozier considered this, probably even accepted it, but held his ground. "I'm seventy-five years old and it's too late for me to be giving new definitions to words I've been using all my life. And I'll bet your friends in New York who are so—" Dozier kept his eyes on the road, but Cam could tell from his expression that he'd drawn a blank. He threw a glance at Josie. "PC? PC? What's that expression mean? Proper conduct?"

"Uh-uh," Josie told him. "It means politically correct."

"Well, politically correct! That's something old-line communists tried to be." His brow puckered in an agony of concentration until he found the thread of his thought. "As I was saying, I'll bet you dollars to doughnuts that your New York friends who want everyone to be so politically correct would call me a redneck in a heartbeat—and you know as well as I that I'm no farmer. The only time my neck gets red is when I'm out on my boat, and even then I wear sunscreen."

"I know you're not prejudiced," Cam said. "I just don't want you to sound as though you are."

"Well, the way I look at it, prejudice is a vagrant opinion without any visible means of support, but I can support my opinions all the way down the line," Dozier asserted with energy, "And you people—"

"Have I become 'you people' just because I live in New York?"

"The most prejudiced people are the ones who fancy themselves exempt from prejudice," Dozier warned.

"Please. Please," Josie said, holding up a hand. "Let's not turn this into an argument."

"Mama, you've never understood! When people argue they define their positions, they listen, and they change."

"Mostly they don't listen," Josie said. "And mostly they don't change. It isn't just what people say. It's the way they say it. You start contradicting each other, not because you're listening to what the other person has to say, but because you don't like the tone in which he's saying it."

"Well, that's true enough," Dozier agreed, thinking about his almost daily feuds with Edna, but, looking at Cam's expression, he couldn't resist getting in a last lick. "Now, I always listen, but Cam here, she does get strident when she argues."

"Hey, Uncle Dozier . . ."

"Just teasing you, Cam," he said lightly. "Just pulling your pigtail like I did when you were little. It's always fun to see you rise up.

And you always do. Lord, girl, you must be a helluva caution to the men you go with."

Cam looked out the window, trying to remember something Sam had said about her need to win an argument. But wasn't that the way men disarmed you? Telling you about your obsessive need to win when that was all *they* really cared about?

"Whoa, you look like that scowling bust of Beethoven on my auntie's piano," Dozier told her. And when she didn't smile, he teased her again. "I would've called old Walt a homo-sex-u-al," he said, drawing in a breath, "but I didn't know he was one."

"Well, he was," she said, crossing her arms over her chest. Then, after a pause, as Dozier pulled her into the parking lot of the Azalealand Nursing Home, "Mama, I know I should've asked you if it was all right to invite Reba down, but you weren't home, and she sounded so distressed and—"

"Nothing to worry about, Cam." Josie collected the presents and the Tupperware bowl with the custard she'd fixed for Mawmaw, and started to get out of the car. When she'd come in from visiting Peatsy, and Cam had told her that she'd invited her friend, Reba, to stay, her first thought had been, *Oh, no, not another complication.* But then she'd reminded herself of something Cam used to say in her teenage years—an expression that had irritated her no end, but upon reflection, didn't seem to be unwise: Go with the flow. She would go with the flow. "It'll be a full house tomorrow night, but I don't suppose you'll mind her bunking in with you."

"Of course not. And by the way . . . I don't think it's important, but Reba's a lesbian." She got out and closed the car door. "I wouldn't want you to ask her why she isn't married or anything."

Josie said, "I don't think you need to teach us our manners with a guest, Cam."

"And you won't mind sleeping with her?" Dozier asked with seeming nonchalance.

"She's a lesbian, not a rapist," Cam said rather too loudly. Dozier looked past her, raised his hand in greeting, flashed a smile bright and wide as a searchlight, and said, "Merry Christmas, folks." Cam turned her head to see a middle-aged couple, ears cocked, hands frozen on the half-opened doors of their black Cadillac.

"And Happy New Year," Cam added, striding off, expecting the sliding glass entrance doors to open automatically, being brought up short when they didn't but refusing to break her stride. And, magically, the doors opened.

Nine

THE FOYER OF the Azalealand Nursing Home looked like a motel that had earned a two-star "very clean with modern fixtures" endorsement from the automobile club—pale blue walls, beige curtains with large flowers in unlikely shades of blues and burgundy, ersatz mahogany furniture. Sunlight streamed through the windows but the heat was turned up high. The air smelled of baking sugar cookies and pine disinfectant with a barely detectable trace of urine. A Christmas tree, decorated with red and green paper chains and tinfoil stars that must've come from a crafts class, had been placed next to a large TV. Two old women sat on the burgundy couch, holding hands and nodding off in front of a game show while a lump of a man hunched over his walker, muttering, "That's not the right answer, you fool," to a stumped contestant.

A young woman stood in the reception area leaning over the desk, chin in one hand, pencil in the other, her rear end bouncing to an inaudible beat coming from the iPod hooked into the waistband of her polyester uniform. Her head, bent over her charts, showed an inch of dark roots fanning into a shock of brassy gold. "Tiffany," Josie greeted her, "how are you, dear?" Tiffany raised her head and pulled out her headphones, causing her candy-cane earrings to jiggle. She had beautiful blue eyes and a tiny ring in her pug nose. A smile puffed her acne-scored cheeks. "Miz Tatternall and Mr. Robido. I figured you'd be in today." She smiled at Cam, waiting for an introduction.

"This is my daughter, Camilla, visiting from New York."

Cam shook Tiffany's hand, noticed it had no wedding ring, said, "Pleased to meet you." Tiffany's face brought to mind trailer parks, scrubby toy-strewn yards, singles nights in country-western bars, Elvis painted on velvet. She might have been twenty-three or pushing forty. And she could see that Tiffany was making similar calculations, trying to guess her age, thinking something like, "Career bitch. Never had kids. Can afford facials and manicures and good clothes. Must be older than she looks." Money was the thing that made the difference, Cam was sure they'd agree on that. Not, Cam thought, that she'd ever had a great deal of it, but what she'd had, apart from contributions to Planned Parenthood, literacy campaigns, arts organizations, and the like, she'd mostly spent on herself. How could she possibly go through a pregnancy, find a bigger apartment, hire a decent nanny to look after the baby when she went back to work? Assuming there was even a job to go back to. She couldn't. And she wouldn't.

"And how're Kayla and Lance?" Josie asked. Tiffany laughed, showing a gap between her molars on the right side. "Oh, they're marking off the calendar to Christmas just like convicts in those ol' prison movies marked off the days till they were gonna be sprung. Kuntry Kids is closed for the holidays so my neighbor's taking care of 'em, so she's markin' off the days too." She leaned, confidential, across the desk. "Your mother's been a lot better since she's had that new medication, Miz Tatternall. 'Member how she used to get all anxious when it started to get dark? Start worrying herself 'bout whether her kids would come home from school or if her husband had been killed in an auto accident? She's a lot calmer toward nightfall since she's on this new medication. Dr. Levinson's on vacation in the Bahamas this week, but I'm sure he'll tell you all about it when he gets back."

"Thank you, Tiffany. And in case I don't see you on the way out"—Josie took a tin box and a smaller package from her shopping bag—"here's a little something. The bourbon balls and coconut cookies are for the entire staff, but the little one's for you."

"Well, aren't you just the sweetest thing! Your mother *is* just the sweetest thing," Tiffany told Cam, as though she had to convince her. "Y'all go on back. She's in her room. Miz Aiken's been reading to her from the Bible."

Josie nodded her thanks and they moved into the corridor. Fluorescent lights caught the whorls the electric polisher had made on the speckled linoleum. Wreaths with crêpe-paper bows and plastic berries (further products of the crafts class, Cam presumed) decorated the doors, most of which were open, droning more TV. "I know Tiffany looks . . ." Josie began (Cam nodded, knowing the words "white trash" would never cross her mother's lips), "but she's really a very sweet girl. Her husband ran off and left her when she'd just weaned one and was pregnant with another and she's had an awful time of it. Oh, there's Beatrice." An Amazonian black woman with cheekbones like Nefertiti was moving toward them, cooing encouragement to the old man who leaned on her arm. She acknowledged Josie with her eyes but kept on with her "Fine. You're doing just fine," and shuffled him past.

"I suppose you brought something for Mrs. Aiken too?" Dozier asked.

"Found a tape of gospel quartets I thought she'd like."

"Wonder if she's still droning through Deuteronomy. Lord, I hope I never get so old I get religious."

"I always thought you were a believer," Cam said. "You used to go to church. You even sang in the choir at St. Helena's, so I assumed . . ."

"Dozier always had a beautiful baritone," Josie said, cutting Cam off from further prying into Dozier's religious beliefs. "Here's Mawmaw's room."

Josie knocked, peeked around the door, then entered, motioning for them to follow. Dozier gave Cam a thumbs-up sign and went in but Cam hesitated, afraid of what she was going to see. Had she ever met anyone who'd survived to ninety-three? In her eyes Mawmaw had always been old—though, she realized, the Mawmaw of her earliest memory had been considerably younger than she was now. At that time, a middle-aged Mawmaw had had heavy-lidded eyes with crinkles around them and cheeks that puffed up like little pillows when she smiled, which wasn't very often. Her hair had been long and pretty, chestnut streaked with gray. Most times she wore it pulled back in a bun, but on special occasions she'd pile it onto the top of her head and pad it out into a fat roll with something she called a rat. Mawmaw wasn't much for smooching, in fact she didn't like to be touched, but she'd let Cam brush her hair before they went to bed. There'd been a photograph on Mawmaw's piano that Mawmaw claimed was her when she was young, but Cam couldn't imagine how that vivacious girl with arched, penciled brows, bee-stung lips, and spit curls had turned into her grandmother.

After her hair turned white, Mawmaw had cut it short—ear length, with Mamie Eisenhower bangs to help disguise the new wrinkles in her forehead. The last time Cam had seen her she'd succumbed to a permanent—a white puff-ball that had made her large head seem more so. Over the years Mawmaw had gained, then lost, flesh. Her dewlap had sagged, her elbows had puckered, her hands had gone veiny. But her bosom had never seemed to change. It was a heavy bosom and she wore it corseted but low-slung, like Eleanor Roosevelt. This had caused Cam no end of embarrassment, and when she was in high school she'd bought Mawmaw an underwire bra for Christmas. Mawmaw had said, "If I pushed them up that high they'd be like a shelf to rest my chin on. It's real pretty, but I just can't wear it." And she never had. Cam crossed her arms over her own breasts, felt the navy blue bra Sam had given her last Valentine's day, and stepped into the room.

There were twin beds with pale blue coverlets, twin chests of drawers, twin night tables cluttered with Kleenex, dry skin lotion in pump bottles, Vicks, an orange plastic water jug, and Styrofoam cups. A standard-issue print—sunset over the marshes—hung near the window where Mrs. Aiken, dressed in gravy colors appropriate to her dumpling shape, sat in an easy chair with an open Bible in her lap. She looked at Cam through thick glasses, showing neither surprise nor curiosity. "So nice of you to come," she said, as though Cam were a regular visitor. Cam nodded and smiled, smiled and nodded, because, from the corner of her eye she could see Josie bending over a small, near-bald figure curled like a shrimp in the other easy chair, and she didn't want to look there.

Dozier stood, hands behind his back, staring out the window. "Now where was I?" Mrs. Aiken asked as though it were a real question. She found her place and quoted: " 'Now the lot of the tribe of the children of Benjamin came up according to their families, and the territory of their lot came out between the children of Judah and the children of Joseph. Their border on the north side began at the Jordan and the border went up to the side of Jericho on the north . . .' "

Dozier winked at Cam. "Real-estate hassles way back when."

"It's Joshua, chapter eighteen, verse eleven," Mrs. Aiken informed him, hoping to evoke further interest. Finding none, she smoothed the ribbon marker onto the page, closed her Bible, braced herself on the arms of the chair, and creaked to her feet. "So nice of you to come," she repeated, shuffling to the door. "I'll just leave you all to visit. If she gets pesky and you need me I'll be in the rec room."

Josie said, "Mama, look who's come to visit you," and moved aside, kneading the old lady's shoulder as though it were dough. Mawmaw jerked up, mouth open, eyes blank, like a four-year-old who'd been interrupted from watching cartoons on a Saturday morning. She looked from Cam to Dozier, then lowered her head and stared at her hands, curled like dead bird claws in her lap. "Sometimes she comes 'round after I've been here for a little while," Josie said without conviction, taking a Tupperware bowl, napkin, and spoon from the shopping bag. "Mama, it's custard," she explained, showing her. "You always liked custard." She held it out, coaxing. She got no response but spooned it into the old lady's mouth, wiping off the dribble with the napkin. Mawmaw accepted another mouthful, seemed to be enjoying it, said, "I like this restaurant." Josie said, "Good," smiled, and dipped into the bowl again. Cam felt she couldn't breathe, found herself counting—one, two, three—mouthfuls. On the fourth, Mawmaw wrenched her head to the side and batted at the spoon. Josie waited, saw Mawmaw's mouth clench into a lipless line and the eyes, sunken under the brows, turn malevolent. Josie sighed, recapped the bowl, burped it, and wiped off the spoon. "I'll just give it to Beatrice. She's used to having Beatrice feed her. Maybe she'll eat it later."

Dozier sat in Mrs. Aiken's chair and took up her Bible. Cam, suddenly feeling very tired, sat down on Mrs. Aiken's bed. Mawmaw tilted her head and studied her. Cam smiled hopefully, but the glimmer she'd hoped might grow into recognition only flared into suspicion. "She's trouble," Mawmaw said darkly. "Always was. Always will be." Cam swallowed, furtively looked at her watch, raised her eyes to the window.

Josie took a manicure set out of her shopping bag, went into the bathroom and returned with a plastic bowl full of warm suds. "The staff . . ." She waved her free hand back and forth, not wanting to put a name to it. "They're really very kind but . . ."

"We'd hoped"—Dozier waved his hand, mirroring Josie's gesture—"but I guess the old saying is true. You can't buy kindness, at least not for two thousand a month."

"Two thousand a month!" Cam was incredulous.

"She has some savings," Josie was quick to put in, "and we just add to that. Mostly, Dozier adds to that. It's the best place we could find. The staff, for the most part, really are kind, but they simply don't have the time for the little niceties of grooming. Remember how important it was to Mama to be well groomed?"

"She was of the 'cleanliness is next to godliness' school," Dozier put in, without looking up from Mrs. Aiken's Bible.

"Long as you could keep things clean you were keeping your head above water, that's the way she thought. I s'pose that was because you had to take over your mother's house when you were so young, wasn't it?" Josie asked her, spreading a towel on the nightstand, setting out her manicure set. "Mawmaw was only thirteen when her mama went off her head and, being the eldest girl, she had to take over."

"Oh," Cam laughed. "Now you confirm my suspicion: there really *was* insanity in the family. I never knew Great-grandma actually went off her head. Was she actually institutionalized?"

"They didn't do that so much in those days," Josie said calmly, putting Mawmaw's fingers into the dish of suds. "Great-grandma was pregnant every two years from the time she got married to the time she went through the change. A lot of her pregnancies ended in miscarriages and I guess she just snapped."

"Nobody ever told me that. I edited a book on women's

reproductive history, so I know that, at the turn of the century, the average sexually active woman could expect at least six pregnancies."

Dozier chuckled. " 'Sexually active'? Just as well Mawmaw can't understand what you're saying. She'd slap you from here to next Sunday."

"She wasn't that shy about sex. She told me about sex before Mama did."

Josie's head jerked up. "Well, she certainly never said much to me and I didn't know she'd ever said anything to you."

"There was an ad in *Vogue* or one of her fashion magazines . . ." Cam could still see it: a full-page photograph of a woman beautifully poised, dressed in a blue satin ballgown, leaning against a grand piano, and a demurely cryptic caption that said "MODESS, because . . ." She'd asked Mawmaw what it meant and that had led to a hushed explanation of "monthlies," followed by stern warnings about the dangers of leading boys on, and seemingly contradictory advice that if a woman wanted to stay married she must never say no to her husband about *that*. Cam laughed. "I don't mean that she talked about sex the way kids are instructed today."

"No. Surely not the way kids are instructed today," Dozier grunted. "State-sponsored textbooks telling ten-year-olds about buggery."

Cam said, "Oh, Uncle Dozier!" then asked Josie, "When did Mawmaw first start to lose it?"

"Lose it? Oh, you mean, when did her mind go. Oh, years and years ago," Josie told her, pushing back Mawmaw's cuticles with gentle nudges of an orange stick. "Strange, but it was your father who noticed it first. Remember how we used to go to Mawmaw's for Sunday dinner?"

"How could I forget?" Sunday dinners at Mawmaw's—a tribal ritual you'd have to die to escape. Josie and Mawmaw bustling in the kitchen, Lila and Evie setting the table, she escaping to read a book, Bear antsy, pacing the porch with hands stuffed into his pockets until the heavy afternoon meal was set on the table, then wolfing down the mashed potatoes, corn, squash casserole, fried chicken, pickled beets, biscuits, home-churned butter, peach cobbler—content while he was eating but even more antsy after he'd finished, tossing the smeared linen napkin aside, eyes searching the room for an exit. And Josie, surveying the wreckage, stoic but a bit disappointed that hours of preparation had been wiped out in twenty minutes. As soon as Mawmaw and Josie started to clear the table, Cam would pick up her book again and escape to the bathroom, since that was the only room that had a door that locked. She would lie on the cool titles reading, ignoring the call of her name but one ear tuned to the scraping and scrubbing so she knew when it was safe to come out. Bear was usually gone by then, pleading work at the base, an obligation to wash the car, sometimes just wandering off, saying he'd be back by nightfall to pick up Josie and the children.

While Josie put away the dishes, Mawmaw and the girls retired to Mawmaw's porch, Evie and Lila sharing the glider, Cam sitting on the steps, Mawmaw in her rocker, massaging almond oil into her cuticles and telling improbable but utterly fascinating stories about her youth—how cousin Joe had drowned, how the hurricane had ripped the roof off the house just like it was a doll's house, how Mildred had run off, how Agnes had died of grief. ("Did Agnes get spots before she died?" Evie asked one night after she'd had a bout of measles. Mawmaw had been derisive—as she often was with Evie: "Have some sense, child. Grief isn't like the measles. It's a disease of the heart." Lila had butted in with, "I don't think you can die of grief. My science teacher says—" and Mawmaw had snapped, "I don't care what your science teacher says. Grief is a disease of the heart and you can die from it.")

In the summer months Mawmaw would talk from sunset into star-spangled dark, and Josie would finally come out carrying a pitcher of iced tea, replenishing everyone's glasses before she walked to the rail. She'd stand there, seeming not to hear their voices, looking out into Mawmaw's garden, not slapping at mosquitoes or scrubbing away at their bites the way everyone else did, but slowly moving her hands up and down her bare arms as though she were rubbing herself with a magic protective ointment. "Don't bother yourself, sister," Mawmaw would say. "He's gone. But he'll be back. They always come back. More's the pity."

"Oh, I can remember those Sunday dinners at Mawmaw's clear as day," Cam said, pulling herself out of her reminiscence. "Mawmaw didn't like Daddy very much, did she?"

"She always held a grudge against him," Dozier said, his eyes narrowing as he studied the motes of sunbeams that danced through the windows of Mawmaw's room. "Mawmaw respected pedigree, money, and education, in that order, and Bear didn't have any of 'em. But I wouldn't exactly say she didn't like him," he added laconically. "I think she was attracted to him. You know what I mean, *attracted*. Battle of the sexes type o' thing. 'Cause he was one of the few people she never could bend to her will."

Cam sat up straighter, but Josie ignored the remark. "You were asking about who noticed Mawmaw's deterioration first," Josie said. "And I was telling you it was your father who saw it even before I did. At first I just thought he was being critical, but then I started noticing little things. She'd forget to put milk in the mashed potatoes, or put away the roasting pan when it still had flakes of chicken skin clinging to the bottom. Then she started calling Ranger—remember Ranger, Cam?—Floppy. Well, Floppy was the name of the dog we had when we were kids. Oh, he was a mean mutt. He even bit me once. You know that little moon-shaped scar right above my knee? That was from Floppy." Josie chuckled, continued to massage oil into Mawmaw's cuticles, then went on. "So the little lapses, forgetting things, calling them by the wrong names, that started way back when, but then she sort of leveled off. Didn't seem any worse than anyone else her age, and in certain respects a lot better. She still had that uncanny intuition about people."

"No one had a sharper eye for human weakness," Dozier put in. "She could spot a philanderer by the way he complimented a woman on her hat, or get the bead on a cheapskate because it took him a second too long to pick up the check. She could meet a four-year-old and predict that he'd end up in prison. And the funny thing was, she was usually right. No one could beat her when it came to spotting the negative. But"—he leaned back, squinting his eyes, dazed and delighted by the sunlight—"she had a lot of trouble seeing the good in people. Edna's like that, too. I mean, she can always spot the negative. But I'm not complaining. She's saved me from more than a few business deals that might've gone sour. She has a real sharp eye for weakness, but . . ." His voice trailed off.

"Mawmaw was always very fond of you," Josie admonished.

"Ah, that's right." Dozier nodded sagely. "I meant to say she was an excellent judge of character."

"I still feel guilty talking about her as though she isn't here," Josie whispered.

"But she's not," Dozier said gently. All three looked at Mawmaw. She stared at nothing.

Josie sighed. "By the time you'd left home, Cam, she'd gotten a bit more quirky. She was always raving against the government, but then weren't we all? And she was always speaking her mind. At first we thought her diatribes were funny. Then she starting saving little packages of salt and sugar she'd picked up from restaurants, things like that. But again, we didn't pay it much mind. Folks who've been through hard times do that sort of thing. Then she started collecting Styrofoam cups and old stockings and rubber bands. Hard to judge when thrift turns into obsession." Josie shook her head and turned her eyes to the window. "I found whole closets full of stuff like that when I cleaned out her house. It just made me weep."

"First time I noticed anything," Cam said, smiling grimly at the remembrance, "was at Daddy's funeral. She was wearing that black polka-dot dress and had a black purse and gloves, but her shoes were brown. And she'd always been so particular."

"I never even noticed," Josie said, "but I remember I didn't have time to help her dress that day." The topic of Bear's funeral was another sore spot and, as if by mutual consent, they all veered away from it. "Why here's a hangnail!" Josie exclaimed as though she'd seen a four-leaf clover, while Cam moved from Mrs. Aiken's bed to kneel in front of Mawmaw. Dozier reached into the shopping bag and suggested, "Why don't we give her the gifts now?"

"Just let me clip this."

"What do you think you're doing, miss?" Mawmaw lashed out as though Josie were assaulting her, knocking aside Josie's hand and the bowl of sudsy water.

Josie righted herself. "You've got a little hangnail," she explained patiently, "and I was just trying to—"

"Should I go get one of the attendants, or Mrs. Aiken?" Cam asked.

"No. No. Just get me a towel from the bathroom." Cam brought the towel, sponged the water from Josie's skirt, mopped up the floor. "We'll just . . . just . . ." Josie shut her eyes and leaned back, hopelessly tired. "All right, Dozier," she said after a pause,

"Go ahead. Let's try to give her the gifts." Dozier had already taken the package wrapped in wedding paper out of the shopping bag.

"Mawmaw," he said in a pay-attention voice, holding up the package, "this is for you. Can you unwrap it, or do you want me to?"

Mawmaw jerked her head in Dozier's direction. "No men allowed in here. That's the rule. Only girls," she warned him, clawing at the package. He put it on her lap. She stared at him, stared at the package, then raised her head again, suspicion changing to a look of sly recognition, and asked, "Where did you put Edna?"

"I think," Josie said, trying to puzzle it out, "that the wrapping paper reminds her of your wedding but she can't quite make the connection. Oh, she was so proud at your wedding. The preparation she put into that!"

"So damned much preparation that I almost changed my mind, but seeing as how she'd spread the word from Wilmington to Valdosta I didn't think it would be gentlemanly to back out," Dozier said ruefully.

"It was one of the high points of her life," Josie continued. "When Edna married you and Mawmaw planned that wedding! Oh, it was wonderful—What a party! I remember the *Charleston Courier* called it one of the most delightful events of the season. Edna looking so fine in that dress we'd traveled all the way to Atlanta to buy. And six bridesmaids."

"Of which you were the best looking," Dozier reminded her. "I always thought Edna chose those girls on the basis of homeliness rather than friendship. Marjorie Chiles in pink silk—Lord, she looked like a side of ham."

"And champagne when you couldn't get champagne for love or money."

"Yes," Dozier agreed. "It was a beautiful wedding."

"The event of the season. Not like mine," Josie said, without any bitterness in her voice. "Mawmaw never forgave me for mine."

"I remember standing in the sacristy," Dozier said, reaching over to slip the ribbon from the package in Mawmaw's lap, tearing off the paper and lifting the lid from the box. "Jeb Amends had a hip flask and he insisted I take a gulp to calm me down. My hands were steady but I could see my knees shake in my uniform. I knew then I wasn't gonna be a war hero. Just a damn supply sergeant, and I had to talk them into taking me because I had flat feet."

"You did more for the war effort than most," Josie reassured him. "Lots of people in supply were skimming off the top. You never did that."

"No. I never did."

"Edna?" Mawmaw said again, looking around expectantly as Josie took the fluffy yellow nightdress out of its tissue bed. Cam looked at the floor, thinking that even if Mawmaw didn't know what she was saying, it must hurt Josie terribly to hear her sister's name when she was the one who'd bothered to come.

Josie said, "Mama, Edna sent you this pretty nightdress." No reaction. "Edna will be coming to visit real soon. Real soon." She separated the words, pronouncing each syllable, hoping it would comfort, but wondering if it was wrong to make a false promise. Mawmaw let the package slip from her lap. "And here's what I've bought you," Josie announced, taking a teddy bear wearing a bowler hat out of the shopping bag. "Look! Don't you like him? Doesn't he make you laugh?"

In an aside to Cam, Josie said, "The last time I was here one of the women had a stuffed bear and Mawmaw seemed to like it."

Mawmaw looked at the bear, turned it upside down, then pulled on the hat. "Edna," she said again, agitated, letting the bear fall to the floor and starting to rock and bounce.

"I think she may have to use the facilities," Josie explained, motioning for Cam to help her. With difficulty, they got her to her feet. They'd advanced a few steps toward the bathroom when she tried to pull away from them and Beatrice came to the door. "I'll take her, Miz Tatternall. She's used to me. You know who I am, don't you, sunshine? Come on now. Come on." Beatrice got behind Mawmaw, propelled her to the bathroom, and closed the door. Josie gathered up the bear, the nightdress, a gift for Mrs. Aiken and one for Beatrice, and put them on Mawmaw's bureau, then held on to the edge with both hands. Her shoulders shook and a soft snuffling sound, more like snoring than crying, came from her. Cam looked at Dozier. Dozier returned the glance, then rested his hand on Josie's shoulder. "I think we should shuffle along now," he told her gently. "Think it's time to go." He gave her another pat, stood close while she repacked the shopping bag with the manicure set and the Tupperware bowl.

Beatrice came to the bathroom door, glancing back and keeping one eye on Mawmaw as she spoke. "You're not to worry, Miz Tatternall. She's been doing real fine but she's just a little agitated today. Like I tolt you when you called a few days ago and asking 'bout taking her home for Christmas—she'd just get disoriented. This is where you live now, isn't it, sunshine?" she asked, moving back into the bathroom, calling, "Y'all have a merry Christmas and we'll see you after the holidays," as she shut the door again.

"There's no point waiting," Dozier said, reading Josie's mind.

Josie shook her head. "A baby you put on your hip and go on, but . . ."

"You're right, sister. There's no light at the end of this tunnel. C'mon. Let's all go out and get some of that sunshine." Without speaking, they walked to the lobby. The two old women and the man on the walker had gone but the TV still droned on. Tiffany, talking on the phone, waved good-bye. As the glass doors slid open, Cam stopped. "Damn, I left my purse in Mawmaw's room. Go on to the car, I'll be right there." She turned and moved fast, almost jogging down the corridor.

Beatrice was easing Mawmaw back into her chair. Cam noticed her arms, the skin dark as eggplant, the muscles as sinewy as an athlete's. "I forgot . . ." Cam began.

"Yes, I saw your purse. Was about to take it down to reception soon's I got her settled."

"Thanks." She felt she should say something but couldn't think what. "It must be terribly hard for you, working here," came out.

Beatrice shrugged. "I don't mind the old folks. It be harder for you to see her like this 'cause she's your grandma. Prob'ly took care of you when you were small."

"She sure did." Cam remembered being seven or eight when Bear was transferred again and Josie had thought the schools weren't good enough in the new place—so she sent Cam back to live with Mawmaw. And how she'd hated it. The big, strange-smelling house, oatmeal for breakfast every single day, even in summer, her hair braided so tight it made her temples ache, non-negotiable bedtimes, no bedside lamp to read by, and constant reminders about good posture and good manners. "Can I?" instead of "May I?" brought an automatic denial of her request. All grown-up men, even the teenager who mowed the lawn, were to be called "sir," and all women, even Sissle, who cleaned the house, were to be called "ma'am." It was socks up, shoulders straight, no hugs, clean your plate, and help with the dishes. "I lived with her for almost a year," she told Beatrice.

Mawmaw looked up, sleepy and benign, and reached out for Cam's hand. Cam kissed it, brought the old woman's head to her chest and stroked it, feeling her skull through the wispy hair. "She had long hair when I first knew her. When she'd take it down to go to bed she used to let me brush it and while I brushed she'd tell me stories. Not children's stories, more likely family gossip. As long as I'd keep brushing she'd keep talking. I hated it when she got her hair cut." But suddenly she remembered: Mawmaw hadn't cut her hair. It had had to grow back. Because it had fallen out. In great chunks. How could she have forgotten! Because it had frightened the living daylights out of her. She hadn't known that such a thing could happen. That a woman could be snatched bald almost overnight.

Sissle had said things like that happened sometimes if too much came down on you too fast. "Nervous shock," Sissle had called it. Mawmaw's younger brother, Billy, had been in a car accident and died out in Phoenix. And that very same week, Mawmaw's best friend, a woman called Flora (who Cam had particularly disliked because she'd said things like "little pitchers have big ears" and sent Cam outdoors to play whenever she visited, which was almost every day) had also died. After Flora's funeral Mawmaw had gone up to her room and stayed there for days. Sissle had left trays of food outside her door and threatened to blister Cam's behind if she disturbed her.

When Mawmaw had finally come downstairs she'd had a bandanna knotted around her head, just like the one Sissle wore when she was cleaning, and she'd refused to go out of the house until a wig she'd ordered had arrived. And one night—a sultry night months later when Cam'd begged Mawmaw to buy her ice cream—they were leaving Mawmaw's old house and Mawmaw had stopped to latch the front gate. She'd raced ahead, calling to Mawmaw to hurry, then run back, huffing. "Baldy, baldy, c'mon, baldy," she'd teased, knowing the minute the words had left her mouth that she'd done something terribly wrong and might actually get that whipping that was often promised but had never materialized. But Mawmaw had just bent, slow motion, over the gatepost. It was the only time she could remember having seen

Mawmaw cry. She knew about hurting—not just with slaps and pinches, but hurting with words, like when she teased Lila—but this was the first time she'd realized that you could hurt without meaning to, that you could get a scar on your heart, just like you could get a scar on your arm or your leg.

"Yes," Cam said, "I lived with her for maybe a year." A shudder went through her. She touched her cheek to Mawmaw's head. "Oh, you poor little thing. You poor little thing." And then she started to cry. She'd always resented the fact that Mawmaw hadn't told her that she loved her, but now she realized it was even worse that she had never told Mawmaw. And now it was too late.

Beatrice put her hands on Cam's shoulders and turned her away. "She'll be all right. You got to realize she doesn't see herself the way you see her. Sometimes she's pretty cheerful. That's why I call you sunshine, in't it, dear?" She took Mawmaw's hand from Cam's and placed it on her lap. "Now you just collect your purse and count your blessings, miss. Remember, the Lord loves you. Just like he loves your Mawmaw."

Cam wiped her eyes with the back of her hand, grabbed up her purse, and walked slowly out of the room.

On the way back to the house, Dozier twisted the dial on the car radio, muttering, "Damn Christmas carols 'bout to make me lose my mind. I'd had enough of 'Rudolph the Red-Nosed Reindeer' a month ago." He found his oldies station. "Hey, Josie, it's the Inkspots," he told her, settling back in the seat, singing along, " 'If I didn't care, would I feel this way? If I didn't care . . .' " Turning his head toward the backseat, he broke off singing and grinned at Cam. "Being a white boy, I had to take my talents to the Episcopal choir, but truth to tell, I always wanted to be an Inkspot."

★ ★ ★

When they pulled into the drive at the house, Cam went in through the sun porch, while Dozier followed Josie into the back garden where she walked, head down, inspecting plants, pulling a dead leaf from a bush. "Do you think about it much?" he asked.

"Enough." She didn't have to ask what he meant. "I suppose I started to really think about it when Papa died. I believe I was dumb enough to feel immortal until that happened. Even through the war—scared as I was—death didn't seem real to me. The hardest thing was a few years back when I realized that I was hoping Mawmaw would die."

"If she had her wits about her she'd be wishing the same thing herself."

"I know that. I don't feel guilty about it anymore."

"It's not death that scares me—death is as natural as birth—it's the dying. I hope to God I keel over one day while I'm out here digging in the garden. You can just put a little compost on me and leave me here."

"I feel the same way."

"I know you do."

"Sun sure feels good, doesn't it?"

Inside, Cam poured herself a glass of juice, walked to the kitchen window, and looked out, wondering what on earth Josie and Dozier were doing. They stood a few feet apart, perfectly still, heads thrown back, eyes closed and lips slightly parted, as though they were sunbathing standing up.

The ringing of the phone made her jump. She picked up the receiver, said, "Hello," and heard, "Cam, babe, it's me. I'm standing outside a liquor store that has a sign in the window that says 'Wise Men Still Praise Him. Bourbon Discount!' so I guess I'm here."

Ten

"You, girl," Cam said, adopting one of Mawmaw's greetings, "are a sight for sore eyes." She was so grateful to see Reba, she got a lump in her throat.

Reba said, "Likewise, I'm sure," ran her fingers through her salt-and-pepper crinkly hair, pecked Cam on the cheek, and looked around the room. "Hey, this is more like it. This is classy." She handed over a worn traveling bag made of carpet fabric. "Sorry about the unfortunate choice of luggage. Cheryl pointed it out when we were loading the car, but it was too late to repack."

"Cam, is that Reba?" Josie called from the kitchen.

"Yes, Mama, come on in and meet her," Cam called back, then dropped her voice. "After the introductions, let's get out of here ASAP."

"Gotcha," Reba whispered. Cam put her arm around Reba's waist and moved her into the room as Josie came in from the dining room. "Mama, this is my dear friend, Reba."

Reba put out her hand. "I've heard about Southern hospitality, but a drop-in for Christmas really tests it to the max. I appreciate your taking me in, Mrs. Tatternall."

"Why, you're more than welcome, Reba." Josie took Reba's hand and held it, her smile of greeting broadening as she looked into Reba's face. It was the sort of face that made you want to smile. Reba's long upper lip and prominent nose ruled out any possibility of beauty, but her keen brown eyes with arched but unplucked brows, and mobile mouth hinted at a mischievous sense of humor. Her outfit was Secondhand-Rose, gypsy-style—Etruscan earrings, a purple cashmere sweater with a hole in the elbow topped with a velveteen vest embroidered with water lilies, scarabs, and hippos with jeweled eyes, a bias-cut vintage skirt with an uneven hem, and red, tooled cowboy boots. "Would you care for some tea or coffee?" Sensing a presence behind her, Josie turned. There was Mrs. Beasley, persistent as garlic breath. "This is my house guest, Mrs. Beasley. Mrs. Beasley, this is Cam's friend, Miss—?"

"Golden. Used to be Goldinsky. My grandparents were in vaudeville. He was a clown and she danced with a troupe called the Floradora Girls. They changed their name when she changed the color of her hair," Reba explained, offering her hand to Mrs. Beasley. Mrs. Beasley looked as though she'd just been asked to kiss E.T.

"Or maybe you'd like something to eat?" Cam suggested, trying to cover Mrs. Beasley's slight.

Reba shook her head, stuffed her hands into the sleeves of her sweater. "I'll just sit for a minute if you don't mind," she said, settling herself on the couch. "I spent last night in a really sleazy motel and didn't get much sleep, and the last hour or so driving down here I had to turn the radio to a rock-and-roll station and hang my head out the window like a dog to stay awake."

"Perhaps you'd like to go upstairs and take a nap," Josie suggested.

"No, thanks, Mrs. Tatternall. Now that I'm here I'll be fine. Just coming into town revived me. I thought, 'Hey, this is more like it.' Big old houses, stuff like old men's beards hanging from the trees"—her arms flew out—"and nobody honking at me when I was driving slow looking for the address."

"Well, Reba, we're glad you're here. And please call me Josie."

"Okay, Josie. You know, I've been reading about the South since I was a kid. And when Cam and I went to see *The Prince of Tides . . .*"

Josie nodded. "Some of it was filmed just a few blocks away."

"Anybody who writes about his family the way Pat Conroy does . . ." Mrs. Beasley began.

"Well, you write what you know, I guess." Reba laughed, scrubbed her head with stubby fingers, and shifted gears. "This is a really lovely house, Mrs. Tatternall, I mean, Josie."

"It was built in 1859 by a family who had a cotton plantation out on St. Helena's Island," Josie put in quickly. "It survived the war, but the family couldn't pay the taxes, so a merchant from Massachusetts bought it. In the 1920s it fell into disrepair and was vacant for a time." Seeing that Mrs. Beasley was still gawking at Reba, she rushed on. "My brother-in-law, Dozier, inherited the house next door, and this house came on the market about the time Cam's daddy was retiring from the military, just when the city started to turn around, so we decided to buy." Josie took a breath. "Forgive me. I'm sounding like a house-proud old woman."

"Don't stop," Reba urged. "There's still a part of me that's like a fourth grader who likes to go on field trips. This is just the sort of story I was hoping for."

"I do think a house is like a person," Josie added. "Much more interesting if it has a history. And, as Cam has probably told you, we moved around a great deal because of my husband's career, so finally having a house like this one was, well, almost a dream come true." Josie's voice had grown soft, and Reba nodded, her expression so curious that Josie was tempted to tell her more.

"All the years I've been coming here," Mrs. Beasley put in, her voice querulous, "I don't think you've really shown me through the entire house or told me its history."

Josie turned to Mrs. Beasley. "I thought your niece was coming to pick you up?"

"She is, but she's late."

"Well, Reba," Josie smiled. "If you're really interested, I'll be happy to show you around later. Just now, why don't I take you up to your room and let you freshen up? If you'll excuse us, Mrs. B." She led the way to the staircase while Mrs. Beasley looked after them with the expression of an abandoned puppy.

"I can give you your own room tonight," Josie explained, mounting the stairs, "but as Cam has probably told you, we're going to have a full house tomorrow night on Christmas Eve. Cam's sister, Lila, and her husband, Orrie, and their children are coming, and so's Orrie's father, Jasper, and Evie, Cam's youngest sister. My housekeeper's choir is giving a Christmas Eve concert, and if you'd like to come along to that you'd be more than welcome, though you shouldn't feel obliged. Lila thought it would be a good idea to open our presents before we go to the concert. That way y'all can sleep in on Christmas morning, then, in the afternoon, we'll have dinner. So, if you'd like your own room for tonight . . ."

"Oh, no. I'll just go on in with Cam right now. It'll give us a chance to talk. We'll have a middle-aged pajama party."

"Are you sure you wouldn't like something to eat or drink?" Josie asked again.

"I'd just . . ." Seeing Cam make a face behind Josie's back, Reba took the cue. "You know what I'd really like? I'd like Cam to show me around town. Will you be my tour guide, Cam?"

"I've been gone so long I probably won't be any good at it," Cam answered innocently, "but I'll give it a shot."

* * *

"Thank God you got me out of there," Cam said as Reba pulled the rental car away from the curb. "Another ten minutes and I would've given that woman a piece of my mind."

"You don't mean your mother?"

"No, Mrs. Beasley. You meet a character like her and you feel like you're in a Dickens novel. Thank God my father didn't live long enough to go through the bed-and-breakfast trip."

"But your mother's great—really sweet without being sugary. Why didn't you tell me she was so nice?"

Cam felt like an adolescent: pleased and flattered that her best friend admired her mother; frustrated that Reba hadn't noticed some of the things that made Josie difficult. "I didn't see much wrong with your mother the first time I met her, either," she said, not altogether honestly. Being in the company of Reba's mother was, as Reba had predicted, about as much fun as being stuck on a runway waiting for flight clearance. "Sure, Mama's gracious, but she's so . . ." Cam tried to lasso the right adjectives, but ended up sputtering, "so depressingly *domestic.*"

"Well, women of that generation were expected to be, weren't they?"

"The point I'm trying to make—"

Reba's hand shot up from the steering wheel in a gesture of exasperation. "Stop trying to make a point and tell me where the hell we're going."

"To a drugstore. Keep on straight, then veer around the curve of the bay."

"A drugstore?"

"I need to get one of those pregnancy tests."

"Oh, shit, I'm sorry. I forgot." She shook her head and snorted. "Who would've thought we'd be spending the Christmas holidays driving around a small Southern town looking for a drugstore to get a pregnancy test?"

"Yeah, life's full of surprises."

"Do you really think . . ."

"What else can I think? I'm five days late now."

"You've never been that regular."

"Okay, but five days!"

"It's just stress. Sam leaves, things are rocky with your job, it's the holidays, *and* you've been traveling. Not to mention the fact that you're at an age when—"

"No. Something's wrong. I feel sick all the time. I feel hungry but I don't want to eat. Every time I go to the bathroom, I'm checking to see if I've started. It comes into my mind about a hundred times a day. I feel pains but I can't tell if they're cramps or gas."

"Have you called Sam yet?"

Cam let air hiss out of her mouth as though she were a balloon that had been let go. "I'm not going to call Sam. Sam is living in another state. Sam's gone."

"You were the one who cut it off completely, you were the one—"

"Whose side are you on?"

"Are we into sides? It's not like Sam treated you the way Cheryl treated me. I feel like roadkill stuck to the wheel of the car."

"You know, I once knew a guy who was indicted for disturbing the peace at a demonstration. His lawyer begged him to cut his hair but he wouldn't do it. Like he'd rather be convicted than make the smallest attempt at conformity."

"What's that supposed to mean?"

"Well, were you wearing what you're wearing now when you met Cheryl's folks? Because you must've known . . ."

"Excuse me, but isn't this an instance of the pot calling the kettle black? I don't recall too many times when you've gone out of your way to conform. Cam, I'm pushing fifty. I don't own a dress with a

Peter Pan collar. I don't own a pair of heels. I wear cowgirl boots winter and summer because my arches have fallen and boots hide my orthotics."

"I didn't know you wore orthotics."

"Just one of the signs of advancing age that I stoically choose to hide, even from my best friends," Reba said airily, turning to look out the window. "Hey, this is really pretty. And it's so quiet. I just can't get used to so few people on the streets."

Why, Cam thought, *am I arguing with Reba?* "What you were saying," she began after a pause, "about not wanting to put on a show for Cheryl's parents? I remember getting up and going to the bathroom the morning after Sam and I first slept together and starting to reach for my makeup and thinking, 'No. Let him see you the way you are.' "

"Your point being?"

"Until I met Sam I always made a *show* of honesty so I could protect all my little secrets."

"No one is as secretive as the person who gives a show of openness. I should know."

"I've always had trouble trusting, you know that. Especially with men."

"Yeah, well, some people you shouldn't trust with lunch money."

"But Sam . . ."

Reba banged the steering wheel. "That's what I'm talking about. You should call him."

"Have you called Cheryl?"

"No. And I'm not going to. She can just stew."

"So what the hell are you doing giving me advice?"

"Well, at least I don't think I'm pregnant."

"Watch out. Watch out."

"What are you talking about? The chances of my being pregnant—"

"No, I mean watch out for the turnoff. The shopping center's here on the right."

"Cam, I can't have a conversation while you're giving me directions."

"Turn. Turn. Turn. Right here! Go into that minimall. Drive to the back of the lot, near where they're selling the Christmas trees. There's a Revco."

The parking lot was jammed. Reba drove up and down the aisles searching for an empty space. "Last time I was at a shopping mall was when I visited my cousin in New Jersey maybe ten years ago. Now I remember why I've avoided them, but hey, that reminds me, could I pick up a present for your mother here?"

"Just send a bread-and-butter gift from New York. There! See the black woman sitting in that green Chevy? She's got her motor on. She's about to pull out." Cam rolled down the window, waved, and called, "Are you leaving?" The woman in the Chevy turned slowly, face haggard.

"She's in shopping shock," Reba said impatiently, about to drive on.

"No, wait," Cam said. "The blonde in the red pants looks like she's getting into the station wagon next to the Chevy." The young blonde, juggling packages, wearing stretch pants that exposed more cellulite than mere nudity could ever reveal, let go the hand of a miserable-looking toddler, fumbled for her keys, threw in the packages, snarled at the kid to climb in, slammed the door, and revved the motor.

"God, it's worse than the post office on April fifteenth," Reba said as she shoved the gears into neutral and waited. "They're like grunion throwing themselves on the beach."

"Last-minute shopping always makes people miserable."

"It's not like they *have* to do it," Reba reasoned. The side of her mouth went up in a devilish grin. "Or are you going to give me another lecture on the need for conformity?"

Cam twisted her head to look out the rear window. "Guy in a Honda," she whispered in a *Mission Impossible* voice. "Pulling up right behind us. He's about to . . . Go! Go! Go!" But it was too late. As the blonde backed out, the man in the Honda zipped around, missing them by inches, and pulled into the empty space. Reba slammed on the brakes. "Talk about your territorial imperative! And look at his face! He gives me a big ol' smile and takes the parking place anyway." They waited until the cautious woman in the Chevy got up the gumption to pull out. "Oh, boy. I need a drink," Reba said as she turned off the motor. "And a cigarette."

"C'mon. C'mon," Cam urged, getting out and walking ahead.

Reba brought up the rear, looking around at the bustle of shoppers. "I feel as though I'm drifting through liquid TV—consumer cyberspace."

"We're just going in here," Cam told her, pushing open the glass door to the drugstore, circling a table of jumbled cards, tree lights, and tinsel with a handwritten sign that said HALF PRICE! STOCK UP FOR NEXT YEAR!

"I think we'll find it under 'feminine needs.' " Cam muttered, scanning signs above the aisles.

" 'Feminine'?" Reba queried. "Shouldn't it be 'female'?"

"For God's sake." Cam strode ahead, came up short at the prescription counter, made a quick turn left, and called, "Okay. Got it."

"Unfortunate placement, wouldn't you say?" Reba asked, seeing the rack of condoms next to the pregnancy tests. "Trojan, Sheik, Ramses, Life Style, Class Act. Class Act?" She leaned closer, examining the package. "Hmmm. This one says it has a ribbed, tickling effect—should that be 'affect' or 'effect'? And this one's in Day-Glo colors. I gotta tell you, all this makes me feel very old. When I was in high school this was all behind the counter. All secret. Boys used to wait for a male clerk. And here they are, on display, in Day-Glo colors, no less. But the illegitimacy rate skyrockets. Go figure. And here"—Reba turned her attention to the right and touched another package—"is the woman's side of things. A bit more in touch with reality, even for Madison Avenue. There's Confirm, FACT, EPT—and Quick Response!" She shook her head. "Wish they'd had these when I was in college. I had to buy a wedding ring at the dime store and go to a doctor for a pregnancy test."

Cam caught her lower lip in her teeth. "Okay, Confirm is on sale for $9.95. I expect they're all pretty much the same. Confirm it is."

As they approached the cashier, Cam stopped, still chewing her lip. Reba handed her the car keys. "Go on, I'll get it. I want to get some cigarettes anyway. Meet you in the car."

Cam sat hunched forward, elbows on knees and head in her hands. The car radio was trumpeting, "For unto us a child is born, Unto us a son is given . . ." from the *Messiah.* Reba got in, switched off the radio, and asked, "Back to the house?"

"No. Let's drive down to Bay Street. I need to look out at the water."

The sky was overcast and a cool breeze came off the bay. Wooden swings were set at a comfortable distance apart on the promenade overlooking the water. Cam sat in one, hands tucked into her armpits, feet planted firmly on the pavement, rocking back and forth. To her right, small pleasure craft were docked near the tourist information center, behind her were an empty bandshell and lawn, the outdoor patios of restaurants, but she was mainly aware of the little playground to her left—whoops and squawks of delight, a woman's voice promising, "Don't be afraid, honey. I'm right here at the bottom of the slide. I'll catch you."

"Here . . ." Reba was beside her, holding two Styrofoam cups. "It's a Bloody Mary. Figured you could use it. Figured I could use it."

"How'd you get them to let you carry it out here?"

"Ordered two drinks, ordered two Styrofoam cups. They looked the other way. Very civilized, I thought."

Cam said, "I shouldn't," but took a long swallow.

"Hey, as Barbara Ehrenreich said, if men knew they'd have to go nearly a year without a drink or a cigarette, or even an aspirin—they'd classify pregnancy as a sexually transmitted disease and abortions would be treated like emergency appendectomies. Cheers." She chugalugged her drink, looked out at the water. "It's so pretty and peaceful here. Don't think I could ever move away from New York, but it sure felt good taking off the winter clothes as we drove south. Gloves and hat off by the time we reached Petersburg, peeled off the coat just outside of Raleigh, felt like Gypsy Rose Lee in slow, slow motion." She took another sip of her drink, studied Cam from the corner of her eye, and gave up the small talk. "Why don't we go back to the house and do the test? I still don't think you're pregnant, but . . ."

"Don't give me the stress lecture." Cam stopped the swing's motion, rested her head on the back of it, and closed her eyes. "I bolted out of the store because I thought I recognized the woman at the cash register. I think she was in my high-school English class. I think her daddy was a preacher or something and she was the one who thought it was okay to make Hester Prynne wear the Scarlet Letter."

"Shit, you're really losing it. Even if she had been," Reba said reasonably, "what are the chances she'd remember you?"

"When you live your whole life in a fifty-mile radius, you remember. It'd be all over town tomorrow morning."

They rocked again, four, five times, swaying gently back and forth, thankful for the slight breeze, warmed by the sun. "So were you?" Cam asked, eyes still closed.

"Was I what?"

"You said you'd had a pregnancy test when you were in college."

"Mmmmm."

"I knew you'd been with men before. But I didn't know . . ."

"It was in my senior year. The fact that I'd never been to bed with anyone was my guilty secret. There was this guy in the peace movement. Remarkably unremarkable, as I recall. Even though I had a smart mouth, I think he guessed I was still a virgin. Ah, the thrill of conquest. But I was open for it. Wanted to think I was desirable. Wanted to think I was normal. Went to bed with him for the first time after a peace march. Well, you remember how those things were—being in a like-minded crowd, all that electricity, the ego trip of feeling you were brave. It was sexy. Very sexy."

"Never for me," Cam told her. "I always thought I was going against everything my father'd taught me."

A couple strolled by, nodded, and said hello. "So," Reba waited until they were out of earshot, "Jerry and I started—I don't know what you'd call it—it wasn't a love affair. No tender words, no exchange of secrets or gifts, no candlelight dinners. It was more like when my uncle threw me into the swimming pool when I was a kid and told me that if I didn't panic, I'd get the hang of it. But I never did get the hang of it with Jerry." She drained her cup, looked around for a trash can, placed the cup on the ground, and lit a cigarette. "We kept on for about six months. I mean, this wasn't a

Movie of the Week, I didn't get pregnant after a one-night stand with an evil seducer."

"So?" Cam said after pause.

"He didn't even want to come to the doctor with me. The sex had happened to *us,* but the consequences only happened to me. I've never felt that alone or that powerless before or since. And scared! You know abortion wasn't legal then. I was sure I was going to either die or go to jail. Or both."

"How come you never told me?"

"If you are pregnant, which I sincerely doubt," Reba said, ignoring the question, "Sam would never treat you like that. Sam's a gentleman."

"You sound like my mother. It's not about Sam being a gentleman. Sam's been married since he was twenty-one and he's already raised two kids."

Reba considered, then nodded. "If you are pregnant, I'll come with you."

"Thanks, kiddo. If that's what I decide to do, I'll be in touch."

"I mean, you don't have much of a choice. Because, what about—?"

"Money? Insurance? My job? Finding a bigger place to live? Getting someone to care for a baby while I work?"

"Those are good questions. And then there's your age, if you'll pardon another splash of reality."

"Funny, though, that you should say I don't have much choice."

"I didn't mean . . . I know you've always been pro-choice. . . ."

"Yeah. And now that I may have to make the choice . . ." She got up and stood for a moment, arms still crossed over her breast, looking out at the water.

"I don't suppose you've told your mother?" A quick look was enough to answer that question.

"Josie's got a ninety-three-year-old mother with Alzheimer's, one of her best friends is in the hospital, my sister Lila is about to blow a gasket, though she doesn't realize it yet, my other sister, Evie, is a complete ditz, and my uncle Dozier, who's the only one Mama can rely on, is going up to Columbia with Aunt Edna to visit their kids. I think she's got enough to cope with right now, don't you?

"You know it's funny. Mama was never really comfortable talking to me about sex, but when I was about fifteen, she said, 'If you're ever in trouble, come to me.' I guess I'm in trouble. Deep trouble. Well." She shook her head, sniffed, and looked up at the sky. The sun had gone behind the clouds and there was a fecund, marshy whiff in the air that signaled rain. "If you're through with that cigarette, let's saddle up, Tonto, and get back to the ranch."

Josie's car wasn't in the driveway, and even Mrs. Beasley was out when they returned, but she and Reba went upstairs without speaking, wincing at every creak of the treads, and let themselves into the bedroom. Reba sat on the bed, pulled off her boots, took the package from the drugstore out of her purse, and began to read: "Results in five minutes. Do not use after the expiration date on the side of the package and blah, blah, blah." She slit the cellophane at the top of the package with her fingernail, opened the box, slid out the instructions, and scanned them. "Says you can use it any time of day but it's most accurate if used first thing in the morning."

Cam was already unzipping her jeans. She put out her hand. "I'm doing it now."

"Of course you are." Reba handed it over, peeled off her socks, and pretended a deep interest in her toenails as Cam went into the bathroom. Thinking she heard a sound in the hall, she moved soundlessly to the door, put her ear to it, then turned the lock and stood quiet as a burglar. She could hear the crinkle of the outer wrapper being torn off, then a moment's hesitation—she guessed that Cam had started to throw the box into the wastebasket, then thought better of it—then the softer sound of the foil being removed from the test stick. A long beat. No sound from the hall, but Reba was so spooked she was sure someone was on the other side of the door. The sound of urine hitting water in the toilet bowl seemed unnaturally loud. She thought about what she'd just read in the instructions: "If there is ANY blue line in the heart-shaped window next to the control window on the test stick, the result is positive and you are probably pregnant." Why had the idiot manufacturers decided to make it a heart-shaped window? "Hey, Cam," she called softly once she'd heard the toilet flush, "hey, come in here." Five minutes was going to be a very long time. "This tree outside the window. What kind of tree is it?"

"I think it's a chinaberry, but I don't really know. My mother could tell you." Cam pressed her forehead to the window. It felt soothingly cool as a smattering of raindrops flew against it. "Mama even knows the Latin names for things, and Mawmaw could walk through the woods and name every tree and plant and tell you which were edible. I never learned things like that."

Reba looked at her watch, tried to think of something to say, but couldn't. They stood side by side watching as the rain fell faster, blurring the view of the garden. Five minutes *was* a very long time. "Guess you could go look now," she said finally.

"Mmmm." Cam turned, shivering, her expression vague but intent, as though she were listening to far-off music. "Hope it doesn't rain tomorrow," she muttered as she went into the bathroom.

It was only a matter of seconds before Reba heard Cam call her name, but long enough for her to think about the nature of time—how it could stretch so that minutes seemed interminable, weighing on you so that you seemed to suffocate, how your fate could be changed in a heartbeat. Standing at the bathroom door, she could see the plastic test stick lying on the tiled countertop, next to a bowl of potpourri, a bar of cucumber soap, and an embroidered guest towel. The little heart shape was definitely blue.

Eleven

IT HAD RAINED on and off throughout the night, washing the streets, soaking the earth, turning the gray Spanish moss greenish. By mid-afternoon, as Lila's Volvo approached her mother's house, the sun was out in a chalky-blue sky, a warm Lady wind tempered the chilly air and shook droplets from the overarching live oaks onto her windshield. She heard a horn honk a happy *Ta-da-ta-da-da,* checked her rearview mirror, saw nothing, then realized that Dozier's Lincoln was coming toward her, Dozier at the wheel and Edna in the passenger seat. He pulled up alongside and rolled down his window. "Merry Christmas, sweetheart."

Edna said, "You looked to drive right by. Didn't you see us?"

Lila rotated her head. "Just tired, I guess. You going up to Columbia now?"

"Getting an early start. Can't wait to see those great-grandchildren."

Edna held up a camera. "Dozier gave me this last night. It's supposed to be idiot-proof. It really feels like Christmas now that we've got young'uns again. I'm going to shoot 'em all."

"That's a great idea," Lila said, smiling at her own joke, and, to cut off any further gabble about cute kiddies, "Orrie and the kids will be coming over later. I wanted to come early and bring the presents"—she inclined her head toward the backseat filled with shiny gold and white boxes—"and see if I could give Mama a hand."

"Your mama's got a full house already," Edna told her. "That Mrs. Beasley's got a migraine so Josie's playing nursemaid to her, and Cuba's sewing machine busted so she came over to use Josie's. She's in there with a couple of her grandchildren, ripping away on some wild-looking outfit for her choir. And some friend of Cam's from New York—gypsy-looking woman—Rita? Rosa?—what's her name, Dozier?—is there too."

"Reba Goldens," Dozier supplied.

"That's it," Edna went on in a confidential voice. "I didn't quite catch the story on her. Seems she was in North Carolina visiting friends and there was some sort of unpleasantness, so Cam invited her here."

"Yes, Mama told me. But I didn't get the full story either. You'd think she'd have the sensitivity to realize that this is a family holiday."

"The more the merrier," Dozier said. "That's what holidays are about. Josie doesn't mind having her. And I know she's real happy to have all you sisters together again. I think it's going to be a real good Christmas for y'all, Lila. All right, ladies." He revved the motor. "I've got to get this show on the road."

" 'Bye, Lila. Wonderful party the other night," Edna called as they drove off.

Lila pulled into Josie's driveway, turned off the ignition, pulled down the visor, and looked at herself in the mirror. Her mouth was pinched, her eyelids heavy, her pupils contracted. No wonder she hadn't seen Edna and Dozier. She looked as though she were in a blind rage. Which she was. Everything she'd planned for Christmas had been fouled up. She was always compromising, always fitting in with other people's wishes and other people's plans, always thinking half a loaf was better than none, and always ending up with the crumbs.

Last night she had felt like a stranger in her own home. She'd hoped that she, Orrie, and the kids would sit down together, finish off the leftovers from the party, and have a talk, but conversation, let alone communication, seemed to be something that only she craved. When she'd told them that they'd be spending the night at Josie's on Christmas Eve, they'd all acted as though *she'd* changed the plans just to cause them grief. After muttering "Oh, shit!" under his breath, then amending it to a surly "Whatever" when she'd glared at him, her son Ricky had, as usual, left without saying good-bye. Susan had whined, "Does this mean we'll have to stay for Christmas dinner, too? And Grandma will fix all that gross food, like turkey and ham, and expect me to eat it?" and flounced off to her room. Orrie had taken a plateful of leftovers and gone into the den to watch TV. Lila'd showered and shampooed her hair, then roamed the house, ending up in the living room, where she'd turned out the lamps and sat, nursing a glass of wine and staring at the blinking Christmas-tree lights. Around eleven she'd gone to bed to read, but found she didn't have the concentration. She got up and took a sleeping pill. But that didn't work either. So she lay, book open on her belly, unable either to think clearly or relax, waiting for *Nightline* to finish so Orrie would come to bed.

But when he crawled in next to her and put his hand on her hip, she grunted and moved away, pretending to be asleep. He turned out the bedside lamp and snuggled up to her back. When he breathed into her ear, she wanted to scream. He'd done that the night he'd asked her to go steady, telling her that a buddy had told him that breathing into a girl's ear got her hot. She'd told him it just tickled. It had become a standing—or rather a lying down—joke. "Can I tickle you pink?" he'd often ask when he wanted to initiate sex. Twenty-five years, and his repertoire hadn't changed! But, she thought, when he gave up and rolled to his own side of the bed, she had to admit that she hadn't done much to expand it.

Sex was never unpleasant, it was just predictable, like the menu at McDonald's. Orrie, being a creature of habit, found this comforting—or so she supposed—though a couple of years ago he had bought one of those *How to Extend Your Orgasmic Ecstasy* books and left it on her night table. There was a photograph of authors, Drs. Hollingsworth and Rosenthal, on the back: a married couple (of course), twin Ph.D.s (of course), with very white teeth and such blandly healthy smiles that they might have been offering "100 New Ways to Fix Tofu." Orrie had highlighted certain passages as though it were a college text on which they'd be tested. Over the next few weeks he'd bought a cheap-smelling musk oil, massaging her back, combing her pubic hair, and sucking on her toes by way of foreplay. At first she'd found it pleasant if a bit silly, but when he'd persisted and she couldn't come up with some wild response to his variations (Chapter 8: "Polarity Switch. Now for the next step!"), she'd found it downright irritating. She hadn't had the heart to tell him to stop, but after a few more weeks he'd gotten the message and gone back to the usual routine. He hadn't seemed to mind. She guessed that he'd bought the book because he'd seen some movie or TV show that had turned him on, or, more likely—he'd guessed her lack of interest but hadn't been able to talk to her about it.

It was true that she had sex with him out of a sense of duty, but she didn't feel that was a sacrifice. It was just accepting a certain course of action because it was the best thing to do. A man's desires were more constant than a woman's, more closely bound up with his ego, and if a woman wanted her marriage to survive, she had to at least be available.

When they were first married, she'd faked it, but after Ricky'd been born they'd fallen into a satisfactory rhythm both in terms of performance and frequency. She didn't kid Orrie and she didn't kid herself. Her body responded and she usually felt good afterward but the same way she'd feel good after a game of tennis or a swim. She'd never in her life felt waves-crashing-against-the-shore, swept-away abandon. Either she was a cold fish, or a lot of people were exaggerating their responses. She suspected the latter. What people expected of sex had a lot to do with the particular time and society into which they'd been born, and her generation put a premium on sex as her mother's hadn't. But common sense told you that even a diamond-hard passion must be worn smooth by decades of cohabitation, and no matter what talk shows, magazines, and psychologists were peddling, marriages didn't survive because a wife wore black teddies and knew the *Kama Sutra*.

If there was something missing, she thought as she rearranged herself and pulled the comforter up to her chin, it was something elusive. Spontaneity. Excitement. Risk. But she didn't think Orrie could grasp such concepts. To Orrie, spontaneity would mean deciding to have hash browns instead of sausage for breakfast. But she could hardly complain that Orrie'd failed her because he'd persisted in the very character traits that had drawn her to him in the first place.

He was everything she'd wanted—steady, quiet, reliable, wealthy. The polar opposite of her father, who'd had such a cluster of negative habits—gambling, drinking and, she strongly suspected (though her mother had never mentioned it), womanizing—that if it hadn't been for the unique force of his personality, Bear would have been a cliché. Of course Cam had idolized him. Cam had cast him as the warrior who could never be vanquished on the battlefield but had been brought low by family responsibilities, refrigerator payments, and garden catalogues. Of course, Cam hadn't been there for the last of it. Cam had already taken off for New York by the time Bear had spent entire afternoons slumped in his easy chair, the ice melting in his bourbon, jumping at the slightest sound. Cam hadn't been there the night the screams and yells had roused her from sleep and she'd felt her way downstairs to see Josie knocked to the kitchen floor, nightdress up over her knees, and Bear, back hunched and eyes crazed as a great ape's, standing over her. As far as she knew, that had only happened that one time. Josie had never mentioned it—had probably blocked it from her mind—but she, Lila, would never forget it.

No, she had no cause to complain about Orrie. Orrie was faithful. He cared about how she felt, let her do pretty much as she liked, had bought her a house worth half a million dollars. And if he breathed in her ear twice a week, then massaged her breasts, then whispered, "Ready?" before he mounted her, could she complain? She kissed him lightly on the shoulder but was relieved when he didn't stir. She did love him. She just didn't want to touch or be touched by him.

At 1:40, when Ricky still hadn't come in, she stroked Orrie's arm and, when that didn't rouse him, she moved her thumbs up and down his spine, the way her masseuse did to loosen her muscles. "Orrie," she'd whispered, "it's almost two. Ricky still hasn't come home." Orrie grunted, jerked up, looked at the clock, muttered, "Hey, he's okay. You know he's okay. Go back to sleep."

"But we agreed that he should be home by one. We both agreed to that. You made him promise."

Orrie stuffed a pillow between his legs, pulled farther away, and rasped, "He'll be home soon. Go to sleep."

She said nothing, but she thought, "Typical! Typical of you. Typical of him. You can't draw a line without blurring it, and he knows it."

He slipped back into steady, sinus-clogged breathing, but she lay awake, her body rigid. She considered taking another sleeping pill but decided against it. Drug-induced sleep would leave her even more fatigued, and tomorrow was Christmas Eve day and she'd have to cope with Cam and her mother, as well as Evie and Jasper. Damn them all! And Ricky. Even Ricky couldn't be so self-involved that he didn't understand that he was making her miserable. But Ricky was like Cam, like Bear—he just did as he wanted, never caring about anyone else. Listening for the sound of his car, her hearing became annoyingly acute. Orrie's snuffling drove her wild. She'd reminded him about taking his sinus medication but he'd forgotten, as usual. She could hear the heat rising from the vents, and the intermittent pattering of rain on the windows, and a maddening drip from the drainpipe in the azalea bed. She willed herself to sleep, but thoughts flew through her mind like the contents of a trash can that had been overturned in a high wind.

When she heard the glass door on the pool side of the house slide back, she sat up as though she'd been shocked with a cattle prod. She looked at the clock. Two-forty-five! In seconds she was up, striding down the hallway, sputtering, "What the hell do you think you're doing?" in a harsh whisper as she reached the living room.

Ricky stood silhouetted against the pool lights, legs apart, one arm on the wall for balance.

"You think you can use this house like a hotel? You think you can come and go as you please?" she demanded. "Leave wet towels on the floor and the bed unmade?"

In the blinking lights of the Christmas tree Ricky's face, blurred with drink or drugs, turned green, then red. "Jeez, am I s'posed to register or somethin'? I thought it was your mother who runs a B & B."

"Let me tell you something, young man: if you keep this up, it's going to be check-out time."

He shook his head. "Oh, Mom," he said, contemptuous and pitying. "Get a life."

"You spoiled little creep." She advanced on him. "You arrogant little son of a bitch!" She swung at him but missed.

He laughed so hard he doubled up. "Son of a bitch! If I'm a son of a bitch, what does that make you?"

This time she connected—*Whap!*—a stunning blow up the side of the head.

"What the hell's going on?" Orrie cut on the lights and stood, bleary-eyed and alarmed, by the hall door.

"Child abuse!" Ricky screeched, stunned but laughing hysterically. "Child abuse! I'm gonna call the cops!"

"What the hell's going on!" Orrie demanded again.

"Your wife"—Ricky pulled himself up, feeling the side of his head—"is having some kind of hot-flash hissy fit."

"Don't talk to your mother like that," Orrie warned. But Ricky was already stumbling past him, weaving down the hallway to his room, one arm flapping dismissively behind him, muttering, "Jesus, I'm going to bed. You guys figure it out."

"Orrie!" Lila screamed as though she were falling off a cliff. "Orrie!"

Orrie looked one way, then the other, wondering if he should try to punish his son or comfort his wife, not trusting himself to do either.

"Do I have to do this all by myself?" she wailed. "Do I have to do everything by myself!"

"No. No, sugar. Of course not." He put his arm around her. She wrenched away. He tried again, holding her this time, guiding her back into the hallway. As they passed Susan's door the stereo was suddenly turned up, but not so loud that they couldn't hear Susan's voice screeching, *"I am not part of this. I am not part of this. Leave me alone!"*

"You're his father," Lila shrieked as they reached their bedroom door. "Don't you know what that means? Don't you have the balls . . ." The second the words passed her lips she realized, like a child who's run into traffic, that she'd done something dangerous and punishable. She almost wished he'd hit her, but instead of becoming enraged, his face crumbled. "Oh, Lila."

"I'll sleep in the other room," she snapped, pulling away.

"Listen, sugar . . ."

"Don't 'listen, sugar' me. Sleep by your goddamn self."

His jaws stretched into a yawn, a reflex that even he knew was damningly inappropriate. "Sorry." He wiped his hand over his mouth trying to hide it, smiled his most engagingly boyish smile—the smile the photographer who'd taken his campaign pictures said would win him the election—and said, "Lila, you know that when you're in a mood like this, no one can satisfy you."

"Least of all you," she screamed, striding down the passageway. She got to the living room, saw the Christmas tree, balled up her fists as though she wanted to punch it down, turned, and moved to the front door, flinging it back. Dammit, she would leave! She would walk out on all of them. Make them notice, finally, all she did for them. Sure she had all the labor-saving machines, she even had help. No one was going to feel sorry for her. But let them see what the drudgery of going through the same routine day after day was like. Let them feel the monotony of repeating the same endless chores. How long would they survive without her restocking the refrigerator, fixing their meals, doing their laundry, answering their phone calls, making their damned dental appointments? She would walk out on all the committees and volunteer services she worked at—with much grief, and no pay. She would even walk out on her mother—stop being taxi driver, confidante, companion, the only dutiful daughter. And when she left, they would—finally—

understand that she had feelings, too. She even took a defiant step outside.

The rain was soft, but the porch light she'd left on for Ricky made it seem like an impenetrable curtain. Her breasts, heaving in her nightdress, looked flaccid and yellow. Where could she possibly go? She couldn't even drive over to her mother's because Cam was there. She turned, closed the door, and crept back down the hallway. No sound from Susan's room or Ricky's. But no, goddammit, she would *not* crawl back into bed with Orrie.

The door to the smaller guest room was ajar. She closed it quietly behind her, realizing that the palm of her right hand was stinging. She had hit her son. Hit him in the face. The same face she'd wiped free of baby food and thought was the most beautiful thing in the world. But, dammit, he'd been pushing her for weeks, he'd been asking for it. Someone had to straighten him out. A couple of years in the military . . . What was she thinking! She hated the military. If it hadn't been for the military . . .

She wiped tears she hadn't known were there from her face and stood in the dark, panting. It had stopped raining and in the soft light coming through the window she saw the bottle of Joy she'd bought for Cam that afternoon sitting on the desk in a mess of ribbons. She grabbed it and hurled it against the wall, then flung herself into the wing chair, sobbing and hiccupping like a three-year-old having a temper tantrum.

When the fumes from the perfume threatened to overwhelm her she got up, opened the window, thought, *Seventy bucks' worth of suffocation!* and started to laugh. The laughter dovetailed into tears. She grabbed the lap rug from the end of the couch and stuffed it into her mouth. The couch was loaded with presents, but she shoved them aside, not caring when some fell onto the carpet, and lay down, balling up in a fetal position.

* * *

She woke up, feeling as stiff and chilled as if she'd slept on the floor, when she heard padding feet—most likely Susan going out for her morning run—in the hallway. She waited a few minutes, closed the window, and crept into the guest bathroom to shower.

She turned on the cold faucet and stepped into a spray of icy needles that made her gasp, stood under it until she was numb, then turned the faucet to a punishing heat that misted the mirrors and scalded her skin. She shaved her legs and armpits, even gave herself a cucumber and sea-kelp mask. Not wanting to disturb Orrie, she wrapped herself in the white terry-cloth robe she left for guests.

By the time Orrie appeared at the kitchen door, his left eye still matted with sleep, barefoot but with his hair combed, dressed in his chinos and lime-green J. Crew shirt, she already had the coffee brewing. Without looking up, she asked, "Toast or croissants?," and she heard the relief in his voice as he said, "Ah, toast is fine." So. It was business as usual. Whatever had happened was better ignored than explored. Any choices to be made came down to toast or croissants, L.L. Bean or Lands' End, red, white, and blue, or just white and blue on the campaign posters. And part of her didn't mind that Orrie was willing to act as though nothing had happened. She *had* behaved badly, and if he wanted to he could call her on it. "Wheat or rye?" she asked, opening the bread bin.

"I think . . ." He looked at her, smiled, then reached for the remote control, and turned on the TV. "I think rye for a change. With cream cheese."

She put the bread into the toaster, pressed down the button, and held her hand on the top of it, almost wishing it would burn her. They'd coast through another day—another week, another year. Well, denial was, if not better, then at least more comfortable than confrontation. Especially during the holidays.

* * *

As she walked through the garden toward Josie's back door she could smell the pungent aroma of onions and celery being sautéed, could hear the whir of the sewing machine, and her mother's voice in conversation with a woman's voice she didn't recognize. She really didn't feel up to dealing with a stranger. She stood still, feeling like a child eavesdropping on adults, because she could tell by the tone that it was an intimate, not to say, secret, conversation. But she could catch only a few words and phrases: her mother saying, "No, I didn't know . . . ," then trailing off, the other voice rising to, "You know Cam wouldn't want. . . ," then dropping. Then, either because they'd come to some revelation that caused them both to contemplate, or because they sensed that someone was listening, there was a long pause, and when the conversation resumed, Josie said, in a cheerful sing-song, as though she were reciting a list, "White gloves. Yes. And calling cards. Whenever we had a new posting I'd put on my white gloves and drop my calling card at the commanding officer's home. I don't know if they do that anymore."

"And aprons. Seeing you in an apron really takes me back. My grandmother always wore housedresses and aprons."

"And did you get milk delivered to the door? Now that's something I really miss."

"And radio instead of television."

"I still prefer radio. I guess I'd rather imagine something than actually see it. Last time I went to the movies with my friend Peatsy, I liked to die of embarrassment. Just can't get used to seeing people naked in bed. Makes me feel like a Peeping Tom."

"My favorite radio show was *Gang Busters*."

"*Gang Busters, The Lone Ranger, The Shadow, Fibber McGee and Molly*. Lila liked *Let's Pretend* but of course she was younger. Cam preferred *Inner Sanctum*."

"I loved that show. Even Stephen King can't send shivers down my spine the way the sound of the creaking door on that show did. Oh, and what else? Girdles! Can you believe my mother tried to get me into a girdle when I was only fifteen and had thirty-four-inch hips?"

Josie laughed. "I confess I did the same thing with Cam. Silly when I think about it now, but those days a wiggle in the fanny was just not acceptable. My husband, Bear, hated them. Whenever I'd wear one he'd call me 'Old Ironsides.' Oh, and I remember Lila nearly had a hissy fit when Cam wouldn't wear a girdle at her wedding. 'Course Cam and Lila have always been as different as chalk and cheese. Even when they were little."

Lila waited to see if any more was going to be said about her, but when she heard the other woman say, "Yes, I will have another cup," she knocked once, called, "Anybody home?" then opened the door.

Josie was at the stove, crumbling cornbread into a large pan of onions and celery. A woman with wild hair and oversized earrings sat at the kitchen table chopping pecans. A little black boy with eyes like a lemur's had just wandered in from the other room. "Oh, Lila," Josie said, gesturing toward the woman, "this is Cam's friend, Reba Golden, visiting us from New York. Reba, this is my daughter, Lila Gadsden."

Reba smiled, put down the knife, and extended her hand, but Lila, damned if she was going to make nice and say pleased-to-meet-you when she wasn't, nodded and said a cool "Hello."

"And this is Cuba's grandson, Antoinne," Josie jumped in. Antoinne eyed Lila suspiciously, shrinking closer to Reba, who put her arm around him and whispered, "If you wash your hands, you could help me break up the pecans."

Josie waved a slotted spoon in the direction of the dining room. "Cuba's sewing machine's broken, so she's here doing some last-minute alterations on a choir robe. Y'all are coming to the service tonight, aren't you? I still haven't decorated the tree. After dinner tonight, I thought we might do that, then open the presents, then go to hear Cuba's choir. Is that all right with you?"

"Fine."

"Cuba's such an unusual name," Reba chimed in. "Do you know where she got it?"

"Her grandfather named her. He was with this all-black unit called the Buffalo Soldiers during the Spanish-American War and he liked Cuba so much he always wanted to go back there, so he got Cuba's mother to name her that. Caused her no end of trouble when Castro took over."

"Where's Cam?" Lila asked, unwilling to be drawn into the small talk.

"She's napping. Looks like she's come down with some sort of virus, or maybe it's just a cold," Josie explained. "We just thought we'd let her sleep."

Typical, Lila thought. *Wasn't it just like Cam to loll around, play sick, and escape the chores?* "Is there anything I can do?"

"Just pull up a chair and relax. Reba and I were just talking about . . . ah, old times." Josie's slight hesitation confirmed Lila's suspicion that something of importance was being discussed when she'd come to the back door. "It's remarkable to think of all the changes we've lived through," Josie went on. "Even more remarkable when I think about Mawmaw being able to talk to her grandparents about the Civil War, and now here we are with helicopters, computers, and this thing called the Internet." Sensing that her efforts to lure Lila into the conversation were foundering, Josie asked, "Where're Orrie and the kids?"

"They'll be here by suppertime. I don't know if they're driving together or separately." She picked up a pecan, looked at Reba, and said, "My kids don't like to ride with me anymore, but I guess it's okay since we're a four-car family." She'd meant to express the frustration of being rejected by her teenage kids, but it came out all wrong, as though she were bragging.

"Do you like to cook?" Reba asked, pulling back another chair and making room for Lila at the table.

Lila shook her head. "Uh-uh. I'm like a Jewish princess. The only thing I like to make for dinner is reservations." And that had come out wrong too. "I didn't mean . . ."

"Oh, I give the lie to that one." Reba's look was more curious than offended. "I make my bread and butter by making bread and butter."

"Reba has a catering business," Josie explained, red-faced at Lila's rudeness.

"That you, Miss Lila?" Cuba called. Lila moved to the dining room. Cuba was bent over the sewing machine, shoulders hunched like an ox in harness, ripping through a voluminous pile of yellow, green, black, and red Kente cloth. "My machine's broke an' I'm fixin' this for Betty Halsy. She so fat"—Cuba shook her head—"when she raise her arms she like to split the seams of a choir robe."

A girl of perhaps eight, her hair braided into cornrows decorated with green and red plastic beads, was sprinkling lemon oil on a cleaning rag and rubbing the sideboard. "Be careful," Lila said to the child, "you might knock something over."

The girl brought the rag to the chest of her JESUS LOVES ME T-shirt, her eyes sullen.

"Don't worry 'bout her," Cuba said, snipping threads. "Shalalla not gonna hurt nothing. Shalalla know how to dust, 'n' make beds, 'n' I'm teaching her to iron. All my grandchildrens know how to pick up after theyselves." Lila couldn't tell if this was bragging or a subtle rebuke of those, like herself, whose children did not pick up after themselves.

Cuba shook the garment and smiled. "You all cleaned up after your party, Miss Lila? That was some fine spread you had."

"Yes. It was." But she'd heard Cuba whispering to Josie that she'd paid too much for the caterers. "Oh, Cuba," she apologized. "I forgot to bring your check."

"That's okay. Can't cash it till after the holidays. See Shalalla's hairdo? That's her Christmas present."

"It looks lovely," Lila told the girl. "Did Grandma take you to the beauty parlor?" Shalalla, knowing when she was being condescended to, stared back without answering.

"The lady's talking to you, Shalalla," Cuba warned, but took her off the hook by answering for her. "Sure. She went to the beauty parlor for the very first time. Wanted to have her nails done too, but we put a stop to that."

Shalalla lifted her chin, picked up a pepper mill, and asked, "What's this, Grandma?"

"Put that down," Cuba said sharply, but motioned for the girl to come to her and put her arm around her. "Long's you get me that check soon, Miss Lila. Otherwise, they be carrying me off to jail for not paying my note."

"We'll be at the church tonight to hear you sing. I'll give it to you then."

"Better come early. They's goin' to be some crowd."

"We will. And I hope you and your family have a happy Christmas." She couldn't think of anything else to say. Leaving the room she heard Cuba say, "That there's a pepper mill. Bring it over here real careful and I'll show you how it works."

Reentering the kitchen, she saw that Josie had pulled up a chair close to Reba's. Reba, who now had Antoinne on her lap, was looking at a 3" x 5" card from Josie's box of recipes. "Go ahead and copy it," Josie was telling her. "I don't know why it's called a

Huguenot Torte, 'cause it's neither Huguenot nor a torte. I prefer a combination of black walnuts and pecans, because walnuts by themselves seem too strong." Reba nodded. They hunched over the butter-stained, handwritten card as though it were one of the Dead Sea Scrolls. Lila felt as useless, out of place, and miserable as she'd ever been on the first day in a new school after one of Bear's many transfers. She didn't care about the great debate of walnuts versus pecans, or the function of a pepper mill. She was sick to death of the company of women and children.

Josie looked up. "Reba's already whipped up the eggnog, but we haven't spiked it yet. But if you want to pour yourself some and put in a jigger . . ."

"I have packages in the car. I'll just go get them."

"Let me help you," Reba volunteered.

"Not necessary. I can carry them in myself."

Going out, she was careful not to let the screen door bang, but when she opened the back door of her car and stared in at the presents, she suddenly slammed it and got into the driver's seat. She turned on the ignition, started to back out of the drive, but couldn't think where to go. If anyone had asked her, she would have said that she had plenty of friends, so many, in fact, that she had trouble keeping up with them. She had friends from the Tidewater to the Florida Keys—college friends, golf friends and tennis friends, club friends and committee friends, friends from Orrie's business and his campaign—but none of them intimate enough that she would feel comfortable turning up unannounced the day before Christmas. None of them so close that she would let them see her in this state.

She turned off the ignition, ran up the electric window, and punched in a CD. As the soprano's voice spiraled like a great plumed bird, she closed her eyes and tried to remember the breathing exercises she'd learned in Lamaze classes long ago. Being alone wasn't so bad. It was being in proximity with people with whom you couldn't communicate that made you feel the misery of isolation.

The tap on the window made her start, and she was even more surprised to see Bedford Bethune, dressed in his customary jeans and denim shirt, his hair loose from its ponytail, motioning for her to roll down the window. "Didn't mean to scare you," he said. "Started to pull in behind you but couldn't figure out if you were coming or going."

"Neither can I. Have you ever had one of those days?"

"I've not only had one of those days, I've had weeks, sometimes months, when I didn't know if I was coming or going." He hunkered down, crossing his arms and leaning into the car, his head cocked to one side to show he was listening. "What's that you have on the tape deck?"

" 'Dome epais' from *Lakme*."

"Wouldn't have taken you for an opera buff."

His lashes were thick as a child's and his right eyebrow had a devilish arch she'd noticed but hadn't really taken in before. "I'm not. I've only seen two operas and that was because I was on a fund-raising committee for the Spoleto festival. And I didn't particularly like them. Guess I'm a dilettante. I just like the arias."

"That one's real pretty." The way he said it seemed to direct the compliment to her. He wasn't flirtatious in the usual way—wasn't given to compliments, smiles, and meaningful looks—in fact his usual demeanor was one of preoccupation verging on surliness. But the other night at the party he'd looked at her as though he found her—well, not mysterious, there was certainly nothing mysterious about her—but interesting. Interesting as a woman. She'd convinced herself that it was just her imagination, plus the fact that when he'd come into the room Ruth Cremori had whispered, "Environmental activist, huh? I wouldn't mind going into the woods with him," and had gone on to say that he'd bedded every single woman (and many who weren't) between the ages of eighteen and sixty in Beaufort and Colleton counties. Bedford was homegrown of prize stock, but his draft-dodging and world travels had given him an exciting otherness. That, plus the fact that there weren't many good-looking, unmarried straight men his age made him a prime target for exaggeration, wishful thinking, gossip. It had nothing to do with her personally.

Suddenly she wondered what he was doing here, at her mother's house. He caught her expression and explained, "When I met Cam the other night, I told her I might drop by when I came into town."

"I believe Cam's sleeping. Seems she's come down with the flu or something."

"In that case . . ."

"I didn't mean to dissuade you. There's a houseful of people and I know my mother would be glad to see you. Just go on in."

"Not important. I was just at loose ends."

"I know. Lag time. Stuck between the preparations and the actual festivities."

"Haven't made any preparations except to get in a load of firewood. I've opted out of the family scene until tomorrow. Then I'll go to my mother's house, listen to my brother preach to me about the constitutional right to bear arms, eat a plate of turkey, and plead a prior engagement."

She smiled because she couldn't think of anything to say. He hitched up his jeans and tossed his head, flicking back his hair. "Want to go down to Emily's and have a drink?"

"Oh, I don't think so. I don't want to be in a public place."

"But you look fine. In fact, that blue sweater sets off the color of your hair."

She wondered if he'd noticed that it was several shades lighter than it had been in high school. Not that he'd have noticed her then. Few people had noticed her, except as Cam's little sister. "It's my daughter's sweater," she said quickly, and could have bitten off her tongue.

He sucked on one cheek and teased her with his eyes. "You mean you don't want to be seen with me because it's politically compromising?"

"Heavens, no." Though the thought had crossed her mind. "It's just that with all the shopping and parties I've just had it with crowds."

"Yeah. I thought about you during Orrie's campaign. Saw you at one of the debates."

"Did I look miserable?"

"Definitely not. You were charming. Very much in control. I just thought how hard it must be to maintain that control all the time."

"I don't maintain it all the time. Political meetings aren't the place to let your hair down."

He pulled his hair back. "Really? I always thought they were." She smiled but looked away. She didn't know how to have this kind of conversation with a man. The nuances and suggestions made her uncomfortable. "Well . . ." She stared at the dashboard. "I'll walk in with you. Maybe Cam's up by now."

"You don't sound too eager."

"It's just that Mama's got a houseful of people and, as I said, I'm worn out with crowds."

"I don't have to see Cam right now. What say we go for a walk?"

"On The Point? And have Mama's neighbors hanging out the windows?"

"No. A walk on the beach. Drive out to Hunting Island with me."

She could have said that she'd come out to get the presents and was going right back in, but she said, "It's too cold."

"Sissy. It's forty-five degrees and the sun is shining. Besides, this is the best time of the year to walk on the beach. No crowds, no umbrellas, no lifeguards, no volleyball players, no teenagers trying to pick each other up, no squalling kids getting sunstroke. Best of all, no radios." He pulled his face into a mask of grim seriousness. "I like to think of myself as a man of peace, but I could pick up one of your father-in-law's rifles in a heartbeat and gun down those fools with their noise. But hey." He grinned like a kid being tickled, "What do you say? The whole beach to ourselves?"

She wrapped her arms around her chest and turned to look at the presents, her overnight bag, and the clothes she planned to change into for Cuba's church service. "I don't think . . ."

"Come on—let's play hooky," he persisted. "Twenty-minute drive out there, twenty-minute walk, twenty-minute drive back. There's so much going on in there, they won't even miss you." Now he opened the door wide, reached for her hand to help her out. She ignored the gesture and got out by herself. She was standing close to him, her eyes level with the second button on his denim shirt. His chest was smoother than she'd supposed it would be, judging by the thick growth of hair on his head and forearms. "So," he said in such a casual voice that she knew he was conscious that they might be seen, "are you coming or going? You know what Thoreau said."

"I guess Thoreau must've said a lot of things." She couldn't trust herself to look at him.

"One thing he said was, 'If I repent of anything, it's very likely to be my good behavior.' " She looked around to make sure no one was watching, then moved ahead of him, down the drive toward his car. She'd expected a Land Rover, or at least a pickup truck, but it was an old BMW. "I quoted that in my high school valedictory speech," he said as he got in beside her. "I'd kind of hoped you'd remember."

Cam lay curled on the bed, eyes shut but nowhere close to sleep, her mind digging into the same ground, hitting packed earth and stone. Was she fit, temperamentally or physically, to be a mother? What arrangements could she possibly make in terms of work, money, insurance, a place to live? But how would she handle an abortion?

Hearing car doors slam and a motor start up, she opened her eyes, wondering vaguely if Cuba and her grandkids were leaving. If so, she should go downstairs. It wasn't right to expect Josie and Reba to entertain each other when they were virtual strangers. She started up, then heard what sounded like a window being closed, followed by a soft patter of feet just outside her door. Mrs. Beasley, no doubt, checking out the comings and goings from the window at the end of the hallway. She sank back onto the pillows and curled onto her side. Cupping her hand over her ear, she was reminded of the first time Sam told her he loved her.

It had been in mid-July, about seven months after they'd met, and the weekend had started badly. Miserable, dog-day weather, near-deserted pavements shimmering with heat, temperatures over a hundred and, wouldn't you know, the air conditioner in her apartment had gone on the fritz. Sam had woken before dawn, automatically pulling her to him, but she'd slept poorly and was feeling clammy and grouchy.

"Okay," he'd sighed. "I can handle rejection. If it only happens once a day. Since we're going downtown later, what say we get up now, walk across the Brooklyn Bridge, and watch the sun come up?" One of the things she enjoyed about Sam was his constant curiosity. He'd learned more about New York architecture than she'd ever bothered to find out and lately he'd been captivated by the Brooklyn Bridge. "All right," she'd yawned. "I guess it'll be our only chance for any exercise. I'll make the supreme effort. Not because I want to, but just because . . ." She'd almost said "because I love you" as she'd wanted to many times before, but she couldn't bring herself to be the first to make such an admission, even in jest.

There was hardly any traffic and no other pedestrians in sight as they walked across the bridge. The sky turned from pewter to pale blue, and there was a relieving touch of dampness in the air. Sam talked about the bridge's design, told her a story about its construction, said that when it was finally completed in 1883, it was the longest suspension bridge in the world, then waxed lyrical about its beauty. Seeing this streak of enthusiasm break through his usual shyness always delighted her. It made her feel as though she'd known him when he was a young man and also brought out her own capacity for simple enthusiasm. He was just plain fun to be with.

They took refuge in an air-conditioned coffee shop on the Brooklyn side, where they drank coffee and read the papers before hailing a cab across the bridge to meet Josh and Betsy in Chinatown. Since it was one of Betsy's first outings since she'd given birth, she wanted to grocery shop after they had dim sum, so they'd obliged, trailing through sweltering streets, wandering into pungent-smelling grocery and herb stores, buying sesame oil and dried mushrooms, and marveling at other, unidentifiable foodstuffs. By the time they were saying good-bye, standing in front of a produce stall on Mott Street, Cam's hair had flattened to her head, her lime linen shift was sticking to her back, and she was sure her deodorant had failed. As Josh and Betsy started to get into a taxi, Cam threw back her arm in an extravagant gesture of farewell . . . and knocked over a pyramid of oranges. Cam, the shopkeeper, and his little son all went scrambling after the tumbling fruit as the taxi pulled away. Betsy laughed and called out, "How can you put up with her?" and

Sam, bending to retrieve an orange, called back, "I've got no choice; I'm in love with the woman," as simply and matter-of-factly as if he were telling a stranger the time of day. Reaching into his wallet to give the shopkeeper a five, he took Cam's arm and said, "I think you've got sunstroke, honey. Gotta get you indoors."

"I dread going back to the apartment," she told him as they got into his car.

"We're not going back to the apartment. Everyone with a brain has left the city. I got us a suite at the Plaza."

"What? I mean, when?"

"When I was paying the check for brunch I made a call."

"But I'm . . ." She looked down at her creased shift and sandals.

"You put on those big ol' sunglasses and toss your head right, everyone'll think you're a celebrity. Marble tub, view of the park, matching robes . . . air-conditioning! Whatta you say? I'll do anything to make my girl happy."

"I say you're wonderful."

"Now you're talking."

He was wrapping her in one of those matching robes after they'd taken a bath, when he stopped, tucked back her hair, and touched her ear. "Know why ears are made in this shape?" She shook her head, feeling as though she were five years old. "Because this is the perfect shape for telling secrets. Can you guess the secret?" He brushed her earlobe with his lips, then whispered, "I love you."

He loved her. He'd do anything to make her happy. But being forced into a lifelong commitment wasn't quite the same thing as a weekend fling at the Plaza.

She could hear more car doors slamming and wheels spinning out fast enough to raise gravel. The sky was darkening, promising storm. Cooking smells. More voices downstairs. And still she couldn't get up.

Twelve

"Won't someone finish this off?" Josie gestured to the serving bowl that still contained a sizable portion of shrimp, spices, sausage, corn, and potatoes that made up a Lowcountry Boil, and looked around the dining room table.

Reba, seated next to Cam, said it was delicious but she'd already had two helpings. Cam studied the embroidery on the tablecloth. Orrie smiled, pressed a finger onto his plate to take up some cornbread crumbs, and shook his head. Susan diddled a fork around the shell of a shrimp it had taken her ten minutes to eat and Evie, predictably, lisped something about diets. Jasper, whose aggressive aftershave all but overwhelmed the smell of the food, pushed himself back from the table, loosened his belt, and patted his belly. Only Ricky, who seemed less in need of nourishment than anyone at the table, reached in front of his sister without excusing himself, and speared another ear of corn. He wore a Braves baseball cap turned backward, a T-shirt, and bib overalls with one strap dangling over a shoulder that still had a layer of quaky baby fat. Josie watched with disgust as his orthodontally corrected teeth and stubbled jaw (Lila had told her that a three-day growth of beard was *de rigueur* with college boys) worked on the corn. My God, she thought, when Bear was no more'n a few years older than you are now, he was flying dangerous missions halfway around the world.

She wanted to say, "Young man, you do not reach in front of someone without excusing yourself. You do not wear a hat at my table. And if you think that you're to walk into Cuba's church in that Little Rascals outfit, you've got another think coming." But this was hardly the time to vent her feelings about Ricky's manners or appearance. Instead, she said, "It's really a summer dish and it's best when all the ingredients are fresh, but since Reba'd never tried it and it's so easy to fix, I thought we might as well have it tonight."

"It was fine, Mama," Orrie assured her. "I'm just not particularly hungry." *And why would you be,* Josie thought, *when it's already dark and your wife's been missing for hours?* "Don't you think . . ." he began.

"No, no, Orrie," Josie soothed. "I'm sure she's all right. Mrs. Beasley told me she saw her talking to some friend outside the house and they went off together. Probably just went down to Bay Street for a drink and forgot about the time."

"Forgot the time on Christmas Eve?" Susan asked in a squeaky voice.

"We had a bit of an altercation last night," Orrie admitted. "Holiday stress, I guess. But she seemed all right when she left the house this afternoon."

"Erratic behavior isn't all that rare during the holidays," Evie told them. "I got so many letters on that article I did last week about stress and depression during the Christmas season."

"She was bent out of shape because I came home late last night," Ricky said. "I mean, like, it's vacation and she still can't get it through her head that I'm an adult and I want to spend time with my friends."

"You might have the courtesy to give us a call when you know you're going to be hours late," Orrie said. "You know how your mother worries."

"Sometimes it helps," Evie advised, "if you don't approach the coming-home-late thing as a power struggle between parents and kids. If you could both just think of each other as roommates."

"Your roommate don't pay your rent," Jasper noted.

"Dad might put up with that, but Mom never would," Susan said.

"Hey, I don't have to tell my roommates when I'm coming home," Ricky gave Evie a smug "gotcha" smirk.

"But just out of courtesy, you might give the roommate a call," Evie persisted.

Cam felt as though she was underwater and didn't have the strength to kick her way to the top.

"Trouble with you kids is that you've had it too damned easy." Jasper swirled the last of the bourbon in his glass. "Good food. Pretty women . . ." He looked at Evie, who gave him an "aw shucks" dip of her head. "Don't see how anyone can be depressed." Not to be thought ungallant, he turned to Reba and asked, "So what do you think of our fine state, Miss Golden?" and, without waiting for an answer, "This isn't the best time of year to see it. You should come down in April or May, see those azaleas blooming."

"Yes, I'm sure it's lovely," Reba replied with a daintiness that made Cam bite her lip.

The table fell quiet again. Orrie looked at his watch. "Mama, I don't care what you say, if she's not back in another twenty minutes, I'm calling over to the police station and asking to talk to Fred."

"She'll be here," Josie assured him, "I told you, Mrs. Beasley said she just went off with a friend." She wondered how much longer she could go without being questioned about who this friend might be. "Dessert, anyone?"

"Like, it's okay for her to go off, but it's not okay for me," Ricky grouched.

"Ricky." Josie felt her temper about to snap. "Despite what Evie thinks, your parents are not your roommates. They're not even your friends."

"They might be your friends in middle age," Reba said, "if either of you has grown up enough to admit you're not perfect."

"My daddy weren't ever my friend," Jasper said into his empty glass. "He was threatening to cut a peach switch and whup me right up till the day he died. Would've done it too, 'cept I was bigger than he was."

"Neither one of my parents would ever lay a hand on me," Susan asserted. "You never hit your kids, did you, Grandma?"

Josie opened her mouth to say no, looked at Cam, and closed it. "Well," she stumbled, creasing her napkin with her thumbnail, "we didn't have the same attitude toward it. Whippin'—I mean physical punishment—was an everyday thing when I was coming up. We didn't think it was so awful. We expected it. And sometimes . . . well, sometimes, you just lose your temper."

"Parents aren't supposed to lose their tempers. They're the adults," Ricky said. "They should set an example."

"Bullshit," Cam muttered. "Just because you reproduce doesn't mean you automatically become a saint." She shut her eyes. "Mama, I think I'll take that bourbon now."

Another silence fell. Josie said, "Why, surely," and got up to go to the liquor cabinet.

Jasper held up his glass. "Might as well give me a refill while you're at it, Josie. Now what's the plan here? We're gonna finish decorating the tree?"

"Yes," Josie said, dipping into the ice bucket. "Cuba's grandchildren decorated the lower branches this afternoon, but there's still some to be done. Then we'll open the presents"—Please, God, Lila would come through the door right now—"and then we're going to go to Cuba's church."

Jasper chuckled. "How we end up going to a nigger church on Christmas Eve is beyond me."

Josie stiffened. "Cuba's choir," she began.

Reba felt as though cold water had just been hurled into her face. Not that she hadn't heard the "N" word—in fact that last time she'd heard it had been when one black man had yelled it at another who'd taken his parking place near Broadway and 86th—but to hear it so casually tossed off . . . "Mr. Gadsden," she began, rising from her chair, not knowing what she was going to say but knowing she had to say something. But suddenly everyone was speaking simultaneously:

"Hey, Pops," Ricky was shaking his head. "It's not politically correct to—"

"Daddy, I wish you wouldn't—" Orrie warned.

Evie pleaded, "Let's not argue."

"You know, Jasper—" Cam began with a "let me tell you something, buster" belligerence.

Reba's voice cut in, loud and articulated as a Shakespearean actor's pitched to the balcony, "Josie, can I help you with the dishes!"

Another silence, broken by Josie saying, after a deep breath, "I wouldn't think of it. I never let my guests help." She touched Susan's shoulder. "But you, miss, are wanted in the kitchen."

"Grandma, that's sexist. How come you don't expect Ricky to help?" Susan whined. "Aunt Cam, isn't that sexist?"

"Sometimes the safest place to be is in the kitchen," Cam said.

"Everyone has to help. You can each bring your plate into the kitchen," Josie told them. "Then you can all clear out because I'd just as soon clean up by myself. Then I'm going upstairs to change and you kids can go upstairs and change too."

"I didn't bring any other clothes," Ricky said.

"Ricky, I told you . . ." Susan started.

"Fine," Josie told him. "If you didn't bring any decent clothes, then you won't be going to the service."

Ricky shrugged. "Wasn't planning to anyway."

Josie's tone was acid. "That's as I'd expected." She reached to the center of the table and picked up the serving bowl. "Why don't y'all go on into the living room. The old record player's in there and Reba might like to hear some of Bear's old seventy-eights."

"You should've seen Daddy dance," Evie said, wiggling her shoulders. "He could really—what did he call it, Mama?—cut a rug?"

"Yes, that's what he called it," Josie said tiredly, exiting to the kitchen. Jasper went to the sideboard to fix himself another drink, but everyone else picked up his or her plate and started to move into the kitchen. As she passed Reba's chair, Susan whispered, "Grandaddy isn't really hateful, he still just talks that way. It's a generational thing."

Reba said, "I'm sure," taking care to keep the sarcasm out of her voice.

"No, it really is," Susan said with conviction. "Grandaddy really likes black people."

"I'm sure," Reba said again.

"He likes them more than I do. Except for Miss Giffens. She's my gym teacher. You remind me a lot of her."

"She's Jewish?" Reba asked quizzically, gathering up Evie's plate as Evie drifted to the living room to kneel beside Jasper, who was fiddling with the record player.

"No. But she's . . . I don't know. You just remind me of her. And you don't understand Grandaddy. He employs lots of black people. And not because the government says he has to, because he hates the government."

"Since your daddy's going to be in the House of Representatives, that may pose a problem."

"No. You still don't understand," Susan persisted, "Grandaddy wanted Daddy to win. He bankrolled Daddy's campaign."

This time Reba laughed before she said, "I'm sure," but the look on Susan's face was so strained that she put her arm around her. "Why do you think my mother's gone?" Susan asked, sotto voce.

"I think, just like your grandmother said, that she was feeling a little bummed out by all the family stuff, so she took off with a friend for a couple of hours. That's not the end of the world, is it?"

"Not if she comes back soon," Susan conceded.

"Why don't you go on into the living room?"

"No, I want to help." Susan trailed Reba into the kitchen, where Josie stood in front of the open refrigerator, staring at its contents as though she were looking at *Guernica* for the first time.

She'd rearranged the shelves and contents several times that afternoon but it was a bulging mess. The turkey, massive and cold as a corpse, had pride of place. A large bowl of cornbread stuffing had been jammed in next to it, along with two cartons of heavy cream, milk, juice, cranberry-orange sauce, and a Jell-O-and-marshmallow mold she would never have fixed had it not been one of Orrie's favorites. On the bottom shelf Saran-Wrapped crudités, olives, cheeses, fixings for salad, snapped green beans, creamed turnips, and a partially cooked sweet-potato casserole crowded by bottles of horseradish, homemade pickled okra, salsa, barbecue sauce, salad dressing, peach chutney, and corn relish. A bottle of wine was wedged in at an odd angle. Oranges and apples, a fresh pineapple, a package of cold cuts were crammed in higgledy-piggledy, along with a cream-cheese-and-salmon spread she hadn't wanted to throw out but that seemed to have developed green-gray blossoms. It was a sin to throw away food, but where was she going to fit leftovers from the Lowcountry Boil? How could she organize it all? And if she couldn't even organize a refrigerator . . .

She glanced over at Cam, who was methodically scraping dishes into the sink. She understood that Cam's afternoon napping had been a simple case of avoidance. Sometimes, when Cam was a little girl and they'd changed bases and Cam hadn't been able to face a new school, she'd develop a tummy ache so she could spend the day in bed reading. Josie had been inclined to let her stay home, but Bear, whose motto was "No slackers or goldbricks permitted in this company," would never let the children miss school unless they had a temperature above a hundred and two. Josie wanted to tuck her into bed now, sit down beside her, and say, "Your friend Reba told me you're having some troubles. Please tell me." Instead, she said, "Don't put the shrimp shells in the garbage disposal, Camilla." Cam nodded without looking at her. It was far from the reunion she'd hoped for. Cam hadn't said a single intimate thing since she'd arrived, but, Josie thought, that was probably her fault. Having Cam brought to Lila's party had been her first mistake, but she'd promised Lila she'd be there. Having Mrs. Beasley in residence hadn't helped. And visiting Mawmaw had hardly afforded an opportunity to find out about Cam's life. No doubt about it, she'd botched it. She'd tried to accommodate too many people, tried to cram in too many things. She looked at the butter dish in her hand and her voice quaked as she said, "I simply don't know where to—"

"Mama." Cam's hand was on her shoulder. "Why don't you go upstairs and have a nice long bath and get dressed for church? Reba and I will clean up."

"I suppose." Josie gave up, put the butter dish on the sink, closed the refrigerator, and moved toward the door, where she turned and ordered, "Don't throw away the leftover shrimp. Just peel it and put it into a Tupperware bowl. I don't know where you'll find room in the refrigerator, but I can use it in something later."

"Mama, go take your bath."

When Josie was out of earshot Cam laughed and shook her

head. "Don't throw anything out. Darn it, patch it, use the bones for soup. Talk about your Depression mentality!"

"You think Grandma's depressed?" Susan asked.

"Depression mentality means something entirely different," Cam explained, taking a gulp of her bourbon. "You see, Susan, Grandma, even Jasper, they were part of another time. When they were growing up, people were actually worried about whether they could pay their loans, whether they'd have enough to eat."

Susan pulled up a stool, wrapped her hands around her bony knees, and muttered, "Ah-huh," encouraging Cam to go on.

"Don't they teach you any of this stuff in school?"

"Well, we were supposed to read *The Grapes of Wrath* which I guess is about all this Depression, but some people thought it was a Communist book so . . ."

Ricky, followed by Orrie, came into the kitchen. "Have you guys finally come to help?" Susan asked sarcastically, but Ricky and Orrie were involved in their own negotiations.

"Oh, Jeee-eez, Dad." Ricky rolled his eyes, laced his fingers together, extended his arms, and cracked his knuckles. "If you don't want to give me the keys to your car, just say so."

"I'll give you the keys. I just want you to promise me . . ."

Not wanting to hear this exchange, Cam switched on the garbage disposal and pushed coleslaw and half-eaten potatoes into its maw, thinking it was a sad day when parents became frightened of their children.

"Are you saying you don't trust me?" Ricky bristled.

"I'm just saying—"

God help the Republic, Cam thought, Orrie's supposed to guide the interests of the state and he can't even stand up to his kid. Turning off the disposal, she heard the keys chink into Ricky's outstretched palm. "I'm outta here," Ricky called, slamming the back door.

"Talk about feeding the mouth that bites you," Reba whispered to Cam, then, in a louder voice, "Am I supposed to shell leftover shrimp, or what?"

"I'll shell them," Susan volunteered. "Grandma taught me how when I was no bigger than a shrimp myself. See, you hold it by its tail, you pull off the legs, then you yank on it so . . ."

Orrie looked at the clock over the kitchen sink. "Anything I can do to help you ladies?"

"Oh, Daddy, you know you break everything you touch in the kitchen," Susan said.

Orrie laughed. "That's how my daddy taught me to avoid housework."

"I think we've got it under control," Cam told him. "Just go on in with Evie and Jasper." Then, catching his look, "Stop worrying, Orrie. She'll be back."

"Well, if she's not back in another twenty minutes . . ." He looked from the clock to his watch.

"She will be," Cam said. "Go pour yourself a drink and relax."

He nodded and shuffled off.

"Daddy hardly ever drinks liquor. At receptions and all he just carries a glass of wine but he doesn't really drink it. He hates liquor," Susan told them. "You know, because of Grandaddy."

"Which grandaddy?" Reba asked.

Susan shrugged. "Both, I guess. Aunt Evie says we've been a dysfunctional family from way back."

"That's the heritage, sugar," Cam said, snapping Susan's legs with a dishtowel. "Try not to abandon it."

Susan grabbed the towel, they went through a mock tug-of-war, then Cam let go, causing Susan to wobble off the stool. "You know," Susan laughed, regaining her balance, "I hardly remembered you, Aunt Cam, but I'm glad you've come home. Mother was all uptight about your coming."

"Is that so?"

"Ah-huh. She thought you'd get into arguments with everyone."

"Yeah," Reba said, winking at Cam, "your aunt Cam's real cantankerous, always spoiling for a fight."

"What sort of arguments?" Cam pressed.

Susan shrugged. "All sorts. Like maybe with Daddy, about girls going to the Citadel. Or the abortion issue. 'Course, Mother argues with Daddy about the abortion thing herself, but only at home. She can't say anything in public because of Daddy's—you know—official position. I'm not sure what I think."

Reba started to sing the Virginia Slims commercial, " 'You've come a long way, baby, to get where you've got to today . . .' "

"I've decided I'm not going to have sex until I'm married," Susan rattled on. "And I'm going to make sure that both of us are virgins. And as far as the abortion thing goes, I know I could never do that. I mean, killing a baby is an awful thing to do. There's this girl at school—"

" 'You've got your own cigarette now, baby, You've come a long, long way,' " Reba sang louder. How could she shut this kid up. She was sure Cam was agonizing over her decision. The last thing she needed was half-baked babble about baby killers. She sighed and said, "I guess we really haven't come a long way. Susan, I hope it's not going to shock you if I have a cigarette." She pulled a pack from the pocket of her skirt, knocked one out, and lit it, asking, "Should I go into the garden, Cam?" Cam shook her head.

"Most of the girls I know smoke," Susan said. "I don't. Well, actually I do." She waited to see what impact her confession would have. "But I don't do it often, because I'm in training."

"Well, don't do it," Reba told her. "I'm glad I'm not a parent so

I don't have to set an example, because this is the single instance in which I'd have to tell you, 'Don't do what I do; do what I say.' It's a shitty habit, Susan. And I'm ashamed of it, but there you go. Nobody's perfect."

Susan looked pleased, whether because an adult had openly admitted weakness or just because Reba had said "shitty," Cam couldn't guess. The raucous strains of a Dixieland band rocked out of the living room.

"So this girl at school," Susan went on, "Chantal is her name—she's black and she's on scholarship 'cause she's real smart—she got pregnant and—"

"How old is she?" Reba asked.

"Sixteen."

"Case closed. Not old enough to be a mother. Not old enough to have sex in the first place."

"But since she did—have sex, I mean—and since—"

"That's an Original Dixieland Jazz Band 1936 recording," Cam cut in. "Why don't you two go into the living room and listen to it?"

"What's it called?" Susan asked.

" 'Tiger Rag.' Your Grandaddy Bear loved it. Oh, when he'd tie one on he'd have us all in stitches. He'd dance and play the harmonica. And the blues? He could croon the blues with so much soul . . ."

"I hardly remember him," Susan said. " 'Cept he used to tell me to stand up straight and salute the flag, and he'd say things like 'front and center' when he wanted us to hurry up and get in the car. Mother didn't like him much, did she? She said he was a bully and a tyrant. I remember once when we were at some kind of a parade he slapped Ricky's behind because Ricky was acting up." Judging by her expression, this was a memory Susan cherished.

"I can't really remember what Grandaddy looked like, but I remember his smells—cigars and shoe polish and some sticky stuff he put on his hair to slick it down. What was he really like?"

"He may have been a tyrant, but he was *never* a bully," Cam corrected. "He hated bullies."

"What's the difference?"

"A tyrant," Reba began, wiping down the countertops, "is someone who exercises power because he—or more rarely, she—is at the top of the pecking order. A bully is someone who preys on those who are weaker."

"I still don't understand."

"Bear had," Cam said in a flat voice, "had a special code of conduct. He lived by it and he expected you to live by it. You didn't argue; you knuckled under. Or you rebelled. I think he secretly respected rebellion more than compliance." She stared out the kitchen window, then turned. "Now, Susan, you're on KP. Know what that means?"

Susan said, "Sure. Even Mother says KP."

"So get off your butt and carry these shrimp shells and corncobs out to that compost pile in your grandma's garden."

"Yes, sir. I mean, ma'am." Susan scrambled down from the stool, collecting the full colander and heading out the back door.

Cam leaned against the sink, head down. Reba put her hand on Cam's shoulder. "I'll finish up here," Cam said, turning to her. "Why don't you go on into the living room?"

"And watch Evie and Jasper do that barnyard courting dance? Talk about strutting and ruffling of feathers!"

"It's pretty disgusting, isn't it? Think Mama's noticed?"

"She'd have to be blind not to. And believe me, your mama's got twenty-twenty when it comes to what's going on."

"Oh, Christ," Cam said with a shudder, "what am I going to do?"

"Until you check with a doctor you won't know for certain if—"

"Sure, sure. And even then I won't have to make a decision, right? I'll just have a convenient miscarriage, like all the sympathetic women characters in the movies always do." She turned the faucet on full and bent forward again, holding her hands under the stream, muttering, "Oh, Christ. What am I going to do?" while Reba picked up a dishtowel.

Thirteen

When she got out of Bedford's car at the corner of her mother's block, Lila felt like Dorothy being dropped back into Kansas after her adventures in Oz. The night air was moist and still, some houses were dark, the residents having gone away for the holiday, others were festooned with colored lights, and Christmas trees could be seen through the windows. There was a single light in an upstairs bathroom of her mother's house but the front of the house was ablaze and she could hear voices raised over a record from Bear's early jazz collection. That's the Original Dixieland Jazz Band doing "Livery Stable Blues," she thought as she heard cowbells clang in the energetic, goosed-up tempo. She complimented herself for recognizing it. Her mind seemed sharp, her senses almost painfully acute, but she had trouble thinking ahead, even to the next simple action. It wasn't until she felt the gravel in the driveway cut into her soles that she realized with a sort of dreamy panic that she was barefoot.

Opening the back door of her car she saw that the presents and her change of clothes and overnight case were gone, but after a flash of concern she realized that someone would have taken them into the house. She moved toward the darkened kitchen. She would sneak upstairs, bathe and change, and . . . then what?

She pulled back the screen door so slowly that its characteristic whine was broken into three small squeaks, turned the doorknob so carefully that her fingers felt sticky and . . . Josie stepped out from behind the kitchen door. Lila's hand went to her throat. "Mama, you like to give me a heart attack!"

"I like to give *you* a heart attack!" Josie whispered furiously. "My God, girl, where have you been?" She grabbed Lila's arm, pulled her in, and closed the door. She smelled of lavender soap and hair-spray and even in the dim light Lila could see that she was dressed in her periwinkle shantung dress with her best pearls, but she looked as distraught as when she'd lurked behind the door in her candlewick robe waiting for Cam to come home in the middle of the night. "I said, where have you been?"

Lila sniffed, wiped her nose with the back of her hand, and kept it close to her mouth, not wanting Josie to smell her breath. "I went for a walk on the beach."

Josie took in her rain-flattened hair and the man's plaid wool shirt. "Christmas Eve and you went for a walk on the beach?"

"Is everybody here?"

"Everybody's been here for hours. Ricky's gone but he's supposed to be right back. We've already had supper. Orrie was about to call the police." Josie drew in her breath. "Mrs. Beasley said she saw you leave from the upstairs window and—"

"Oh, Mrs. Beasley!"

"—she thought you'd been abducted."

"Abducted?" She snorted. "From The Point?" The music stopped. They both froze. From the living room, laughter like a small explosion of a glass being dropped. Cam's voice dominating, "And Bear always loved this," then "Minnie the Moocher" blaring out.

Josie said, "Dear God, you look like something the cat dragged in. Your clothes and overnight bag are upstairs in my room. Go on! Get upstairs. Get cleaned up. Fix yourself." She propelled Lila into the hallway, guiding her to the foot of the stairs. "Do you need me to help you?" she muttered, so close that her breath tickled Lila's ear.

"No. I'm a grown woman."

Josie fixed her with a basilisk stare, hissed, "Then, dammit, act like one. Go!" and waited, watching Lila hold onto the banister as she climbed. She walked back into the kitchen with heavy steps, switched on the light, and said, in a voice that carried, "Oh, Lila, you're back! We were all so worried." Paused, then said, "Surely. Go on upstairs and get ready. I'll tell everyone you're here." But what was she going to tell them? That Lila had gone off with some friends and (thank God Mrs. Beasley had finally gone over to her niece's and wasn't expected back until tomorrow afternoon) the storm . . . she would say Lila had been caught in the storm and hadn't been able to call because the power had been knocked out. Plausible enough, and Lila would just have to take it from there. She'd just mention the storm. What else could she possibly say? Because she knew, sure as God made little apples, that Lila had not just been out with, but had *been with,* a man.

Lila pulled her sweater over her head, then sniffed it. She thought she could detect the smell of marijuana but couldn't be sure. Her slacks, still damp from the rain, were hard to get off and as she pulled at them, the sand lodged in the cuffs spilled onto the tiles. She reached behind her, found her bra already unhooked, realized she hadn't done it up after Bedford had undone it, shook it loose, and let it drop to the floor. She didn't feel cold but goose bumps stood out all over her flesh and her nipples were the color of strawberries. She looked at herself in the mirror. She *did* look like something the cat had dragged in. Her hair, tangled and flattened, looked darker, more like her natural color. Her face had a smudge of mascara under her right eye, her mouth was swollen and pink as a child's. Worst of all, she couldn't read her own expression. If she could just sink into a hot bath for twenty minutes, then take a nap . . . But she couldn't do that. She had to construct some sort of alibi. Stepping out of her underpants and turning on the shower, she wondered how much Mrs. Beasley—damn her eyes—had seen. But she couldn't concentrate on Mrs. Beasley either.

Pictures flashed in her mind as though she were watching a movie—or, more accurately, a movie preview—because she saw only quick cuts—his bare chest in the firelight, the black-and-red Indian blanket, the storm squalling out of the sky as the two of them raced for cover, the fish hook on the sleeve of her sweater—all vivid, but disjointed, out of sequence. She tried to put the images in order, to remember what had led up to and come after them. The drive out to the island was pretty much a blur—realizing that she'd actually gone with him had left her in a kind of shock. The conversation had started innocuously enough—something about sighting dolphins, and shrimpers' fighting the imposition of the Turtle Exclusion Devices. Neither Cam nor Orrie had been mentioned, for which she'd been extremely grateful.

The first thing she could remember with clarity was Bedford's hand—sunburned, with dark hairs, a moonstone ring on his index finger—switching off the ignition as he'd pulled into the sandy drive next to the cabin. She'd said, "I thought we were going to the beach," sounding so much like a teenager afraid that she was about to be seduced that she'd felt like a fool when he'd shrugged and said, "The beach is right over there. I thought you wanted a jacket."

The cabin was on stilts. She followed him up rickety stairs, surprised when he opened the door without a key, asking, "You don't lock up?"

"I've finally got to the point where I don't have anything worth stealing."

"Like Mahatma Gandhi," she said slyly, remembering gossip about his Wall Street killings. "You don't own stocks?"

"Sure, but I understand those thieves better."

The place smelled of woodsmoke and coffee grounds with a sweetish overlay. The living room had a battered wicker couch and chair with pillows in expensive but faded upholstery with a palm-tree motif (his mother's?), a fireplace that needed to be cleaned, and a prodigious woodpile. Next to it, stacks of books and magazines on the bare pine floor, a coffee table that looked like a shrine holding a semicircle of sand dollars, the tail feather of a grackle, a stalk of sea oats, and a bone shaped like a fish hook. Nothing on the walls but a bulletin board with a snapshot of a turtle thumbtacked alongside a Parks Department schedule of tides.

Hearing him rooting around in the other room, she'd looked through the door, seen a double bed covered in a red and black Indian blanket. She'd turned her attention back to the tide.

He came out carrying a red-and-green wool shirt, patting the pockets. He unearthed a joint and held it out to her. She shook her head with what she hoped was nonchalance but he laughed and said, "Oh, Lila, from the look in your eyes you'd think you'd just seen *Reefer Madness* at a high-school assembly. If you don't want to, do you mind if I do?" She did mind but she couldn't say so without sounding like a prude, besides which, he'd already taken a wooden match from a container on the mantel and lit up. The sweet, resinous smell filled the room. She'd smelled it on her son's clothes but Ricky had looked her straight in the eye and denied it. She said, "We'd better hurry."

He grinned and took a deep drag. "Lila, you're hurrying your life away." His voice sounded strangulated because he was holding in the smoke. More annoyed with herself than with him, she went out to sit on the steps. If she'd shown Orrie such an open annoyance, he would have hurried, or at least offered an apology, but Bedford took his time. Strangely, after sitting there for a while, listening to the surf, her impatience evaporated. Maybe she had what the kids called a "contact high." Maybe she should have had a few drags. Oh, sure. The middle-aged wife of a state representative lighting up in a beach cabin! What was she thinking of?

"Ready?" he asked, going past her down the stairs, as though she'd been the one who was holding things up. "Just leave your shoes here." So, she'd thought, relieved, it wasn't going to be a seduction, it was going to be a guided tour. She slipped out of her shoes, rolled up the cuffs of her slacks, and followed him to the beach.

There wasn't a soul in sight. He strode ahead of her, pointing out the marvelous visibility of the winter sky, the erosion that left powdery piles of sand on the high beach. "Hey, there . . ." He took her elbow and looked up. "See those sentinel gulls?" She smiled as though she were an eleven-year-old on a field trip, wondering why she never went to the beach in winter, in fact, rarely went in summer unless she and Orrie had out-of-town visitors. He released her arm and she moved away from him, splashing into the water, feeling a delicious shock as it hit her ankles, shins, and thighs. Feeling him watching her, she stood firm, fearless against the waves, holding up the tails of his wool shirt as water drenched her crotch. She looked out to sea, pretending to ignore him until she realized he wasn't watching her anymore. Turning, she saw that he'd left her and was walking along the beach.

She straggled out of the surf and waved; he waved back and kept walking. But that was all right. It was like Robinson Crusoe and his man Friday, or better yet, like *Blue Lagoon*—one of the sexiest movies she'd ever seen—where a boy and girl were shipwrecked on an island, built a hut, lived on fruit and fish, got rid of their tattered clothes and inhibitions, and went about near-naked and wildly in love. Now she was thinking like an eleven-year-old! But she didn't care. The anxiety of playing hooky dissolved into the sheer excitement of freedom.

She ambled along, admiring the ripple marks in the sand, poking her toe into pinholes and sand domes, bending to examine the flotsam of seaweed, cast-off crab claws, and coral, watching the miniature deltas drain swash back into the sea.

There was no sunset to speak of, just a gradual waning of light so that it became harder to see him, even though he was only thirty or forty feet from her, crouched down to examine a piece of driftwood.

"See," he said, running his hand over it as she came up behind him, "it's been worn by the surf and sand blast, and if you look closely, you can see where the shipworms have burrowed."

The sky had gone dark and squally and the wind picked up, puffing his shirt out from his back, blowing his hair around his face and shoulders.

"It's getting too dark to see anything," she told him, backing off.

"Then feel it." He reached up, pulling her down next to him, guiding her hand onto the driftwood. It was damp, silky smooth, and hard.

She stood up and hugged herself. "I have to be getting back."

It was that moment of absolute stillness that comes just before a storm, producing a curious blend of fear and anticipation.

And then the rain came cracking down.

"C'mon," he yelled, rising in one svelte movement, grabbing her hand, and pulling her close to the shoreline so they could run faster on the hard-packed sand.

It came down in sheets.

She let go of his hand, running against the wind, outdistancing him—oh, so free—barely hearing him shout, "Here! Here!" as he turned toward the treeline and ploughed up to the cabin.

★ ★ ★

"Want a fire?" he asked, as she stood drenched and heaving at the door.

"No . . . I . . . uh . . ." She laughed, breathless, shaking herself like a dog. "I, uh . . ."

He rubbed her head with an oversized towel that was already damp, blotted her forehead and neck. Their eyes met briefly, then locked and she felt a shock run through her. He draped the towel around her shoulders like a shawl, and went to the fireplace, kneeling and blowing onto the kindling. "There's a bottle of Courvoisier near the toaster. Why don't you pour us one?"

She peeled off the sopping wool jacket, wiped back her hair, and went to the kitchenette. A bottle of Courvoisier was shoved next to a toaster that looked as though it had come from the Salvation Army. She opened the cabinets: a package of blue corn chips, brown rice, Yucatan Instant Black Beans, a strangely shaped tin of imported liver paté with truffles and green peppercorns (she'd assumed he was a vegetarian), two plastic plates, two plastic glasses, and a single crystal snifter. "There's only one . . ."

"You got something against sharing?" he called, poking at the fire, bringing it to flame, sitting back on the red-and-black Indian blanket he'd carried in from the bedroom. "I s'pose you do. Of course you do. Being a Republican, I guess you want your own glass."

"Oh, Bedford, give it a rest," she said with a tired drawl that made him laugh. She carried the bottle and snifter to the coffee table and took a seat on the wicker couch. He poured a double shot and offered it to her. She shook her head.

"You don't drink either?"

"Rarely. I've seen how much trouble it can cause."

"Haven't we all, but, as the politician said: if by liquor you mean that destroyer of homes, that wrecker of dignity, that curse upon mankind, why, then I'm against it; but if, by liquor, you mean that healer of pain, that balm of conviviality, that sweet sharing of pleasure, why then I'm for it." He took a sip, opening his mouth slightly and sucking in air as he swallowed. "That's the way to get the full effect," he explained. "Pool it between your bottom teeth and the root of your tongue, then breathe in to aerate it."

"I know how to drink it"—though in fact she'd never seen anyone do that before—"I just choose not to."

"Lila." He looked into her eyes again. "You can't possibly think I give a damn about Republicans and Democrats, can you? I just can't resist teasing you 'cause you rise to the bait every time and when you do, you're so"—he shrugged—"cute. There's no other word for it. You're cute." She wished he'd said beautiful or interesting. "Don't you want to get out of those clothes? I mean . . ." Seeing her reaction, he shook his head at how that might have sounded. "I mean, I have a robe in the bedroom and you could let your things dry in front of the fire."

"No. I can't stay that long. In fact—"

"Well, I'm drenched." He unbuttoned his shirt, loosened his belt buckle, snapped open the top studs of his jeans. For a minute she thought he was going to strip them off too, but he gave her another "gotcha" smile, pulled his shirt free and peeled it off so unselfconsciously that it would have seemed prudish for her to react or even seem to notice. Different people had different standards of conduct. What seemed seductive to her was probably no more than sociable ease with someone like Bedford. When he offered the snifter again, she took a small sip, holding it between her bottom teeth and the root of her tongue—had she ever been aware of that sensitive little cavern before?—sucking in, swallowing the sweet fiery liquid. Tears came to her eyes.

"Seems strange having Cam back," he said, settling cross-legged on the blanket.

"I've hardly spoken to her. She disappeared from my party with H.A."

He chuckled. "That's Cam for you. Hardly changed at all."

"You think not?"

"Well, sure she's changed. She's got that patina, that shiny lacquer now. Comes from being a career woman in the big city. They can't avoid it. That sort of independent savvy doesn't appeal to me. I'm more attracted to—" He broke off, but looked at her with the clear implication that he found her, for all her inhibitions, more alluring.

"Do you think she and H.A. . . . ? I mean in the past. Do you think they ever . . ." She couldn't finish the question.

He took a pillow from the couch, put it beneath his head, and lay back, stretching, arms behind his head. "How would I know? Does it matter?"

She wanted to know if he and Cam had been lovers but couldn't bring herself to ask. His belly was lean and flat. In the firelight his chest was gold bronze. She noticed the dark feathering in his armpits, the peculiar pattern of growth on his chest, the hair curly near his collarbone but shorter and straight around his erect nipples, his chest silky smooth, hardly any hair around the belly button but another vibrant sprouting where the studs of his jeans had been undone. She looked out the window. It couldn't have been more than five o'clock but the storm made it seem later. "I ought to be getting back," she told him, taking another sip.

He seemed not have heard her, his eyes slits as he stared into the fire. " 'And the rain doth fall, a weeping and a blessing.' "

It seemed such a beautiful thing to say, so appropriate to her own mood that she tried to neutralize it by saying, "My grandmother told me never to trust a man who talked poetry."

"She was probably right. Hey, don't you ever relax? We can't drive till the storm's over. Come toast your toes." He took hold of her big toe and gave it a this-little-piggy wiggle, then suddenly released it. "Oh, I guess you have to report in. There's a phone next to the bed."

She bristled. "I don't have to report in"—though that was exactly what she knew she should do.

He patted the space next to him. She felt both unnatural and uncomfortable sitting on the couch so she moved to the blanket, tucking her legs underneath her. "You know how these storms are," he went on. "It'll be over in ten minutes. Then we'll leave. Promise."

That seemed reasonable. Besides she didn't want to leave. Not just yet. The darkness outside, the flickering fire, the rain pelting the roof, the cognac—all gave a cocoonlike feeling of privacy and protection that soothed her anxiety, made her want to relish every second. He closed his eyes and reached for her hand, found it without fumbling and patted it in a friendly way. "Little Lila Tatternall. Hang your clothes on a mulberry bush but don't go near the water."

The storm lashed the roof. An ooze of resin caught fire and sizzled. He was so still he might have fallen asleep. She lay on her side, curled and almost prone, feet toward the fire, propping herself up on an elbow, looking at his profile, his hair spread on the pillow. Feeling an almost irresistible impulse to touch him, she turned to the coffee table, picking up the first object she touched. "What's this?" she asked, though its probable function was apparent from its shape. He turned his head, peering at it through dreamy eyes. "It's a fish hook carved out of bone," he said laconically. "Lots of Indian artifacts on the beach." He took it from her, holding it up for mutual examination, then reached over, catching it on the sleeve of her sweater, tugging ever so gently, whispering, "Caught you," as he pulled her down. Their lips were inches apart.

She expected him to kiss her but he removed the hook with an easy twist, let it drop to the floor, moved slightly, making a space next to him.

They lay close and still, breathing together and then, as though guessing her thoughts, he took her hand and placed it on his chest. She remembered the thing he'd said earlier, the thing that had made her go with him in the first place: "If I repent of anything, it's very likely to be my good behavior." Her hand moved, skimming the muscles in his arm, finding the hollow of his neck, easing upward, fingertips on his scalp, fingers entangling his thick damp hair. His entire body arched as a pet animal's would, rising to her touch. He rolled toward her, taking her head in his hands, pulling gently on the roots of her hair, twisting, tangling, untangling it so that the tingling in her scalp set off a more delicious tingling between her legs. Her lips found his mouth—already open, his tongue snaky with anticipation. It was one of the few times in her life that she'd kissed rather than been kissed and it gave her a tremendous charge of energy that brought her body on top of his, mouth to mouth, rib cage to rib cage, her sweater riding up so that she felt naked flesh belly to belly—hers surprisingly hot, his cool, as though all the blood had rushed to his genitals.

She pulled up, amazed and breathless, blinking down into his face. His eyes were closed, his mouth open, but he wasn't gulping air as she was, but breathing slow and steady, like a trained swimmer, pacing himself. His hand moved so slowly she thought she'd scream out with anticipation, easing one of her breasts out of her bra, already kissing it as he reached behind, unhooking her with a single deft movement. Her mind went back to something she'd said to Orrie a few weeks ago when, coming home from a party, he'd varied his usual routine and tried to undress her, fumbling with her bra so long that she'd finally undone it herself and they'd both laughed when she'd said, "Honey, you could never have a woman without her total cooperation."

Pushing his hands away, she arched back, panting, astride him, trying to recover. She tumbled off. He didn't come after her, but lay there, reaching down to hold himself, then, slowly, rolling toward her, pulling her buttocks close, kissing her again and again, unzipping her slacks, pulsing her with his fingers, his tongue in her mouth, her ear, lapping her neck, slithering past her breasts to her belly. He eased up, releasing her. Now he was breathing hard too, but his caresses were teasing, light as a butterfly, waiting until he'd roused her, then kneading, demanding, then releasing again. It went on and on, beyond anything that could be called foreplay—more like the ritual petting of decades before. He brought her to such a pitch that she was aching, bruised and yearning, desperate for release, knowing that she'd explode with his first thrusts. She pulled at him, grinding into him, offering herself completely. "Tell me," he whispered. "Tell me you want me."

She could have killed him. She pushed away, squirming, crawling toward the couch, pulling herself up into a sitting position, holding the front of her slacks together. She didn't know why his words had shattered the spell, but suddenly the dynamic had changed and she'd sensed something threatening: more than he wanted her, he needed to know that she wanted him. He wanted an admission of outright surrender. She burst into tears, not knowing which of them she hated the most.

He got up, patted her shoulder, refilled the snifter, and held it to her lips. "Hey, girl, hey. You kinda lost it there. You all right?" She shook her head violently, gulping down the contents of the snifter. He patted her head and turned, stuffing himself into his jeans, moving to the fireplace to poke the logs apart, then resting his arms on the mantelpiece, head down, waiting for her to recover.

"You want . . . I mean, you want . . . ," she blubbered, trying to explain.

"Hey," he said gently, "I know what I want. You're the one who's confused. But I know all this is new to you."

The storm had stopped. Only her sobs could be heard over the crackling of the dying fire. "Right," he said when she'd subsided, her head sagging between her legs. "Time to leave."

When she'd rearranged her clothes, he put his wool jacket over her shoulders and guided her out the door. He looked up as he flicked on the flashlight. "Hey, look at that sky." It was navy blue, without stars, the moon hiding behind a drift of watery clouds. She felt dizzy and looked down, holding on to the railing, following the bouncing circle of light down the rickety stairs.

The moment of truth couldn't be delayed any longer. She sprinkled herself with talcum powder, rolled the clothes she'd worn to the beach into a ball and stuffed them into her overnight bag, put on fresh underwear, searched for Josie's hair dryer, which was nowhere to be found. She sat on the toilet and pulled on her hose, zipped up her cocoa velveteen skirt, buttoned her gold satin big-sleeved blouse and cinched it with the topaz-studded belt. Her newly washed face still looked pale and strangely open, as though every thought and feeling could be read on it. Applying her makeup more liberally than usual, she realized she was humming, the words to the song running through her mind, insistent as a commercial jingle, "Oh, my love, my darling, I've hungered for your touch, A long lonely time . . ." She slipped into her heels, clasped on her gold charm bracelet, which she'd brought along because it was Orrie's custom to add a new charm each Christmas, and stepped into the hallway.

The music downstairs had been turned off and she could hear

them talking, not, she hoped, about her, though the odds were that her disappearance would be the topic of choice. Walking to the landing, she realized she was still wobbly. She felt like a kid on her way to the principal's office and resentment bubbled up. Didn't she have a right to go her own way for a few hours? But who was she kidding? Her conduct had been shameful, inexplicable even to herself, so how could she possibly explain it to anyone else? She still hadn't constructed a plausible story, but as she started down the stairs, all she could think of was the last thing Bedford had said to her as she'd opened his car door: "Next time we go to the beach, maybe there won't be a storm." And she'd nodded, as though there would be a next time.

Fourteen

ORRIE WAS STANDING in the archway to the living room as though on lookout. Seeing her, he came to the foot of the stairs, his anxious look easing into a wan smile. "Hey, sugar, where in the world have you been? I was really worried about you." There was no accusation in his voice, only relief.

"I'm sorry," she said as lightly as if she'd forgotten to buy his favorite cookies, but looking into his face she thought she might burst into tears. Maybe she should ask him to take her home right now, tell him about the whole sordid mess, beg him to forgive her. "Orrie," she began, but Jasper's voice boomed out, "Where the hell have you been, girl? We were about to call out the militia."

"It's just not like you to go off without telling anyone," Orrie reasoned, leading her into the living room. Susan, cross-legged on the floor next to the tree, chided, "Really, Mother!" Ricky, sprawled next to her, smirked, "This is the woman who gives lectures about responsibility."

"We thought you'd been abducted by gypsies," Evie chimed in while Cam, sitting on a couch next to her friend, Reba, added, "We really were worried. Mrs. Beasley said . . ."

"I know I should have called but . . ." Lila began, then stalled.

"No matter," Josie cut in, putting on an old *Perry Como Sings Your Christmas Favorites*, adjusting the volume to the level of background music. "We're all here now and . . ." she checked her wristwatch. "We still have time to open the presents before we go to Cuba's church service. I've been like a kid, reading all the tags and shaking them," she went on, cheerful as a camp counselor. She handed a present to Susan, then turned to Reba, explaining, "It's always been our custom to let the youngest hand out the presents. I know most people wait till Christmas morning but when the children were little, Lila, or maybe it was Cam, got out of bed one Christmas Eve and caught Bear red-handed, so ever since then we've opened them on Christmas Eve. I guess it was Cam. Yes, that was the year she figured out there wasn't a Santa Claus."

"Cam was a cynic at five," Evie told Jasper.

"No, she wasn't a cynic. If fact, she asked me not to tell you kids because she didn't want to spoil it for you. So ever since then . . ." She was babbling and she knew it. Susan overlapped her with, "Hey, this first present is for me, from Grandma. I can tell it's a book," and started to untie the bow. For a minute it seemed as though things might proceed as though nothing had happened, then Evie asked, "So, Lila, where were you?" and all eyes were on her again.

"Yeah. Where were you? We were sick with worry," Ricky mimicked her voice. "Didn't you know we'd be anxious? Couldn't you have called?"

"Well, it was so spontaneous, I . . . I'd just started to unload the presents from my car when"—Lila took the plunge—"a couple I know drove by and—"

"Who?" Orrie wanted to know.

"You don't know them." Not likely. "That is, I think you've met them but you probably wouldn't remember," she foundered. "Jim and Constance Tidewell? They're from Charleston. I worked with her on that fund-raiser for the Spoleto festival, remember?"

Orrie shrugged. "Can't say as I do, but what—"

"Didn't I meet her?" Josie rushed to Lila's rescue. "Tall dark-haired woman with a lovely complexion?"

God bless you, Mama! "Yes. That's her. She's maybe five-foot-eleven, used to be a model." Without realizing she could do it so quickly, she began inventing. "I hadn't seen her since last summer, but she and Jim were on their way out to visit relatives on Fripp and they were driving around The Point because Jim had never seen it before, and—"

"They're from Charleston and he'd never seen The Point?" Evie asked.

"No. They're not *from* Charleston, they're from Los Angeles." From the corner of her eye she saw Reba studying her over the rim of her eggnog cup. Cam put her head down, examining her hands. "I think maybe she was born here but she went to Hollywood. That's where she met Jim. He used to be in TV. A producer, I think." Evie swallowed that scrap of information like a seal who'd been thrown a fish and wanted more. "They're retired. Of course, they don't look old enough to be retired, at least"—What name had she given the woman?—". . . *she* doesn't, but I guess she's a lot younger than he is. They moved here a few years ago and they like the area so much that they talked his brother into taking a time-share on Fripp." Jasper, already bored, blotted a drop of bourbon from his vest. ". . . quite a nice condo, though it only has a marsh view . . ." Susan rolled her eyes with impatience. ". . . but they like the Lowcountry so much they're thinking of buying . . ." Ricky yawned and pulled his cap down over his eyes. ". . . but I told them they should investigate Hilton Head as well, because they play both golf . . ." Josie nodded encouragement as though waiting for the punch line of a familiar joke. ". . . in fact, I even asked them to come visit us . . ." She was flowing with details and asides, veering so far from the original story that she had to rein herself in. ". . . but I don't suppose they will, because they're only here until the New Year. So: they were just driving around The Point on their way out to Fripp, and they were so surprised to see me in Mama's driveway, and they asked me about The Point, so . . ."

"Why didn't you bring them in and show them Mama's house?" Evie persisted.

Lila wanted to slap her.

"Just as well she didn't," Josie came to the rescue again. "It was like hell with the lid off this afternoon. Cam wasn't feeling well, Cuba and a couple of her grandkids were here, Reba and I were cooking . . ."

". . . so I showed them around The Point," Lila went on, "and then they said, why didn't I drive out to Fripp with them and meet his relatives. They said the sister-in-law was an actress, so I couldn't resist."

"Who was she?" Evie wanted to know.

"Turns out I didn't recognize her, but just to be polite I pretended I did. Anyway, I thought I'd be back within the hour, but then the storm started and—"

"And you couldn't call because what?" Ricky sneered. "They were too poor to have a phone? Your hand was broken?"

"No, Mr. Smartie. The power went out. Since it wasn't their condo, they didn't know where the fuse box was and we were all scrambling around hunting for candles, which we couldn't find."

Cam raised her head and gave her the "big sister" smile. Its combination of amusement, warning, and scorn said, "I don't buy a word of it." *You bitch,* Lila thought. *The only reason you know I'm making this up is because you've told so many lies yourself.* But she knew that wasn't true. Cam had always gotten into trouble because she'd told the truth.

"Oh, pull-ese," Susan whined. "Can't I open this present now?" Without waiting for an okay she tore off the paper and held up a book. "It's about Billie Jean King," she told everyone. "Oh,

Grandma, I knew you were going to give me this, 'cause I remember when we saw it at the bookstore and I know you're always trying to get me to read." She crawled over to Josie, who had seated herself in a wing-backed chair, and gave her a kiss.

"Am I next?" Ricky asked.

"No, you're not," Susan told him, searching through the pile. "I'm the youngest and I get to choose the order."

"How 'bout another round?" Jasper asked, heaving himself up. Evie put her hand over her glass, Reba said she was fine, Orrie said he'd stick with the ginger ale. Though she desperately wanted to ask for a double, Cam shook her head. A pregnant woman couldn't drink or smoke. She was—she clasped her hands until the knuckles showed white, trying to assimilate the reality—a pregnant woman. She felt a cramp in her abdomen and wanted to run upstairs, check and see if she might not have started. A line from a book of poetry she'd edited—"No man has ever looked for his future in the crotch of his pants"—kept running through her brain.

"Don't get up, dear lady," Jasper told Josie, though she'd made no attempt to move. He walked with drunken deliberation toward the drinks cart.

"Here, Mother." Susan handed a large box to Lila. "This is for you, from Daddy."

"Go on, open it," Orrie encouraged. His face was still full of questions, but he didn't voice them.

"Open it," Josie seconded.

"You can pour me one," Lila called as she slipped the ribbon from the box. She was home free. Off the hook. Dizzy with relief. Nothing more need be mentioned. Nothing at all. And, given today's standards, had she really done anything so terrible? A little heavy petting after more than twenty years of marriage. It wasn't as though she'd actually had sex with him. "A light bourbon."

Jasper raised his eyebrows at this unusual request, then laughed and said, "All right, girl, you're starting to loosen up and get into the spirit. Merry Christmas."

"I'll have one too," Ricky said.

Lila, slipping her fingernail under the Scotch tape and pulling the wrapping from her present, gave him a warning look but Jasper, fumbling in the ice bucket, pronounced, "Hell, Lila, he's old enough to drink. At his age . . ."

"Oh, yeah. A pint of white lightnin' a day never hurt a country boy," Orrie said so softly that Cam was sure she was the only one who'd heard him. His boyish features were crumpled with uneasy acceptance. You poor SOB, she thought: Jasper for a father, Ricky for a son, and now it looks like Lila, of all people, is getting it on the side, and you'll never have the guts either to see the truth or to call her on it.

Lila, smiling even before she lifted the lid from the box, drew out a black silk Natori nightdress and peignoir with appliqués of gold butterflies. "Now that's an eyeful," Jasper said approvingly, handing her a huge tumbler of bourbon with just a few ice cubes floating in it. "That's enough to make Orrie forget he's been a married man for twenty years."

"Twenty-three, but who's counting?" Orrie smiled as Lila planted a kiss on his cheek. "She's still my number-one girl."

"Oh, gross," Susan groaned, reaching for another gift. "This one's to Grandma from Daddy. Not Mother and Daddy, just Daddy."

"Why, Orrie, thank you." Josie slipped the ribbon from the box, rolled it up and put it into her lap, then carefully eased off the wrapping paper and began to fold it. Cam winked at Evie, who smiled knowingly at Lila. Lila looked at Cam and they all started to giggle as though they were kids playing Pass It On and whispering at a birthday party.

"What?" Josie asked innocently.

Cam said, "Depression mentality," and all three sisters broke up laughing.

"There's nothing wrong with saving ribbons," Josie said with dignity.

"Or old wrappings," Cam added, covering her mouth.

"Or rubber bands," Lila chimed in, ducking her head.

Evie, overcome with laughter, squirmed and pulled her skirt down over her thighs. "Remember when Mawmaw used to tell us not to throw out old nylons because we could use them to dust the furniture?"

"Well, girls, it's a sin to waste things," Josie began as though they were still children. "If you'd—"

" '—lived through the Depression,' " her daughters said in unison. They fell about in another paroxysm of laughter, kids again, united in gleeful scorn at their mother's crazy obsessions.

"I know this is for me." Ricky grabbed one of the gold-and-white packages. The way he tore at the ribbons and ripped off the paper was such a boorish contrast to Josie's gentle thrift that Cam stopped laughing and stared at him, unable to mask her distaste. Where could such a sense of greedy privilege ever hope to find a foothold in the world outside his parents' indulgence?

Josie lifted a china figurine from its bed of tissue paper. "Oh, thank you so much, son," she said, holding up the figurine for general approval. Cam expected that even her mother's tastes were too sophisticated for a bluebird sitting on a cherry branch, but Josie's face was soft with gratitude.

"I picked it out myself," Ollie told her as Ricky yanked a navy blue crew sweater from his box, smiled, and shook his head. "I knew you'd get me something that looked preppie, Mom."

Lila shrugged and took another swallow of her drink. "If you don't like it, I can take it back. Or maybe I'll keep it for myself. Unisex is in."

Cam thought about the navy cashmere sweater she'd bought Sam for Christmas. Months before, when they'd been taking one of their long Saturday afternoon walks, they'd seen one in a shop window and Sam had mentioned he'd never owned a cashmere sweater. He'd been a scholarship student, always living on the cheap, never having more than a couple of pairs of chinos and Orlon sweaters, and by the time he'd left the service and was going to graduate school, he'd had a wife and baby to support. Even though he now made good money, he had two kids approaching college age. He bought expensive suits because that was essential, but he'd never indulged himself with fancy casual clothes. She hadn't wrapped up the sweater because she'd planned to give it to him as he'd come out of the shower. She'd wanted to towel him off, tell him to close his eyes, then slip it over his head, easing it over his shoulders—he still had wonderful shoulders—kissing him before she told him to open his eyes. She decided she wouldn't return the sweater. Even if her job was on the line, she wanted him to have it. She'd find out his address in Atlanta and send it. Damn, but she wanted a drink! Damn, but she wanted to be out of her mother's house. And maybe Reba was right. Maybe she had an obligation to tell Sam she was pregnant. She felt an overwhelming desire not just to talk to him but to see him, in the flesh.

Perry Como was singing "Have Yourself a Merry Little Christmas" for the second time. Lost in her own thoughts, Cam realized that the exchange of gifts had progressed: Susan had a pile around her—the Billie Jean King book, a tennis racket, a set of aromatic candles, a vegetarian cookbook, two sweaters, several T-shirts, CDs, running shoes, perfume, a telephone in the shape of a 1950s car, a museum reproduction of a pre-Columbian bowl with tiny feet as supports, a stuffed dinosaur that she held in her lap. Evie, Jasper, Orrie, Josie, and Ricky had all amassed their own loot. She dimly recalled that there'd been some shift in the wind—Lila surprised, Josie silently disapproving—when Jasper had given Evie an inappropriately expensive watch. And now Lila was taking a gold charm in the shape of the statehouse from a jewelry box and reading the attached note: " 'To my sweet wife: A replica of our new house. All my love and thanks for helping me get there.' "

"Shit, I hope we never have to go through another campaign," Ricky complained. "That was really the pits."

"Get used to it, boy," Jasper told him, beaming. "This is only the beginning."

Lila leaned into Orrie, draping an arm around his neck, whispering, "Thank you." Cam's quick look at Josie confirmed that she wasn't the only one who'd noticed that Lila's words were slurred. What a little hypocrite Lila is, Cam thought; she's got affection beaming from one eye, calculation shining out of the other. And yet Cam felt sorry for her. Hypocrisy was a full-time job.

"Susie. Susie, darlin', hand over that green envelope to your daddy," Jasper ordered. Susan did as she was told, Orrie tore open the envelope and read: "Caribbean vacation—you pick the dates. Five days and four nights on St. Kitts. You both deserve it after the campaign. Congratulations, Dad." More whoops of surprise, kisses and hugs.

"Cam and Reba are being neglected here," Josie said. "Susan, give our guest that red box—the one underneath that big silver package." Susan handed it over and Reba opened it, finding a copy of Josie's *Lowcountry Cooking*, a jar of homemade pepper jelly, and another of peach jam. "Had I known you were coming," Josie began, but Reba got up and went to her, putting her arms around her and saying, "Hey, you took me in. I can't tell you how much that means to me."

"Now for Cam," Josie said. "Susan, please give your aunt Camilla that little package with the sprig of holly on it. Now Cam, be careful," she warned as Cam peeled off the wrapping paper. "It's real old." It was a small leather-bound, hand-sewn volume. "*The Pharmaceutic Practical Recipe Book*," Cam read aloud. "There's no copyright date but the inscription says, 'To Wallice Houseman, Esq.' and it's dated 1800. Oh, Mama, wherever did you get this?"

"I found it with Mawmaw's things. Don't have the vaguest clue as to who Wallice Houseman, Esq., was, though I did hear Mawmaw tell that we had a distant uncle who was a pharmacist, or apothecary, I think they called them back then."

"It says here: 'For The Use of Druggists, Apothecaries, Perfumers, Confectioners, Patent Medicine Factors and Dealers in Fancy Articles for the Toilet, Compiled with Great Care from Recipes Now In Use by the Most Popular Houses in France.' Oh, Mama, this is wonderful." Reba leaned over her shoulder as Cam gingerly turned the age-spotted pages. "Oh, listen to this. This is under 'Preparations For The Hair': To Make Pomade Divine: Take Mutton Suet, 2 ounces; White Wax, half an ounce. Perfume with Oil of Lavender.' "

Reba laughed. "If we can get our hands on some mutton suet, we could try it."

"Oh, it's marvelous, Mama. And look at this: 'Paints for the Face, Which May be Used Without Danger' and 'Pimple Wash' and 'Eye Waters', 'Almost Paste for the Hands' and 'Portuguese Rouge.' I love it. I'd never sell it, but I think it's probably worth something."

"I have a cousin in the rare-book business," Reba told her. "We could get him to look at it."

Cam sucked in her cheeks. "Reba, you have a cousin in everything from heart transplants to auto repair."

Reba hunched her shoulders, raised her eyebrows, turned her hands palms upward. "What can I tell you? They were fertile a couple of generations ago."

Cam laughed and hugged her, then asked, "Isn't this great?" turning and offering the book to Lila.

Lila, fumbling unsuccessfully to attach the new charm to her bracelet, pretended not to see the book and offered her wrist up to Orrie. Anger rose in her throat like undigested grease. She and Josie had come across the apothecary book while going through Mawmaw's trunks just before Mawmaw had been taken to the rest home. She'd asked Josie if she could have it, but Josie had said she wouldn't feel right giving away Mawmaw's possessions until Mawmaw had died. But then, Josie had assured her, Lila could have anything she wanted. And she'd specifically said she wanted the book. She could only suppose that Josie, scrounging around for a gift in the face of Cam's sudden appearance, had forgotten her promise.

"That little package," Lila said, pointing impatiently, "Yes, that one, gold and white, like all my presents. That's for Ricky. Give it to him, Susan. It's not just from me and Daddy, it's from Grandaddy too."

Susan grudgingly obliged, holding out, then pulling back the package, teasing Ricky as he lunged and grabbed it.

"Okay! Okay!" Ricky yelped, shaking out a set of keys. "I didn't think you'd do it but you did. Damn! Keys. Keys to a new car, right?" Jasper, Orrie, and Lila all nodded. "Damn! I've been driving this clunker used to belong to Mom for two years," Ricky explained in an aside to Reba. "So what is it? Where is it?"

"It's a new red Saturn," Orrie said.

Jasper, helping himself to another refill at the drinks cart, raised the bottle and said, "Buy American!"

"It's back at the house, sitting in our driveway," Lila, flushed with satisfaction at Ricky's pleasure, said. "That is, if the dealer put it there this afternoon, like he was s'posed to."

"He did," Orrie confirmed. "I called him to check."

"Way to go!" Ricky yelped again, pounding his chest as though congratulating himself.

"As Ivan Boesky says," Reba whispered to Cam, " 'Greed is all right. Greed is healthy.' "

Susan pouted. "You're always saying how he drives like a maniac."

"You'll get one too, blossom," Jasper assured her. "Like all good things, it's just a matter of time."

"When I graduate?" Susan pressed.

Ricky leapt around, punching Orrie's shoulder, slapping palms with Jasper. "Can I take your car and go get it now, Dad?"

"Most certainly not," Lila said. "You just sit tight and wait for everyone else to open their presents, then we're all going to Cuba's church."

"Grandma said she didn't want me to go dressed like this, so why can't I just—"

"Now you've got some new clothes, you can just trot upstairs and put them on," Orrie told him.

"Aw, come on, Dad. Why can't I—"

"Sit down, Ricky," Jasper ordered, short and sharp, as though training a dog. "Just sit down." Ricky skulked back to the floor, jiggling the car keys in Susan's face. "I can't go to the church service and neither can Miss Evie," Jasper went on, "so later, when I carry Miss Evie back to Savannah, we'll drop you off."

Josie looked up in surprise. "I was expecting you all to stay overnight."

"Thought I'd better go check my boat 'cause of this storm," Jasper said. "And since Evie said she had to get back to Savannah to work, thought I'd kill two birds with one stone."

"Evie?" Josie said, half questioning, half warning.

"Oh, Mama, you know I'd love to come to church with you,"

Evie started in her little girl voice, "but I've been so stressed out I haven't finished working on my column."

Reba and Cam exchanged a quick glance.

"And you're going home to work on your column on Christmas Eve?" Josie asked with quiet incredulity. She wanted Evie to know she wasn't getting away with this paltry excuse. No, not excuse. Lie. She felt both exploited and defeated. How could it be that she, who'd only lied in petty, altruistic ways—telling an overweight friend that she looked slim, putting off the phone company by saying she hadn't received a bill—had raised children who were liars? Lila had just lied—and she'd helped her to do it, thinking that a little inaccuracy could save a ton of painful explanation—and now Evie was lying, stupidly, clumsily. "Evie," she said again, her voice a dying fall, wondering when Evie and Jasper had planned their getaway.

"We'll be coming back for Christmas dinner tomorrow," Evie said brightly.

"Evie," Josie said again. But what could she do? The older her children had gotten, the more inhibited she'd become about stating the obvious. Even if she took Evie aside, could she bring her into line by demanding, "How dare you?" Could she make Evie's conscience smart by asking, "Don't you know it's wrong to go off with your sister's father-in-law, a man who's old enough to be . . ." She didn't think so. If her lecture that "petting won't make you popular" had fallen on deaf ears when Evie was sixteen, how could she hope to stop her from going off with a man when she was forty plus?

"Mama, how come you look so sad?" Lila asked. She was on that dangerous cusp of drunkenness, acutely aware of the feelings of others because she was about to plunge into her own universe of self-pity. "Mama, don't be sad. Wait'll you see what I've got you." She went down on all fours, crawled toward the tree, picked up one of the few remaining presents, and crawled to Josie, already easing off the gold ribbon as she handed it to her. "Mama, I really think you're going to like it." She leaned back on her haunches as Josie undid the package, rolling up the ribbon and folding the wrapping paper in slow motion.

"See, she's still doing it," Ricky pointed out. "Depression mentality." But this time only Evie laughed.

Josie lifted out the woolen plaid robe. "Why, Lila, this is lovely. It's so nice and warm and—"

Susan laughed. "It looks like the blanket my friend Melissa puts over her horse."

"You said it." Ricky guffawed, tossing his head and neighing.

"It's bright and cheery," Evie said, seeing Lila's face crushed with disappointment.

"Just the thing to wear when you're sitting in front of the fire," Reba said, sensing the sudden squall.

"Warm and comfortable," Jasper muttered, so far gone that he tapped Evie's knee before he leaned back, closing his eyes.

"I bought it at a specialty import shop in Atlanta. It's made in Scotland," Lila announced.

"Yes, it's bright and cheery," Josie agreed, smiling, refolding it. "Just the thing I need."

"It's got pockets," Lila persisted. "You're always saying you like pockets because they're practical. It's a Stewart tartan, imported from Scotland. See the label?" She stopped herself from mentioning the price.

"Yeah, Grandma, you'll look like a happy old mare in that," Ricky neighed again, then leaned toward his grandfather, asking, "Are we going to be leaving soon?"

Lila said, "Shut up, Ricky," and cuffed him, none too playfully, as she crawled back to the tree. "And this is for you, Cam." She picked up one of the last packages and tossed it into Cam's lap. "I hope you like Chanel. I'd bought you some Joy but . . ." She pulled back her hair, shook her head as if to clear it, and groaned, "Whoa!"

"Of course I like Chanel. Thank you," Cam said, sniffing one of the bars of soap. "Did you get the Mary Cassatt book I sent you yet, Lila? And, Evie, I sent you another museum book, *Fashion Through the Ages*, and one to Mama about Victorian gardens. You see, I didn't realize I was going to come home so—"

"Why should you?" Lila muttered. "You haven't come home in ten years."

"You don't have to give us anything, Aunt Cam." Susan snuggled her stuffed dinosaur. "Your presence is present enough."

Reba gave her a thumbs-up for the pun and dove in. "Once I get back to New York, I'm going to send you all a big old package from Zabar's or Balducci's. Coffee from Jamaica, frogs' legs from France, triple virgin olive oil from Italy, newts' eyes and turtles' eggs—something really special."

"We don't need no foreign foods," Jasper muttered with such unexpected belligerence that Evie patted his knee, then leaned to whisper in his ear.

Leaning in Reba's direction, Orrie grimaced an apology. "Don't mind Daddy. When he's had a few, he gets—"

"Oh, that's all right," Reba said archly, flashing her brightest smile, "I don't expect all Southerners to be gracious—after all, that would be a cliché."

"There's one more," Cam gestured to Susan, desperately wanting the whole charade to be done with, fighting an impulse to just get up and head for the door.

"It's from Aunt Cam to Grandma," Susan said, examining the Lord & Taylor box.

"I just had time to get the one present before I left," Cam began to explain.

"Just look at this mess!" Lila exclaimed, grabbing up discarded wrappings and ribbons and crunching them into a ball.

Josie signaled Orrie with her eyes and he bent forward, whispering, "Just let that go, sugar," and easing Lila back onto the couch.

"I hope you're not planning to drive, Jasper," Josie said, "because you look"—she covered her warning with threadbare politeness—"too tired to drive."

"Of course not," Evie said indignantly. "I'm going to drive. Jasper, where're your keys?"

"I've only had one drink, I can drive," Ricky volunteered.

"Hush up," Susan said, "Can't you see Grandma is opening her present?"

As Josie drew the rose-colored dressing gown out of the package she said nothing, but as she held it up, a soft exhalation of breath showed her pleasure. "Why, it's . . . it's . . ."

"Beautiful," Reba said for her.

"Oh, yes," Josie agreed. "The color's like something from a real sunrise and the fabric . . . see how these gathers from the shoulder pads and these pleats from the waistband just . . ."

"Cascade," Reba supplied. "Oh, it's all flow and slither. You'll feel like a nymph standing in a waterfall when you wear that."

"Super pretty. Super sexy," Orrie agreed.

"Isn't it, you know, for somebody younger?" Susan asked.

"In the privacy of my bedroom, I don't see why I can't be any age I wish to be," Josie declared with a smile.

"Hey, I feel the same way," Jasper croaked with a more lecherous intent.

"Oh, Camilla," Josie said, pointedly ignoring Jasper's boorishness, holding the dressing gown up to her breasts. "It's just . . ."

"So now I guess you have something else to play dress-up in. You can finally throw out that ragtag lizard-green thing that looks like it belongs in a bordello." Lila's voice rasped like chalk scraping on a blackboard. "I've been telling her to throw that green thing out for years, but she can't bring herself to do it because it was from her darling prodigal daughter." She hauled herself up and went to the drinks cart, sloshing another bourbon into her glass.

"Lila, I don't think—" Josie started.

"You don't think what, Mama? What don't you think? Women so rarely say what they think. They just yammer and simper and make nice, like you taught us to do. Except Cam. She always says what she thinks and does what she wants to do, just like Daddy always did. And she doesn't care who it hurts."

"Oh, God," Cam groaned.

"She's . . ." Reba whispered.

"I know."

"What are you saying?" Lila challenged, spinning around. "What are you whispering to the friend you imported from the big city so you'd have someone to talk to instead of us dumb home folks?"

"Hey, I don't want to be part of a family brouhaha." Reba, raising her hands as though someone had a knife in her ribs, making a clown's grimace to ease the general embarrassment, got up and started to back out of the room. "I'll just go upstairs."

"And pack," Lila said.

Josie got up from her chair. "Lila, *please*. Reba, don't."

"No, Reba," Cam started after her friend but thought better of it, calling, "I'll be up soon," then turning back, her rage giving way to icy calm. "Lila," she said, evenly and quietly, "you're drunk."

"Takes one to know one, Cam. You were drunk at my wedding and drunk at Bear's funeral. If you think I'm ever going to forgive the terrible things you said—"

"Mother!" Susan admonished.

Ricky got up, tossing his keys in the air. "I'll wait in Granddaddy's car. You all are comin', aren't you? Or do you want to watch a crazy woman go off the deep end the way I have to every night?" The front door slammed behind him.

"Couldn't we just—" Evie, close to tears, begged.

"—'All just get along,' like Rodney King's lawyer told him to say?" Jasper wheezed, dragging himself up, feeling in his pockets. "I don't hardly want to sit around listening to contentious females scratchin' in a cat fight. You comin', Evie?"

"Just as soon's I find my purse." She stared after him, feeling along the edge of the couch until she'd found it. "Mama, I just—" she apologized, getting up. "I mean, I love you all but I just can't . . ."

"Oh, cut the crap," Lila barked. "You wouldn't even be here if your married boyfriend had been able to get away from his family."

Evie stood, helpless as a doe caught in headlights. "Lila, why are you so hateful? What have I ever—"

"It's all right, Evie." Josie went to her. "Go on along. Don't let either of those boys drive."

"Mama, you don't think—?"

"Go on along." Josie reached into her pocket for a handkerchief. "You never could find a handkerchief," she said, dabbing at Evie's eyes. "Go on along. Call me later." Evie, sniffling, gave a weak parting shot—"You're both so hateful I'm ashamed to call you my sisters," and left the room. Josie went to the drinks cart, gently taking the bottle from Lila's hand. "Don't," she said gently. "Just go upstairs and—"

"Take a little nap," Orrie suggested helplessly, straggling up, then slumping back down.

"I don't need a nap! Cam's the one who takes naps," Lila snapped. "She's only here once every ten years but it's all so terribly trying for her special sensitivities"—her voice rose into a na-na heckle—"that she gets a case of the vapors and disappears for the afternoon while the rest of us are trying to"—she gulped—"trying to . . ."

"Moth-er," Susan shrieked.

"Trying to what?" Cam taunted with sudden vehemence. "What were you trying to do this afternoon, Lila? Have a little fun? Get . . ."

Both Orrie and Josie turned to Cam as though they'd heard a gunshot. "Cam!" Josie threatened. "Cam, you sit right back down and hush up."

"Wait a little minute here," Cam said, shaking with indignation. "Wait just a little minute! What have I done wrong?" She stood rigid, hands at her sides. "You beg me to come home at the last minute. I buy a ticket to the tune of seven hundred dollars. Seven hundred-some dollars!—which, since I don't have a rich husband, I can hardly afford, and when I get here, this uptight, goody-goody hypocrite is snotty to me at her stupid party, insults my friends . . ." Her voice seemed to be coming from some crazyhouse echo chamber. She was a five-year-old who'd been pushed down the slide, sent to bed without supper, a victim of unfairness and stolen love, yowling a tantrum of indignation. "I don't know why I was stupid enough to think that I could come back here. But I'm sure as hell not going to be stupid enough to stay."

"That's right, run off," Lila screamed. "Run off like you always do. You're only around for the big scenes, aren't you, Cam? You're the center of the universe. Just like Daddy. Just here long enough to spoil everything. Well, I didn't want you back this time and I hope you never come back again."

"Lila, stop it. Stop it this minute." Josie shook her. "This is my house. I won't have either of you talking like this."

"You don't have to worry about me, Mama, 'cause I'm out of here." Cam turned and walked deliberately to the stairs.

Josie muttered, "Oh, my God. Oh, my dear God." Lila collapsed into her arms, sobbing, "She's always been the favorite. I looked so hard for the right present, then she . . . she can't do anything wrong and I can't . . . I try so hard, Mama and . . . it's just *not fair.*"

Patting Lila's back as though she were burping her, Josie motioned to Orrie."I don't know, son. Do you think—?"

"Yes, I think we'd better go on home. Susan? You want to gather up your things or . . ."

"I don't care about my shitty things. You're all hateful. All of you. Mother, how could you?"

"I'm sorry," Lila gulped. "I'm so very, very—"

"Sorry doesn't count," Susan shouted.

"Sorry *does* count," Orrie said with unexpected firmness. "Now you, miss, you get your butt out to the car and wait. Your mother and I will be right along."

Lila, snuffling, weaving on her feet, wiping water from her nose and eyes, said, "If you think I'm going to apologize to Cam—"

"It's too late for apologies. I don't need apologies and I don't want explanations," Josie said with dreadful tiredness. "I'd just like some peace and quiet."

After they'd left she sat on the couch, staring at the treasures and debris that cluttered the carpet. Perry Como was singing "Have Yourself a Merry Little Christmas" for the fifth time and she lifted the needle from the record, took it off the turntable, and cracked it in two, cleanly and quietly as though she was cracking an egg, and let it drop to the floor.

She thought she should go upstairs, try to smooth things over, convince Cam to stay, but she was too tired for that too. She turned out all the lights except those on the Christmas tree. She looked at her watch, found her purse, and straightened her hair in the hall mirror, though the only light she had to see by was the moonglow coming through the fanlight above the front door. She would have to leave right now if she was going to be on time for Cuba's service. She wasn't sure she had the strength to walk to the church, though it was only a few blocks away. But of course, she'd find the strength. She'd promised to be there, and a military wife always fulfilled her obligations.

Fifteen

Though residents of The Point were almost exclusively white, the First African Baptist Church had been built just after the Civil War and still had a black congregation. It was a substantial two-story wooden structure with a steeple, well maintained and appealing in its simplicity, located on a large corner lot. Painted white, with pale yellow light shining from the windows, it looked almost luminous in the moonlight. Since there were no sidewalks in the neighborhood, cars were parked higgledy-piggledy on the sides of the streets, and people, mostly black, but a sizable minority of whites who'd come to hear the choir, were streaming toward the church. It had stopped raining but the wind was still gusting and a few carried umbrellas to protect themselves from the drops shaken by overarching oaks.

As she went up the three steps to the open doors, Josie held her hands at belly level as though she were toting a Bible and looked straight ahead, acknowledging greetings of "Hey there" and "Merry Christmas" with a smile and a slight bow of the head, not bothering to see if those who spoke were acquaintances or merely friendly strangers. Shalalla and Antoinne were behind a card table that held a stack of music tapes, a cigar box filled with bills and coins, a notebook and pencil. Antoinne, so scrubbed his small nose and forehead seemed to glow, looked like a midget man in his bright blue three-piece suit with a red polka dot bow tie. Shalalla wore a full-skirted green taffeta dress bound in red, to match the beads in her hair. Her little arms, poking out of the flounced sleeves, had goose bumps. "It's cold in here," Josie said, "I think you should be wearing a sweater."

Shalalla shrugged her shoulders. "Heat never come up tonight." She took a step closer, eyes bright with amusement, covering her mouth with her hand to hide a giggle. "Preacher got so mad he said 'damn.' "

Josie smiled. "Then you'd best put on a sweater or a coat."

"But I wants to show my dress," Shalalla explained, and, pointing her toe, "See my shoes and socks?" Josie nodded appreciatively at the black, patent-leather Mary Janes with lace-cuffed white socks.

"Miss Josie, we're playin' store," Antoinne told her, stacking dimes in a pile.

"We aren't playing nothing," Shalalla corrected him. "We're selling tapes of the choir. Want to buy one?"

" 'Member what Grandma said?" Antoinne pinched Shalalla's arm. "You're not s'posed to ask. Just s'posed to say Merry Christmas and wait and see if they buys one."

"Well, let me see . . ." Josie picked up a tape. She hadn't known that Cuba's choir had been enterprising enough to have tapes produced, or, more likely, judging from the look of them—the label had a typewritten quote ("In shady green pastures God leads His children along"), and a primitive drawing of a lamb sitting beside a cross—Cuba had made them herself. "How much are they?"

"Eight dollars. No tax," Shalalla said.

"Why, then I guess I'll take two." She thought Dozier would get a kick out of having one.

"That'll be sixteen, right?" Shalalla printed the figure in the notebook.

"Right. And I'm going to give you a twenty-dollar bill, so I'll get back . . . how many?"

Shalalla concentrated, biting her tongue. "That'd be four?"

"That's right."

"You be a teacher, Miss Josie?" Antoinne asked. "You always talks like a teacher."

"No, I'm just a mama and a grandma."

"Then how come you don't have childrens with you?"

Josie paused, wondering how to phrase her explanation, but Shalalla, showing a precocious social grace, reminded Antoinne, "Not s'posed to ask questions from the customers either."

Antoinne moved from foot to foot, indicating that he either had to go to the bathroom or had something exciting to say. "Guess what?" he blurted. "My mama come home. She come on the train this morning and she brought me stuff all the way from . . ."

"Philadelphia," Shalalla prompted.

"No. From . . ." The pencil in his cousin's hand jogged his memory. ". . . from Pencilannia."

"Pennsylvania's a state. Philadelphia's a city," Shalalla told him. "Philadelphia is *in* Pennsylvania, dummy."

"Shouldn't fuss in front of the customers, either," Josie said, sotto voce, dropping the tapes into her purse. "Tell your grandma to call me in the morning, will you?" Feeling a presence at her elbow, she added, "I think maybe this gentleman wants to buy a tape."

"Yes, I do." It was H.A. Staples. "And how are you this evening, Mrs. Tatternall?"

"Just fine. And you?"

"This is my wife, Constance"—H.A. touched the hand of a handsome woman with her hair ironed into a pageboy, wearing a tailored cream suit with a floral challis scarf draped over her shoulder—"and my daughter, Christine. Christine's home from

Howard University for the holidays." A young woman with a close-cropped Afro, dressed in a preppie skirt and navy blazer that didn't quite cover a T-shirt that said FREE ABU-JAMAL, said hello. Her features, potentially even prettier than her mother's, had an expression of amused condescension, as though she found this small-town Baptist church and its congregation too quaint for words. "I expected Cam would be here," H.A. said, and, turning to his wife. "Cam's Mrs. Tatternall's daughter. The old high-school friend I told you I'd bumped into at Orrie Gadsden's party the other night, remember?"

"Cam's come down with some sort of bug," Josie said, and lest H.A. inquire after the rest of the family, she looked around and added, "Nice turnout. I guess we'd best go in if we want a seat. Pleasure to meet you, Mrs. Staples, Christine. Merry Christmas. And children," she leaned across the card table and straightened Antoinne's bow tie, "don't forget to tell Cuba to call me first thing in the morning." After what had just happened, she knew her Christmas feast wasn't going to happen and she had four pies and a twenty-pound turkey to get rid of.

She turned to the stairs, thinking she'd be less likely to be seen if she sat in the balcony, but the staircase was so crowded as to present a fire hazard. The downstairs was packed, too, humming with whispered conversation. She paused, looking for a place, saying, "Excuse me" to a man in jeans who was toting a television camera, and the good-looking blonde she recognized from the local nightly newscast. She didn't like the notion of a TV camera in a church, but supposed nowadays people couldn't believe something had happened unless they saw it on TV. She inched down a side aisle, hands clutching elbows—Lord, it was chilly in here!—until a moon-faced black woman she thought she recognized moved over to make a space for her. Sliding into the pew, she muttered her thanks, trying to remember where she knew the woman from.

Maybe it was a sign of age, or maybe it was because the town was growing so fast, but she was always bumping into people she recognized but couldn't quite place. Then she remembered: the moon-faced woman was a teller at NationsBank, and the teenager sitting next to her, obviously her son, was the boy who sometimes mowed Josie's neighbor's lawn. She looked around surreptitiously and, thankfully, didn't see anyone else she knew. She was safe here.

Then she felt a prickly sensation at the back of her neck, and turning, saw Margaret Crosby, a member of her garden club who planted more gossip than azaleas, flanked by her husband and her bug-eyed daughter. Margaret gave her a smug little smile. So. Now the whole town would know that she'd been alone on Christmas Eve, and conjecture would sprout faster than Jack's beanstalk. She could imagine the conversations beginning with tutted sympathy—"She always tried to be a good mother, but . . ." Her cheeks burned and her throat tightened, imagining what might be said about her. What might be said about her girls hurt her even more. Thank God Bear wasn't alive!

But the root of her pain was not what others would say, but what she herself knew and feared. What if Evie kept running around with Jasper? What if anyone had seen Lila in that drunken state with that man—whoever he was (she'd combed her mind for possibilities but hadn't come up with any). She would never have guessed that Lila would be unfaithful to Orrie. How could the girl hurt the poor man so? Why would she take the risk of compromising her own reputation and wrecking Orrie's future? Because if it came out, it wouldn't just be local gossip; it would be statewide news. And who would have thought that Lila would be the catalyst for that awful fight? It was as though Lila were paying them all back for a lifetime of deeply held grudges Josie hadn't even known were there. And Cam. She'd known from the moment she'd seen her that something was wrong, but of course Cam hadn't seen fit to tell her. Cam had never confided in her, and she'd best face the fact that she never would. Thank goodness Reba had told her, in strictest confidence, that Cam was worried about her job and had just broken up with a man she was still in love with. Her intuition told her that there was even more to it, though it was hard to imagine what problem could top a failed love affair and financial insecurity. But now Cam had left—just as Bear had always left—without apology, probably without regret, without even a decent good-bye.

The pressure of Margaret Crosby's eyes almost made her want to shrink down so that she could not be seen. Cam always said it was superficial to care what people thought of you, but what was wrong with wanting the good opinion of your neighbors, or being proud of your reputation? It was a fine thing to rise above pride; but you had to *have pride* to do it.

Glancing across the center aisle, she saw Cuba's family. They took up an entire pew. As she looked at them she could hear Cuba's comments on each of them. Sitting closest to the center aisle was Thalia, Cuba's eldest, so much like her mother that she might as well have been a clone. A high-school principal, Thalia usually dressed conservatively, but tonight she was sporting a Carol Little ensemble in a jungle print. She'd been the first in the family to get a degree, but had never married. ("Smart as a tack, but unlucky in love. Part be her own fault—she won't hardly look at a man 'less he be a professional, an' how many black professional men you see lining the streets callin' out for a wife.") Josie guessed that the infant on Thalia's lap must belong to Cuba's eldest son, Russell, who sat next to her.

Both Russell and his wife, Eugenia, who was bending to whisper a warning into the ear of their fidgety six-year-old son, were stiff as mannequins in a department-store window. Russell wore a light-weight tan suit, suitable for either winter or summer; Eugenia in a beige shirtwaist with a cocoa blazer, showing no more flash than sizable engagement and wedding rings and gold-rimmed glasses. ("They be squeezed in the middle-middle class, like some two-hundred-pound woman trying to wear a waist cinch. Both workin' extra jobs 'cause they got to have a house with *two* bathrooms, they both got to have *new* cars, Russell got to have his computer. And half the time they forgets to give me anything for taking care of their childrens, an' you know how groceries do mount up.")

Shalalla's mother, Bernice, still so country that she was wearing a large "lady" hat, sat next to her fidgety nephew. In her late twenties, the best-looking of the bunch, she'd dropped out of college to marry a star basketball player who'd never made it into the big leagues. Now she was living back with Cuba, chasing her ex for child support, and studying to pass a civil-service exam. ("I tolt her that being good-lookin' could be more bad news than good, but did she listen?") Cuba's younger son, Seth, was beside Bernice, his dreadlocks tucked into a red, black, green, and yellow knitted cap, a ring in one ear. He was, Cuba said without apparent irony, her "black sheep"—arrested for possession, now on parole, living out of a van and peddling posters and handmade jewelry at concerts and county fairs. Next to Seth, a young woman who must be Alethea, Antoinne's mother, her hair braided and piled high, gold loops almost sweeping her shoulders, painted eyebrows raised to show she was there under sufferance ("She think she the queen of the Nile, her head held so high she don't see the leaks in her boat"). And finally, Cuba's father, who also lived with her, sitting ramrod straight but looking frail and ashy. Dear God, Josie thought, Cuba has raised five children, mostly by herself. She's buried two husbands, seen her son arrested, and now she's raising her grandchildren and taking care of her father. Who am I to complain? She turned her eyes to the altar.

The lights dimmed. A skinny woman in a pink dress with glasses as thick as the bottom of Coke bottles, her hair ironed into marcelled waves, came out from a side door behind the altar and took her place at the piano surrounded by pots of poinsettias and baskets of food. A big-bellied man followed her and sat down behind a set of drums. Shalalla and Antoinne scooted up the aisle and squeezed in next to their great-grandpa. Josie expected the choir to file out onto the altar, but nothing happened. A baby whimpered. Someone coughed. Children started to wiggle and whisper. Then, as though she'd purposely waited until the audience was off-guard so as to shock them into attention, Cuba's voice rang out from the rear of the church in a heartbreaking, powerful call: "Oh, Lord, you know I won't turn back . . ." (Josie remembered Cuba saying that the other choir members had wanted to start with "Silent Night" but either by force of personality, or because she'd done the lion's share of work sewing the new robes, Cuba had prevailed.) "Oh, Lord, you know I won't turn back . . . ," Cuba sang again. She was echoed by a deep baritone, then a pure as sunlight soprano repeated the call, as though they were singing out to one another across the marshes. The accompanist brought three resonant chords from the piano, and the choir started down the aisle, each carrying a lighted candle, their voices joined in harmony. Cuba, resplendent in her multicolored dashiki bound with gold tape, her head wrapped in a twist of matching fabric, led the way, chin thrust forward, so that her dewlap disappeared and she looked like a younger, stronger woman. As she passed Josie's pew she cut her eyes over to her for the briefest moment, taking it all in, and giving, though her expression hardly changed, a look of understanding. Josie swallowed hard. A white couple, obviously tourists, sitting in front of her, clapped their hands self-consciously in time to the music.

After placing the candles in a sand tray in front of the wooden cross, the choir arranged itself in a double semicircle. Cuba led them through hymn after hymn, each more confident and heartfelt than the last. Some of the congregation clapped along, others hummed or called assent. Some took off their sweaters and jackets. The emotional temperature also rose and Josie, alone in her thoughts, had a strange sensation: it was as though she were sitting at a campfire on a very dark night, protected not only by the animal warmth of the others, but by the realization that each and every one of them had hopes and fears, sorrows and joys, unique in their particulars, but somehow shared.

The choir swayed and hummed as Cuba raised her hand, and, in a sad and sonorous voice, said, "As we think about the birth of the baby Jesus, we also think about His mother. When she birthed Him this night, she didn't know what she'd have to face down the line, when they brought His body down from the cross and laid it in her arms. This night, her labor was over, and she held Him in her arms, all squallin' and new—and all she felt was joy. You mothers out there you knows what I mean." The drummer beat a swift, syncopated rhythm and the choir rocked into a vibrant, joyful reggae: "Mary had a little baby, yes, she did, yes, she did . . ." Josie was smiling, hands folded in her lap, her head down. It wasn't until she felt a tear drop onto her hand that she realized she was weeping. She reached into her purse and, not finding a handkerchief, wiped her cheeks with her index finger. The moon-faced woman pressed a pocket-size package of Kleenex into her hand and patted it. Josie felt no sense of embarrassment, only a gratitude that further opened the floodgates. Her tears flowed silently and easily, washing her clean, releasing all her heartache like a long, gentle sigh. She understood it all. And she could forgive them all. She could even forgive herself, because, after all, as Dozier had said, she'd done the best she could.

Sixteen

"Eureka!" Reba yelled when she saw the lights of the ramshackle country store with a deserted fruit stand at the side and a single gas pump in front. "It looks like something out of a horror movie, but at least it's open. I was afraid we were going to run out of gas and have to sleep in a ditch." Cam had said she didn't want to get on the highway so they'd been driving on back roads to Charleston for over an hour.

"I'll get the windshield, you get the gas," Cam said as they rolled up and got out. Slapping at her left buttock, which had developed pins and needles, Reba squinted at the self-serve instructions. "When I was a kid, men in little caps and bow ties used to run out and do all this for you," she complained, struggling with the nozzle.

"Yeah. Yeah. When you were a kid you could get candy for a nickel and everybody who graduated from high school could read." Cam yawned, pressed her hands into the small of her back, and looked up at the moon above the piney woods. " 'That is the land of lost content, I see it shining plain, The happy highways where I went, And cannot come again.' "

"You make that up?"

"Hardly. Think it's A. E. Housman. In high school I had this tough old English teacher who thought memorization was a mental discipline. Made us learn poems and famous speeches. We hated her for it, but you know, they're about the only things I can quote. When we get back on the road, I'll give you Lincoln's Gettysburg Address."

"I don't think you can top your rendition of 'Me and Bobby McGee,' but you can try." Not wanting to talk about their swift and unhappy departure, they'd been singing ever since they'd left Josie's house—working their way through the Beatles, Joni Mitchell, Bob Dylan, the Supremes, moving back to Gershwin, Porter, Berlin, and, finally, harmonizing on patriotic songs and TV jingles.

"I'm not going to take sarcasm from a Jew who can't remember 'Hava Nagila.' " Cam bent forward and stared at the ground next to the pump. "There's a bucket of water here, but no sponge. Guess I'll go get some paper towels from the ladies' room. You want anything?"

"I was saving my appetite for tomorrow's sumptuous feast but I guess I might as well break down and have a Snickers."

"Look, I'm sorry we had to leave."

"Hey, it's all right. I mean, I thought I was going to be in a production of *The Christmas Carol*, but it turns out I'm in a remake of *Thelma and Louise*."

"You think we shouldn't have left?"

"Not like that. Not without even saying good-bye to your mother."

"I told her I was leaving before I went upstairs. And when we came back down they'd all gone to church. What were we going to do? Stick around for the next round? I mean, Reba, both Jasper and Lila were so rude to you and—"

"Cam." Reba got the nozzle into the tank and pushed up the lever to start the gas pumping. "I cater upscale soirées, remember?

If I got my feathers ruffled every time some drunk insulted me . . . okay, they may do it with a little more style in New York, but hey, what's the diff? A drunk with a chip on his shoulder is a drunk with a chip on his shoulder."

"I'm sorry."

"It wasn't your fault."

Cam was grim. "Right. For once it wasn't my fault."

"I mean, you weren't the one who was boozed up."

"Yes, that was an unexpected reversal. Jasper's always lit up, but Lila? I've told you she's always been Miss Priss. And to disappear like that, then turn up drunk after she'd clearly been out with some guy? It's crack-up time. But I still don't understand why she took it out on me. She and I have had some major fights in the past, but I thought she'd forgiven and forgotten."

"Hey, the grass may grow and the flowers may sprout, but nobody ever forgets where they buried the hatchet." The trigger of the nozzle kicked back in Reba's hand. "What the hell's wrong with this?"

"Don't clutch it, just apply steady pressure."

"Oh, like you know a lot about not clutching and being steady," Reba teased.

"Here, I'll pump the gas, you go pay and get us something to drink."

"What do you want?"

"I'll decide when I come in. I have to use the ladies' anyway."

By the time Cam went into the sloppy little store, Reba was already deep in a conversation with the lank-haired female clerk behind the counter. Cam nodded hello and looked around for the RESTROOM sign. The woman said, "You gotta have the key," and held up same, tied to a piece of wood almost as big as a walking stick. Cam took it and headed toward the back of the store, passing a stand of girlie magazines, *TV Guides*, tabloids devoted to murders, incest, 350-pound Siamese twins, nine-year-old pregnant girls, and the ever-pressing question of "What Does Oprah Want?" There were wire racks of paperbacks and country-and-western tapes, a spattered HELP YOURSELF counter with Styrofoam cups, a pot of coffee the color of tar, paper napkins, packets of sugar, Cremora, relish and catsup, a two-gallon container of neon-yellow mustard, and hot dogs like huge, diseased fingers revolving on a spit in a plexiglass heat box. The restroom reeked of Lysol and stale cigarette smoke. The rusted "Sani-seat for Your Protection!" container on the wall was empty. Not trusting what she knew to be true—that your chances of contracting a disease from a toilet seat were about a million to one—she heard Josie's early warnings and used the last of the paper towels to cover the commode. After washing her hands with several squirts of foul-smelling industrial-strength pink soap, she shook off the water, dried her hands on the seat of her pants, and started back toward the cash register, this time going down an aisle crammed with canned corn, Chef Boyardee SpaghettiOs, chili, evaporated milk, cold remedies, No-Doz, Pampers, potato chips, pork rinds, and Cracker Jacks, and a stand-up freezer crammed with Popsicles, six-packs of beer, Coke, Eskimo Pies, busted boxes of fried chicken, and milk, which was what she was looking for. She reached to the back of the shelf, checked the date on a quart carton, and carried it up to the cash register.

"You'd be surprised," the clerk was saying to Reba. "Quite a few folk driving through, even on Christmas Eve. Some, you know, jes' needin' to get out of the house for a bit, but others . . . Hey, a man I know drives a hire car come through 'bout ten minutes ago, carrying some outta town fella all the way from Walterboro to the Charleston airport. Fella come down for some family do and there was some kinda bust-up an' the fella's cousin wouldn't take him to the airport." She shrugged as though she understood chaos to be the natural order of things, her ice blue eyes wandering back to the tiny TV perched above her head in the rack of cigarettes.

"You aren't afraid being here alone?" Reba asked.

"Well, sure. All kinda holdups and murders in convenience stores, but . . ." Without taking her eyes from the TV, she reached underneath the counter and pulled out a gun. Seeing Cam wince, she put it back, said, "Didn't mean to scare you ladies," and started toting up the bill. "Including gas, that'll be forty-one-fifty."

"Forty-one-fifty!" Cam gasped.

"Well, now, thirty for the gas, four for these li'l ol' flags, three for the snuff . . ."

Cam stared at the mess on the counter: two miniature Confederate flags, a couple of tins of Peach Tree snuff, a package of something called Road Kill Snack.

"Souvenirs," Reba explained with a hunch of her shoulders. "And this Snickers bar and a pack of Marlboros."

"And the milk." The woman snapped open a brown paper bag, held it at the edge of the counter, and scooped in everything except the quart of milk, which Cam was still holding. "You gonna drink that now?"

Cam nodded.

"Mostly it's men an' kids that be into milk. I s'pect it's because they weren't proper breastfed. Got this trucker comes through—looks like Sylvester Stallone—but he downs 'bout a gallon of milk standin' right here in front of me—but most women, they won't be into milk less they're pregnant. Don't want the calories. I know when I was carryin' Erika I jest couldn't get enough. Craved milk and ice cream. Hell I woulda eaten chalk, any damned thing that . . ."

"Gave you calcium," Cam said as Reba pulled bills from her wallet and shifted her weight, showing that she was anxious to leave.

"Don't know about that, but I sure did crave milk." The woman gave them their change and a tired smile. "Merry Christmas. Now you girls take care."

"Thanks, we will," Reba said over her shoulder.

"Good God!" Cam shuddered as they walked into the night. "Have you ever seen anything like the crap in that store?"

"Yeah. Everything that you'd need to sustain a life that'd make you want to kill yourself."

"Want me to take over now?"

"No. I'll keep on," Reba said, getting into the driver's seat and snapping her seatbelt shut.

"And you know what's crazy?" Cam asked, prying open the quart of milk and taking a long swallow.

"It was *all* crazy, Cam," Reba told her, flipping on the high beams and pulling on to the darkened country road.

"She was right. I usually don't like milk, but I really craved this. Isn't it amazing that the hormones would kick in this fast?"

Reba nodded glumly. "Okay if I turn on the radio?"

"Please don't," Cam said. "You most likely won't be able to get anything except Christmas carols and I'd either scream or cry if I heard a Christmas carol right now." They rode on in silence, Cam deep in thought, sipping the milk. "You think it was wrong to leave like that, don't you?" she asked suddenly.

"You already asked me that. It didn't seem fair to punish your mother."

"I wasn't punishing my mother. I just couldn't stand to be there any longer. I mean, they insulted you, too."

"I told you, Cam, we didn't have to leave because of me."

Cam knew Reba meant it. "I just couldn't . . . I mean, the state I'm in . . ."

"Hey, I'm not on your case. You asked, I told you."

Cam finished off the milk, wiped her upper lip, and turned. "You're right," she said in a dull voice. "Leaving like that. Mama's the one who'll feel it most, and I wasn't even mad at Mama. In fact, I had more loving feelings for her than I've had since I was a kid. The other morning, when I was in the house alone, I started to think about all she's been through."

"So, she'll forgive you," Reba reassured, seeing her miserable expression. "She's a mother."

"You mean that's part of the job description? Because if it is I'm not going to be qualified. In fact, I'm not qualified personally, financially, or socially."

"But you're still thinking about going ahead with it?"

"I don't know. Yesterday I thought absolutely. Today I've been . . ." She shook her head. "I don't think I've ever been this miserable. I just don't know. 'Course, if I go through with it, Mama will have to deal with that too. Poor Mama. She's always had to forgive everyone. I used to think that was so weak of her."

"Even when she forgave your father?" Seeing that would take a while to sink in, Reba went on, "Sometimes I think forgiveness is weak, you know, just a way of manipulating the wrongdoer so they're in your debt. But I don't think that's the case with Josie. I think she's just loving, maybe in a way that people like you and me can't be."

"God, they were so mismatched," Cam said. "Daddy off in the wild blue yonder, while Mama was worrying about school lunches. I always wanted to be like him. Always thought she was the one who brought him down. But lately I've started thinking, Mama could have made lots of men happy, but Daddy? He should never have gotten married. No woman could ever satisfy him. Ugh." She shuddered. "Marriage is the pits." She slumped down, folding her arms around her chest, leaning her head on the back of the seat, her chin thrust forward, her lips tight, her eyes mere slits as she stared through the windshield. Like a boxer with a glass jaw, Reba thought.

"Listen, Cam, I didn't mean to make you feel bad. In fact, don't feel bad. I know Josie will forgive you because I had a long talk with her this afternoon while you were sleeping."

Cam sat up. "You what?"

"All right, so be pissed at me. She was worried about you so I told her—"

"You *told* her!"

"Not about the pregnancy, idiot. I just told her that you were having troubles at work and that you and Sam had broken up. I mean, the woman's not stupid. She knew something was wrong and you weren't telling her anything, so it seemed only fair to relieve her mind by giving her some of the facts." Cam opened her mouth but didn't say anything. "And don't get on my case," Reba warned, "because if you'd been in my place, you would've done the same thing. And once you think about it, I bet you'll thank me."

Cam considered this. Though she didn't like the idea of Reba and Josie talking about her, she had to admit that it gave her a sense of relief. In fact, she was downright grateful. "Okay, so you talked to her. I guess that was all right."

"And I also called information in Atlanta. Sam's listed," Reba said quickly.

Cam's eyes flashed. "Well, haven't you been a busy little bee."

"And . . ." Reba took a breath. "I talked to him."

"You what!"

"So call me a buttinski! So tell me I've ruined our friendship!"

Reba threw up her hands in exasperation. "So say you'll never forgive me!"

"Dammit, Reba, keep your hands on the wheel!"

"Don't worry about me. I only look like I'm out of control, whereas you look like you're in control, but I know and you know you're not."

Cam was seething. "So," she got out, mimicking Reba's voice, " 'I talked to Sam.' When did you call Sam and what did you tell him?"

"I called him when I went upstairs, 'cause I knew we'd be leaving. I told him we were at your mother's and we'd be rolling into Atlanta sometime tomorrow." A pause. "He sounded excited about it." A longer pause. "So. Either you can call and tell him we're not coming, or you can reach into that glove compartment and get out the maps to Atlanta. Now will you peel that Snickers bar for me?"

PART *Two*

Seventeen

"High of fifty-three today and the weatherman says we'll have clear skies throughout the holiday." Mary Gebhardt shuffled the cards and turned to her sister-in-law, Esther, who was visiting from Cleveland and had been brought along to make a fourth for the game. "Sure beats last year. You wouldn't have believed last year. It rained the whole damned holiday."

"It surely did," Peatsy remembered, rearranging the cardigan of her magenta twin set. "And there I was with tubes jabbed into me like banderillas stuck into a bull. Lord, what a time." She gathered up her cards, fanned them in front of her face with her usual geishalike coyness and turned to look at Josie, who was coming from the kitchen to the sun porch with a coffee carafe in one hand and a teapot in the other. "Josie, come sit. I can't hardly win if my partner's not paying attention."

"For dessert," Josie offered, "I have rum balls, pecan sandies, or Pomona. Do you have a sweet tooth, Esther?"

Esther, whose size suggested that she probably did, asked, "What's Pomona?"

"It's mixed fruit and nuts, sort of like an old-fashioned sugarplum," Peatsy told her. "Takes about half a day to make so nobody but Josie bothers to fix it anymore."

"I'd love some," Mary sighed, reaching into her purse for her packet of Nicorette gum, "but since I've quit smoking I've gained at least ten pounds."

"Oh, Mary." Peatsy shook her head. "First you slapped those nicotine patches all over your body, and you were allergic to them and swelled up like a poisoned pup, and now you're chompin' on this drug gum that's going to yank out your fillings. If you weren't such a hardheaded Yankee, you'd know you're too old to reform."

"My doctor told me . . ."

"And a year ago my doctor gave me a few days to live, then," Peatsy laughed, "when he saw how much money he was making, he decided to stretch it out a little longer. What do doctors know?"

"Oh, Peatsy, you're so cynical," Mary admonished her. "You can't say you didn't get the best medical care. Those doctors saved your life."

"Sure I got the best medical care. But how's somebody I've just met gonna know more about my body than I've been able to figure out in . . ." Able to face all harsh realities except her actual age, Peatsy stopped short, then added, ". . . in a lifetime. Josie, will you sit down! You see, Esther, Josie spent most of her life waiting hand and foot on her husband and children, and when they were out of the way she couldn't get out of the habit, so she opened a bed-and-breakfast."

"The main reason I started taking in paying guests," Josie explained, "was because I didn't want to give up the house and I needed the money." She knew most people, Peatsy included, would tell you about their sex lives before they'd tell you about their finances, and there had been a time when she'd have been embarrassed to admit she was having money troubles. But lately she'd become much less hesitant about speaking the truth on any and all subjects. "I'd built up quite a good clientele," she told Esther, "but so much has happened in the last year that I've had to turn down most of my guests, and I don't know if I have the energy to start it up again."

Mary nodded. "This last year has been an awful roller coaster ride for you, Josie."

"Like *Days of Our Lives* on fast forward," Peatsy put in.

"Josie's mother died right after New Years," Mary told Esther. "Then . . ."

"Oh, let's not get into all that," Peatsy insisted.

"I'm sorry to hear you lost your mother," Esther said to Josie.

"She didn't *lose* her," Peatsy corrected. "I hate it when people say you 'lost' someone—like they were a package you misplaced or something. Mawmaw *died.* And it was a blessed relief."

"It *was* a blessed release," Josie said, trying to smooth things over. "My mother was very old and we'd been expecting her to go for a long time."

"Still . . ." Esther began. Afraid that any conventional expressions of condolence would bring about another outburst from Peatsy, she smiled and looked around. "You certainly do have a beautiful house and garden here, Josie. I can see where you'd attract a lot of guests."

"Why, thank you," Josie said. "I confess I am proud of it, but it's way too big for a single person."

Peatsy raised her eyebrows. "Single person? Dozier's here 'most every time I come around."

"Yes, he is," Josie said blithely. "More coffee, Esther?"

"And I predict you'll start up with the paying guests again," Peatsy said, " 'cause you'll never get out of the habit of waiting on other people."

"It's not just a habit," Josie told her, "or, if it is, it's a habit I choose to continue." Since serving people was so alien to Peatsy's nature, Josie didn't expect her to understand the special satisfaction she found in doing it.

"Josie, sit!" Peatsy ordered again. "I can't spend all afternoon lolling around here trying to extort pin money from you girls. I've got things to do, places to go, people to meet. Waring . . . that's my son, my only child," she informed Esther, "Waring, and his friend, Alonzo, have already arrived and they're expecting guests from D.C.—some couple in the antique business. I guess they'll all be scampering around my house asking cute, cryptic questions, trying to figure out what they can sell once I've croaked."

Josie said, "Peatsy, that's not fair. Waring has never given any indication that he's—"

"Of course he hasn't given any *indication,*" Peatsy said indignantly. "After all, I brought him up to be a gentleman. But it's only natural for him to wonder about the division of the spoils. I know I did when my elders and betters were about to shuffle off this mortal coil. And it's only natural for those who are about to exit to want to hold on to the final trump card. I don't mind Waring pawing the chiffonniers and hefting the silver. He's going to get everything in the house. What he doesn't know"—she rearranged the cards—"is that I've left everything except the furnishings to the United Negro College Fund."

Mary was incredulous. "You have?"

"Maybe I have, and maybe I haven't." Peatsy put on her Mona Lisa smile. "You all will just have to wait and see."

"Peatsy, you were born a tease and you'll die a tease," Josie chastised her. She suspected Peatsy was just tweaking Esther and Mary because they were Yankees; then again, even after a lifetime of association, it was impossible to guess what Peatsy might do.

"But don't you worry, Josie," Peatsy drawled, her eyes twinkling over the top of her hand. "I'm leaving you that silver tea service you've always admired, and also that bronze statue you're so fond of. Never did understand why you love that statue so. Can't imagine why you'd identify with a bare-breasted girl carrying a torch."

"Imagining what other people feel has never been your strong suit," Josie said lightly.

Esther, not being able to determine what was serious and what was a joke, said, "I think I will try a piece of that . . . Pomona, is it? And maybe just one rum ball."

"You can't have just one ball. Balls come in pairs." Peatsy laughed. "Hey, have you heard the joke about Marilyn Monroe after she married Arthur Miller?" None had. "Miller, of course, was a Jew, and Miller's mother served matzoh ball soup, and Marilyn said, 'Matzoh ball soup! I've never had it before. What do you do with the rest of the matzoh?' "

"Peatsy!" Mary pretended to be shocked.

"Oh, come on, Mary. It's a little late in life to be pretending we can't tell the difference between a jock strap and a slingshot. And talking about sex . . ."

"Were we?" Esther asked, shy but titillated.

"A couple of weeks ago this little grandniece of mine came to see me because she's planning to get married. We talked about her wedding plans and all, because you know and I know that staging a wedding is pretty much akin to mounting a Broadway production—but after I'd wet her down with a couple of bourbons she asked me"—Peatsy shook her head—"she asked me about orgasms. Would you believe it? I figured girls of her generation would know. But then I pulled back and thought, why should they? I mean, they've got their sex education classes and they're always yammering about it on TV, but it's not something you learn about in a class or the TV, now is it? Turns out she was ignorant as a boiled egg. She's gone to bed with him a few times but she didn't feel anything like she thought she would. But she's still crazy to marry him. Besides, the invitations have already gone out. So I told her, 'Darlin', maybe you'll feel it and maybe you won't, but if you don't, just roll your eyes back in your head and act like you're havin' a little asthma attack.' 'But,' she says, all indignant, 'that would be dishonest.' 'Get real,' I told her—that's what they say these days—'Get real.' 'Fakin' it is one of the few advantages a woman has. 'Cause a man can't hardly bear to think he can't satisfy a woman—though most never care enough to learn how to do it, and the few who do can make your life hell.' "

Josie laughed. If anyone had thought that Peatsy's brush with death was going to reform or soften her, or, as Mary put it, "put her in touch with her spiritual side," they'd been sadly disappointed. As soon as she'd recovered, Peatsy had made some changes in her life: she'd gone, with Waring and Alonzo in tow, on a trip to Paris. Upon returning home, she'd had her house painted and her living room furniture reupholstered and she'd bought a little dog—a miniature purebred something-or-other she'd christened Scarlett, who, true to her namesake, trotted about with eyes bright and well-groomed tail wagging but refused to be housebroken. (Josie had finally had to ask Peatsy not to bring the animal with her because it piddled on her carpets, and Peatsy had not taken too kindly to the request.) Peatsy now went to the beauty parlor not once, but twice, a week. And she was planning another trip, to London for the new theater season. Other than that . . .

Josie held the carafe over Peatsy's cup and asked, "More coffee?"

"No. Would you have the makings of a vodka tonic?"

"I'll check."

"I know it's a summer drink," Peatsy called after her, as Josie started into the kitchen, "but who knows if I'll be here next summer? So if you have the makings . . ."

Josie put the carafe and teapot on the sink, filled a glass with ice, cut a wedge of lemon, and started into the dining-room liquor cabinet, but paused as she heard Mary's voice saying, "Yes, almost a year to the day. Right here where we're sitting now. We were in the middle of a rubber and Peatsy just collapsed, flung herself right across the table . . ." Josie moved to the window that overlooked the sun porch, standing where she could see but not be seen, as Mary continued, "I'll never forget the look on Edna's face and the sound of all the coins hitting the floor. Edna grabbed Peatsy's feet and I grabbed her shoulders—or maybe it was the other way 'round—in any event"—Mary started to giggle—"we struggled into the living room to lay her on the couch, arguing about whether we should move her, frightened we were going to drop her."

Peatsy laughed too. "I bet you *did* drop me and you just never admitted it."

"Almost," Mary agreed. "I remember thinking you were like fine bone china and if we dropped you, you'd shatter. But Josie was marvelous. It was almost as if she were clairvoyant. She was on the phone to 911 before we even got Peatsy off the sun porch. Then Edna started fussing at me about smoking and I was on the verge of tears and Josie was trying to calm us down and then the emergency rescue people came in and Edna . . ." Mary stopped laughing and chewed reflectively on her gum. "Oh, poor Edna. I mean, who would have thought that you . . ."

"Mmmm. Who would've thought that I'd pull through and Edna would be gone inside a couple of months. February, wasn't it?"

Mary nodded. "Mid-February. I remember because Cam got married in Atlanta on Valentine's Day, and Dozier had to call Josie and tell her to come home."

Josie stepped back from the window. What a time it had been! She really had felt as though she'd been strapped into a roller coaster. She had no sooner lain Mawmaw to rest than she'd got a call from Cam confessing that the real reason she hadn't attended the funeral was not, as she'd originally said, because she was stricken with a virus but because she was six weeks pregnant, had breakthrough bleeding, and been ordered to bed by her gynecologist. Josie had barely had time to recover from that news when Cam had told her that she'd quit her job, was leaving New York for Atlanta, and that she and Sam planned to be married on Valentine's Day ("Sam's idea. He's a hopeless romantic"). They wanted Josie to be present ("When I say 'immediate family' I mean immediate. Just you.").

Sam had picked Josie up at the airport, striding toward her as though he already knew her, planting a kiss on her cheek, and getting right to the nub of it by saying, "Thank God you're here. Cam's a wreck." She intuited that Sam was, by nature, as reticent as she, but circumstances pushed both of them into an uncharacteristic openness. On the drive to his apartment, he'd talked about Cam—laconically, and certainly not uncritically, but with such affection and humor that she knew he loved her difficult daughter almost as much as she did. She expressed fears to him that she'd withheld from Cam, but he assured her they had a doctor who specialized in late-life pregnancies and he, Sam, planned to pamper her throughout.

After depositing her in his apartment—an expensive, prefurnished bachelor high-rise that would have been bare as an executive office had it not been crammed with boxes of Cam's belongings, which Reba and her friend, Cheryl, had been good enough to cart down from New York in a large U-Haul—Sam kissed both Josie and Cam good-bye and went back to work. Cam, strained and listless, but obviously happy to see her, suggested they go shopping. Cam still hadn't found a suitable wedding outfit and she and Josie'd shopped for hours. Josie, remembering the disappointment of her own wedding costume, had suggested something flowing and full-length, but Cam, neurotically concerned that she might be "showing," had rejected anything festive. ("If I'm a blushing bride, I'm blushing for all the wrong reasons.") Finally, they'd selected a pale yellow silk suit with a tailored, hip-length jacket and slim skirt. Reba and Cheryl, who met them for afternoon tea, presented Cam with a set of lipstick-red underwear. "You've already got something old—your birth certificate—and something new—your new life in Atlanta—and something borrowed—I can't imagine you'll ever do anything more than borrow respectability—and you've had enough blues—the blues are all over for you, so red," Reba'd explained.

That night, as Josie had tried to sleep on Sam's living-room couch, she'd heard him get up to take Cam water and soda crackers to settle her stomach, heard them talking quietly, and had a surge of optimism. They were going to be all right.

The next morning they'd gathered at the courthouse: Cam quaky, Sam resolute, Reba sailing through with a quirky smile, Cheryl wiping away sentimental tears, and an old Navy pal of Sam's, appropriately called Buddy, providing the ballast. They'd had an elegant lunch at the Ritz-Carlton, Cam hoeing into the salmon and caviar, Reba making wisecracks, Sam looking relieved, and Buddy so blissfully unaware after the first bottle of champagne that he'd made a pass at freckle-faced Cheryl.

Sam was treating Reba and Cheryl to a few nights at the hotel, and Josie was supposed to stay at Sam's apartment, unpacking and arranging Cam's things while Cam and Sam went on a two-week honeymoon in Italy. But that very evening, Dozier had called to say Edna had been admitted to the hospital.

"Cam and her husband offered to give up their honeymoon and come help, but Josie told them not to because it didn't look that serious," Josie heard Mary say. "I mean, who would have thought that Edna was in bad shape? Because if there was ever anybody who'd tell you how they were feeling, it was Edna. But nobody, not even her husband, guessed that she was ill."

"What did she die of?" Esther asked.

"Perforated peptic ulcer," Mary explained. "She was only in the hospital for a week or so, and Josie was planning to bring her home and nurse her here, but then complications set in and she went"—Mary snapped her fingers—"like that."

"Edna was always decisive," Peatsy said. "I have to congratulate her on a nice, clean exit."

Josie braced her hands on the dining-room table and bent her head. She may have been clairvoyant where Peatsy's heart attack had been concerned, but she hadn't even suspected that Edna had any major health problems, though when she and Dozier had spoken to Edna's doctor, they'd found out that Edna had been under treatment for some time. Also, unbeknownst to either of them, Edna had already made a living will. The night before she was to have surgery she'd told Josie that she was ready to go and asked her to take care of Dozier. Josie had put her arms around her and told her, as she'd fully believed, that she was being silly, she'd be up and around in no time. Just as Josie'd predicted, the operation was pronounced a success. There'd been talk of releasing Edna within days. Then pneumonia had set in.

It had all happened so fast that Josie had been in a state of dazed disbelief. Seventy-two hours of round-the-clock vigils, Edna surrounded by hissing respirators, multicolored electronic signals, beeping monitors . . . then the final word coming around dawn, no more than a half hour after she, Dozier, and Edna's son, Skip, her daughter, Marilyn, and her husband had left the hospital and come back to her place after an all-night watch. They'd been in Josie's kitchen, deciding whether she should make them an early breakfast or if they'd be better off getting some sleep when the phone had rung and the doctor had told them.

Dozier had been immobilized with shock and grief; neither Marilyn nor Skip knew their way around Beaufort anymore, so Josie had taken over. It was a time of chores and crowds, burial arrangements to be made, food to be prepared, hands to be shaken.

It wasn't until a day after the funeral, when she'd woken up in the middle of the night and thought, "I must remember to tell Edna . . . ," that reality had hit her. She'd cried out her sister's name in the pleading voice she'd had over sixty years ago, when Edna would race ahead and leave her behind on the way home from school. Edna hadn't stopped then and Josie's sobs couldn't bring her back now.

The next morning, when Dozier came over for breakfast, she told him. "I know," he said, draining his coffee. "Several times a day I remind myself to tell her this or that. Even found myself calling out to tell her I was home when I came back from the gas station yesterday. Marilyn was upstairs going through some of Edna's things and she heard me. She got all shook up. Thought I was losing it. You know, Marilyn's got that marvelous practical streak Edna has—I mean *had*—there I go, getting my tenses mixed up again . . ."

"Oh, that happens to everyone."

"I know that. But Marilyn . . . as I was saying, she's got Edna's practical streak, but sometimes she lacks imagination."

And sensitivity, Josie thought. The idea that anyone, especially his daughter, would be critical of Dozier, who'd borne up with such manly grace! "She ought to realize that when you've lived with someone for more'n half your life . . ." Hearing incipient indignation in her voice, she said more softly, "I don't know if you ever get over it. Bear's been gone all these years and sometimes I still hear him in my head. Or I'll be at the store and see something he'd fancy, like a Porterhouse steak, and I'll almost put it in my shopping cart."

"Would you please top off this coffee?"

"I was about to mix up a batch of blueberry pancakes. Will they all be coming over for breakfast soon?"

"I don't think so. Skip's tribe are packing up. Said they'd like to get on the road back home. But Skip's staying for another day so he can talk to the lawyer about the lease on Edna's shop."

Josie noticed how tired he looked. "I'm glad he's going to take care of that for you."

"And Marilyn says she'd going down to the shop to help the girl take inventory."

I bet she'll take more than inventory, Josie thought as she refilled his cup. "And you?"

"You know what I'd really like to do?"

"Eat a stack of blueberry pancakes?"

"Sure. And then . . ." He touched her hand as she poured herself a cup of coffee and sat down. "If the weather holds, I went by Buds 'N Bloom yesterday. Walked around their greenhouse for damned near an hour, so I felt obliged to buy something." He gave her a sheepish grin. "Hell, Josie, I went wild. Bought every new strain of spring bulb they had. Spent about a hundred dollars." He shook his head and passed his hand through his hair. "A hundred dollars! Bought tulips, iris, narcissus. Partly bought them because of their names: Gold-throated Trumpet, Lady Murasaki's Dream."

She nodded. "I bought a lipstick a couple of months ago just because it was called Spiced Peach."

"So. Think you'd have time to garden this afternoon?"

"Prob'ly. I'm expecting some guests around two."

Dozier stared into the mid-distance and she thought he was

going to say something profound, but after some rumination he said, "You've lost a lot of money on your guests over the last couple of weeks. And the money is the least of what I owe you."

She said, "Pay it no never-mind, Dozier," though, in fact, the bills had been piling up.

He sighed. "Would you think it was awful if I said I'll be glad when the kids and grandkids are gone?"

"I surely would." She feigned shock, then smiled. "But I'd completely understand. I'll fix those pancakes now."

She was as relieved as he when Skip, Marilyn, and their families left. At Dozier's request, she and Cuba went over to pack up Edna's clothing and other belongings. They made four piles: one for things that Dozier might, upon consideration, want to keep, the other three for her, Cuba, and the Goodwill. "Looks pretty well scavenged already," Cuba grunted, handing Josie a jewelry box as they stood in Edna and Dozier's bedroom. "And," Cuba added dryly, rummaging through the closet, "I see Miss Edna's fur coat and hat be gone." Josie said it was only natural that Marilyn would want most of her mother's things. Cuba hunched her shoulders and said, "Uh-huh. Just wonder if when we be cleaning out the sideboard in the dining room, we don't find Mr. Dozier be eatin' wif' plastic knifes and forks." Josie laughed and said that was a possibility, but she knew Dozier wouldn't care. Lots of people were fond of declaring that they didn't care about material things, but, she knew, Dozier really *didn't* care. Though he'd worked like a demon to made a success of the lumber business he'd inherited, he'd always handed over the bulk of his earnings to Edna, and just kept out enough for books and tools.

Josie had found little she'd wanted in the treasures her sister had amassed. Edna, thinking reminders of the past were sentimental, had already given her most of Mawmaw's memorabilia. Josie took only a tarnished gold brooch of hands clasped in friendship (which, apparently, Marilyn had found unworthy), and a box of early photographs, which Edna had always been meaning to put into albums, but never had. Sorting through them, she'd come across one that made her tear up: she, Edna, and Mawmaw, at the beach, in old-fashioned bathing suits; Mawmaw, holding an umbrella, squinting angrily against the sun; Edna (who must've been around eleven), protected by Mawmaw's arm, bumps showing through the chest of her tank suit; and she—Josie—standing one step behind, holding a sand pail close to her crotch, looking isolated and confused. She kept that photo, but pasted the others into an album, which she put on a top shelf in Dozier's library, thinking Dozier might give it to his grandchildren.

Following his children's departure, Dozier rattled around, tying up the loose ends of Edna's business, paying off doctors and lawyers. Determined not to give in to grief, or to lean on Josie as his sole source of companionship, he made a concerted effort to keep busy: he joined the Friends of the Library, volunteered to teach a class on furniture restoration at the Episcopal church, drove up to visit Marilyn and her family, but came back after less than a week, telling Josie, "They eat in front of TV." He turned down countless dinner invitations from divorcees and widows (Peatsy chief among them); then accepted an invitation to a college reunion, but decided not to go at the last minute. Josie noted, with some concern, that he was taking afternoon naps and wasn't always clean-shaven when he came though her back door for breakfast, though, trying to be cheerful, he usually greeted her with, "Wake up and smell the coffee." Since there was just the two of them, they often talked about all the others—the parents, mates, and children—the living and the dead who'd shaped their lives. Like most men, Dozier was reluctant to start intimate conversations, but if she slid into them slowly, he'd join in, and seemed to find some relief in talking. Sometimes they'd have tea, or even a drink, in the late afternoon, and if she didn't have guests, she'd usually convince him to stay for supper. More rarely, he'd treat her to hamburgers at Shoney's, and once in a while, they'd dress up and drive into Savannah for Sunday brunch at the DeSoto Hilton.

In late May, Lila, being on the Arts Council, gave them some tickets for the Spoleto Festival. Thinking it would be too tiring to drive back to Beaufort after a full day and evening in Charleston, they decided to spend the night at a hotel, and, shocked by inflated rates for the Festival, concluded that it was only common sense to reserve a single room. With twin beds.

The weather was balmy and they were so elated to be going on a trip, if only seventy miles away, that they acted like tourists, taking a carriage tour and smiling at one another as their guide, a hefty young woman in white shirt and too-tight gray slacks that were supposed to be a replica of a Confederate uniform, told cute but inaccurate stories about the city and the Civil War. They went to an art show they both thought was trash, then walked through an old church graveyard, wandering away from one another, Dozier drawn to the monuments of famous men, Josie bending low to see the small, overgrown headstones that marked the graves of children. As the sun was starting to go down, the sound of an organ playing Bach's *Toccata and Fugue* drew them into the empty church. They sat in a back pew, the marvelous music swirling about them. Knowing that they had dinner reservations, and remembering how uncomfortable any departure from a planned schedule had made Bear (unless he was off on one of his cut-loose toots), she gave Dozier a questioning look. "It's like a command performance," he whispered. She nodded agreement and sat back, relishing the music and watching the light change in the stained-glass windows. Dozier was so easy, so spontaneous. It was like being with your best friend. But not quite.

They stayed for the entire rehearsal, looking up and nodding a speechless thanks to the organist as he'd packed up his scores. Since they'd gotten back to the hotel late, whatever embarrassment they might have felt changing into their evening clothes had been ignored in the rush to get to the jazz concert on time.

After the concert they'd shuffled their way out of the departing crowd. "Nothing like a concert of Duke Ellington hits," she'd said. "That sax player—"

"He was good, but that organ music this afternoon," he'd said, taking her arm, "you can't beat serendipity. Would you like to go to that restaurant Lila recommended?"

"Not unless it's in the next block" she told him. She was wearing the teal blue jersey dress with matching heels that she'd worn to Cam's wedding. "My belt already feels too tight and my feet are killing me."

"Heard the food at the hotel is good. Shall we just relax and have room service?"

"I haven't had room service in—not years, decades. In fact I've only had it about three times in my life."

"Then let's do room service."

She'd gone in to the bathroom and changed into her nightdress and robe while he'd made the call, then she'd sat on one of the beds, self-consciously reading the concert program while he'd gone in to change. Silly to feel self-conscious, she told herself. He'd seen her in her robe and nightdress countless times, but there was something about hearing a man undress in the bathroom of a hotel room . . . When the waiter arrived, they drew chairs up to the little table and lifted the bell-shaped covers from the plates. Shrimp and crab salad, oysters (both Casino and Rockefeller), hot French bread, a bottle of Chardonnay. "Perfect," she told him. They clinked glasses. He gave her a smile she could feel right between her breasts. The food was delicious and she was mellow and sleepy after a single glass of wine. He smiled at her again when she covered a yawn, and said, "I can't think of when I've had a more perfect day." Their eyes met and held, affection inviting touch, but *This man is your sister's husband*—so quick it was more subliminal message than thought—flashed through her. She looked away, and felt something like a reprieve when he asked, "Mind if I watch the late news."

"Of course not," she said, and went into the bathroom, brushed her teeth, and took off her makeup. He sat near the TV, the volume turned low. She got into her bed without saying anything and closed her eyes. After a while he turned off the TV and got into his bed. He knew she wasn't asleep because he reached across the space between them. She took his hand, squeezing it tight before releasing it and turning onto her side. Each knew what the other was thinking and feeling; they didn't need words.

As if by mutual agreement they saw less of one another during the ensuing months, though they still worked in their yards together, digging up the spring flowers—the best showing ever, Josie winning a prize at the garden club for Lady Murasaki's Dream—and planting summer herbs and vegetables. Agreeing that it was uncivilized to eat alone, they still shared breakfasts, oftentimes with Josie's guests. But, increasingly, Dozier broke down and started to accept dinner invitations, even to Peatsy's. When Josie said it had been at least a decade since she'd been invited to Peatsy's for dinner and teased him about being an eligible bachelor, he said, looking wise and blank as an owl, "You gotta eat somewhere." She noticed, however, that he always came home nights, because she could see the ghostly blue glow of the television in his living-room window as he watched the late news. Sometimes she was tempted to go over, but she resisted the impulse.

Then, one evening in mid-September . . . it was after seven and the sun still hadn't gone down. The humidity was so heavy it felt like a blanket. She had no guests, so she turned off the air conditioner, not just to conserve on the electric bill but because she wanted to. Though she was consciously grateful for all modern conveniences, especially air-conditioning, there was something about being without it that brought back sensations of her youth. She took a shower, dusted herself with talcum, put on fresh underwear and a loose dress, pinned her damp hair to the top of her head, but her skin was pleasantly moist with perspiration by the time she reached the bottom of the stairs. Not wanting to deal with neighbors who might be out for a stroll, she decided not to sit on the front veranda, but found her palmetto fan and went into the back garden, settling into the hammock. The air was dense but sweet with honeysuckle and jasmine and she swung gently, thinking how strange it was that one changed so much on the outside while the inner self remained essentially the same. She was in a thoughtful, sultry haze, content to be alone, but not at all surprised when she heard Dozier cutting across the lawn, saying, "Only way to get a breath of air is to go out to the beach. Want to come?"

The sun was going down over the marshes, washing the sky with a glorious palette of gold, pink, and coral. They took off their sandals and walked to the shore. Invigorated by the cool water lapping their feet and a refreshing breeze, they walked, barely speaking, Dozier looking out to sea, Josie watching a family pack up scorched and cranky children, a lifeguard taking down a volleyball net, a grimly determined jogger, a young couple buttoning one another's shirts. They had walked perhaps a mile when their conversation turned, as it often did, to Edna. "I was always trying to get her to come out to the beach, but it didn't have much appeal for her," Dozier said. "She didn't like feeling sandy and getting her hair mussed."

"I love being outdoors, just walking along like this, but when

Bear wanted to go camping it always seemed more chore than adventure to me. Having to cook out made me feel like a cavewoman. I guess I should've been more flexible."

"I think you were more than flexible when it came to accommodating Bear." His tone implied a wealth of knowledge. "I'm the one who should've tried harder. You know, Edna and I got along fine all the time I was working, but once I retired . . . I guess I believed all that Golden Years' crap. I'd been in harness so long I just wanted to stay close to home. I didn't understand—didn't really try to understand—her restlessness. I didn't give her much support when she opened the gift shop."

"You financed it."

"Sure. But I didn't understand why she needed to earn her own money, and I didn't praise her when she made a success of it. I didn't realize it at the time, but it hurt my—I s'pose you'd say male ego. I thought she didn't need me, and I resented her being gone so much."

"I guess," Josie said after a pause, "whenever someone we love dies, even if we've treated them well, we still feel guilt. The other day I was thinking about how annoyed I'd get when Edna fussed at us about cholesterol and all. If I'd known she had stomach troubles . . . And I used to think she was so cold when she wouldn't go visit Mawmaw. I'd forgotten what a time she'd had—well, you'd both had—helping Mawmaw nurse Daddy while Bear and I were off in the Philippines."

"I was busy with work, so it mostly fell to Edna. And you know Mawmaw never even thanked her."

"Well, she wouldn't, would she? Mawmaw didn't think you had to thank a family member for doing what was expected of them. And God knows," she added ruefully, "Mawmaw expected a lot." They shared a laugh. "If I'd known how much being around sick people frightened Edna . . ." Josie went on, "But we never talked about things like that. Never really talked about anything important."

They stopped walking. The beach was virtually deserted, palms silhouetted against an almost navy blue sky, the ocean silvery in the light of a rising moon. "Carolina moon," Dozier said, looking up at it. "Most beautiful moon in the whole wide world." He put his arm around her. "Talking about things is good. You've made me realize that. But there's a limit to it. You can never talk about the deepest things. Only poets can do that. And that's not conversation."

She tucked her head close to his chest and turned up her face. He pulled her closer, looking down at her. "Do you know what you are? You are"—he stroked her windblown hair back from her forehead—"a marvelous woman, and . . ." She thought he'd kiss her, but he moved away, holding her at arms' length. ". . . the best friend I've ever had."

She wrapped her arms around her chest, turned away from him. and mumbled, "Don't you think we should be getting back?" He fell in next to her. She was glad it was dark because the darkness hid the humiliation she knew must show on her face. How could she have shown herself like that—wide open, anticipating—like a moonstruck teenager asking to be kissed! They walked without speaking until she saw the palmetto that had been knocked over in the last hurricane. "This is the turnoff to the car," she told him. He said he thought it was further on, closer to the lighthouse. "If you say so," she said, her tone unintentionally pesky. He was right.

He started the motor immediately. They rolled down the windows, letting the night air rush in. If her life had depended on it, she couldn't have made conversation. They had almost reached the highway when a deer, starting out of the wood, was caught in the headlights. She clutched his legs, he slammed on the brakes, the deer froze, wheeled, then crashed back into the underbrush. The tension between them was dissipated by the thrill of having seen the animal, rigid with fear, but quivering with life, close up. "Did I tell you about the pet raccoon when I was a kid?" he asked her. She shook her head. "I knew about your hunting dog, and that turtle you brought home that you used to hide in the icehouse, but you never told me about a raccoon."

"Mean little varmint. Chewed its way right through the floor in my bedroom, and my mother . . ."

They were back on track, easy with one another again. Friendship, she'd once read or heard someone say, was love without wings. At this stage of her life, she'd best content herself with flights of imagination. Because he too was the dearest friend she'd ever had.

Her hand was already on the door handle when he pulled into his driveway. "Thanks. That was a lovely walk. I'm all relaxed, and it's cool enough to sleep now," she told him, planting a sisterly kiss on his cheek. "See you for breakfast in the morning." She closed her kitchen door, threw the bolt and leaned against it, kicking off her sandals, reaching for a dishtowel to wipe the grit from between her toes. Though it was almost eleven, she decided to take a bath. She went up to her bedroom, flicked on the bedside lamp, then went into the bathroom without turning on the light. She turned the faucets to full, poured in lavender salts, opened the window, and stripped off her clothes so slowly that the tub was almost full when she lowered herself into it. She lay back, filling and squeezing the sponge, sudsing it and stroking her outstretched arm. Firm-muscled from gardening, it looked quite lovely in the shadowy light. Everyone, she thought, remembers their first real kiss, but no one ever talks about the last kiss, because they can't know which kiss will be the last.

After soaking for a long time, she got out of the tub and walked, without drying off, to her chest of drawers. As she'd told her granddaughter last Christmas, in the privacy of her bedroom she could be whatever age she chose to be. The rose-colored gown Cam had given her was there, still wrapped in tissue paper. The fabric had a magic weight and feel, rich as satin, but gossamer light, and as she put it on, it seemed to take on a life of its own, slithering over her, clinging to her damp arms and breasts, but swirling as she did a half-turn. She put up her arms to an imaginary partner, closed her eyes and swayed, humming, "Sometimes I wonder why I spend the lonely night, dreaming of a star, The melody haunts my reverie, and I am once again with you . . ."

She stopped and listened. Perhaps imagination was taking her to a place she didn't want to go. She listened again. The knock was real. And insistent.

When she opened the back door he stepped in, taking her in his arms and gently kicking the door shut with one motion. "You know . . ." he began.

"Yes, I know," she amazed herself by saying.

"You feel like . . ."

"I know . . ." she said again. And then she was truly amazed.

Eighteen

"OH, THANK YOU, dear heart," Peatsy said as Josie placed the vodka tonic next to her elbow and set a plate of rum balls and Pomona in the center of the table. "Now will you sit down?"

"Yes, Josie, do sit," Mary echoed. "I've talked Mort into having a Christmas tree this year"—Esther looked none to pleased with this—"and we've got to get it this afternoon because the best ones are already picked over. Then I've got to do a major grocery shop. I swear, it's been rush, rush, rush. It's like Evie wrote in her last column: Christmas is nothing but stress. It's consternation, not celebration."

"Consternation, not celebration? For God's sake, Mary," Peatsy drawled, "you sound like Jesse Jackson."

"I'm really going to miss Evie's columns," Mary went on. "I was a big fan of hers and I'm sorry she quit her job at the paper."

"Well," Josie said, "newspaper work is notoriously underpaid. She's looking around and I'm sure she'll find something else soon." Josie's newfound frankness had its limits. In fact, Evie had not quit her job but had been asked to leave because she'd taken too much time off, mainly to go on trips with Jasper. At first Evie had been coy about her travels, saying she'd had a surprise offer to go to Las Vegas, a sudden chance to see Hawaii, an unexpected invitation to

Dallas. She never explained how these happy opportunities came about or gave Josie any particulars, she just asked, in a rhetorical whine, "How can I possibly pass this up?" Initially she'd claimed that her trips were working vacations and she'd incorporated her travels into her column; initially her editor had put up with it. But after Evie had missed several deadlines, the editor had pointed out that Evie hadn't been hired as a travel writer and that her articles, confined as they invariably were to descriptions of expensive hotels and restaurants, were not of great interest to the readership. Complaining to Josie about this lack of editorial sensitivity, Evie had slipped, or seemed to slip—one could never be sure with Evie—and announced that Jasper was going back to Dallas on business and wanted her to go with him, and since they were treating her "so mean" at the newspaper, she was going to go even if it meant losing her job. Which it had. In her final column, which had appeared last week, she'd advised her readers to break with tradition, escape the traumas of family, and make Christmas vacation a real vacation by leaving town.

"Well, give Evie my regards," Mary said. "She's coming to your place for Christmas, isn't she?"

"Actually, no. She had an opportunity to go to the islands—St. Kitts, I think it is—with friends." Lila and Orrie had never used the vacation package that Jasper had given them last Christmas, and Jasper was determined not to let it go to waste.

"Yes," Peatsy said, "Gloria Seymour told me she ran into them at the airport a couple of days ago when they were leaving town." She gave a subtle emphasis to "them," letting Josie know that Jasper and Evie's affair was no longer a secret.

Josie said, "Sorry, I'm not paying attention," and picked up her cards. Not only did she disapprove of Evie's affair, she thought it was downright disgusting. To imagine any woman—let alone her baby daughter—going to bed with Jasper Gadsden made her flesh crawl. Evie had never outright admitted the affair, but her references to Jasper, though casual, were increasingly frequent and she had new clothes, luggage, and jewelry she could never have afforded herself. The last time Evie'd come to visit, she'd switched on some afternoon soap about a tycoon and his young mistress; when Josie'd expressed disapproval, Evie had said blithely, "Better to be an old man's sweetheart than a young man's slave." The cynicism of the remark had knocked Josie back. On the other hand, for once, maybe Evie wasn't going to let herself be taken advantage of. And even Josie had to admit that Evie seemed happier than she'd ever been. "I'm just glad Bear wasn't alive to see his daughter become a kept woman," she'd complained to Dozier, the only one in whom she confided, "because he would have knocked her from here to next Sunday and taken a horsewhip to Jasper. I just can't understand it. You know how I raised my girls, but you'd think Zsa Zsa Gabor had brought them up." Dozier had reminded her that since her "girls" were all over forty, her opportunity for moral instruction was long gone. The smartest thing she could do was to recite that Alcoholics Anonymous prayer and ask God to give her the serenity to accept things she could not change.

"Josie, are you with us?" Peatsy demanded.

"Sorry," Josie apologized, realizing that they'd lost the hand.

"How about one more round?" Mary asked. "We want to give you girls a chance to catch up."

Peatsy rose to the challenge. "Go on and deal."

"All right," Josie acquiesced. "But it has to be the last because Lila's dropping by on her way home from Columbia and we're going to do some last-minute shopping."

"Saw Lila being interviewed on TV the other night," Mary said, shuffling the cards. "She was talking about wetlands preservation. I liked her new hairdo."

"Josie, are you with me?" Peatsy prodded. "Please pay attention."

Josie tried to put her mind to the game, bidding and slapping down cards, making the expected grunts and sighs and maneuvers. But her mind was not on bridge. She was wondering if Lila would live up to her promise and come by. There had been a bizarre and totally unexpected reversal in her relationships with her two eldest daughters: now it was Cam who stayed in touch, calling her a couple of times a week, while Lila kept the emotional distance that had separated them since last year's awful fight. For weeks after that sorry event, Lila hadn't even returned her phone calls, but after Orrie had insisted that Josie come up to Columbia for his swearing-in, they'd all made nice and smiled for the photo ops. She and Lila had resumed their round of phone calls, lunches, and shopping but there was an indefinable distance between them. The only time Josie had dared broach the subject of what had happened last Christmas Eve, Lila had stonewalled, saying, "I'd just like to put it behind me and get on with the rest of my life." That was, Josie realized, the line guilty celebrities, criminals, and politicians used when being interviewed, as though their personal actions had nothing to do with events, as though any unpleasantness was no more than a cruel and inexplicable act of nature—like a hurricane they could not have predicted but were happy to have survived.

Josie's intuition still told her Lila had been involved with a man that night, but she was relatively certain that whatever had happened had been an aberration—a one time thing brought about by marital boredom, maternal frustration, and sibling rivalry that Lila was either unaware of or couldn't admit. But things seemed to have resolved themselves. At last Lila and Orrie seemed to be flourishing, so . . . let sleeping dogs lie. She had enough to think about, knowing, as she did, that she was going to make an announcement that would cause another furor.

"Looks like we've won again," Mary told Esther, scooping the pile of quarters to her edge of the table.

"It was all your chompin' and chewin' on that drug gum that distracted us," Peatsy said, pulling her pearls from the neck of her magenta twin set. "Shall we play one last winner-take-all?"

Esther was confused. "But I thought you were anxious to leave."

"I am, but I just can't stand to lose," Peatsy admitted.

Mary checked her watch, snapped her purse shut, and got up. "I'd love to, but we've really got to be going. Esther?" They said their good-byes and Merry Christmases to Peatsy, Esther eyeing the last rum ball before following Mary and Josie to the kitchen. "Oh, before I go." Mary reached up to the shelf above the China cabinet. "Would you mind terribly if I copied out your recipe for cornbread stuffing?" Josie handed her a pen and a sheet of note paper. Mary scribbled the recipe as Josie wrapped up some Pomona for them to take home. "This is such a great cookbook," Mary said as she recapped the pen. "You know, Esther, you really must buy a copy to take back to Cleveland with you next week." Having killed two birds with one stone (by praising Josie's book, which she was never going to buy herself, and reminding her sister-in-law that she'd visited long enough), Mary kissed the air near Josie's cheek and, after another round of good-byes, they went out the back door.

Josie picked up a tray and returned to the sun porch where Peatsy sat, fingering her pearls and staring out at the garden. "Can I get you anything else?" Josie asked, already stacking cups and plates on the tray.

"I guess not. I should be going, but, truth to tell, I'm not up to dealing with guests. I've lived alone so long now that I'm not fit company. If anyone—even Waring—stays more'n a day, I feel like I've been invaded. Thank heaven Cuba's been available to help, 'cause I'm not about to be foolin' and fixin' for houseguests."

"I know Cuba appreciates the work," Josie said, though Cuba had told her that, despite the fact that Peatsy's home had appeared in *Southern Living,* her cupboards and closets were a fearful mess, and her refrigerator hadn't been defrosted for so long that cleaning it was like hacking her way to the North Pole.

"Come, sit for a spell."

Believing that life should never be so rushed that you couldn't find time for a friend, Josie sat, but cautioned, "Just for a few minutes."

"I was wondering how Cam's doing, living with a man after all those years of freedom. I don't mean a man, I mean a husband."

"A husband's not a man?"

"I've always thought they were different."

"You never really loved Gibbs, did you?"

Peatsy snorted. "I don't think anyone but his aide ever cared for Gibbs, and that was only because he had to suck up to him for promotions. What a little dog-robber he was! Always snooping around, checking up on me so he could report back to Gibbs."

"Why did you marry him?"

"Oh, Josie, don't be naive. I married him because I was s'posed to, because he was considered a catch. At twenty-one, how could I be expected to know that the only power and personality the man had, he put on and took off with his uniform. But I was asking you about Cam."

"She seems happy. More'n happy, she seems content. And that's not a word I've ever associated with Cam. Her husband's a prize. Can't think of any man I'd rather have for a son-in-law, but it makes me sad to think that Bear didn't live long enough to see her settled. He never told her, but he worried about her so. And I know Bear would have liked Sam. Sam's his kind of man."

"Then he might be my kind of man." Peatsy fished the lime out of her drink and sucked on it. "I'd like to meet him."

"Are you angling for an invitation?"

"I thought you'd never ask."

"They'll all be here for Christmas, all except Evie, that is. Even Dozier's kids and their families are coming down."

"You're fixing for the whole damn tribe of them?"

"It's okay. I volunteered. So, just give a call day after tomorrow and if things here have settled down to a dull roar, come on by with Waring and his friend."

"I might just do that."

Peatsy's mention of "her kind of man" hit her. She thought, *I've been waiting for forty years to ask; if not now, then when?* And with the abandon of a fledgling swimmer hurling herself from the high dive, she said, "I've often wondered if Bear was your kind of man."

"Bear was every woman's kind of man."

"Yes. He was undeniably attractive. I mean . . ."

They looked at one another. "You know," Peatsy said slowly, "you've changed a lot in the last year or so. You've gone and got yourself liberated."

"Maybe I've just gotten so old I don't care much about what people think anymore."

"That's liberated, isn't it? I didn't mean you were marching around without a bra carrying a placard."

"I was asking you . . ."

Peatsy blotted her lips with her napkin, then smoothed it. "You still use linen napkins. And you still iron them, don't you?" she said, as though this was to be a deciding factor in her answer.

"Always have, always will. So. You were saying . . ."

"Oh, men!" Peatsy sighed, tilting back her head, her eyes hooded but sharp. "I've always figured a real man needed two women: one to bring out the best in him, and the other to make him forget it."

"And I was the former and you were the latter?" Josie asked, keeping her voice calm though she couldn't control the twitch in her left eyelid.

"Josie." Peatsy looked out at the garden. "I suppose I always knew that one day—"

The front door slammed, making both of them jump. A man's voice called out, "Hey, sweet lady, where you hiding? I got something special for you." Dozier appeared in the archway leading to the sun porch, eyes shining, carrying a sprig of mistletoe. "Well . . . if it isn't Peatsy Gibbs!" He masked his embarrassment with a look of pleased surprise and, not being able to hide the mistletoe, held it over Peatsy's head, pecked her cheek, and said, "Merry Christmas."

Her face flaming, Josie blurted, "Didn't you see Peatsy's car in the driveway?"

"Didn't pull into the drive. Parked at the front of your house because I went and picked up the Christmas tree and I planned to carry it straight into the living room. So, Peatsy"—Dozier sat, dropping the mistletoe onto the table and putting his hands in the back pockets of his jeans—"good to see you. Are you feeling as fine as you're looking in that pretty purple sweater?"

"It's magenta," was all Josie could get out.

Peatsy wiggled her shoulders and raised her eyebrows. "Oh, Josie, you know men never learn more'n the primary colors."

"Poor, simple souls that we are," Dozier said with a feather touch of sarcasm.

"Can I get you anything to eat or drink, Dozier?" Josie asked.

"No, thank you, ma'am. I dropped by the Steamer for lunch. Figured you ladies would have finished your game by now."

"You know how women are," Peatsy said. "We just love to gossip."

"I heard more'n an earful from the fellows at the Steamer, but we men don't call it gossip. We call it an exchange of information and ideas."

Peatsy laughed and slapped his hand. Josie got up. "Sure you don't want anything else, Peatsy?"

"Oh, maybe just a splash." Peatsy handed up her glass. "Then I really will have to be going along."

I wish, Josie thought.

Dozier said, "If it's not too much trouble, I guess I'll have a cup of tea."

She went to the dining-room liquor cabinet to pour another—very small—shot of vodka. Interruptions like this only happened in plays. "Unbelievable," she muttered, shaking her head as she went into the kitchen, dumped ice into the glass, and cut off another slice of lime, nicking her index finger in the process. Filling the kettle, she heard Peatsy's trilling laugh (the one reserved for men) and Dozier's answering chuckle. She slammed down the kettle onto the gas ring. Flirting . . . at her age! And Dozier lapping it up like a puppy. She crossed her arms over her breast and sucked her finger, waiting for the kettle to boil. And jealous . . . at her age! It was just too pitiful to think that she could still be in the grip of such a humiliating emotion. But, she'd read somewhere that when jealousy went out the window, Eros went out of the bed. So be it. It was part of the human condition, and unless you were a saint, you were doomed to suffer it until the very end. On the other hand—she poured the boiling water over the Constant Comment and waited for it to steep—she didn't have to indulge it and make a fool of herself. She could maintain at least a modicum of dignity, even if she was churning inside. Chin high, her lips forming a slight smile, she carried the tea and Peatsy's vodka tonic to the sun porch.

Dozier and Peatsy had fallen silent, both looking through the archway as though they were strangers on a platform looking down the track for a late train. Dozier got up, excusing himself and saying he was going to untie the Christmas tree from the roof of his car and would call when he needed help to carry it in. Peatsy, conspicuously checking her watch and saying that maybe she didn't have time for the drink after all, got up, too. Putting her bag over her shoulder, she walked without speaking through the archway and the kitchen, reaching for the knob on the back door.

"Peatsy?" Josie put her hand on her shoulder. "Is anything—"

Without turning, Peatsy said, "What you were asking me about . . ." She put one hand on the doorjamb and rested her forehead on the glass. "Bear would never have left you." She turned slowly, giving Josie an enigmatic and not totally friendly smile. "He really loved you. And now . . ." She raised her chin and shrugged. "It looks as though you're going to be the woman who brings out the best in a man *and* makes him forget. Congratulations." Josie's mouth opened. "No, I mean it. Congratulations. And good luck." Peatsy's smile showed just a shadow of a smirk as she opened the door. "Because when you make this public, the shit's really going to hit the fan. Give me a call when you can, dear heart. I left your Christmas gift on the table."

Josie sank down into a chair, biting her injured finger. She didn't hear him come in, but suddenly Dozier was behind her, massaging her shoulders, saying, "I hope you don't mind that I told her. I just felt it was time to cut to the chase." She nodded, grabbed his hand, and held it to her cheek.

Nineteen

As Lila started to turn her car into her mother's driveway a black Cadillac backed out, swung around—almost hitting her—then took off at such speed that it seemed its driver hadn't heard her horn. Looking after it she realized it had been Peatsy Gibbs. If the police could take away Ricky's license for reckless driving (for which she'd been more than grateful) then they ought to be able to keep wacko senior citizens like Peatsy Gibbs off the roads.

Shaken, she pulled into the drive, cut off the motor, and turned to look at the presents that had tumbled off the backseat when she'd slammed on the brakes. She closed her eyes. Almost a year to the day since he'd stood here, leaning into her car, asking her what was on the tape deck. Almost a year since she'd fallen madly in love for the first, and surely the last, time in her life. Her emotions had the uncontrollable force of a natural phenomenon, like the storm at the beach. But if the storm had been over within an hour, it had taken the better part of a year for her affair with Bedford to play itself out.

The first time he'd made love to her—no, she corrected herself—the first time he'd had sex with her, she'd fallen back onto the bed, panting, wild-eyed, trembling as though she'd survived a minor earthquake, and he'd said—she would never forget this—"Gotcha!" That should've warned her that his ego was more involved than his heart, but she'd believed, because she'd wanted to believe, that it was a passionate cry of possession because he was as crazy about her as she was about him. And, no doubt about it, he had got her as she'd never been gotten before. From that first afternoon in early January, through the spring and summer and into September, she'd gone to him whenever he'd asked her to come. She'd taken chances that even at the time she'd known were on the other side of madness. But the adrenaline rush of danger had only increased the excitement of going to bed with him.

At first they'd met only at his cabin, then she'd met him in towns where he was speaking on environmental issues, and they'd end up in motels or the apartments of his friends. Once they'd even gone to his mother's. And several times, when the House was in session and she'd gone up to the capital with Orrie, they'd risked a hotel right in downtown Columbia. At last she'd understood that desire could come on you like a sickness and you had no more chance of controlling it than you could control your temperature when you had the flu. The sexual experimentation she'd found ridiculous with Orrie seemed wonderfully liberating with Bedford. She lived from meeting to meeting, wild memories of the last encounter spilling over into anticipation of the next. Her daily life, even deaths in the family, were no more than a backdrop to her secret life with Bedford.

At times she'd been sure that Orrie knew. Even though he was wrapped up in his own life, how could he not know? He'd taken his responsibilities as a representative far more seriously than she'd thought he would, had told her that though his motives hadn't been the best (indeed, he'd run more to satisfy Jasper's ambitions than his own), now that he'd taken the oath of office, he was going to work to be worthy of the people's trust. But even though he was away from home much of the time and, even if, after twenty-four years of marriage, he thought of her more as an appendage than an individual, how could he not see her as different when she even looked different—skin tighter, eyes brighter? How could he overlook the whispered phone calls, the absences that couldn't reasonably be explained as shopping trips or committee meetings, the new sets of Victoria's Secret underwear?

There had been times when she'd thought *Caught!,* shuddering but strangely relieved, her confession already in her mouth: the time he'd dropped her off at the beauty salon but she'd ducked out for an hour with Bedford and had arrived late at the reception at the governor's mansion, hair pulled back into a headband. Or the time she told him she'd been playing golf and he'd hung up her jacket and found shells in the pocket. That had been touch and go for a while, but she'd turned his questions around and, borrowing heavily from Bedford's lectures, made a speech about the unique beauty of the coastline and urged him to take a more statesmanlike attitude toward preservation. Since Orrie hated confrontation of any kind, the whole thing had blown over. They'd bumped along as usual, actually better than usual, because she had more time to herself, and when he was home she made sure that the sex was regular and the comforts constant. Ironically, she'd even increased his constituency because people who saw her at environmental meetings cast her as the concerned wife, forced to keep a low profile because of her husband's conservatism but likely to pillow-talk him into more liberal views.

Sometimes she and Orrie had run into Bedford at various functions. The polite and casually friendly way she and Bedford related to one another gave her a secret sizzle, but the sizzle was often doused by watching other women come on to him and, worse, seeing him come on to other women. When she'd first questioned him about these flirtations, he'd tease, "Why would I bother with other women when I've turned a virtuous, socially upstanding matron into my love slave?" That should have been a red flag, but she'd ignored it. Later, when she'd first started to notice the signs of his disinterest (the increased speed with which he took off her clothes and put his own back on, the excuse that he hadn't bought her a birthday present because he couldn't think of anything that Orrie wouldn't discover, even though she'd given him some expensive Indian pottery it had taken weeks of creative accounting to hide), she'd asked, her gut churning, knowing it was a mistake, if he was seeing other women. Of course he was "seeing" other women, but that was part of his social life, superficial, didn't mean anything at all.

Sometime in July "I only have eyes for you" had changed into "For Chrissake, Lila, you still sleep with Orrie, don't you?" But it was early August before he'd stopped calling when he was supposed to, and well into September before he'd failed to meet her at the cabin as promised. Later that night, when she'd told Orrie she was out of Tampax and had driven to a gas station to call him, he'd said, irritably, that something unexpected had come up and, damn it, he couldn't call her because he knew Orrie was home. When she'd reminded him of the code they'd used in the past to warn one another of a change in plans, he'd said, "Oh, Lila, please" in an irritated voice. Panicked, *she'd* apologized, saying she'd cancel all appointments so they could meet the next day and he'd said—her stomach still turned at the humiliation of it—"When a woman's hot for a man she can come up with more opportunities in an hour than he can come up with in a month." He didn't know if he could juggle his schedule, but he'd call her in the morning.

It was over and she knew it. But she couldn't accept it any more than a patient could accept the first announcement of a fatal diagnosis. She'd had to play it out, to put herself through the final rejection.

All the next day she'd stayed home, waiting for the promised phone call. Desperately wanting to keep busy, she'd gone through her closets, selecting clothes to donate to the Junior League, shaved her legs, balanced her checkbook, watched the men from Waterworld clean the pool, followed the gardener around while he mulched and dead-headed the flowers. In the afternoon she went through the laundry hamper and instead of bundling Orrie's shirts to go to the dry cleaner, washed and ironed them herself. In the late afternoon she cooked, which she rarely did of late, fixing chicken pot pie, one of Orrie's favorites. Knowing it would just be the two of them for dinner (Susan's psychiatrist had said they shouldn't make a big deal and insist she eat with them), she set the table with candles and flowers, and after the meal, when Orrie was leaving to go back to Columbia, she hung the fresh shirts in his car and kissed him good-bye.

She watched television with Susan, resisting the impulse to ask her what she'd eaten that day, not even questioning her about how things were going with the psychiatrist they'd taken her to after her weight had dropped to 105. She let Susan have control of the remote and suffered through *Beverly Hills 90210*, MTV, the ten o'clock news, and David Letterman. "Am I the only one in America who thinks this man is insufferably smug and totally unfunny?" she'd asked when she'd felt she was about to scream. Susan, yawning, had said, "You've never had much of a sense of humor, Mom." She said, "Bedtime." Susan bristled but acquiesced. As soon as she was sure Susan was asleep she called Bedford's cabin, and hung up when he answered. She took a hot shower, changed out of her robe into jeans and a sweatshirt, and got into her car. Driving over the bridge to Hunting Island, she looked out at the moonlit water and wondered what it would feel like to have it close over her head.

She knocked until her knuckles stung. A light came on. Blinking, irritable, wearing only his jockey shorts, Bedford threw open the door, saw her, said, "Oh, shit!" then stumbled back into the living room, one hand flapping behind him, motioning for her to follow. She stepped in, feeling as though she was going to throw up. Ignoring her, he moved to the kitchenette, opening the refrigerator, drinking from a carton of juice. After wiping his mouth, he scratched his chest and asked, "What time is it anyway?"

She couldn't speak. He rolled his eyes in a show of boredom. "I guess you want to talk. Women always want to talk. Especially when there's nothing to talk about."

"I thought . . ."

"That it was going to go on forever?"

"I thought . . ."

"No, Lila," he cut her off again. "You didn't think. You never did think."

His brutality literally stunned her. She felt dizzy, unable to catch her breath. "You mean, cold-hearted bastard. At least you could have had the decency to—" She choked.

He extended his arms and hung his head to one side in a parody of crucifixion. "All right. Pound away. But you can only do it for a little while because I really do have to get some sleep tonight."

If she'd had a gun she would have shot him. She took a step toward him, mouth open, hand raised—and then the miracle happened—she could only describe it as a miracle: suddenly she saw herself and despised what she was doing even more than she despised him, and that restored her dignity. She turned and went out the door without bothering to close it behind her. He called, "Lila, Lila, come back," coming to the top of the stairs as she kept moving, slow motion, down them. As she got to her car he cursed and slammed the door shut.

She couldn't get out of bed or keep anything in her stomach for days. She cried, took tranquilizers and slept, slept and cried, until Susan told her, "I've always known you were the one who really needed a shrink." Orrie, though he put it more gently, thought so too. Wouldn't she get up, wash her hair, get dressed, go "talk" to someone? And did she want to see a man or a woman? Sex, she said, smiling weakly at her private joke, was unimportant. Orrie took the initiative, made an appointment, and drove her to Dr. Dareher's office. She sat through her first session staring at the seascape behind his head, saying next to nothing. At the end of the fifty minutes he asked if she would be willing to try an antidepressant. She grunted assent. He cautioned that it would take several weeks for the medication to kick in, but chemistry was no substitute for insight and he expected to see her twice a week.

By mid-October she'd resumed most of her activities and, though by no means happy, at least she didn't feel dead to the world. Dr. Dareher was patient, intelligent, genuinely concerned. At last she began to talk, but only in the abstract, about self-delusion, manipulation, betrayal. When he pressed her for instances in her own experience, she shut down. She could never bring herself to talk about Bedford, though she still thought about him constantly. How, she asked herself, had she let herself be seduced (there was no other word for it) by such a cliché (there was no other word for it) character? Admittedly, she hadn't had much experience with men, but she wasn't an idiot. Why hadn't she seen it coming? But, to be honest, she *had* seen it coming—that very first afternoon after the storm she'd had enough sense to get up and leave, then, God only knew . . . "Why," she asked Dr. Dareher, "do we deny our strongest intuitions?" As expected, he turned the question around and made it more personal, "Why do you think *you* deny yours?" Over the next couple of months, as he'd guided her through the maze of childhood memories and traumas, she'd pondered that question. But she'd never been able to come up with an answer that satisfied. She'd answered his questions about how she felt being Orrie's wife, Susan and Ricky's mother, Bear and Josie's daughter, Cam and Evie's sister. "And who, apart from all these roles, are you?" he asked. "Who is Lila when she's all by herself?" Staring at the seascape behind his head, she'd thought for a long time, then said, apologizing because it sounded so corny, "I really do love nature." She'd been driving to a beach close to her house every day after breakfast, or before breakfast if Orrie wasn't home. Walking in the early hours, listening to the ocean, watching birds, studying shells and plants calmed her and took her out of herself. She put her hands behind her head, still studying the painting. "I thought I was in love with this man. Isn't it strange that someone who's a real bastard can still have wonderful ideas?" Dr. Dareher leaned forward, encouraging her to go on. After a pause she said, "So."

"So?" he prodded gently.

"So I've been thinking that I might go back to college. I never finished, you know. I'd like to take some classes in marine biology."

"About the man?"

"Oh, he was a real clam worm."

"A what?"

"A clam worm. They live buried in the mud and rocks, and they have bristly legs and powerful horny jaws. They dig in for defense but they're aggressive hunters when it comes to young clams." She thought about this. "Ah, well. All things exist in nature."

When she didn't go on, he smiled and said, "Clams? As in 'clam up'?"

She checked her watch, got up from the couch, picked up her shoulder bag. "I think my time's up." She didn't suppose, even with the help of a psychiatrist, that she could plum the murky depths. Because she really didn't want to. At the door she turned and said, "You've never seen a clam worm? You know, doctor, you really ought to get out of the office more."

* * *

Big band music was drifting from the house. Opening Josie's kitchen door, Lila called, "I'm here, Mama," and walked through to the living room. Dozier and Josie were jitterbugging, so engrossed that at first they didn't notice her. "That was a slinky move," Dozier, spinning Josie away from him, said. "Now roll in tight and we'll cross hands and . . ." Lila watched, vaguely envious. Maybe that generation didn't have the Pill, but they sure got a lot of pleasure out of dancing and, as far as relations between the sexes went, maybe it was a toss-up. "Ah, Lila . . ." Seeing her, Dozier put out his hand, motioning for her to join in. "Come trip the light fantastic with us."

"Don't have time if I'm going to go grocery shopping with Mama."

Josie disengaged herself and turned off the record player. "I'll be right with you, Lila. Soon's I comb my hair and grab my bag. Oh, no. I forgot. First we have to help Dozier with the Christmas tree. His car's parked out front."

"I didn't notice. Reason being, Peatsy Gibbs about ran me down as I tried to pull into the drive."

"That's Peatsy for you," Dozier chuckled as the three of them walked to the front door. "Thinks she's queen of the road and every other thing. Oh, looky here." He bent to the floor near the mail slot, picked up a scattering of envelopes, and handed them to Josie. "Mailman's been while we've been dancing the afternoon away."

"Christmas cards," Josie said, examining the envelopes. "Here's one from Joan Christianson—'member the Christiansons, Lila?"

"No, Mama, I don't."

"They were stationed in Norfolk same time we were. You used to play with the little boy, Roger. That little boy who had more freckles than a turkey egg? Then they were transferred to—"

"I don't remember, Mama," Lila said impatiently, meaning she didn't care. Josie had her wits about her, but she still insisted on going through the old person's litany of neighbors and friends you couldn't possibly remember and had no interest in.

"And here's one from Mrs. Beasley . . ." Josie reached for the letter opener on the hall table, ripped open the envelope, and pulled out a card showing barnyard animals smiling at an infant Jesus who looked like the chubby-cheeked child in the old Campbell's soup advertisements.

Dozier said, "Mrs. Beastly wanted to come again this Christmas, but I told your mother definitely not."

"Thank God someone can penetrate Mama's stubborn streak," Lila congratulated him.

" 'Dear Mrs. Tatternall,' " Josie read, " 'I hope this year's holidays will be better for you than the last. I was so disappointed to hear that you were not feeling well enough to accept guests . . .' "

Lila groaned. "The Mouth of the South. Please don't take time to read anything from Mrs. Beasley now."

" '. . . I expect you will be, as I am, very lonely, but . . .' " Josie continued.

Dozier said, "Some people deserve to be lonely. What else have you got?"

"Oh, this is from Evie." As Josie opened the letter, a photograph fell to the floor. "She says—" Josie perused the note, willing to censor it if need be, while Dozier picked up the photo. " 'Having a wonderful time . . .' "

"Originality was never her long suit," Lila cut in.

"She doesn't have a long suit," Dozier said. "She's got a Morse code bathing suit."

"A what?"

"Two dots and a dash." He winked and showed them both the photo: Evie in a shocking-pink bikini, tanned as toast, with sunglasses as big as aviator's goggles, and a smile as big as all outdoors, lolling in front of a beachfront cabana.

Lila shook her head. "I'm surprised Jasper was sober enough to hold the camera."

Josie took the photo. "We won't show it to Orrie."

"Oh, Orrie's dealing with it better than I am," Lila said. "Or maybe he's just happy that Jasper's out of town and doesn't know how he voted on that wetlands preservation issue."

"You tell Orrie I'm proud of him about that vote," Dozier told her. "When he was elected—and I guess you know that, much as I like him, I didn't vote for him—I said, this dog won't hunt. But he's surprised me. He's come good."

"Yes," Lila said, with just a tad of condescension. Orrie had "come good," as Dozier put it. He'd assembled an eclectic staff who knew about the issues, and he had a "gee-golly-whiz" earnestness that made her feel renewed affection and respect for him. Much to her surprise, she was beginning to enjoy being a politician's wife. "Personally," she said, handing the photograph back to Josie, "I think Evie and Jasper are pathetic, but Orrie says not to worry. In an era of television, voters like dirt."

"Voters have always liked dirt," Dozier told her. "Just they used to feel some shame for flapping around in it like birds in a dust bath."

"I wish they'd damn move to St. Kitts," Lila said. "Just as long as they stay out of our lives and the old goat doesn't leave everything to my Barbie-doll sister and cut my kids out of his will."

"Oh, tidings of comfort and joy," Dozier teased, and, seeing Josie's discomfort, "Shall we haul in that tree?"

"Please. Let's." Josie said. "You know Cam and Sam are due in tomorrow afternoon and I want—"

"Cam and Sam. Sounds like some new brand of cat food." Lila

laughed to take the edge off the remark. Cam still came first in Josie's heart, and now that she'd gotten married and moved to Atlanta, Josie acted as though Cam'd hung the moon. But what Lila had perceived as favoritism didn't hurt her as it once had. And if, as she knew was the case, she'd lived in Cam's shadow and chosen a life of conformity not only to protect herself but to save her mother from the pain Cam and Bear had given her, she could hardly blame Cam. And she wasn't going to be like Evie, perpetually replaying the injustices of childhood in order to explain away her problems. Now that she and Orrie were getting along so well, and she was looking forward to going back to school, she just wanted to get on with the rest of her life. "All right," she said, a smile creasing one corner of her mouth, "let's go get that tree."

It was a crisp, clear day, the sun beaming through the windshield of the Volvo highlighting the tips of Sam's lashes and the silver at his temples. They were cruising at a smooth sixty miles an hour, the windows rolled down to let in the fresh breeze, the heater on to warm Cam's chronically chilly feet. Her head was on his shoulder, his hand was on her thigh. Mozart was playing on the tape deck. "This is a perfect moment," she said, almost to herself.

"What?"

"A perfect moment. Like the first time I wrote a short story and banged out *The End* on my old Underwood, or when I heard Ray Charles sing 'Georgia' in person, or when I went to the Museum of Modern Art for the first time and saw Rousseau's sleeping Arab with the lion standing over him."

"Oh, yeah. The sleeping Arab and the lion. I'd sure put that on my top-ten favorite things."

"Philistine." She pinched his arm but nestled closer. "You know what I mean. Special moments of great pleasure. Why are those moments so short-lived? Why can't we hold on to them?"

"Just tough luck, sweetheart." He talked out of the side of his mouth. "What a smart dame like you calls the human condition."

"Don't try to do Bogart. You can't do Bogart. You can't even do Elvis or John Wayne. You're a lousy impersonator."

"I thought I did a pretty credible Don Juan last night."

"You did," she whispered in his ear.

"Whoa, girl, you want me to go off the road?"

"Only if you see a cheap motel." She laughed, but her laughter ended in a sigh.

"You going strange on me because we're getting close to your mama's house?"

"No. I can't wait to see Mama. I'm a little worried about her. When we talked on the phone last night, she said she had something important to tell me but she was going to wait until we were all together. Her health's been fine, but I wonder . . ."

"Don't worry. If anything was wrong she would've said so. Josie's a straight-shooter."

"Much more than she used to be. You can't imagine how white-gloves, make-nice, and salute-the-flag she used to be." She smiled and shook her head. "Evie running off to the islands with Jasper! There was a time when Mama would have drawn the shades and put her head in the oven because of that, but she seemed to take it in stride. It's too bad you won't get to meet Evie and Jasper. They're the dog-and-pony show of the Tatternall circus. Jasper would Bubba-and-turkey-shoot you to death, and Evie would shake her boobies and bat her eyelashes, and if you were friendly, she'd think you were coming on to her. And if you weren't, she'd say you were passive-aggressive and had trouble relating to women. And then there's Lila. Haven't heard from her since I called to thank her for my birthday gift."

"You said she sounded fine."

"Sure, she sounded fine, but that doesn't mean she isn't going to be mad at me when she sees me in person. She's always mad at me when she sees me in person, though after last Christmas I expect she'll be on her best behavior."

"As will you."

"As will I," she agreed. "Unless Lila's kids fray my patience. Susan isn't too bad. In fact, I could develop some affection for her, but Ricky? He's a real Generation X poster boy, twenty going on three. Likes to hurl himself on the floor and have a temper tantrum if cable goes out on the TV. 'Course Lila and Orrie have no one but themselves to blame for that. Now Orrie . . . as I've told you, you wouldn't want to be stranded on a desert island with him, but I don't think you'll actually dislike him."

"Why don't you just let me form my own impressions?"

"Well, excuse me!" she said grandly, but kept on. "And Uncle Dozier. You can't help but love Uncle Dozier. Want an apple?" He shook his head. She reached into the brown bag at her feet, took an apple, and polished it on the sleeve of her cable-knit sweater. "So, I'm glad we're going."

"You'd better be, it was your idea. I would've been just as happy to stay home and put up bookshelves in your office."

The wrinkle in the center of her forehead creased. "I sure hope we haven't bitten off more than we can chew. The world isn't exactly crying out for another small-press operation."

"You trust Jane and Fred. You've said yourself that between the three of you, you have more publishing experience than a staff of eight."

"Since we're going to be doing the work of eight, I guess we'll need it."

"You also said the idea of starting a grass-roots publishing house excited you."

"I still think 'Root Hog' would be a better name than 'Annabell Lee.' "

"The stationery isn't printed yet. Maybe you can convince your partners. You can be very convincing when you put your mind to it."

She munched on the apple, thinking out loud. "Fred's so stuck on publishing poetry, and I do want to publish poetry, but we can't be so artsy-fartsy that we can't pay the bills. I've been wondering if maybe we couldn't bring out a new edition of Mama's cookbook. Distribute it through independent bookstores, tourist shops, chambers of commerce. A good Southern cookbook might be the cash-cow to see us through all those wonderful, unappreciated poets. I don't know." She tossed the core of the apple into the paper bag. "The whole thing makes me antsy."

He felt her emotional temperature drop. "It's not just worrying about business that's getting to you, is it?"

"I don't know. I'm glad we're going to Mama's but there's still a part of me that's jealous of our time together."

"We've got the rest of our lives together."

"You know, Sam, sometimes you sound like dialogue from a Disney movie."

"I happen to like those Disney movies where animals mate for life."

"Well, maybe we will be able to mate for life," she said in a world-weary growl, "seeing as how we're already halfway through it. You know what Bear used to say."

"I've heard a helluva lot of what Bear used to say."

"He used to say: 'A man isn't complete until he's married; and then he's finished.' Finished meaning washed up, ruined."

Sam laughed. "You've told me. And how was it supposed to be for a woman?"

"The woman's whole life is supposed to be focused on legally snaring the man, bringing him to earth, caging him up."

"I don't feel caged. Do you?"

"No. I just feel . . ." She felt superstitious; to admit happiness was to court disaster.

"You know, Cam, when things are going wrong you never believe they'll go right, but when things are going right, you're always anticipating disaster."

Now she was downright gloomy. "I just wonder if we'd ever have gotten married if—"

His voice took on an edge. "I've told you I was miserable when I left New York, but you weren't exactly hanging on my neck begging me not to go. Nor did you give any indication that you'd be willing to come with me. I figured you'd never give up your career, or living in that damned cesspool."

She bristled. "I still love New York. There are a lot of wonderful things about New York. New York is—"

"Can we stick to the subject? Can we?"

"What," she demanded, "is the subject?"

He pulled over to the side of the road, stopping next to a scraggly palmetto and a gully of dormant ferns. "How many times do I have to tell you? I didn't marry you just because of . . ." He didn't want to say 'the baby,' though by the time she'd lost it he'd started to think of it that way. ". . . because you were pregnant. For Chrissake, we've talked about all this a hundred times."

"I know." She turned away. "But if I hadn't been pregnant . . . If you hadn't felt sorry for me. I mean, you have to admit, it *was* the catalyst."

"Yes, it was the catalyst." When Reba had brought her to Atlanta they'd talked for two days straight, admitting the improbability of it all, considering the alternatives, then, in a scene that had started with angry words and ended with tears and admissions of love, they'd decided, against all sense, to go through with it. The obstetrician, a specialist in late pregnancies, had warned them about the risks but said that with care and caution, and probably a

C-section, Cam would make it through. Then, after two months of waning nausea but increasing fatigue and boredom, on the very day before she was supposed to have amniocentesis, she'd cramped up, fainted, and had a spontaneous abortion.

"Admit it, you were relieved," she said, quietly. "Just admit that you were relieved."

"In a way, yes," he said, not without guilt. "But I'd been honest with you. You know I'd already gone through raising kids, and, yes, I was worried about doing it again, both financially and emotionally. And I was worried about you. Sometimes you're a goddamn Amazon, but you were so tired and worried. You were so . . ." His fist clenched in frustration. "You don't have to have a baby to be a woman."

"I know that!" she said vehemently. "I don't think—"

"But maybe you still *feel* . . ." He pulled her head onto his shoulder and stroked back her hair. "For everything there is a season. We were just in the wrong season. There's still a lot we can look forward to together."

Her tears soaked his shirt. "I love you. I love you so much. I don't know why—after all we've been through—after you've proven—I don't know why I'm still afraid. I don't know why I still don't trust. When I wake up in the morning and you're not there I still think you've gone away and maybe you won't come back."

"Shush. Shush."

"Why is that?"

"Oh, baby, you know all the reasons why. You don't believe in roots." He rocked her gently. "But we've grown vines, and vines are so resilient and so strong . . ." Feeling his eyes water, he took her by the shoulders, shook her, rubbed the top of her head with his knuckles, and said, "Shape up. We're due to report at your Mama's at seventeen hundred hours," and started the car.

Twenty

THE LATE AFTERNOON sun slanted in the kitchen window and the air was warm with delicious smells of baking cloves, cinnamon, raisins, apples, and pumpkin.

"Mama, you'd better stop dirtying bowls and pans 'cause I'm about to stop washing them." Cam, at the sink, looked out the window, raised a sudsy hand, and pointed. "Come see Dozier and Sam." Josie stopped crimping the piecrust, wiped her hands on her apron, and came to look. The men stood on either side of the live oak, hands stuffed into their back pockets, heads tilted back, sizing up the overhanging branches. "Don't they just look like bookends?"

"Neighbor woman had a tree surgeon in and I was going to get him to come by, but Dozier said to save the money. He's been wanting to prune that tree for ages, but I question the wisdom of him being up a ladder by himself."

"Sam'll help him. Sam'd do anything to be outdoors," Cam said. "First thing he comes home at night, no matter what the weather's like, he wants to go out and sit on the deck. Next summer we plan to expand it so's it'll take up most of the backyard."

"So you won't put in a garden after all?"

"Oh, Mama, a garden's too much like hard work. We'd rather sleep in on the weekends."

"And how's the rest of your house coming?"

"We're gradually getting it together," Cam said, though she didn't imagine Josie would think it prudent that they'd bought office equipment and an original painting of a nude instead of investing in a dining-room set. She'd been pleased that they'd been able to find a neighborhood near downtown Atlanta that fitted both their budget and their tastes. It was called Little Five Points, had mostly older homes that were being restored, bookstores, specialty shops, ethnic restaurants, and a mixed population. Since Sam had lived in country-club comfort during his first marriage, he didn't find the house particularly grand, but she, having lived most of her adult life in New York apartments, found it airy, private, and spacious. "I never thought I'd have my own bathroom and my own office. And we're fixing up the extra bedroom for when his kids come to visit."

They watched as the two men chatted, seemed to come to some conclusion, and started toward the house. "Sam may not be able to help Dozier prune the tree this trip, but there's no reason why we can't come back for a long weekend in a couple of months."

The timer went off and Josie grabbed potholders and went to the oven, lifting out another pumpkin pie.

"Mama, this is starting to look like that *I Love Lucy* skit where they can't keep up with the candy coming off the assembly line."

"This is the last one." Josie put in a mincemeat pie. "Who knows, maybe this'll be the last year I'll be up to it."

"Fat chance."

"Maybe next year you'll do it."

"I got married, Mama, I didn't get reincarnated as Martha Stewart."

Josie patted the perspiration on her neck with her apron and looked around. "That'll make seven. Seven ought to be enough, don't you think? Let's see, there's me and Dozier, you and Sam,

Lila, Orrie, and their kids, Skip and his wife and their kids, Marilyn, her husband, their daughter and son-in-law and their kids. S'pose I can put the children on the sun porch?"

"Please do. Drooling and squealing doesn't do a thing for my appetite."

The men came in through the back door. "Smells great in here," Sam said, eyeing the pies but moving close to Cam and sniffing her neck.

"We were just looking over the tree," Dozier told Josie as he pulled up a chair. "Speculating as to how old it is. Time was, nobody'd cut down a tree. Knew they'd go to hell if they did."

Cam dried her hands and slipped her arm around Sam's neck. "Why don't you open one of the bottles of wine we brought and we'll all have a quiet drink before Orrie and Lila get here."

"Where's the bottle opener?"

Josie said, "It's in the hide-nasty."

"She means that second drawer down." Dozier pointed. "The one where she keeps old rubber bands and string and bottle stoppers and buttons that don't belong to anything and gas bills from a quarter century ago."

Josie sniffed. "You're mighty critical for a man who has a toolshed that looks like fish guts."

"Mama, sit!" Cam said as though she were training a recalcitrant puppy.

"Oh, all right. It's just that I hate to quit before everything's—"

"Ship-shape," Sam said.

"Squared away," Dozier added. "It's the military influence."

"No," Josie corrected, "good housekeeping started with Mawmaw. She used to say, 'When a thing is once begun, never leave it till it's done, Be the labor great or small, Do it well—' "

" '—or not at all,' " Cam finished, laughing.

"Judging from the way our house looks," Sam said, easing the cork out of the wine bottle, "I would never have guessed that Cam had been taught anything like that."

"Just because I was born with a uterus doesn't mean I'm condemned to scrubbing and fetching," Cam told him.

"Of course not, precious," Sam teased as he poured the wine. Josie and Dozier, a bit embarrassed by this exchange, raised their glasses.

"A toast?" Dozier asked.

"Sure, why not start now?" Sam agreed. "How about 'To Love.' "

"You sound like you've already had a few," Cam said.

"How'd you raise such a cynic?" Sam asked Josie.

Josie's eyes twinkled. "Tried not to, but she was just smarter than the rest of us."

"All right. A toast to love," Dozier agreed. "We can get into all the Christmas cheer stuff tomorrow."

"If all goes well," Josie said softly.

"Why, yes. If all goes well," Dozier said, touching his glass to Josie's and giving her a look that Cam had trouble reading.

After draining his glass, Dozier got up, hitched his pants, and said, "My kids should be driving in any time now, so I guess I'll shuffle off next door and leave you folks alone."

Cam said, "I thought you all were coming over tonight."

"No. God willin' an' the creek don't rise, we'll all have the Christmas feast together tomorrow, but tonight I'm just ordering four large pizzas with the works. Want to talk to my kids alone."

"As do I," Josie said. "Sure you won't take some of this marvelous stuff Reba sent us?" She gestured toward the sideboard where the contents of the package ("Xmas C.A.R.E. Package to Depressed Southern States, From the Yenta and the Redneck") were stacked. "I'm not even fixing supper. I'm just going to put all these wonderful things on the table with a big salad and a loaf of bread. Why don't you take some?"

Dozier eyed the salmon with a dill sauce, Greek olives, green pepper paté, hard salami, Kosher smoked turkey, brie, goat cheese, pickled calamari, Noël log, and almond biscotti. "I think I'd better stay with the pizza."

"Stick in the mud," Josie chided, touching his shoulder before he left, turning as she shut the door behind him, her gaze drifting, then recovering herself to say, "You two must be tired after that drive from Atlanta. Why don't you go upstairs, clean up, and rest while I finish up here?"

Cam was about to say no, but she sensed that Josie wanted some time alone; besides, Sam had touched her knee under the table. "Okay, Mama. We'll take a late siesta. Call us down soon as Lila and Orrie get here."

Josie hadn't used the fireplace in her bedroom all season, but after she'd kissed Cam and Lila and their husbands good night and shown them to their respective rooms, she knew she needed a fire. She was exhausted but too keyed up to sleep, too restless to read, too full of plans to relax. A fire would be just the thing. Setting her cup of cocoa on the mantelpiece, she struck a match to the kindling. She thought of putting on her rose dressing gown, but practicality overcame the desire for glamour and she reached for her blue flannel nightdress. By the time she'd changed into it, let down her hair, turned off the light, settled into the armchair, put her slippered feet on the ottoman, and covered herself with a lap rug, the kindling was licking the bark of the big log.

The flickering light made the silver frames of the photographs on her chest of drawers glint. She couldn't make out the photos, but they were clear in her mind's eye; in fact, Bear had been gone so long that when she imagined him it was usually as he appeared in their wedding photo. But she no longer thought of her marriage with remorse and disappointment. No one got through life without regrets. The best you could hope for was that they'd be the *right* regrets, that no matter what you'd suffered, you had taken a chance on love or whatever else you'd most wanted. And since Bear had been the great love, and the great sorrow, of her life, it seemed right that she should remember him as forever young and ready to take on the world. She wondered what he'd think about her and Dozier. He had never been able to master his own discontents, but he'd had great generosity of spirit. She believed he'd be happy for her.

A pinecone caught and flared, drops of resin sizzled. There was something special about a fire. Center of the home since the cave days. Looking into it, she drifted into a dreamy but concentrated state, relaxed but so attuned that she could hear the ticking of the grandfather clock, like the heartbeat of the house.

The blaze had mostly settled into embers when the door creaked open and shut. She startled, but he put a finger to his lips and moved silently to her, sitting on the ottoman, his arms around her legs, his head in her lap. She stroked on his head and whispered, "What time is it?"

"After one."

"I thought you weren't coming. How did it go?"

"Better'n I thought it would. Had to wait until they put the kids to bed and that took some doing because they were all excited being in such a big house. Then I sat them down and told them. Funny. Marilyn was the most shocked. Wondered if we shouldn't wait. Wondered how she'd explain it to the kids, which really meant she wanted me to explain it to her. I told her it was a little late in the game for us to be waiting for anything. She should just tell the kids they were lucky to be getting a grandma and great-grandma they already knew. Skip's wife, well, you know how she is since she's been turned religious." He chuckled softly. "The religious ones are always so damned interested in sex. Hinted around to find out if we'd already consummated the union."

"You didn't—?"

"Just said we loved one another. After that it more or less changed into a business seminar. Wanted to know if I was going to sell the house. I told them yes, I planned to move in with you, so unless they want to make some arrangements to take over my place as part of their inheritance I'd be putting it up for sale. Wanted to know if we'd have a prenuptial agreement and if I'd change my will. Truth to tell, their practicality struck me as kind of chilly. And speaking of chilly, your hands are cold, sister." He kissed them, linking his fingers with hers.

"I don't feel cold. Just old age I guess."

"You still look beautiful to me. Come on, let's get you under the covers and I'll tell you the rest of it." He took off her slippers, put his arm around her, and walked her to the bed, pulling up the covers to her chin after she'd got in. Taking the fire iron, he scattered the cinders and put the screen around the hearth, then started to take off his clothes. She raised up on one elbow. "Think it'll be all right if you sleep here?"

"Going to have to be, since that's what I'm doing. Don't worry. When you get up at dawn to put the turkey in I'll sneak back over to my place." He stripped to his boxers and undershirt, shivering. "Damn it's cold!"

She pulled back the covers to welcome him. "Then come get toasty."

"Now," he pulled her close, putting her head in the crook of his arm, "tell me how it went for you. Girls get along all right?"

"Friendly as puppies, much to my surprise. I doled out that eggnog like prescription medicine, not too much, not too little. Everyone seemed very mellow. We decorated the tree . . . and then I told them. Cam took it best."

"As you thought."

Josie nodded. "She just kept saying, 'Why didn't I guess before?' She wanted to go over and fetch you but I told her not to and she listened, for once."

"And Lila?"

"Didn't like it at all at first. You know she pretends not to care, but she's smarting from the Evie and Jasper situation. Said the family was as incestuous as something out of *God's Little Acre*."

"Incestuous?"

"Shush! Sam smoothed things over. Told her when people were first immigrating from the old country it was quite common for things like this to happen. He said—I don't know if he was just making it up—that his great-grandfather had married his great-grandmother's sister when she'd died. Said it strengthened family ties." Holding in a laugh, her shoulders shook. "I don't think Lila was won over, but I did the best I could with them. Can't do any more. Didn't end too badly. Sam got everyone laughing by saying I'd have no cause for complaint if I wasn't happy because I couldn't claim I didn't know what I'd be getting."

"I figure you do know what you're getting." He kissed her cheek. "Orrie?"

"Now, that was a surprise. Orrie wondered why we'd want to get married at all. Said we ought to check with an accountant because it was probably smarter tax-wise to keep our money separate. I didn't admit that I'd told you much the same thing. I just gave him the speech you'd given me, about marriage being more than a financial arrangement."

"You give him the whole speech?"

"No. Didn't want to get into the mushy stuff." He yawned so wide his jaw cracked. "You look like the MGM lion," she told him. "You real tired?"

"That I am. Besides . . ."

"I know. It's inhibiting having the kids in the house. But they'll be gone tomorrow night."

"Mmmm."

She shifted into the curl of his arm, her hand on his heart, feeling its beat as he slowly relaxed into sleep. "I think"—her sigh was blissfully content—"this is going to be the best Christmas yet."

A PENGUIN READERS GUIDE TO

BED & BREAKFAST

Lois Battle

An Introduction to *Bed & Breakfast*

When a family gathers for the holidays, putting aside personal differences can seem nearly impossible. Josie Tatternall has certainly felt that way before. These days, though, these differences seem more insurmountable than ever. Josie has no delusions that her family is perfect. Her late husband had been a Marine and, if the constant moving from place to place wasn't enough of a strain on their three daughters, there was also his alcoholism and abusive behavior to contend with.

Out of the three, Josie ought to be closest to her daughter Lila, who lives nearby. But Lila has always felt that her mother favored her older sister, Cam. And Josie's youngest daughter Evie is another problem altogether. Evie has always been content to let her beauty trump her brains, even at the expense of her dignity. Now she makes her living airing people's dirty laundry, including her family's, in a tart newspaper column. And then there's Cam—rebellious, independent, and strong willed—who works for a feminist press in New York City and has vowed never to come back home.

But when Josie witnesses her best friend's brush with death, she decides that life is too precious to let anything stand in the way of family togetherness, especially at Christmas. She resolves to do what even a week before had seemed unthinkable: get her three daughters together again at the bed and breakfast she runs in Beaufort, South Carolina.

Of course, it's not the idyllic Christmas gathering Josie

might have imagined. Unhealed wounds, jealousies, bad judgments, and the inevitable stress associated with the holidays threaten to destroy any hopes of unity. But could this Christmas be just the beginning of her family's rebirth—the first of many happier gatherings to come? And can Josie, with the love of her children, family, and friends, finally come to terms with her less-than-perfect life and be content with simply doing the best she can?

About Lois Battle

Lois Battle's seven novels include *Bed and Breakfast, Florabama Ladies' Auxiliary & Sewing Circle, Storyville, War Brides,* and *A Habit of the Blood* (all available from Penguin). She lives in Beaufort, South Carolina.

A Conversation with Lois Battle

You explore cultural differences between the North and South in your books. Do you have experience living in, forgive the expression, Yankee territory? Do you think Cam might have been a different person if she had not moved to New York?

I left home for New York when I was nineteen and lived there, on and off, until I was over forty. At that time I moved first to Savannah, then to Beaufort, where I've now lived for more than twenty years. I still miss New York and try to get back there at least once a year. Even though our country has become increasingly homogenized, there are still some cultural differences. No, I tell Southerners who have never been there, New Yorkers are *not* unfriendly; they're just crowded and in a hurry, and they actually enjoy arguments as mental exercise. And no, I tell folks who've never ventured to the South, there is a genuine graciousness and courtesy even if some of it is candy coated. I love New Yorkers because they're sharp and diverse, always looking for what's next, but I also value the South's deep sense of history and tradition, and love of the land. Bagel with schmear or Mama's hot biscuits and gravy? I'll take 'em both.

Young people come to New York because they're ambitious (one day you may play the violin in Carnegie Hall, dance in a Broadway show, become a stock market whiz) or curious (it is one of the world's great cities), want to find (or lose) themselves, or maybe just want to get away from home. All of the above apply to young Cam. I shudder to think what trouble she might have caused for herself and her family if she'd stayed in Beaufort.

There are likely some readers who will find Josie and Dozier's relationship scandalous. How would you respond to them?

I have come to the point where I don't disapprove of any relationships that are founded on affection and mutual satisfaction. Many older couples have affairs or live together these days. It's also interesting to note that a hundred years ago marriage to the brother or sister of a deceased relative was quite common. Dozier and Josie will give one another more understanding and tender care than either of their spouses did.

Cam and Reba have a strong and mutually beneficial friendship. What inspired you to write Reba as a lesbian? In what ways does having one character be a lesbian and the other character be straight affect how a writer can explore their relationship?

I think I must've been about fifteen when I first heard homosexuality openly discussed. At first it confused and shocked me but then I realized that I'd known "people like that" all my life, had intuited their difference, but just hadn't had words for it except "fairy" or "queer."

Sexual preference doesn't have much to do with the qualities I seek in a friend. Sense of humor, loyalty, mutual experience or interests, trust, or simply enjoying one another's company—all have much more to do with the bond of friendship.

Bed & Breakfast *takes place during the Christmas holiday. What are some holiday traditions—long standing or new—that you observe? Or do you boycott the holidays entirely?*

At Christmas, I love decorating the tree, hearing choirs, or singing carols. The fiftieth Muzak rendition of "Little Drummer Boy" makes me want to break his drumsticks over his tiny head. Though I send few Christmas cards, and usually late ones at that, my mother always sent a slew of cards and updates to her many friends and distant family members. She would scotch-tape their replies all around the fireplace. It was a cheery and affectionate tradition that I miss.

Is there a particular character with whom you identify the most? How did that affect the way you wrote him/her?

I identify to some extent with all my characters. It's part of the enjoyment of writing to imagine other people—though naturally I like some more than others and have to be careful not to punish them just because I don't like them.

Have you been at all surprised by your readers' demographics? Is there an unexpected age group or region where your novels have gained popularity?

I don't know all the demographics of sales. Surely my novels are popular in the South. People like to read about places they know, and see if the author got it right. Then again, people like to read about the South. I read *Gone with the Wind*, under the covers, when I was eleven or twelve and vowed that one day I'd get to Savannah, which I did. Far as I know, my audience is mainly female, mainly middle aged and college educated, but I've been surprised by the number of women I've met who'll say, "I've read you so I'm giving you to my daughter." That pleases me because it suggests I have a generational reach. Sometimes I even get letters from men—especially on *Storyville*, which is about prostitution in New Orleans.

Is there a particular routine—time of day, place, music you listen to—that you follow when you're writing? What advice would you give to aspiring novelists?

Hints about writing? Wish I had something smart to say. I know that setting a particular time of day is helpful because then it feels more like a job. Which it is. Unless your muse visits more often than mine, you can't rely on inspiration. John Gregory Dunne said, "Writing is manual labor of the mind. A job, like laying pipe." It nearly always goes much slower than I hope. Stick at it. Don't throw away work you don't like, just put it in a bottom drawer and reassess it after a week or so. And, ah yes . . . best of luck.

Questions for Discussion

1. Do you think you would be successful at running a bed and breakfast? What are the challenges and rewards associated with that line of work? In what ways might Mrs. Beasley's behavior be seen as inappropriate? Do you think she was treated fairly by Josie and her family?

2. Josie reflects that Peatsy is her friend despite the pain she has caused over the years (p. 34). Are there friends with whom you have a similar relationship? Why do you think it is in our nature as humans to continue friendships that might be dysfunctional? Knowing about Peatsy's involvement with Josie's husband, do you think you could be as gracious as Josie? Why or why not?

3. Compare each of Josie's daughters. Which do you find to be most sympathetic? Why? If you chose one of them to be a friend, whom would it be? Why?

4. Cam obviously has a one-sided view of her parents' relationship. How do you think Josie could have made her understand earlier how her father's alcoholism and abuse were affecting their family? When are children old enough to learn unpleasant truths? Are there some issues—substance abuse, infidelity, etc.—that should never be revealed to children, no matter their age?

5. Lila's son isn't depicted in the best light. Do you think he's indicative of "kids today"? Or does he act especially spoiled? What changes in Lila's parenting style do you think you would make if you were her?

6. Do you think Orrie bears any responsibility for his father's behavior with Evie? If he were your husband, would you ask him to intervene and speak to his father? At what point do you think you would reach your limit of tolerance?

7. Lila is upset with Cam's behavior at her party, even though Lila was really just jumping to conclusions. What are some instances when you might have been looking for a reason, any reason at all, to get angry or upset with someone? Did you realize you were doing it at the time? What are some times when people might have been spoiling for a fight with you? Were you able to diffuse the situation?

8. If your son or daughter asked to invite a friend who happened to be gay or lesbian home for the holidays, how would you react? Do you think Reba judged her partner's family too harshly before she came to Beaufort? What are some ways she could have improved the situation? How might her partner have helped make her feel more at home?

9. When Josie is at Cuba's church service, she feels as if she "were sitting by a campfire on a very dark night, protected not only by the animal warmth of others, but by the realization that each and every one of them had hopes and fears, sorrows and joys, unique in their particulars, but somehow shared" (p. 302). In what ways might this have been a turning point for her? Can you remember times that you felt especially connected to a group of people you did not know well? From where do you think that feeling of connectedness comes?

10. How do you think Cam and Sam's relationship will fare?

11. As Reba and Cam drive away from Beaufort, Reba says that forgiveness is just part of motherhood. In what ways is

that true? Do you think it is part of the mothering instinct? Cam replies, "Poor Mama. She's always had to forgive everyone. I used to think that was so weak of her" (p. 309). Why do you think she might say this? How could a willingness to forgive seem weak? Are there situations when it is?

12. There are quite a few instances in the book where characters bemoan "progress"—urbanization, increased traffic, malls, and the changing face of small-town America. In what way is such progress destructive? Is there a happy medium to be found between boom and bust?

[illegible]

13. There are quite a few instances in Gogol's fiction where [illegible] [illegible] good and bad.

For more information about or to order other Penguin Readers Guides, please e-mail the Penguin Marketing Department at [illegible] or write to:

Penguin Books Marketing Dept.
Readers Guides
375 Hudson Street
New York, NY 10014-3657

Please allow 4–6 weeks for delivery.

To access Penguin Readers Guides online, visit the Penguin Group (USA) Inc. Web site at www.penguin.com.